Ly... has
...er teens. She is very
...ng husband who has
...ed to write! Her five
...he has a very large dog
... a very small terrier who
...hen time allows, Lynne is

# The Rumours
## COLLECTION

July 2019

August 2019

September 2019

October 2019

November 2019

December 2019

# Rumours: The Billion-Dollar Brides

LYNNE GRAHAM

MILLS & BOON

First Published in Great Britain 2019
By Mills & Boon, an imprint of HarperCollins *Publishers*
1 London Bridge Street, London, SE1 9GF



ISBN: 978-0-263-27669-5

0919

FSC
www.fsc.org
MIX
Paper from responsible sources
FSC™ C007454

This book is produced from independently certified FSC™ paper to ensure responsible forest management.

For more information visit: www.harpercollins.co.uk/green

Printed and bound in Spain
by CPI, Barcelona

# THE DESERT KING'S BLACKMAILED BRIDE

# CHAPTER ONE

KING RASHAD EL-AMIN QUARAISHI studied the photos spread across his office desk. Six feet three inches tall, he dominated most gatherings, having inherited his grandfather's unusual height. Black-haired and possessed of long-lashed dark eyes, he had also inherited the perfect bone structure that had made his mother a renowned beauty in the Middle East. Indeed, his smouldering dark good looks continually inspired admiring comments on social media and he was greatly embarrassed by the fact.

'A cornucopia of feminine perfection,' his chief adviser, Hakim, remarked with fervour. 'A new reign, a new queen and, we trust, a new *dynasty*! Truthfully, fortune will smile now on the fortunes of Dharia.'

Although his royal employer appeared somewhat less enthusiastic, he did not disagree. But then Rashad had always known that it was his duty to marry and father a child. Unfortunately it was not a project that inspired him. After all, he had married before and at a very young age and he knew the pitfalls. Living with a woman with whom he might not have the smallest thing in common would be stressful. Misunderstandings and personality clashes would abound in such a relationship and if the desired conception did not occur in record time the stress would multiply and the unhappiness and dissatisfaction would settle in.

No, marriage held very little appeal for Rashad. The best he could hope for in a future bride was that she would have sufficient sense and practicality to enable them to live their separate lives in relative peace. He did not expect much in the way of support from a wife because his first wife had clung to him like superglue. Nor was he likely to forget his parents' famously stormy marriage. Regardless, he also understood and accepted that the very stability of his country rested on his capacity to act as a respected role model for his people.

Over the past twenty-odd years the population of Dharia had suffered a great deal and change and innovation were no longer welcome because in the desire for peace everybody had rushed to re-embrace the traditional relaxed Dharian outlook and customs. The heady years of his father's extravagance and his blind determination to force Western ways on an extremely traditional country had resulted in a government that became increasingly tyrannical and inevitably clashed with the army, who acted to defend the constitution with the support of the people. The history of that popular revolution was etched in the ruins of the former dictator's palace in the city of Kashan and in the prompt restoration of the monarchy.

Tragically, a car bomb had killed off almost all of

Rashad's family. In the aftermath his uncle had hidden him in the desert to keep him safe. He had only been six years old, a frightened little boy more attached to his English nanny than to the distant parents he rarely saw and in the turmoil following the bomb and the instigation of martial law even his nanny had vanished. The palace had been looted, their loyal staff dispersed and life as Rashad had come to know it had changed out of all recognition.

'Your Majesty, may I make a suggestion?' Hakim asked.

Rashad thought for an instant that his adviser was going to suggest that he flung all the photos of potentially suitable brides into a lucky dip and chose blind. It would be a random form of selection and very disrespectful of the candidates, he acknowledged wryly, but he was cynically convinced that his chances of a happy union would be just as good with that method as with any other. Marriage, after all, was a very risky game of chance.

His wide sensual mouth compressed. 'Please…' he urged.

Hakim smiled and withdrew the file he carried below his arm to open it and extend it to show off a highly detailed picture of an item of jewellery. 'I have taken the liberty of asking the royal jeweller if he could reproduce the Hope of Dharia…'

Rashad stared at him in astonishment. 'But it is lost. How can it be reproduced?'

'What harm would there be in having a replacement ring created? It is a powerful symbol of the monarchy. It was the family's most important heirloom but after this long there is very little likelihood that the original ring will ever be found,' Hakim pointed out seriously. 'I feel that this is the optimum time to do this. Our people feel safer when old traditions are upheld—'

'Our people would prefer a fairy tale to the reality that my late father was a rotten ruler, who put together a corrupt and power-hungry government,' Rashad interposed with the bluntness that was his trademark and which never failed to horrify the more diplomatic Hakim.

While consternation at such frankness froze the older man's bearded face, Rashad walked over to the window, which overlooked the gardens being industriously watered by the palace's army of staff.

He was thinking about the ring superstitiously nicknamed the Hope of Dharia by the Dharian people. The ring had been a gorgeous fire opal of fiery hue, always worn by the King at ceremonial events. Set in gold and inscribed with holy words, the ring had acquired an almost mystical aura after being brought into the family by his saintly great-grandmother, whose devotion to charitable enterprises had ensured that she was adored throughout the kingdom. In other countries a king might wear a crown or wield a sceptre but in Dharia the monarchy's strength and authority had rested historically and emotionally in that ancient ring. It had vanished after the palace had been looted and, in spite of intensive searches, no indication of the opal's whereabouts had ever been established. No, the ring was gone for good and Rashad could see Hakim's point: a well-designed replacement would undeniably be better than nothing.

'Order the ring,' he instructed ruefully.

A fake ring for a fake king, he reflected with innate cynicism. He could never shake off the knowledge that he had not been born to sit on the throne of Dharia. The youngest of three sons, he had been an afterthought until his brothers died along with his parents. He had been left at home that day because he was an excessively energetic and noisy little boy and that reality had saved his life. Rashad's massive popularity with the public still shook him even while it persuaded him to bend his own ideals to become the man his country needed him to be.

Once he had wanted to fall in love and then he had got married. Love had been glorious for all of five minutes and then it had died slowly and painfully. No, he wasn't in the market for that experience again. Yet he had also once believed that lust was wrong until he fell in lust many times over while he was finishing his education at a British university. Whatever, he was still grateful to have enjoyed that fleeting period of sexual freedom before he had to return home to take up his duties. And unfortunately home signified the rigid court protocols that ensured that Rashad was forced to live in a little gilded soap bubble of perceived perfection as a figurehead that inspired the most ridiculous awe. Yes, his people would enjoy the restoration of the ring and all the hoopla of dreams and expectations that went with it…but he would not.

* * *

Polly glanced at her sister, Ellie, and managed a strained smile as a middle-aged blonde woman approached them after their mother's short funeral, which had taken place in an almost empty church.

Both young women had found the ritual a sad and frustrating event. Ellie, who was two years younger than Polly, had no memory of their mother while Polly had vague memories of an occasional perfumed smiling presence while she was still very young. Their grandmother had raised the two girls and the older woman had passed away only a few months earlier. For more than ten years the Dixon sisters had not even known if their mother was still alive. That was why it had been a considerable shock to be contacted out of the blue by a complete stranger to be told of Annabel Dixon's passing.

That stranger, a volunteer at the hospice where their mother had died, Vanessa James, was only marginally more comfortable with the situation than they were, having frankly admitted on the phone that she had tried hard to persuade their long-lost parent to contact her daughters and speak to them *before* her death. At the same time she acknowledged that Annabel had struggled to make herself understood in the later stages of her illness and such a meeting could have been frustrating and upsetting for all of them.

'I've booked us a table at the hotel for lunch,' Vanessa James announced with a determined smile as she shook hands firmly with both young women.

'I am so sorry that we are meeting in such unhappy circumstances.'

Polly had never felt less like eating and she made an awkward attempt to admit that.

'It was your mother's last wish and she set aside the money to cover the meal,' the older woman told her gently. 'It's her treat, not mine.'

Polly's pale skin flushed red with embarrassment, her white-blonde hair acting as a foil to accentuate her discomfiture. 'I didn't mean to be ungracious—'

'Well, even if you didn't you would have every excuse to feel uneasy about this situation,' Vanessa remarked wryly. 'Let me tell you a little about your mother's last years.'

And the sisters listened while the older woman told them about the terminal illness that had begun to deprive their mother of independent life and mobility while she was still only in her forties. She had lived in a nursing home and had died in the hospice where Vanessa had got to know her well.

'That's so very sad,' Ellie lamented, flicking her red hair back off her troubled brow, her green eyes full of compassion. 'We could have done so much to help her…if only we had known—'

'But Annabel didn't *want* you to know. She was aware that you had already spent years nursing your grandmother through her decline and she was determined not to come into your life and become another burden and responsibility. She was very independent.'

The three women sat down at the table in a quiet

corner of the restaurant and rather blankly studied the menus presented to them.

'I understand you're studying to be a doctor,' Vanessa said to Ellie. 'Annabel was so proud when she heard about that.'

'How did she find out?' Ellie pressed. 'It has been years since she last contacted our grandmother.'

'One of your mother's cousins was a nurse and recognised Annabel a couple of years ago when she was hospitalised. She brought her up to date with family developments. Annabel also made her promise not to approach you.'

'But why? We would have understood how she felt!' Ellie burst out in frustration.

'She didn't want you to see her like that or to remember her that way. Having always been a rather beautiful woman she was a little vain about her looks,' Vanessa explained gently.

Polly's mind was wandering. Thinking of her sibling's studies, she was very conscious that she had never achieved anything of note in the academic stakes and had done nothing to inspire a mother with pride. But then one way or another, life had always got in the way of her hopes and dreams. She had stayed home to take care of their ailing grandmother while Ellie had gone off to university to study medicine and she was proud that she had not been selfish. After all, her kid sister had always been very clever and she had a true vocation to help others. She knew just how guilty Ellie had felt about leaving her to cope alone with their grandmother but, really, what would have been the point of *both* of them losing out on their education? At school, Polly had been an average student, only plodding along while Ellie streaked ahead.

'I did so hope that you were in touch with your younger sister and that you would bring her with you today,' Vanessa James remarked, startling both women into looking across the table at her with wide eyes.

'What younger sister?' Polly exclaimed with wide blue eyes the colour of gentian violets.

Vanessa surveyed them in dismay before telling them about how their sibling had gone into foster care when Annabel could no longer look after her. She was four years younger than Polly and apparently their grandmother had refused to take her in.

'We had no idea we had another sister,' Ellie admitted heavily. 'We really know nothing about our mother's life…well, only what Gran told us and that wasn't much and none of it was flattering. She certainly never mentioned that there were *three* of us!'

'When Annabel was young she led quite an exciting life,' Vanessa volunteered ruefully. 'She was a highly qualified nanny and she travelled a great deal and lived abroad for long periods. She worked for some very wealthy families and earned an excellent salary, often with lots of perks thrown in. But obviously when she had children of her own she couldn't take them to work with her, which is why you ended up in your grandmother's care. But when you were both still quite young, Annabel *did* return to London, where she tried to set up a childcare facility. She poured all her savings into it. She was planning to bring the two of you home to live with her. But, sadly, it all went wrong. The business failed, the relationship she was in fell apart and she discovered that she was pregnant again.'

'And she gave birth to another girl? What's our sister called? Why are we only hearing about her now?' Polly gasped, only a little touched by the news that the mother she had never known had actually once planned to raise her own children. Indeed that struck her as a very remote possibility because it had seemed to her as a child that she had a mother who ran away from responsibility. Even worse, her outlook was coloured by the reality that she and Ellie had been brought up by a woman who bitterly resented the responsibility of having to raise her granddaughters at a time in her life when she had expected to take life at an easier pace.

Their sister's name was Penelope Dixon and Vanessa had no further information to offer. 'I did approach social services but as I'm not a blood relative I wasn't in a position to push. One of you would have to make enquiries. Penelope could have been adopted but I understand that if that proves to be the case you could leave a letter on file for her should she ever enquire about her birth family.'

Their meals were brought to the table. Vanessa withdrew three envelopes from her bag. 'Your mother has left each of you a ring and I must ask you to take charge of your youngest sister's ring for her—'

'A...*ring*?' Polly repeated in a renewed daze of astonishment.

'And with each a name. I assume, your fathers'

names…although Annabel was very evasive on that score,' the older woman revealed uncomfortably. 'I should warn you now that I'm not sure that Annabel actually *knew* who your fathers were beyond any shadow of doubt.'

Polly paled. 'Oh…' she said, in a voice that spoke volumes.

'She wasn't specific but I did receive the impression that when she was living the high life, looking after her rich employers' children, she may…er…possibly have been a little free with her favours,' the other woman advanced in a very quiet voice of apology.

'Sorry…? You mean…?' Polly began uncertainly.

'She slept around,' Ellie translated bluntly with a grimace. 'Well, thank you for being honest enough to tell us that before we get excited about those names. But with that particular disease, I know that Annabel may have had problems accessing her memories and she may have become confused when she tried to focus on the past.'

The instant Vanessa handed Polly her envelope, Polly ripped it open, patience never having been one of her virtues. A heavy and ornate gold ring with a large stone fell out and she threaded it on her finger but it was far too large. It was, she finally registered, a man's ring, not a woman's. She peered down at the stone, which flickered with changeable hues of red, orange and yellow.

'It's a fire opal, very unusual but not, I understand, particularly valuable,' Vanessa proffered. 'It's also an antique and foreign made.'

'Right…' Polly muttered blankly, returning to extract the small sheet of paper enclosed in the envelope and frown down at it.

*Zahir Basara… Dharia.*

'My…my father may be of Arabic descent?' Polly murmured in sheer wonderment, because, in the most obvious terms, she looked as though she had not a drop of more exotic climes in her veins and indeed had been asked several times if she was from Scandinavia. 'I have heard of Dharia—'

'Your mother was a nanny in the royal household there…right up until the royal family died,' Vanessa volunteered.

And Polly immediately wondered if there was a connection to her birth name, which had been Zariyah and which was on her passport. Her grandmother had always called her Polly, having disliked her foreign name.

'I've got an emerald!' Ellie announced as if she had just opened a Christmas cracker, her whole demeanour suggesting that she had no intention of taking either ring or name too seriously.

'And the name?' Polly pressed with rampant curiosity, hoping that it would be the same as her own putative father's because at least that would suggest that the relationship had been more than a passing fling.

'Possibly a name of Italian extraction. I'll keep it to myself for now though.' Ellie dug the envelope into her bag with an air of finality but she was unusually pale. At Vanessa's instigation she also took charge of the envelope intended for their sister, Penelope. 'Maybe our mother *collected* engagement rings—'

'My ring is a man's,' Polly argued.

'Yes, but there could have been an intention to make it smaller,' Ellie pointed out calmly. 'I wish she'd left us a letter telling us about herself. Would it be possible for us to visit the hospice, Vanessa? I'd very much like to see where Annabel spent her last days and speak to the staff.'

And while the two other women became involved in an intense discussion about the hospice, the disease that had taken Annabel's life and the research that Vanessa's charity raised funds to support, Polly drifted off inside her head, something that she did frequently when her imagination was caught.

Just then she was thinking about the fire opal and wondering if it had been a symbol of love. Ellie was of a more practical bent but Polly liked to think she had, at least, been born to parents who had been in love at the time of her conception. Love between two people of different cultures would have been testing, she reflected, and perhaps those differences had become too great to surmount. Even so, that name in the envelope had sparked a mad craving inside her for facts about the country of Dharia.

Did she have Dharian blood running in her veins? Was it even possible that her father could still be alive? And that he might want to get to know her?

Polly had a deep longing to have a real parent. Her mother had virtually abandoned them and while her grandmother had not mistreated Polly and Ellie she certainly hadn't loved them. Polly thought it would be absolutely wonderful to have a parent who actually cared for her as an individual, someone who would celebrate her strengths and overlook and forgive her weaknesses.

'You're not charging off to some foreign country to make enquiries,' Ellie said drily, having perused her sister's ring and the name on the piece of paper and surmised exactly where her sister's fertile imagination was taking her. 'It would be insane.'

And Polly had never ever done anything insane, *never ever…*

No, she had not defied her grandmother when she had won a place at art college and the older woman told her that she couldn't take it up because it was her duty to go out and get a paying job to help support the household. While suitably employed in a lowly but enjoyable position for a charitable enterprise, Polly had contented herself with the outlet of evening art classes shared with other enthusiastic amateurs.

Polly had never been particularly adventurous, so she knew then with a sinking heart that it was very unlikely that she would ever get to visit Dharia. She didn't have the money for air fares or holidays, she wouldn't have the cash to chase up some father armed only with what could well prove to be as common a name in Dharia as John Smith. No, it was a dream and Polly knew dreams didn't come true unless you were willing to take risks and seize the moment…

Polly was aware of being stared at in the passport queue at the airport outside Kashan. It was the blonde hair, she thought ruefully, aware as she looked around her with eager curiosity that her pale colouring seemed rare in Dharia.

She was here in her father's country, she was finally *here* and she still couldn't believe it! Ellie had made it possible, taking on part-time work in spite of her heavy study schedule and insisting that she could get by for one term at least without her sister's financial help. Even so, it had still taken Polly months of saving to acquire sufficient funds for such a trip. Her budget was tiny and she would be staying in a little bed-and-breakfast establishment near the bazaar in Kashan. As long as it was clean, she would be happy, and if it wasn't clean she would clean it for herself.

Encountering another prolonged stare from a dark-eyed male, Polly flushed and wished she had braided her hair. When she went out and about tomorrow, she promised herself, she would put on a sunhat to cover her head. After all, Dharia wasn't a tourist-orientated country and was kind of old-fashioned. She definitely wouldn't be wearing the shorts and vest top she had packed, for while there were no veiled women around those she had seen wore unrevealing clothes with longer hemlines than were fashionable.

Finally she reached the head of the queue and handed over her passport. That seemed to be the signal for another couple of men to approach the booth and a split second later one addressed her. 'Will you come this way, please?'

To her bewilderment she was accompanied to the baggage hall to reclaim her luggage and then her case and her bag were taken from her and she was shown into a bare little room containing several chairs and a table. Her case and bag were then searched in her presence while she wondered why her passport had not been returned. What were they looking for in her luggage? Drugs? A cold shiver of fear ran through Polly even though she had nothing stronger than headache tablets in her possession. She had heard horror stories about people being strip-searched and when a female airport security guard entered, her slight frame stiffened into defensive mode. There was an exclamation as one of the men removed the fire-opal ring from her handbag and held it high where it caught the bare light bulb above and sent a cascade of colour flickering across the drab grey walls. The trio burst out into excited speech in their own language and seconds later the two men slammed out, taking the ring with them. The female officer stared fixedly at her and Polly breathed in slow and deep in an effort to calm herself.

'You are very beautiful,' the woman said, startling her.

A sickly smile pulled at Polly's tense mouth because she didn't know how to respond to that remark in such trying circumstances. 'Thank you,' she said finally, reluctant to be rude.

The minutes ticked by like a hammer slowly beating down on her nerves. Her companion answered her phone. Polly linked her hands together on her lap and wondered why they had all seemed so excited about the ring. Was it a stolen ring? Was that possible? But what sort of ring could possibly attract such immediate recognition when according to Vanessa it was not worth much money?

Another woman entered with a tray of aromatic tea. Polly's companion stood up and offered her a cup. It smelled of mint and her hand shook as she lifted the glass up to her tense mouth to sip the fragrant brew.

'Why am I being kept here?' she dared to ask then.

'We are waiting for instructions,' she was told.

'And the ring?'

Both women exchanged looks and neither made an answer. Polly was angry that her ring had been taken from her because she treasured it as her sole remaining link with the mother she had never known. When would her ring be returned to her? At the same time she was trying to take encouragement from the fact that she had not been strip-searched and that tea had been brought. It was a misunderstanding. What else could it be? She had done nothing wrong. But had her mother done something wrong years back in the past?

How was she supposed to answer that question? In many ways, her mother remained a complete mystery to her eldest daughter. Annabel had travelled the world in luxury to look after other people's children while abandoning her own to the tender mercies of her own mother, who had been a most reluctant guardian. She had, however, dutifully provided financial support for Polly's grandmother and her daughters for many years. When that support came to a sudden unannounced halt, Polly had learned a lot about how to live on a very tight budget.

The sisters had inherited nothing from their grandmother. She had left the contents of her house, all that she possessed, to her son, Polly's uncle, complaining bitterly that her daughter had ruined her retirement by forcing her to raise her illegitimate children. It was a label Polly had always hated, a word the younger generation rarely used because it wasn't fair to tag a child with something that they had played no active part in creating. But it was a word that had meant a great deal to her staunchly conservative and judgemental grandmother, who had been ashamed that her only grandchildren had been born out of wedlock.

While Polly agonised on the other side of Kashan, Hakim, who rarely moved fast, was positively racing down the main corridor of the palace in his haste to reach his King. His rounded face was beaming and flushed, his little goatee beard quivering. Rashad was in his office, working diligently as usual.

'The ring!' Hakim carolled out of breath, holding it high in the air like a trophy before hurrying over to lay it down reverently on the top of the desk. 'It is found.'

Rashad frowned and sprang upright, carrying the ring in one lean brown hand to scrutinise it in the sunlight pouring through the window. 'How was it found? Where was it?'

Hakim explained about the British woman being held at the airport.

Rashad's dark as jet eyes hardened. 'Why is she not in prison?'

'This must be carefully handled,' Hakim urged. 'We would not want to cause a diplomatic incident—'

'A thief is a thief and must be held accountable,' his King assured him without hesitation.

'The woman is young. She could not have been the thief. She has not been questioned yet. The airport police wished to first ascertain with the palace that the ring was the genuine article. There is great excitement in Kashan. Crowds are already forming at the airport.'

Rashad frowned. 'Why? How could word of this discovery already have spread?'

'The airport grapevine was most thoroughly aired on social media,' his adviser told him wryly. 'There will be no keeping a lid on this story—'

'Crowds?' Rashad prompted in bewilderment.

'The woman concerned is not being viewed as a thief but as the woman who has brought the Hope of Dharia home to our King. When I add that she is young and apparently beautiful...well, if you think about how your great-grandmother came to your great-grandfather and brought the Hope with her, you can see why our people are thrilled.'

But Rashad was still frowning. A large gathering of thrilled people could translate all too easily into civil unrest. He could barely comprehend his aide's fervent attitude to what was, after all, only a legend, polished up by the next generation to enhance and romanticise the monarchy and their alliances. 'But that was a century ago in another age and it was a set-up to achieve exactly what it did achieve...a marriage that suited both countries at the time.'

'It is dangerous to have crowds congregating at the airport. I would humbly suggest that you have the woman brought here to be questioned. It will keep the whole matter under wraps without causing undue comment.'

Rashad was thinking with regret of the old dungeons in the palace basement. He didn't think Hakim wanted the British woman put in the basement. He reminded himself that the ring had come home and that the woman was apparently too young to have been responsible for its disappearance. 'Very well. I suppose it will be interesting to hear her story.'

'It is a complete miracle that the Hope of Dharia has been returned to us,' Hakim declared fervently. 'And a wonderful portent of good events yet to come.'

Sadly, there was nothing miraculous about Polly's feelings as she was herded out of the airport by what looked suspiciously like a rear entrance as they emerged into a loading bay surrounded by crates. She was clammy with fright in spite of the presence of the female security guard but her rarely roused temper was also beginning to rise. She was a law-abiding, well-behaved traveller. How dared they force her to endure such treatment?

'You are going to the palace!' the woman told her in a voice that suggested that she expected Polly to turn cartwheels of joy at the news. 'It is a great honour. They have even sent a car and a military escort for you.'

Polly climbed into the rear passenger seat of a shiny white four-wheel drive. She linked her hands tightly together on her lap. Over twenty years ago her mother had been employed at the palace and now she was receiving an unexpected opportunity to see the place, she told herself, striving to take a more positive view of her circumstances. If she got the chance to ask questions she might even meet someone who *remembered* her mother working at the palace. Of course, that could only lead to a very awkward exchange, she acknowledged reluctantly. Had her mother slept around? Had she been involved with more than one man? And how on earth was she supposed to find *that* out without seriously embarrassing herself and other people? For the first time, Ellie's forecast that seeking out her father would be like looking for a needle in a haystack returned to haunt Polly and she resolved to keep her personal business strictly private until she was confident of her reception.

A military truck crammed with armed soldiers led the way out of the airport and Polly's nervous tension increased as a big crowd of people surrounded the convoy when it slowed down to leave the complex. Faces pressed against the blacked-out windows, hands thumped noisily on the outside of the car and there was a great deal of shouting. Something akin to panic briefly gripped Polly's slender frame and perspiration beaded her brow. She shut her eyes tightly and prayed while the car pulled away slowly and then mercifully speeded up.

The car drove down a modern thoroughfare lined with tall buildings and lots of people standing around, apparently there to stare at the car she was travelling in. There were masses of people everywhere and a surprising suggestion of a general holiday mood, she thought in surprise as people waved in a seemingly friendly and enthusiastic fashion as the convoy passed by.

They left the city of Kashan and the crowds behind to travel into a desert landscape empty of human habitation. Flat plains of sand ornamented with rocky outcrops stretched in every direction and in the distance she could see giant dunes. There was something about that view stretched taut below a bright blue sky and the burning sun that made her want to paint in a medium different from her usual dreamy pastels. Distracted, Polly blinked as the car purred through giant gates into a startlingly green and lush spread of gardens dotted with trees and shrubs and colourful flowers.

Ahead loomed a very old building that was topped by a variety of large and small domes and which spread in all directions in a haphazard design.

The door beside her opened and Polly eased back out into the simmering heat, her lightweight trousers and tee shirt instantly sticking to her dampening skin. It was incredibly hot. A single female figure stood beneath the huge entrance portico and as Polly approached she bowed very low and motioned a hand in silent request that she follow her.

Clearly, she wasn't under arrest, Polly reflected with intense relief, her curiosity flying as high as her imagination as she entered the palace, but her anger at the fearful uncertainty she had endured remained. They padded down a very long and very broad hallway lined with ornately carved stone columns. Her sandals squeaked as she trekked after the woman into the depths of the great sprawling building. They traversed a shallow staircase and crossed a scantily furnished large room towards French windows that stood wide open.

Oh, dear, Polly thought in dismay, back to the horribly hot outdoors and the unforgiving burn of the midday sun.

She walked hesitantly out into a walled courtyard and her companion departed. Water gushed down into a fountain overhung by palm trees. The tiles on the ground formed an elaborate pattern faded by time. Polly moved straight into the shade by the fountain, desperate for the cooler air.

A young woman in a long fashionable dress appeared and dealt her a small tight smile, sweeping a hand helpfully at the table and two chairs sited in full sun. Suppressing a groan, Polly moved closer just as quick steps sounded from behind her. The young woman immediately dropped down onto her knees and bowed her head. Polly blinked in astonishment and slowly turned round.

A very tall man with blue-black hair and eyes as keen as a hawk's surveyed her. The hunting analogy was apt, she conceded, because she felt cornered and intimidated. He emanated authority and danger like a force field. He was also, very probably, the best-looking man she had ever seen outside a modelling advert and she knew who he was, thanks to her Internet research on the country of Dharia. He was the recently crowned ruler of Dharia, King Rashad. She swallowed hard, thoroughly disconcerted and shaken that she was being granted a personal meeting with such an important individual.

Her mouth had run dry and she parted her lips, struggling to think of something to say but he got there before her.

'I am Rashad, Miss Dixon. I would like to hear how the ring came into your possession.'

*I am Rashad,* she thought, as if there were only one Rashad in the whole world. And looking at him, she thought there might well only be one man quite like him in the Arab world, a remarkable man who had single-handedly united his country's different factions to bring about peace and who was universally and quite slavishly adored for that commendable achievement.

'The truth is…there's not much I *can* explain,' Polly admitted shakily, for the instant she connected with those striking dark brown eyes as luminescent as liquid gold in the sunlight she could barely breathe, never mind think and vocalise.

## CHAPTER TWO

'PLEASE SIT DOWN,' Rashad urged in a harshened undertone because he was finding it a challenge to maintain his normal self-discipline.

An instantaneous lust to possess was flaming through his lean, powerful frame and the uniqueness of that experience in a woman's radius thoroughly unsettled him. But then the woman in front of him was, admittedly, quite exceptional. Polly Dixon was blindingly beautiful with hair of that silvery white-blonde shade that so rarely survived childhood. Her wealth of hair fell in a loose tangle of waves halfway to her waist. Her skin was equally fair, moulded over a heart-shaped face brought alive by delft blue eyes and a sultry full pink mouth. She wasn't very tall. In fact she was rather tiny in stature, Rashad acknowledged abstractedly, doubting that she would reach any higher than his chest, but the ripe curves of her figure at breast and hip were defiantly female and mature.

Polly gazed back at him, dry-mouthed with nervous tension. He had amazing cheekbones, a perfect narrow-bridged nose and a full wide sensual mouth enhanced by the dark shadow of stubble already visible on his bronzed skin. With difficulty she recollected her thoughts and spoke up. 'I gather all this fuss is about the ring that I had in my bag,' she assumed. 'I'm afraid I know very little about it. It only recently came into my possession after my mother died and I think that she had had it for a long time—'

Rashad's sister-in-law, Hayat, brought tea to the table, acting as a discreet chaperone and stepping back out of view.

'What was your mother's name?' Rashad enquired, watching Polly lick a drop of mint tea off her lower lip and imagining that tiny pink tongue flicking against his own flesh with such driving and colourful immediacy that he was glad of the table that concealed the all too masculine swelling at his groin.

Polly was starting to feel incredibly tired as well as desperately thirsty and she sipped constantly at the tea, wishing that it were cold enough to gulp down. 'Annabel Dixon,' she admitted heavily. 'But I don't see what that—'

Rashad had frozen into position. Lush black lashes swooped down to hide his eyes and then skimmed upward again to frame startled gold chips of enquiry, his surprise unconcealed. 'When I was a child I had a nanny called Annabel Dixon,' he revealed flatly. 'Are you saying that that woman was your mother?'

'Yes...but I know very little about her and nothing at all about her time here in Dharia because I was brought up by my grandmother, not by my mother,' Polly told him grudgingly while marvelling at the idea that her mother had looked after Rashad as a little boy. 'Why is the ring so important?'

'It is the ceremonial ring of the Kings of Dharia, a symbol of their right to rule,' Rashad explained. 'It has great emotional significance for my people. The ring went missing over twenty-five years ago when my family died and the dictator Arak staged a coup to take power here. Who is your father?'

Polly stiffened at his question. A headache was forming behind her brow and she was wishing she had access to the medication in her case while also dimly wondering when she could hope to be reunited with her luggage. 'I don't know but if all this happened twenty-five years ago it must've happened around the time I was conceived, so you see I have no further information to offer. I had no idea the ring was a lost treasure, nor do I know how my mother got hold of it or why she kept it. Surely she would've known how important it was?'

'I would've assumed so,' Rashad conceded. 'I was in her care with my brothers from birth to the age of six and during that period your mother must have learned a great deal about my family.'

'What was she like?' Polly was betrayed into asking.

He looked at her in surprise.

'I don't really remember her…at least I have only the vaguest of recollections. Perhaps you don't remember anything about her,' Polly added hastily, her very pale face flushing as she gave him that escape clause.

'She was always smiling, laughing,' Rashad recounted quietly. 'I was fond of her…as were my brothers. She was not blonde, like you…she had red hair—'

Polly nodded stiffly, thinking about her sister's red hair, which Ellie hated. 'Is there anyone else here who would still remember her?' she asked daringly. 'Naturally I'm very curious about her.'

'Few of the staff from that era remain in the household,' Rashad responded with regret, his lean dark face shadowing because so many of the palace staff had died in the coup.

'So what happens to the ring now?' Polly pressed tautly.

'It must remain here in Dharia,' Rashad pointed out in some surprise, as if she should have grasped that reality immediately. 'This is where it belongs.'

Polly lifted her chin, her blue eyes darkening with annoyance even as a mortifying trickle of sweat ran down between her breasts below her loose tee shirt. She might be feeling hot and bothered and impossibly tired but there was nothing wrong with her wits. 'But it is *my* ring and it's the only token I will ever have from my mother.'

Rashad was taken aback by her statement. 'That is most unfortunate but—'

'For me, *not* for you!' Polly interrupted fierily, her anger sparking at his immense assurance and his assumption that she would simply accept the situation.

Rashad was unaccustomed to being interrupted and even less familiar with the challenge of dealing with an angry woman. An ebony brow lifted at a derisive slant. 'You are more fortunate than you appreciate,' he told her levelly. 'You could have been accused of theft simply for having the ring in your possession—'

Polly rammed back her chair and stood up, bracing her hands down on the table to steady herself because that quick impulsive movement had left her a little dizzy. 'Well, go ahead and have me charged with theft!' she urged furiously. 'How *dare* you treat me like a criminal? My journey has been interrupted. I was marched off by security staff in front of an audience at the airport, held against my will in a nasty little room for hours and had the life threatened out of me when a crowd mobbed the car on the way here—'

'You were selected at random at the airport to be searched in a drug-screening scheme we have recently established,' Rashad interposed smooth as glass. 'I regret that you have been inconvenienced and embarrassed and will ensure that what remains of your holiday compensates you for the experience.'

Backing further away from the table and its support, Polly valiantly straightened her back and squared her shoulders to lift her head high. 'I want my mother's ring back!' she declared stridently.

Rashad rose fluidly upright, shamefully entertained by the sheer fury that had erupted in her face, flushing the skin to a delicious shade of pink, darkening her bright blue eyes to violet and compressing her lips into a surprisingly tough line. 'You must know that that is not true. The ring did not belong either to your mother or your family—'

'It was left to me. Therefore it belongs to me.'

Rashad raised a black brow as he strode towards

her and she warily backed away, her legs feeling oddly weak and unusually clumsy.

'The most basic law is that a stolen item may not be considered the legal possession of the person it is given or sold to because the individual who gave or sold it did not have the right of ownership to do so.'

Polly wasn't listening to him. After all, now he was talking like a lawyer and, even in his light grey designer suit, he looked like a fantasy against the colourful backdrop of the courtyard. He didn't look real, indeed none of what had happened to her since she first set foot on the soil of Dharia felt remotely real, so far did those events lie outside her experience. And all of it, *him*, her surroundings and the whole complex problem of the wretched ring, not to mention the heat, which she was finding unbearable, was becoming too much for her.

'I'm not going to discuss it with you because it's *my* ring, not yours!' Polly flung back at him dizzily while she wondered why her fantasy image of him was turning a little fuzzy round the edges and putting him into a soft focus that did very little to blur the hard cast of his lean, darkly handsome features.

'You are being most unreasonable,' Rashad told her without skipping a beat while he stared at her, fascinated by the firebrand personality hidden beneath that beautiful fragile outer shell. 'You are even being—forgive me for saying it—a little childish.'

Perspiration trickling down her forehead, Polly's small hands balled into fists. 'If you weren't who you are I'd thump you for saying that!'

A harried knock sounded on the French windows that led back into the palace and Hayat rose to answer it, bowing backwards out of his presence in the same way the staff had behaved over a century ago. The old ways were not always the *right* ways, Rashad reflected with a sigh. Polly shouting at him and threatening him with a ludicrous assault had had a wonderfully refreshing effect on his mood. Had she any idea how many Dharian laws she had just broken? No, nor would she care were she to be informed because she was angry with him and felt free to express her anger openly and honestly. Rashad had never enjoyed such freedom of expression or action. All he had learned about from the age of six was duty and the always dire consequences of *not* doing one's duty.

Hakim was framed breathless in the doorway, frantically indicating a need to speak to him.

Rashad suppressed his irritation at the interruption. After all, whatever good or bad thing had happened, it was his job to deal with it, regardless of mood and timing. For one final self-indulgent moment, he focused on Polly, marvelling at her pale perfection in the sunlight. 'I don't think you could hit me even if you tried to do so,' he responded silkily. 'I am highly skilled in almost every form of combat.'

'But you talk like a textbook,' Polly mumbled shakily, moving jerkily forward as if she was struggling to walk back to the table.

But she didn't make it. Her small frame crumpled down on the tiles in a heap. Hayat released a small startled scream but Rashad was a lot more practical.

He bent down and scooped Polly up off the ground, astonished by how little her slight body weighed. Hayat went from screaming to wailing an urgent cry for help indoors so that a squad of guards came running in an unnecessary panic that their King was in danger.

Rashad refused to put Polly down when others offered to release him from his burden. Hakim was already calling the palace doctor. 'I will speak to you when we are alone,' he murmured guardedly.

'What is the matter with her? Bad temper!' Hayat remarked to no one in particular in the lift, which was uncomfortably full of people. 'She shouted at the King. I could not believe my eyes or ears.'

Rashad wondered idly whether Hayat had been a playground sneak, who told tales on her peers. She was very snide about other women and always in his vicinity as if she feared he might not notice female flaws without her drawing them to his attention. He knew that as the sister of his late wife she regarded herself as a superior being. She belonged to a leading Dharian family. And every prominent Dharian family had put forward their daughters as potential brides for the King, a dangerous state of affairs that had convinced Rashad that he had to choose a bride from another country to maintain the peace between the various clans all jockeying for social position.

Rashad laid Polly down on a silk-clad bed. She was starting to recover consciousness, her eyelids flickering, little formless sounds emerging from her full pink lips. But even in that condition she contrived to look remarkably like an idealised image of an angel he had once seen in a book.

'Dr Wasem is here,' Hakim said at his elbow, and Rashad stepped back from the bed, suffering one of those weird 'moment out of time' sensations and momentarily spooked by it.

Being men, they retreated to the corridor while the female contingent of the household took charge.

'I wonder what is wrong with her,' Rashad said tautly.

'I wonder what our excitable crowds will make of this latest development. One of your guards used his phone in the lift. I frowned at him. He should have desisted immediately. What kind of discipline have we here when even the men dedicated to protecting you are taking a part in this media gossip nonsense?' Hakim was steadily working himself up into a rant.

'She was so pale. I should have realised it wasn't natural for her to be that pale,' Rashad breathed as if his adviser hadn't spoken.

Minutes later, Dr Wasem joined them. 'Heatstroke,' he pronounced with a hint of satisfaction at the speed of his diagnosis. 'Normally I would suggest our guest be taken to hospital but I am aware of the current mood in our city. The women will ensure that she is rapidly cooled down and rehydrated. I wonder whose idea it was to take a woman who had already endured a long flight outside during the hottest part of the day? Even our constitutions are taxed in such temperatures as we have in summer.'

A slight flare of colour outlined Rashad's stunning cheekbones. Sunstroke.

'That is serious—'

'Not as serious as what I have to tell you,' Hakim whispered once the doctor turned away to reel off further instructions to the cluster of women at the bedroom door.

With difficulty, Rashad rose above the guilt he was experiencing because sunstroke could be very serious and his guest could have had a fit, convulsions or even a heart attack if her temperature were not speedily reduced. He was appalled by his own thoughtlessness. 'And what is that?'

'Our guest may say she is called Polly but the name on her passport is Zariyah,' Hakim divulged in an even lower-pitched whisper.

'But that is…that is my great-grandmother's name. It is rarely used,' Rashad framed in shock, for the name was not used in Dharia out of respect for his ancestor's memory. 'How can her birth name be Zariyah?'

'My suspicions have taken me in a direction I really do not wish to go,' Hakim admitted heavily. 'But her mother's possession of that ring and her use of that name for her child, added to her unexplained disappearance all those years ago, deeply concerns me…'

'It is not possible that she could be a relative!' Rashad protested with rare vehemence.

'With the timing, added to your father's predilection for dallying with pretty women on the staff, it is sadly…possible,' Hakim spelt out grimly. 'A DNA test must be taken. Our guest could be your half-sister.'

'My…' Half-sister? Reeling with shock, Rashad had frozen into position by the wall as he struggled mightily to handle that shattering possibility while instinctively swallowing back any repetition of that familial designation.

That was not a result he wanted. No, he didn't want that, he definitely *didn't* want to discover that he had been sexually attracted to a long-lost family member. The very idea made him feel sick. But hadn't he once read somewhere about such unnatural attachments forming between adults who had not been raised together as children?

'It must be confirmed one way or another. We must know,' Hakim repeated doggedly. 'Annabel Dixon was a flirtatious woman and your father was—'

The strong bones of Rashad's bronzed face set hard as granite as he spoke. 'I *know* what he was.'

# CHAPTER THREE

POLLY SURGED BACK to recovery to find herself naked and being sponged down. In horror at her condition and the strange faces surrounding her she began to struggle to sit up and cover herself.

'I am sorry but this treatment is necessary to bring your temperature down quickly,' a pretty young brunette explained from the head of the bath in which she had been lain. 'I'm Azel and I'm a nurse. You are suffering from heatstroke and although this must be unpleasant for you, it is not as unpleasant as more serious complications would be.'

Heatstroke? Polly recalled the claustrophobic burning heat of that courtyard and suppressed a groan, knowing she should have admitted that she was far too hot out there. She was embarrassed by the fact that she had fainted and caused a whole fuss. Furthermore she had a vague memory of shouting at King Rashad and of threatening to thump him. Her cheeks prickled with mortification and she said nothing until the treatment was complete. The nurse took her temperature and blood pressure and pronounced both satisfactory before she was finally patted dry with a towel. She was then eased into some sort of silky garment and tucked into a very comfortable bed as if she were a young child.

An older man entered and introduced himself as Dr Wasem. He took a sample of her blood and a swab from her mouth before advising her to have a light meal and rest.

As if she were going to just lie there and sleep after all that had happened, Polly thought in disbelief. But once she had drunk as much water as she could manage her eyelids began to slide down as though weights were attached to them, her body sinking into the comfy mattress, and she was asleep before she knew it.

When she wakened, darkness had fallen and she focused in bemusement on the woman seated in a small pool of light near the door. It was Azel, the nurse who had addressed her earlier. Slowly she sat up and voiced her most pressing need. Urged to leave the bed with care in case she felt dizzy, she padded into the bathroom and freshened up with relief. It was after midnight and the silence within the palace walls was unfamiliar to a born and bred Londoner, accustomed to the sound of traffic and the outside glow of street lights.

A knock sounded on the door. 'Do you want anything out of your case?' Azel asked helpfully.

Grateful to finally be reunited with her luggage, Polly retrieved the necessities.

'I've ordered a light meal for you. You must be very hungry.'

'It's the early hours of the morning here,' Polly pointed out in surprise.

'The palace is staffed round the clock. It's a very convenient place to live,' Azel imparted with a smile.

A tray was brought and Polly tucked happily into a chicken salad. She wondered what time it was at home, not having yet got her head around the time difference. She would phone Ellie in the morning, she thought ruefully. In spite of her sleep, she still felt ridiculously tired and tomorrow when she got back to her interrupted holiday she would feel better able to explain how her unexpected inheritance from their late mother had brought her nothing but trouble. Her sister would be unsurprised, she thought fondly, for Ellie had a more cynical outlook on life than her older sister.

The next time she wakened, she could see the brightness of day lightening the wall above the curtains and she was alone. Rising, she dug clean clothes out of her case and she went for a shower. Well, this would be a tale to tell, she reflected with rueful amusement, flying out to Dharia in the hope of exploring her parentage only to end up spending the night in the royal palace.

A maid appeared with a trolley once she had returned to the bedroom and she chose a selection of foods from what was on offer and ate with appetite while she planned what she would say to her sister when she called her. She was reluctant to say anything that would wind up Ellie's fiery temper and more aggressive nature. Placed in the same position, Ellie would have been screaming for the assistance of the

British Embassy before they even got her out of the airport.

But when she dug into her handbag for her phone she couldn't find it even after emptying the bag contents out onto the bed. Her mobile had clearly been stolen. Her money was intact, as was her passport, but her phone was gone. She was furious. It was a cheap phone too, not one she would've believed anyone would think worth stealing. Well, she would take that up with King Rashad when she next saw him. In the meantime, she still needed to ring Ellie, who would be panicking because she hadn't got in touch when she had promised to do so. Honestly, even though Polly was older, Ellie treated her like such an innocent just because she had never been abroad before, Polly mused, shaking her head.

She opened the bedroom door and found a maid and an armed guard standing outside, which took her aback. She was even more disconcerted when the soldier wheeled round and dropped to his knees, bowing his head, muttering something in his own language. Well, good luck with that, whatever it was or meant, Polly decided, politely ignoring his display when it occurred to her that perhaps it was a prayer time of day and he was devout.

'I need a phone,' she told the maid. 'I have to phone my sister.'

The maid beamed and took her back into her bedroom to show her the landline by the bed. Polly suppressed a groan, not wishing to mention that she had wanted a mobile phone to make a free call on an app because she wasn't sure the young woman's English would be up to that explanation. With a sigh, reflecting that Dharia with its oil wealth could surely afford one phone call after the ordeal she had been put through, she lifted the handset.

Ellie answered her call at predictable speed. 'Where are you? Why has it taken you so long to phone me? I've been really worried about you!'

And Polly proceeded to give her sibling the watered-down version of the truth that she had already decided on but she did have to explain that their mother had apparently had no right to even have the fire-opal ring, never mind bequeath it to anyone.

'Well, I think a lawyer would need to decide that, not some jumped-up foreign ruler!' Ellie exclaimed, angrily unimpressed. 'You have to fight this, Polly. Are you sure you're free to leave the palace? Why have they a guard stationed outside your door? Try going for a walk and see what happens. I'm very suspicious about the set-up you've described and I think I may approach the Foreign Office to ascertain what your position is and ask for advice—'

'Do you really think that's necessary?' Polly prompted ruefully. 'Don't you think you're taking this all too seriously?'

'Polly…you don't pick up on warning signals!' Ellie condemned with heartfelt concern. 'You're always making excuses for the bad things people do…I'm not sure I could trust you as a judge of human character!'

Polly completed the call, her face flushed and sheepish. Now Ellie was up in arms and ready to do battle!

Although she believed her sister's concern was groundless she was willing to test Ellie's suggestion that she try going for a walk. She grabbed her sunhat and sunglasses and left the room, turning left at random and moving along a stone corridor, pausing to look down at an inner hall covered with the most eye-catching mosaic tiles she had ever seen.

She traversed a wide stone staircase and stilled again to admire a big wide corridor of elaborate arches that stretched away into the distance to frame the far vista of a lush garden at the end. As she set off to explore she noted that the guard was following her but not closely and he was so busy chattering to the maid that had accompanied him that Polly reckoned she could've turned cartwheels without him noticing. She wandered down the corridor and peered out into the gorgeous garden that shaded a pool in the shape of a star. The stone arches surrounding the courtyard were as exquisitely carved and detailed as handmade lace. It was truly beautiful and had she had her phone with its camera she would have loved to take photographs.

Her exploration ranged deeper into the building until she finally recognised the main hall where she had arrived the day before, and she was approaching the entrance when the woman who had served tea to her and the King appeared out of a doorway.

'Miss Dixon?' she called with a very artificial smile. 'The King asks that you join him for lunch.'

'How lovely,' Polly responded with a rather more natural smile, her face heating as she recalled her first meeting with Rashad, the gorgeous talker of textbook English.

Turning to follow the woman, she faltered only slightly when she finally registered that her guard of one had turned into a guard of six while she was wandering and all of them backed away in concert and flattened themselves back against the wall and averted their eyes as she passed by. Weird, *really* weird—maybe it was considered impolite to look too directly at a female, she pondered uncertainly. Certainly, her companion's jaw had tightened so much in response to that display that it might have been carved from stone.

Lunch was mercifully being served indoors, Polly appreciated as she entered a room with a polished marble floor and contemporary furnishings that fitted in surprisingly well with the ancient walls. Rashad appeared without warning, striding in through a connecting door to the left only to stop dead the instant he saw her. Her feet stopped too and without her meaning to still them where she stood. And there he was, she thought rather giddily, jaw-droppingly gorgeous and breathtakingly sexy. Sexy wasn't a word she normally applied to or indeed even *thought* of around men, but it rushed to her brain the minute she saw Rashad and it made her wonder if that was the main drawback of being a virgin and essentially inexperienced. Did sheer curiosity about sex give her a more impressionable response to men? But it had never happened to Polly around any other man, she reasoned, irritated by her wandering thoughts.

'Please sit here,' her companion interposed, tugging out a chair at the table Polly hadn't even noticed ahead of her.

'You look better today,' Rashad commented quietly as he settled down opposite her, his attention locked to the delicate colour in her cheeks and the sparkle in her blue eyes.

'Yes, feeling better too. Sorry about the fuss I caused,' Polly responded dismissively, trying not to look directly at him, utterly unnerved by the effect he had on her usual calm state of mind.

Rashad was disappointed that her hair was braided. He had never seen such beautiful hair before. Simply the novelty of different colouring in a country where most people had black hair, he told himself doggedly. She was wearing trousers again and a loose white top and he would not allow himself to wonder the things that his brain wanted to wonder. He angrily shut that side of himself down and began to make excruciatingly polite conversation of the sort he was accustomed to making at foreign dinner parties.

'My phone wasn't in my bag when it was returned to me,' Polly announced without warning, encountering eyes so dark they glittered like stars in the light filtering through the open doors behind him.

'Enquiries will be made on your behalf,' Rashad fielded smoothly, well aware that the phone had most probably been confiscated as a security precaution at Hakim's order. 'I am sure it will be found and returned to you.'

'Thank you,' Polly said equally politely, wondering why he seemed so different from the man he had seemed to be the day before.

He was more controlled, almost stiff and expressionless, the lean strong bones of his face cool and set, his jawline hard. Wary? Hostile? Offended? She marvelled at the extent of her own curiosity and scolded herself for it. Why should she care? She would soon be taking up residence in her little bed-and-breakfast place near the bazaar in Kashan and she could be fairly sure that she would never meet an actual reigning king again in her lifetime. He could only be lowering himself to sharing a meal with a foreign commoner to pursue the controversial topic of the fire-opal ring he wanted to retain.

'About the ring,' she began abruptly.

'We will not discuss that now,' Rashad decreed without hesitation. 'When you have fully recovered from your illness we will discuss it.'

Off-balance at the flat refusal, Polly studied him for several tense seconds. He was the most infuriating man. She could see that he expected the subject to be dropped simply because he had issued an embargo and his sheer level of assurance hugely annoyed her. 'I *am* fully recovered,' she traded quietly. 'And grateful as I am for the care I received when I took ill and the hospitality which has been offered to me here, I would like to return to my holiday plans as soon as possible.'

'Perhaps we will discuss that tomorrow,' Rashad fielded without batting a single lush black eyelash.

'You do realise,' Polly whispered, because that hard-eyed brunette she couldn't quite warm to was seated only ten feet away, 'that you are making me want to thump you again? I thought it might be my high temperature that caused my loss of temper yesterday but I can now see that it was merely you being you—'

A brilliant smile unexpectedly stole the grim aspect from his lean, dark, brooding features. 'Me being me?' he queried with perceptible amusement in a clear encouragement for her to expand on her feelings.

'Horribly bossy. And I can see you're used to people doing exactly as you say—'

'Because I am the King,' Rashad filled in helpfully.

'But you're not *my* King.' Polly made that distinction with a slow sweet smile of mingled exasperation and reluctant amusement.

When he saw that smile, Rashad froze and leant back into his chair, squaring his shoulders while he wondered if she was flirting with him. Probably not, his brain told him. The British women he had been intimate with a few years earlier had used methods that were considerably more direct to attract and hold his attention.

'But you are still my guest,' Rashad retorted with lashings of cool. 'And the Dharian rules of hospitality are strict. One should never make a guest uncomfortable—'

'But you're doing exactly that right now!' Polly hissed at him in frustration.

His long brown fingers clenched taut round the cutlery. He tore his gaze from her lovely face, painfully aware that she made him very uncomfortable. With the discipline of years strengthening him, he studied his plate and he ate in complete silence.

'In fact, you're only making me want to stick a fork in you,' Polly whispered across the table.

And that was it—Rashad lost that minor battle. A wholly inappropriate laugh broke from his lips when he failed to stifle his enjoyment. Polly studied him in surprise and then encountered the brunette's chilling appraisal, which suggested that amusing the King could well be a capital offence.

'We will talk again tomorrow,' Rashad informed her quietly as they vacated the table they had shared.

Polly had to forcibly put a lid on her growing frustration with him. She was being too polite, she told herself. He had blocked her questions and refused to discuss the matter of the ring or tell her when she could leave. But did that really matter? After all, she was being treated like an honoured guest. Staying in the lap of luxury in a truly magical royal palace, another little inner voice chipped in gently, was scarcely a penance. It was a gift to be housed in such a gorgeous building, to be waited on hand and foot and to be wonderfully well fed. How could she possibly form a bad opinion of her host? It wasn't as though she had been stashed in some primitive prison cell. Moreover she was being granted an intriguing glimpse of a very different and far more colourful lifestyle.

Satisfied by that more positive take on her unexpected stopover in a royal dwelling, Polly wandered off to enjoy all that the exotic palace had to offer. She ignored the troop of men, armed to the teeth, and the maid following close behind her, and roamed from the magnificent desert views available from the recently built rooftop terrace down through the state rooms, with their superb intricate brass-covered arched doors and elaborate interiors, right down to the kitchen, with its army of busy staff, who fell silent and froze in shock when she first appeared.

With the maid acting as an interpreter, Polly ended up seated in yet another shaded courtyard, being plied with chilled strawberry and honey tea and an array of fantastic little pastries. Somewhere about then she decided that she was having a truly wonderful holiday even if it was not advancing her an inch in her unlikely search to find out more about her father.

Possibly that had always been an unrealistic goal, she thought in disappointment. Too much time had passed. How did she even risk voicing the name she had been given when the poor man might not be her father at all and was probably long since married? She didn't want to upset anyone and the mother she barely remembered had been sufficiently dysfunctional in her relationships even with her own family that she did not feel she could place much faith in Annabel Dixon's judgement.

Later that afternoon a dialogue that would have very much shocked Polly was about to take place. Hakim had collected the DNA results and had received such a shock that he had passed much of the afternoon at prayer, wrestling with his guilt and with sentiments it was too late to express. Having unburdened himself, he had then received a shock almost as great when events that had taken place a quarter of a century earlier were clarified for him by an unexpected source. Sharing that information with his King was almost more than Hakim could bear but he did not have a choice.

'Our guest is *your* granddaughter?' Rashad repeated with incredulity. 'How is that even possible, Hakim?'

The older man sighed heavily. 'At the time my son Zahir died we were estranged. That has been a lifelong source of regret to me. I was aware that he was involved with the nanny but I also suspected her of having other male interests on the staff at the time. I knew that my son wished to marry her and he refused to listen to my objections. I urged him not to marry her—citing the example of my own parents, who married across the cultural divide—and my son took offence.'

Rashad was silent while his trusted adviser unburdened his troubled conscience. Zahir had been Hakim's only child and that much more precious for that reason, and the day after the death of Rashad's family Zahir had died heroically trying to defend the palace and its inhabitants from Arak's squad of hired mercenaries.

'And now you see the consequences of my miscalculation. I spoke to my son from my head instead of from my heart. He loved this woman and she was already pregnant. He would not have told me *that*,' Hakim acknowledged hoarsely, his emotions roughening his usually steady voice. 'When the nanny vanished after his death I never thought about her again...why would I have? But I have only now learnt that Zahir married her privately and secretly only the day before he died. May I humbly request some time off to go home and discuss this astounding discovery with my wife—?'

'Of course,' Rashad breathed tautly, struggling to absorb the apparent truth that Polly, in spite of her misleading colouring, actually carried Dharian blood in her veins. 'But who does she resemble?'

'*My* mother,' Hakim confided tremulously. 'That hair. I should have suspected it the instant I laid eyes on her. I must also ask you to put all matters pertaining to my grandchild and the current unrest in the streets in the hands of my two deputies, because I am no longer a suitably independent and disinterested third party—'

'That I refuse to do,' Rashad responded instantaneously. 'I trust you as I trust no other man close to me.'

'You do me great honour in saying so but I—'

'Go home to your wife, Hakim,' Rashad urged gently. 'For today at least put family first and official duty second.'

Freed from the risk that Polly could be a half-sibling, Rashad smiled thoughtfully. Well, surprisingly, he was *her* King because although she did not know it her paternity granted her dual citizenship. He wished he could tell her that but it was her grandfather's right to break such news, not his.

The following morning other concerns swiftly consumed him when one of Hakim's aides brought the most popular newspaper in Dharia to him. The secret of Polly's true name on her passport was a secret no longer and it was just the kind of nonsense liable to inflame the superstitious with fanciful ideas. A single king, a single woman named Zariyah after his great-grandmother, the return of the Hope of Dharia... Such coincidences were being interpreted as supernatural signposts of heavenly endorsement in the home of his birth.

Rashad heaved a sigh. It was little wonder that Polly's birth name was now being chanted in the streets. He could not possibly let her leave the palace, for there was no chance of her enjoying an anonymous holiday after her passport photograph had been printed in the newspaper. Proving that the hysteria was generalised throughout every strata of Dharian society, the usually sensible editor had totally ignored all safety concerns when he put such information into the public domain.

And Rashad's day only darkened in tenor when he was informed that an official from the British Embassy was currently waiting to be seen. The diplomatic incident that Hakim had feared was beginning to happen...

Polly was watching the local television station as she ate her breakfast and wishing she could speak the language. She had tried and failed to access a European television channel. But she did not need Arabic to recognise that the massed crowds in the streets of the capital city were on the edge of overexcited. She wished she could read the placards some of them carried and waved along with the Dharian national flag.

Having promised to phone Ellie again, she did so. Her sibling startled her by admitting that she had spoken to a man from the Foreign Office and that official enquiries were being made about her so-called arrest and imprisonment at the royal palace.

'Oh, my goodness, Ellie!' Polly fielded in consternation. 'How could you *do* that? I'm having a really interesting time here—'

'This ring business you're involved in stinks to high heaven of some sort of a cover-up. I don't think you have a clue what's happening out there. As usual you're just sailing along and letting people push you around—'

Polly let her sister state her case and finally agreed that it was time she returned to the holiday she had booked and that she would *demand* the right to leave the palace and return to Kashan. Before she could lose her nerve she used the palace switchboard and asked to be put through to the King, wryly amused by her own daring.

'I have to speak to you,' Polly declared boldly as soon as she heard his dark deep drawl. 'And as I may shout, it would be better if we didn't have an audience.'

At his end of the phone, Rashad almost groaned out loud for palace protocol stated that he should never ever be left alone with a member of the female sex. He knew it was to protect him from the slurs and scandals caused by his father's debauchery but it was not easy to escape the tightly linked net of strict procedure.

'Meet me on the roof terrace,' he urged abruptly. 'I hear you were there yesterday and it is shaded. I'll join you as soon as I can.'

The strangest shred of compassion infiltrated Polly. It was clearly a no-no for him to meet up with her alone. When did the Dharian King ever get to be alone? She had seen the security team that followed him everywhere he went and she wondered what it was like to live in such a goldfish bowl where every word and every action was monitored.

Polly left her room and told the maid she wanted to walk alone. The three men guarding her room studied her in wonderment but when she moved off, she was not followed and relief spread through her because she felt really free for the first time within the royal walls with no one watching over her.

The shade on the roof terrace took what she believed to be a rather odd form. A giant tent had been set up at one corner. Within it opulent floor cushions surrounded a fire pit and there was an array of the implements she assumed were required to brew the traditional tea. Walking out of the bright sunshine, Polly sank down with relief on a cushion to enjoy the view. It was fifteen minutes before Rashad appeared through another entrance onto the terrace.

'We are breaking rules,' he told her with a sudden flashing smile of such charisma that her heart jumped inside her. 'This is not allowed.'

'Sometimes it's fun to break rules,' sensible Polly heard herself say dry-mouthed because for the first time Rashad was wearing traditional clothing, a muslin cloth bound by a gold rope hiding his black hair, a pristine white long buttoned robe replacing Western clothing. And that cloth merely accentuated his stunning dark eyes and arresting bone structure, so that breathing was barely an option for her as he sank with fluid animal grace down opposite her.

'And sometimes there is a price to pay for breaking

those rules,' Rashad murmured with wry amusement. 'Why did you want to speak to me?'

'I want to leave the palace and start my holiday,' Polly told him simply, even though she knew that somewhere down deep inside her she really didn't want that at all. It was the rational thing to do, she reminded herself doggedly. She did not belong in a royal palace.

Rashad linked long brown fingers and flexed them. 'I'm afraid I can't agree to that.'

He even had beautiful hands, Polly was thinking abstractedly before she engaged with what he had actually said and it galvanised her into leaping upright in disbelief. 'So, I *am* a prisoner here?' She gasped in horror that her sister could have been correct in her far-fetched suspicions.

'Do not lose your temper,' Rashad urged levelly. 'Allow me first to explain the situation we are all in—'

'The only person in a situation here is *me*!' Polly exclaimed angrily.

'There is great unrest in Kashan. You would not be safe…you would be mobbed. While no one would wish to harm you in any way, excited crowds are very hard to control.'

'I don't know what you are talking about.'

'Sit down, listen and I will explain,' Rashad instructed with quiet strength.

'No, you can explain while I stay standing,' Polly responded, determined not to give way on every point.

'Very well.' Rising as gracefully as he had sat down, Rashad stepped back out of the tent and strode over to the rail bounding the terrace. 'A century ago—'

*'A century ago?'* Polly practically screeched at him, gripped by incredulity that that could possibly be the starting point of any acceptable explanation for her apparent loss of all freedom.

'Close your mouth and sit down!' Rashad raked back at her in sudden frustration, his dark deep voice startlingly like a whiplash in the silence. 'If you refuse to listen, how can I speak and explain?'

Polly compressed her lips and sat down with a look of scornful reluctance on her heart-shaped face. 'Well, if you're going to shout about it—'

'I must make you aware of the most powerful legend in Dharian history. A hundred years ago, my great-grandmother, Zariyah, came to Dharia with the fire-opal ring and gave it to my great-grandfather, who then married her. My people think it was love at first sight,' Rashad advanced. 'But in actuality it was an arranged marriage, which was very popular and which ushered in a long period of peace and prosperity for Dharia—'

'That name,' Polly whispered with an indeterminate frown. 'Zariyah. That's the name I was given at birth.'

'The ring is also invested with enormous significance in the eyes of my people. The name on your passport was *noticed.* It may even be the reason why you were singled out for the drug screening process we have begun. You also brought the ring back to Dharia—'

'Not to give to you!' Polly objected vehemently.

'You are much given to interruption,' Rashad fired back at her rawly.

'And you are much given to being quietly listened to.'

'My country endured dark times for over twenty years. My people suffered greatly under the dictator, Arak,' Rashad told her in a curt undertone. 'They are very superstitious. Your appearance, your name and your possession of the ring has led to a hysterical outpouring of sentiment in the streets. At this moment in Kashan, people are waving signs bearing the name Zariyah because my great-grandmother was very much loved. If you left the palace, you would be mobbed and it would be extremely dangerous.'

Polly stared back at him with a dropped jaw. She could barely get her head around what he was trying to tell her. 'You mean, the coincidence of me having that name and the ring is sufficient—?'

'To cause all that excitement? Yes,' Rashad confirmed heavily.

Polly stared numbly into the fire pit, genuinely bemused by what he had explained. People were demonstrating in the city and waving those placards on her behalf? It was beyond her comprehension and her lashes flickered over blue eyes widening in growing amazement.

'But I don't understand. What do they want from me?' she queried numbly.

'In a nutshell, they want you to marry their King,' Rashad replied very drily. 'A single monarch, a single woman with the name of a famous queen…in their eyes it's a simple equation.'

'They want me to *marry* you?' Polly cried incredulously.

'And everything about you plays into their fantasy conclusion,' Rashad imparted with an edge of bitterness because the more he watched those crowds waving flags in the streets, the more his sense of duty warred with his brain. 'You are very beautiful. What man would not wish to marry such a beauty? And while you could have followed some inappropriate career as a stripper or a lap dancer, which would admittedly have doused their enthusiasm somewhat—'

'I beg your pardon?' Polly exclaimed furiously, jumping upright again.

'Instead you work in a homeless shelter helping the underprivileged,' Rashad completed. 'Yes, our media are every bit as given to spying as your own. You have been framed even in the newspapers as the perfect wife in the eyes of my people.'

Polly bolted out of the shade of the tent to stand by the rail in the golden sunshine, staring out at the lines of the shallow sand dunes gradually shifting into larger ones in the distance. 'I'm mortified—'

'I am trapped,' Rashad traded without sympathy, raging at the fates that had created such a disturbing and difficult situation. When he was crowned he had sworn to do whatever it took to make the people of Dharia secure and happy and he had never once considered that sacrifice of freedom as a personal constraint. Only now when it came to the question of his marriage was he finally appreciating the true cost of that pledge. But it also gave him a great deal to think over, he acknowledged, studying Polly and wondering what it would be like to go with the flow of popular sentiment rather than sit it out and hope it eventually died a natural death.

'Certainly not by me!' Polly lashed back at him, one small hand lifting in emphasis off the rail.

Without warning Rashad caught her hand in his, studying the slender bones below the skin that was so pale against his bronzed colouring and the intricate tracing of blue veins at her inner wrist. As if under a compulsion, he bent his proud head and pressed his mouth to that soft, smooth, delicate skin.

Polly studied that down-bent head in complete shock while tiny little tendrils of prickling awareness traversed her entire body. That one little contact was so screamingly sensual she couldn't believe it. She had had passionate kisses that left her cold as ice but the brush of Rashad's mouth across her wrist made her nipples tighten almost painfully inside her bra and forced a surge of hot liquid heat to rise between her thighs in a manner that made her rigid with discomfort. She quivered, shaken, aroused, suddenly out of her depth with him in a way she had never been before. When that skilled mouth roved across her palm and shifted to enclose a single fingertip and suck it, her knees trembled and her legs almost gave way beneath her in response.

Mesmerised, Polly looked up into shimmering golden eyes alight with raw sexual hunger.

An urgent burst of Arabic sounded from somewhere

behind them and she flinched in surprise while Rashad immediately dropped her hand.

Hakim was outraged by what he had seen. He had trusted his King. He had overlooked the reality that his King was a young man with all the appetites of a young man in the company of a beautiful young woman.

'This meeting is most improper,' Hakim informed his granddaughter unhappily. 'But I do not blame you for it.'

Further exchanges took place over Polly's head, which was bent because she was seriously embarrassed. After all, she had requested the private meeting and was guilty of disrespecting what appeared to be the cultural norms of Dharia. Rashad had only kissed her hand though, for goodness' sake, she thought angrily, thoroughly disliking the old man who had intervened and who was contriving to behave as though he had interrupted a raw and shocking sex scene.

'I am Hakim, Miss Dixon,' the older man informed her gently as he led her off the terrace. 'May I call you Polly? Or is it Zariyah?'

With difficulty, Polly recalled her manners. 'No, my grandmother wouldn't call me by my birth name. When I was old enough to understand it *was* my true name, she told me it was foreign and outlandish and she refused to use it, so she gave me the name Polly instead.'

'That is a great pity but perhaps in time that could be remedied,' Hakim remarked incomprehensibly above her head. 'Would you be willing to talk to me? I have something of very great importance to tell you…'

# CHAPTER FOUR

HAKIM ESCORTED HER to a room that he described as his office but which more closely resembled an old library.

Polly sank down in a comfortable armchair but sat bolt upright again, eyes wide with astonishment, when Hakim informed her that he was her grandfather.

'But how could you possibly know that?' she whispered unevenly.

'My mother…' Hakim handed her a creased old photo of a smiling blonde woman. 'My son, your father…'

Polly peered down in wonder at the photo of the attractive dark-eyed young man in the photograph. 'Is his name Zahir Basara?'

Hakim gently corrected her pronunciation and regretfully informed her of her father's death when the palace had been overrun twenty-odd years earlier. Tears stung Polly's eyes as he broke that news while frankly admitting that he and his only child had been at odds at the time of his demise.

'He wanted to marry your mother,' he explained. 'But I refused to support him. My own parents had a mixed marriage. My mother was the daughter of a

Swedish missionary working here. Although my parents stayed together they were not happy. My prejudice blinded me towards the woman my son loved—'

'I can understand that…but are you really sure that your son was my father? His is the name my mother left me with the ring, but—'

Tears dampened Polly's cheeks as her emotions spilled over because she felt so horribly guilty for doubting that name now. How much had she let her grandmother's bitterness colour her own attitude towards her mother? Annabel Dixon had not been lying, nor had she been unsure of who had fathered her first child. Her late mother had told her the truth.

'There can be no doubt because we did a DNA test. A sample was taken from you by the doctor without your permission,' Hakim confided gravely. 'DNA samples of the dead were conserved after the coup that killed our King's family and many others at the palace. I am very sorry that we ordered the test to be done without your awareness—'

'But why *did* you order it?' Polly murmured in bewilderment, too preoccupied by what he had told her to be angry when it had resulted in her finding an actual blood relative of her late father's. 'Why would you do such a thing?'

With quiet assurance, he explained that her arrival with both the Hope of Dharia ring and the name of a former queen had roused the suspicion that she could be a child of Rashad's late father. 'He was a most unscrupulous man with women. He had many extramarital relationships. We are not aware of any children born from those liaisons but it has always been a possibility. Imagine my astonishment when the computer found a match with my own son…'

Polly was just beginning to adapt to the shattering idea that she was in the company of her actual grandfather, who appeared to be a great deal more warm and pleasant in character than her maternal grandmother had proved to be. 'It must have been a nasty shock—'

'No, it was wonderful,' Hakim contradicted with a wide smile. 'My wife, your grandmother, wept with joy and cannot wait to meet you. We are strangers but we would dearly love to be considered family…'

At that generous statement, Polly's eyes flooded with tears again. 'I think I would like that too. Apart from my sister, I've never really had what people call a family. But doesn't it make a difference to you that Zahir and my mother weren't married?'

'But they *were* married,' her grandfather countered and he explained.

'My mother must've been devastated,' Polly commented sickly, trying to imagine the pure horror of marrying the man you loved and losing him again the next day.

'Dharia was in uproar and naturally Annabel fled home to the UK. There was nothing here for her to stay for. She must also have been aware that Zahir's family were hostile to her,' he completed sadly. 'I was very much in the wrong in the way I dealt with their relationship, Polly.'

A small hand covered his and squeezed comfortingly. 'You didn't know. You made a mistake. You wanted the best for your son. You didn't know what the future held…none of us do,' she pointed out quietly.

Hakim beamed at her, his rounded face flushed with pleasure. 'Will you give my wife and myself the opportunity to get to know you?' he asked humbly. 'We would be very grateful.'

Polly mumbled that she would be equally grateful. Tears were tripping her up again and she blinked them back in exasperation but her needle-in-a-haystack search for her father had come to an amazing conclusion. Her father was gone, as was her mother, but she had discovered other relatives to comfort her for that loss. It was more, she felt, than she could have hoped for before she set out on her journey.

'But do not be holding hands with the King again,' Hakim advised in an undertone. 'The fault was his, not yours, but I will not have your reputation soiled.'

'Are relations here in Dharia between single men and women so strict, then?'

'Only when the King is involved,' her grandfather admitted wryly. 'He is a public figure. He must not be seen to resemble his late father by practising any over-familiarity with a female. Once he is safely married, he will not need to be so concerned about appearances.'

Polly's right hand tingled and her face warmed while she distractedly recalled what Rashad had done with her finger. She wondered what an actual kiss would have felt like. With her imagination catching fire at the idea, a wanton charge of heat filtered through her lower limbs and filled her with self-loathing embarrassment. 'Is he planning to get married, then? Has he a wife lined up?'

'Not as yet but he *must* marry,' Hakim told her cheerfully. 'It is a monarch's duty to take a wife and have children to provide stability for the next generation.'

As far as Rashad was concerned, there was definitely a high price to be paid for all that bowing and scraping and luxurious privilege, Polly acknowledged ruefully. She remembered him saying that breaking the rules brought consequences and remembered how quickly Hakim's censure had brought those consequences home. Rashad had known exactly what he was talking about. She had been naïve and thoughtless, she reckoned ruefully, and, if Rashad was never allowed to be alone with a woman, surely it was little wonder that he had got a little carried away with her hand?

Wasn't it even possible that her request to see him alone had given him the wrong impression? Polly winced at the suspicion that he might have believed she was deliberately inviting that kind of attention. But on another level, warmth was still pooling in her pelvis at the recollection. He was a very handsome, very sexy guy and, for Polly, it had been an educational experience to finally realise why other people made such a fuss about the act of sex. If a man just kissing your hand could make you feel that overheated… At that point, she broke off her wandering thoughts and buried them deep.

Her maid wakened her with breakfast at what appeared to be dawn the next morning and told her with eyes that danced with mischief that she was going on a trip. Polly was not told where she was going or why or whose company she would be in and she assumed that that was probably because the young woman's small stock of English wasn't up to that challenge. She wondered if Rashad had managed to contrive some discreet way of returning her to her holiday plans but, when she began packing, the maid's confusion suggested that that was not the explanation. Had her kindly grandfather made some arrangement for her? Regardless, Polly was delighted by the prospect of seeing a little more of her father's country because all she had so far seen were the city streets and the view from the palace rooftop.

The maid led her down a service staircase and through a long tracery of quiet corridors and courtyards that suggested they were taking a more than usually circuitous route through the sprawling palace. They finally emerged into a garage packed with opulent vehicles and with noticeable ceremony she was ushered into an SUV. As they filtered out through the palace gates she noted that another two cars were accompanying them.

She would phone Ellie later, she promised herself guiltily. In truth she didn't want to hear any more of her sister's dire predictions after Rashad had bluntly explained the status quo. She didn't like the situation and neither did he, but there really wasn't very much that could be done about it, was there? It wasn't his fault or hers that his people had chosen to weave her into the legend of his great-grandmother and the fire-opal ring.

While the convoy of vehicles drove out into the desert, Polly settled back in the air-conditioned cool to enjoy her sightseeing. When they began to trundle up and down dunes, she told herself it was exciting although in reality the steep inclines and declines unnerved her. At one stage they passed by a long train of camels laden with goods and there was much hooting of car horns and shouted exchanges. When they descended the last dune she saw the oasis and her breath caught in her throat because that lush spread of green dotted by palm trees and a natural pool was so very beautiful and inviting in such an arid dusty landscape. The car came to a halt and the door was opened.

Without warning, Polly was engulfed in a whooping and chattering crowd of women. It unsettled her but the sociable smiles were a universal language of intent and she smiled as much as she could in response. That tolerance became a little more taxed when she was led into a tent and a long dress was presented to her with the evident hope that she would take off her trousers and tee shirt to put it on. Briefly, Polly froze while she wondered if trousers on a woman were a cultural no-no in such company and she decided to change for the sake of peace. Furthermore the dress, which was covered with blue embroidery, was really very pretty and she surrendered, not even objecting when her hair was unbraided and brushed out because it seemed to give her companions so much pleasure and satisfaction.

Ellie would tell her that she was much too busy being a people-pleaser to do as she liked but Polly loved to make those around her happy, she conceded guiltily as she was escorted between black capacious tents and taken into a very large one overlooking the pool. She sank down in the merciful shade and then Rashad strode in, as informally dressed in jeans and an open shirt as she was formally dressed.

'Rashad…' she murmured in sincere surprise, feeling her entire body heat as hot as the sun outside and her muscles pull taut in reaction to his sudden appearance. 'I suppose I shouldn't call you that. It's too familiar. What do—?'

'You call me Rashad,' he interposed without hesitation. 'How are you feeling after what Hakim told you last night?'

'Still shocked but mainly…' Polly considered thoughtfully '…incredibly happy to have discovered who I am even if I feel very sad that my father is no longer with us. I also like my grandfather.'

'He is a fine man, fiercely loyal and wise.' Rashad tilted his arrogant dark head to one side and lifted a broad shoulder and dropped it again in a sort of fluid fatalistic shrug that was as electrifyingly sexy as all his lithe physical movements. 'When he finds you gone from the palace this morning, however, he will be ready to kill me—'

'You arranged for me to be brought out here?' Polly frowned. 'Why?'

'It was bring you here or jump balconies to visit you in your bedroom. The bedroom would have been the worst option of all,' he told her with derisive amusement lancing through his stunning dark golden eyes.

In truth, very little amused Rashad in the sardonic and cynical mood he was in. He had spent most of the night thinking rather than sleeping, angrily confronting the issue that Polly's arrival with the ring had created and coming to terms with his own position. And the truth of what he should be doing had soon faced him. *There was no choice.* She was the woman his people wished him to marry. No other woman could even hope to fit into a legend. In reality he did not wish to marry at all but that was *his* problem, scarcely the problem of the people he ruled. His sense of duty, moreover, was strong. He would not be a selfish ruler like his father; he would put his people first and foremost in his life. It would be a challenge to remarry even though he could see decided advantages to marrying Polly, whom he, at least, *desired.* He believed that choosing an unknown wife from a photograph, basing the decision on her heritage and what others with a vested interest said about her, would be much more likely to lead to a dissatisfactory marriage. After all, at least he had got to *meet* Polly and draw his own conclusions...

Rashad's eyes were surrounded by the blackest, thickest, longest lashes she had ever seen on a man, Polly was acknowledging giddily, briefly wondering why every cutting edge in his lean dark features was set so hard, from his exotic cheekbones to his aggressive jawline, lending a tough, angry edge to his face. Assuming that that could only be a misapprehension on her part, she savoured the truth that he was still drop-dead beautiful in a way she had never known a man could be.

It was a serious challenge to drag her attention away from either his lean, darkly handsome features or his tall, powerfully muscled body. Indeed the sheer pull of Rashad's erotic allure thoroughly unsettled Polly because she could now feel and recognise the desire he incited in her and it was like nothing she had ever felt in her life before. That physical hunger that she had tried and failed to feel with other men was much more powerful and all-consuming than she had expected.

'I had you brought out here to the oasis so that I could ask you to marry me,' Rashad informed her levelly.

'But we're strangers!' Polly exclaimed in disbelief, totally unable to understand what he had just said and take it seriously.

'No, we are not. I already know much more about you than I would know about a bride I chose from a photograph...which, by the way, is my only other option,' Rashad admitted, choosing to tell her that unattractive truth. 'An arranged marriage would be considered normal for a man in my position although the practice has died out in our society. I've already had one arranged marriage and I don't want another—'

'You've already had *one*? You've been married before?' Polly whispered in wonderment, because she knew he was only thirty-one years old.

'I was married at sixteen—'

'I'm sorry but I think that's...barbaric,' she muttered helplessly. 'You were far too young—'

'We both were but those were more dangerous times and alliances had to be made and marriage was how it was done,' Rashad explained. 'I had no choice and I would very much prefer to have a choice this time.'

'But you said you felt *trapped* by your people's expectations,' Polly reminded him, dancing round the whole topic of his proposal rather than actually getting to grips with it because she just couldn't comprehend the enormity of what he was suggesting. 'Now you say you *want* to meet those expectations—'

'Why not? They chose you but I choose you too,' Rashad murmured huskily, his dark eyes flashing gold over her intent and expressive face. 'I want you.'

And his earthy appraisal left her in no doubt of what he was referring to. That hungry sensation surged and pulsed along her nerve endings and flipped her tummy over to leave her breathless. Her skin flushed, her body coming alive, and she shut her eyes because she could no longer withstand the intensity of his hot gaze.

'And you want me,' Rashad told her with maddening confidence.

Polly's eyes opened and her hands knotted into fists. 'I think you've—'

'No, don't fight me…it turns me on and if you do that I can't promise to keep my hands off you as I should,' Rashad framed in a roughened tone of warning.

*'It turns you on...'* Polly repeated in wonderment.

'Because nobody *ever* fights or argues with me. You can have no idea how boring that becomes,' Rashad admitted grimly.

In possession of a very sparky and forceful sister, Polly almost disagreed because she could not imagine finding pleasure in the apparently stimulating effect of dissension. Instead she said nothing, she simply shook her head. 'Sexual attraction is not a good basis for marriage—'

'It is for me,' Rashad countered without hesitation. 'I am convinced that you would make me the perfect wife.'

'But nobody's perfect!'

'More perfect than flawed,' Rashad qualified smoothly. 'The discovery that you have Dharian blood in your veins only adds to your appeal. This is your world now as much as it is mine and you have a family who will love and support you here.'

Polly bent her head down to escape the temptation of his glittering dark eyes. It was a powerful argument to know that there was another world and another family for her to explore. Apart from her sister she had never had a caring family to lean on, which was why Hakim's welcome had meant so much to her. She wanted to get to know that family and their culture, she wanted to spend time with them, which, with the cost of travel set against her low salary, would be very difficult once she returned home as scheduled at the end of the week.

'There would be advantages and disadvantages to marrying me,' Rashad outlined with dry practicality. 'I do not believe you would be unduly influenced by my wealth but as my wife you would be very rich. On the other hand, you would lose the freedom to do and say exactly as you wish because royals are expected to behave according to protocol. Sometimes that protocol feels stifling but it is there for our protection.'

Polly flushed very pink because although he had

said he hoped she would not be unduly influenced by his wealth, her mind had immediately flown to the good she could do with more money and she was mortified by that embarrassing moment of unwelcome self-truth. But poor Ellie was steeped in student debt and struggling and would be for many more years to come. Moreover, both sisters were desperately keen to trace their missing youngest sister, Penelope, and get to know her, but the hiring of a private detective was utterly beyond their financial means at present. She swallowed hard, ashamed of her thoughts and deciding that money had to be, in truth, the root of all evil and temptation.

'What happened to your first wife?' she asked him abruptly to escape those shameful thoughts of wealth and what she could do with it.

'Ferah contracted blood poisoning from a snake bite and died five years ago,' Rashad revealed in a harshened undertone. 'She did not receive medical attention quickly enough.'

'I'm sorry,' she murmured automatically because her mind was reeling under the burden of all that he had said and her own desperate confusion.

'Do you have an answer for me?' Rashad prompted with an air of expectancy on his lean, strong face.

'Not yet,' she admitted, matching his honesty.

Her brain had flatly rejected marrying him at first. They barely knew each other and it would be insane… *and yet*? She did want him, in fact she wanted him more than she had ever wanted any man and she was not an impressionable teenager any longer. In fact, what if she *never* met another man who made her feel the same way that Rashad did? That terrible fear held her still and turned her hollow inside because he made her feel alive and wanton and all sorts of things she had never felt before. And what was more, she was discovering that she *liked* the way he made her feel.

'Perhaps I can help you to make up your mind,' Rashad murmured with silken softness. 'You will see it as a form of blackmail but in reality it is the only possible alternative if you do not wish to marry me—'

Polly's head reared up, blue eyes wide and bright. 'Blackmail?' she exclaimed in dismay. 'What are you talking about?'

'If you don't marry me, you will have to leave Dharia immediately. Only your departure will end this madness on the streets and in the media.'

Polly was aghast at that cold-blooded conclusion. 'You're willing to throw me out of the country?'

Hard dark eyes held hers. 'If that is what it takes, yes…and naturally I would not wish you to return in the near future,' he decreed harshly.

Polly was shaken by that solution because she had been planning to get to know her grandparents, her newly discovered Dharian family. She had no doubt that Hakim and his wife would be willing to visit her at least once in London but it would not be the same as staying on in Dharia and having the chance to explore her father's heritage and culture for herself.

'I cannot allow the current security situation to continue,' Rashad informed her grimly and he went to the doorway of the tent to clap his hands. 'We will have tea while you consider your options.'

Polly didn't see how tea was going to be the answer to anything but the sheer amount of entertaining ritual involved in the brewing of tea by two robed men at least gave her something to watch while her brain struggled to deal with a rising tide of anxiety. He was using blackmail even if on one level she could understand his position. It was very unfair from her point of view, though, that she should have to suffer for something that was in no way her fault. In many ways by piling on that extra pressure of an immediate departure, he was taking her right to choose away from her.

'Seriously…' she began furiously, 'you would actually force me to go home?'

'When it comes to what is best for my country I will always do it,' Rashad countered with a roughened edge to his dark deep drawl. 'That is my duty.'

Polly compressed her taut lips, her hand clenching angrily round her cup. She knew he meant it. It was stamped in the resolve that had hardened his lean, darkly handsome face. Either she stayed on in Dharia and agreed to marry him or she went home again and stayed there. She didn't need to be pregnant to be offered a shotgun marriage, she reflected angrily. That was what he was offering her with the crowds providing the firepower of pressure.

Yet when it came to marriage all that went with Rashad in terms of baggage and culture and his people's expectations was simply huge. Even so, she quite understood why he was willing when his next-best option was a marriage to a complete stranger about whom he would essentially know nothing.

'Of course, you'd get the ring back if you married me,' she said with a flat lack of humour.

'And gain a gorgeous blonde wife,' Rashad traded with a sudden charismatic smile that lit up his bronzed face, illuminating the hard cheekbones and hollows that gave his features such strong definition.

Polly glanced across the fire pit at him and the knowledge that if she said no she would never see him again sliced into her like the sudden slash of a knife blade. That prospect, she registered in mortification, was not something she wanted to think about. No more easily could she imagine being forced to walk away from the new family she had found. Perspiration beaded her upper lip as she fretted.

Marrying Rashad would be like taking a huge blind leap in the dark and she wasn't the sort of woman who took risks of that nature, was she? But if it worked, there would be much to gain, she reasoned ruefully. She would have her grandparents for support. She was already powerfully attracted by Rashad.

'The answer is…yes. It's insane but…*yes*,' Polly muttered almost feverishly before she could lose her nerve.

Although relief slivered through Rashad at her agreement that relief was threaded with undeniable resentment over his predicament. After all, he had been backed into a corner and forced to marry again. This was *his* choice, he reminded himself sternly. *She* was his choice and far superior to a bride who would have been a complete stranger, but the stubborn streak of volatility Rashad always kept suppressed had flickered from a spark into a sudden burning flame, for it was impossible for him to forget how very much he had hated being married.

# CHAPTER FIVE

'IT'S NOT TOO late to change your mind,' Ellie said with a hint of desperation while she watched the television to see the partying taking place in the streets of Kashan to celebrate Rashad and Polly's wedding day. 'Well, they probably do have you on the tea towels and you would need to be smuggled out of the country in disguise if you *jilted* him!'

'Obviously, I'm not going to jilt him,' Polly said quietly, wishing her sister would stop winding up her nerves with her dire forecasts.

Ellie had landed in Dharia forty-eight hours earlier and she had given her elder sister every conceivable lecture against marriage since her arrival.

*'Marry in haste, repent at leisure. Do you realise what you're getting into? Are you even sure you will be his only wife? What if everything Rashad shows you on the surface is simply a front to persuade you to marry him? Look at those people partying at the announcement! He needs you more than you need him. That should make you suspicious. What if he has another woman hidden somewhere? A woman he really loves?'*

Polly had dutifully listened to every possible argument but she had absorbed few of her sibling's warnings for the simple reason that she suspected that she was falling in love with Rashad. Yes, she had finally worked that out all on her own. How else had she contrived to overlook his threat to throw her out of the country if she didn't agree to marry him?

On her side of the fence, her reasons for marrying Rashad had become resolutely practical over the two short weeks that had passed since his proposal. One, her grandfather spoke very highly of his ruler, and she trusted Hakim and his wife Dursa because she was genuinely convinced that they would rate her need for happiness higher than any desire to see their grandchild wed their King. Two, Rashad had been honest with her. He had paid her no extravagant compliments and had made no mention of love and she had accepted that latter handicap with the strength of a patient, optimistic woman because she hoped that in time his feelings for her would change. Three, there was just something very powerful about Rashad that called to Polly on a very deep level and she couldn't put it into words or explain it, so she had come to think of it as the start of love. She simply knew that she wasn't capable of walking away from him.

And how did she know that? she asked herself as the cluster of chattering maids surrounding her twitched at the skirts of her elaborate wedding outfit and attached more jewellery to her, although she was already laden down with gold and precious gems because Rashad's uncle had saved the family jewel collection along with his youngest nephew. How the fire-opal ring had become detached from that collection would probably never be known but Hakim believed that his son had very possibly taken it and given it to Polly's mother, Annabel, for safekeeping during the chaos following the explosion that had claimed the lives of Rashad's family. Her father, Zahir, had after all been the most senior soldier in the palace that awful day and had died himself within twenty-four hours.

She could never walk away from Rashad when her own family was so deeply involved with the country of Dharia. No, she knew that even if her marriage turned out to be a bad marriage she was very likely stuck with it until the day she died because her grandfather had spelt out to her that she had to think in terms of for ever when it came to marrying a ruling king. Rashad's father had divorced twice before wedding Rashad's mother and those matrimonial breakdowns had been interpreted as signs of his general instability and his lack of staying power and sense of duty as a monarch.

'And even worse, you've hardly seen Rashad since you agreed to marry him,' Ellie reminded her with anxious green eyes.

'He's had so many people to meet and so many arrangements to make,' Polly responded quietly, for Rashad had spent the last fortnight travelling around Dharia. 'He has to consult with others about everything he does to come up with a consensus. It's the way he operates to keep everybody happy that they've had their say and Grandad says it works beautifully.'

Ellie stood back a step to examine her sister's gorgeous appearance. Traditional red and gold embroidery and rich blues had been laid down on the finest cream silk fabric that flowed like liquid and screamed designer just like the matching shoes. Her head was bare, her hair loose, as was the norm in Dharia for a bride. A magnificent set of sapphires glittered at her ears, her throat, her neck and her wrists. Delicate henna swirls decorated her hands and her feet and beneath the dress she wore a chemise with a hundred buttons for her groom to undo on the wedding night. Ellie was more intimidated than she wanted to admit by the pomp and ceremony of Rashad and Polly's wedding and the deep fear that she was losing her sister to another world and another family. She knew that Polly's affections ran loyal and true but how could she possibly compete?

As for Rashad? Well, it went without saying that he was very, very nice to look at, very well spoken as well as educated and civilised but, like the buttons waiting to be undone beneath Polly's dress, what was her future brother-in-law *really* like below the smooth polished façade? That was the main source of Ellie's concern because in her one brief meeting with Rashad she had reckoned that a great deal more went on below that smooth surface than trusting, caring Polly was probably willing to recognise. A man traumatised as a boy by the loss of his entire family, forced into marriage at sixteen, widowed ten years later and then raised to a throne over a population who worshipped him like a god because he had rescued them from a dictator's tyranny? That was quite a challenging life curve to have survived. How much did her sister genuinely know about the man she had agreed to marry?

'Would you *please* stop worrying about me?' Polly urged Ellie with troubled blue eyes. 'I want this to be a happy day.'

'I'm always happy if you're happy,' Ellie declared, giving her a gentle but fond hug of apology.

But Polly knew different. Ellie had always been a worrier, expecting the worst outcome in most situations. She refused to borrow that outlook, wanting to look forward with all the hope and optimism that her wonderful discovery of her loving grandparents had already fanned into enthusiasm. Why shouldn't their marriage work out? She wasn't expecting an easy ride. Of course there would be obstacles and surprises and disappointments but surely there would also be joys and unexpected benefits along the way?

She refused to admit even to her sister how isolated and rejected she had felt at having barely spent even a moment with Rashad since agreeing to marry him. And worse still and far too private for her to share, how very apprehensive she actually felt at the prospect of having sex for the first time with a man she had yet to even kiss…

The wedding was to be very much a public event and screened on television. Refusing to give way to nerves, Polly went downstairs with her sister and her bevy of chattering companions to be ushered into the throne room that had been set up to stage the ceremony.

A sharp pang of regret pierced her that she should still have an unknown sister who could not be part of her day and she wondered how soon after their marriage it would be acceptable for her to ask Rashad for his financial help with that problem. How else was she to locate their missing sister, Penelope?

As she strove to ignore the camera lenses while at the same time studiously trying not to do anything unsightly with her face, her nervous tension surged to an all-time high. And then she saw Rashad, exotically garbed in magnificent red and gold ceremonial robes, and all her anxiety was swallowed alive by a sense of awe and wonder that she was on the very brink of marrying such a divinely handsome male. She felt ridiculously schoolgirlish when she looked at him but, on another, much more intimate level, she also felt surprisingly wanton.

Rashad made her wonder about stuff that she had truly never wasted time thinking about before because for so long sex had been part of other people's lives but never hers. That was just how it had been while her freedom was restricted by her grandmother's long illness. Her gaze locked onto the wide sensual curve of Rashad's mouth and she simply tingled as she wondered what he would taste like, what that glorious long bronzed muscular physique of his would look like naked and, inevitably, what it would be like to be in bed with him. As her colour fluctuated wildly, a tide of heat claimed her innermost depths to encourage an embarrassing dampness at the heart of her and she pressed her thighs together and stood rigid as a rod to discourage her colourful imagination. It embarrassed her to be so very impressionable.

'Wow…' Ellie mumbled at her elbow, overpowered by the sheer medieval splendour of their surroundings. 'Who's that guy with the bridegroom?'

'Some Italian Rashad went to uni with. I haven't met him but I think his name is Rio,' Polly whispered, unable to focus on anyone but Rashad because she was now wondering why her future husband looked so impossibly moody and tense. Didn't he realise that he should be smiling for the cameras? Or was any show of human emotion forbidden to him as a ruler? Or was it even possible that he genuinely loathed figuring as a leading light in such a public event?

The ceremony was short and sweet, translated into both their languages. Polly's hand trembled in the firm hold of Rashad's when he slid the ring onto her slender ring finger. His slightest touch invoked a storm of churning, rippling awareness throughout her entire body and she was embarrassed by it, questioning that it could be normal to be so susceptible to a man. But that anxiety was squashed by her astonishment when she belatedly registered that her wedding ring was a feminised miniature of the famous fire-opal ring that Rashad wore on his hand. It seemed deeply symbolic to Polly that he had deliberately made a feature of the ring that had first brought them together and a brilliantly warm and happy smile softened her previously tense mouth as she looked up at him with starry eyes of appreciation.

His wide sensual lips almost made it into an answering smile of acknowledgement but his shimmering dark eyes remained cool and evasive and a faint pang of disappointment touched Polly. Yet somehow she sensed that his self-discipline was so inflexible and so intrinsic to his character that he would not allow any relaxation of his innate reserve to betray his true feelings. Simultaneously and for the very first time she wondered what those feelings actually were…

Of course she knew and accepted that he wasn't in love with her, even respected his essentially honest nature because he had not tried to deceive her with any false show or foolish promises. But there was something so distinct about his obvious emotional withdrawal that she felt guiltily unnerved by it.

At least Polly was pleased about the ring, Rashad was thinking wryly. It was very probably the first *positive* thought he had had in the two frantic weeks of meetings and reorganisation required before it was possible for him to free up the time to become a husband. And future father, he reflected joylessly. Back to the life of being a sperm donor and praying that the seed took root this time around, he reflected with a pang of distaste. That was, after all, he believed, the *only* reason for him to even get married: to father a child and create the generational continuity for the throne that his people needed to feel safe in the future. He recalled Ferah's heartbreak when she had learned that she had a medical condition that made conception a virtual impossibility and guilt engulfed him over his derisive musings. The ability to have a child would have meant the world to his first wife.

Did Polly have any idea what she had got herself into? And why hadn't he made the effort to warn her?

Why hadn't he? he asked himself afresh, disconcerted by that truth and belatedly recognising that he could have told Polly many things that would have put her off marrying him but that, inexplicably, he had shared not a single one of them. He breathed in slow and deep, more than a little disturbed by the worrying nature of his failure to discuss something so very crucial to the likely success of their marriage. His conscience was suddenly laden down by that awareness.

Admittedly it was a sore subject from his point of view and he saw no good reason to dangerously overshadow the present with the tragic clouds of the past. In truth he had never shared his feelings about marriage with any living person and loyalty and honour demanded that he protect his first wife's memory. After all, Ferah had suffered horribly from the stigma of a ten-year childless marriage and in death she deserved his respect at the very least.

'You need to smile,' Polly whispered under her breath as Rashad guided her out of the throne room in front of an audience of clapping and cheering well-wishers.

'Why?' he whispered back, long-lashed dark golden eyes narrowed. 'It is a solemn occasion.'

'But you're behaving as though you're at a funeral,' Polly muttered in instinctive complaint while they took their seats at a massive long top table in a giant banqueting room already filled with tables.

No, not a funeral but possibly the bonfire of his most

unrealistic hopes, Rashad labelled cynically, his facial muscles tightening so that his bronzed skin traced his sculpted features even more closely. He had hoped to stave off marriage for at least another few months but Polly's explosive effect on the Dharian population had killed that possibility in its tracks. But now that he had fallen dutifully into line, hopefully everybody would be happy for a while and he could relax again. With another person beside him though, with a *wife*... His lean, darkly handsome face tensed again, his dark eyes flashing gold with disquiet until he looked at her afresh. His very beautiful wife, who had shivered with excitement when he'd kissed her hand. He almost groaned at how hard that tantalising memory made him.

As the reception wore on Polly became increasingly troubled by Rashad's grave demeanour. For a split second she glimpsed Ellie laughing uproariously at the side of Rashad's friend, Rio, and that stark contrast sobered her even more. Surely the bride and groom should appear even happier? But Rashad wasn't talking, he wasn't smiling, he was the very antithesis of happy and she was shocked and unnerved by it. Most particularly, Ellie's warnings were haunting her again.

*How much do you really know about Rashad?*

And all of a sudden Polly was in the deeply unenviable position of admitting that she knew virtually nothing about the man she had just married. As soon as the meal was done she submersed herself in her grandparents' sincere happiness on her behalf and their evident conviction that she had married a man who would move heaven and earth to make her happy. Seemingly they saw nothing amiss with Rashad's behaviour.

Was he one of those very moody men one heard about? Oh, dear…oh, no, she thought in dismay at the prospect of being wed to a man who switched from sun to shade at the roll of a dice. Or was it only her that was noticing—or *imagining*—that something was wrong? Was she seeing Rashad from a different perspective now? After all, Hakim was very much a man who served his King and as long as Rashad was courteous her grandfather would be content with the surface show and question no deeper. But it was a little more complicated for a wife, Polly reasoned anxiously, particularly a wife, who suddenly felt as though she had married a stranger…or a Jekyll and Hyde character.

A white open-topped limousine, accompanied by a heavy escort, drove them slowly through the streets of the capital city to the airport. Hundreds of soldiers and police held the excited crowds back behind barriers. Polly waved and smiled as her grandfather had told her she must while marvelling that Rashad's marriage could ignite such demonstrations of sheer joy. She could only hope that she would somehow manage to live up to the people's no doubt high expectations of her and in an undertone, above the loud clamour, she shared that thought with Rashad.

'Get pregnant. That's probably the only thing they really want,' Rashad pronounced very drily.

Polly's blue eyes widened to their fullest extent as her head whipped round to stare at his lean, darkly handsome face in shock. 'Are you serious?' she framed, shrinking not just from his blunt words but from the harshness with which he voiced them.

'You can't be that naïve,' Rashad responded drily. 'It's not as though either of us have a choice in that department and that cliché about honeymoon babies would be a real feat to pull off.'

Polly had paled, the delicate lines of her face freezing as she carefully turned her head away again to dutifully continue waving and smiling. But neither the wave nor the smile came as freely or as easily as earlier because her heart had frozen inside her and her tummy had turned over sickly at his response.

When Rashad had said, 'I want you' was that why? He simply needed a wife to impregnate as quickly as possible? And why, oh, why was she only now thinking about something that should have been obvious to her from the outset? Obviously a king wanted and needed an heir. She hadn't even thought about birth control and now she could see that even the mention of it would go down like a lead balloon. Was she ready to get immediately pregnant? Were they to have no time to become accustomed to living together as a couple before they became a family?

Rashad noticed that Polly had transformed into a still little statue by his side and faint dark colour flared along his cheekbones because he was discomfited by the reality that he had taken his bitterness out on her. 'I'm sorry,' he said instantly. 'I didn't mean that quite the way it sounded.'

As if from a distance, Polly looked down at the lean brown hand suddenly resting warmly on hers but it was too little, too late from a bridegroom who had avoided all physical contact throughout the long and exhausting day they had shared.

Freeing her hand without making a drama of doing so, she said flatly, for the sake of peace, 'I'm sure you didn't.'

*I'm sure you didn't mean to be that blunt and insensitive.*

*I'm sure you didn't mean to make me feel like a rent-a-womb.*

*I'm sure you didn't mean to pile so much pressure on me when conception is not something I can control.*

*I'm sure you didn't mean me to see just how ruthlessly pragmatic you are about conception.*

*But you did.*

She kept up her valiant smile but her eyes stung with tears and her heart felt as if he had taken it in his hand and crushed it. What remained of her determination to have a happy wedding day drained away as well.

If he wasn't prepared to make any effort, why should she?

## CHAPTER SIX

POLLY DROPPED OFF into a nap on the helicopter flight. The noise of the engine combined with her fatigue to simply knock her out. She surfaced when Rashad shook her shoulder. Flushed and bewildered, briefly not even aware of *where* she was, she stumbled stiffly upright to move to the exit, only to be scooped out and carried away from the craft like a bundle. But the natural heat of Rashad's body penetrated even through their clothing and she stiffened in dismay, engulfed by the glorious scent of him. It was a typical Eastern layered fragrance and the already familiar hints of sandalwood, saffron and spice were outrageously exotic and she breathed him in dizzily, all her senses firing as he settled her firmly into the vehicle awaiting them.

'Where are we?' she framed slightly unsteadily when Rashad climbed in after her.

'By the sea. My grandfather used to come here to fish,' Rashad proffered, sounding rather more animated than he had earlier.

And in reality, he was feeling much more relaxed than he had been at the outset of the day. Haunted as he was by destructive memories, the wedding had been like a long dark tunnel of recollection he'd had to fight his way through without betraying himself. But then he would feast his gaze on his bride and the wild seething hunger she incited would claim his brain like an intoxicating drug that made rational thought impossible.

In the midst of recalling their last conversation, Polly stiffened and glanced at him from beneath her eyelashes in a quick sidewise foray, noting the classic purity of his strong profile and the more relaxed line of his beautiful mouth. Evidently escaping the wedding fervour at the palace and the street celebrations in Kashan had revitalised him.

'When I was a little boy, my grandfather brought me here to stay with him several times,' he told her.

'So, you're into fishing?' Polly gathered, forcing herself to speak, to make the effort, although it was hard when she herself was in a remarkably tough and unforgiving mood. He had spoiled her day. He had ridden roughshod over her feelings. But then maybe Rashad didn't have much in the way of feelings, she reflected, feeling downright nasty because he had hurt her. Get knocked up on the honeymoon and please everyone? He had very much picked the wrong bride for that little project. And yet that brief instant when he had carried her out of the helicopter had enveloped her in a cascade of erotic anticipation that made her want to lock herself away because she wasn't quite sure she could trust herself to maintain restraint around him.

'No, I'm not,' Rashad admitted. 'Fishing is too slow a pastime for me. I only have such good memories of those trips because it was rare for me to receive any male attention in those days. I literally never saw my father…and for that matter, I seldom saw my mother. I was my father's third son by his third marriage and of very little importance in the royal household.'

'So, there was a sort of hierarchy in your family?' she remarked, her curiosity engaged in spite of her mood. She was taken aback to learn that he had had little contact with his royal parents even before their death. Yes, she had grasped that her mother had been his nanny but she had still possibly naively assumed that he had continued to enjoy regular interaction with his mother and father.

'Of course. Nobody ever said no to my eldest half-brother because they believed that one day he would be King. Naturally as third in line behind two healthy siblings it was not considered possible that I would ever inherit the Dharian throne.'

Polly watched his lips part and then close again, his strong jaw clenching. She knew that he was remembering the two half-brothers who had died with his parents and her soft heart was pierced on his behalf. 'I'm sorry that you had to lose your family to become what you are today.'

'As God wills,' he murmured with husky finality.

Night was folding in fast around them. The sun was going down in scarlet splendour over the dark shimmering sea while against that backdrop and raised on a rocky outcrop above the beach she could see the silhouette of a battlemented stone building. 'A…castle…?' Polly mumbled. 'We're going to stay in a castle?'

'My grandfather and his friends once used it as a fishing lodge. Don't worry,' Rashad told her, misinterpreting her reaction. 'It's not as medieval as it looks. Our private apartments were renovated soon after I became King. The castle is one of our national treasures—'

'You mean it's open to the public?' she prompted in surprise.

'Only when we're not using it—which means it's open most of the year. It's a Crusader castle and if we want to attract tourists we must offer historic sites. The royal family owns all the sites but from now on we will share them with our people.'

Minutes later, Polly slid out of the car in a stone courtyard while staff rushed around them bowing and grabbing up luggage and smiling endlessly to display their pleasure at their arrival. And Polly thought in wonderment, Rashad's *talking* again. Was that because it was their wedding night with all the expectations that that signified? What else could it be? Her chin lifted and her mouth compressed.

They were ushered into a giant stone room furnished like a very opulent historical set piece. She gazed in awe at the huge scarlet and gold fabric-draped four-poster bed and the matching silver and mother-of-pearl-inlaid furniture. 'Please tell me there are modern washing facilities somewhere,' she whispered.

With a husky laugh, Rashad opened a small arched door in one corner and spread it wide to display the marble-tiled bathroom, presumably custom built to fit the circular turret room.

His laugh and that spontaneous smile brought her head up again, silvery blonde hair spilling across her shoulders, and she connected with black-lashed golden eyes so heated in their steady regard that something in her pelvis burned, liquefied and positively ached. Her heart raced and her face hurt with the effort it took not to smile back but how could she smile and forgive and forget when all her husband wanted her for was to provide him with an heir? He had pretty much ignored her throughout their wedding day, she reminded herself stubbornly, and if his outlook had improved it could only be because he now expected to have sex with her.

Momentarily, as she freshened up at the vanity unit, she paused when she caught a glimpse of her hectically flushed face in the mirror. She couldn't do it—she *couldn't* do the sex thing coldly, on demand, not the way she felt now!

She had always wanted that first experience to be special and she had expected it to be special with Rashad right up until he had made her feel like an anonymous female body to be impregnated. Was she being unfair? Even unreasonable? She knew he needed an heir but following on from his behaviour throughout their wedding that had been a step too far into the dark for her to accept.

Her body was hers alone to share or deny. She had always been the least likely woman to be coaxed into doing anything she didn't want to do because for all her eagerness to please she had always had a very strong sense of self. But until she met Rashad she hadn't actually *wanted* to have sex with anyone, not that acting as her grandmother's carer for years had given her many opportunities in that department, she conceded ruefully. But right now, this night, *this* moment felt very wrong to her because she needed more from Rashad than he had so far given her to feel safe with him…and yet?

Deep down inside she wanted him, *craved* him as much as her next breath of air, she acknowledged in driven discomfiture. Her brain might say one thing but her body was singing an entirely different tune. Her breasts were full and tight and there was something like a little flame burning low in her pelvis that had made her all tender and damp and aching in a place she had literally never thought about before. But it wasn't right, she reminded herself doggedly. Where was her self-respect? Her courage?

*Well, what are you waiting for?* she asked her now wildly flushed reflection in the mirror. She had to tell him before expectations got out of control.

Rashad watched Polly emerge from the turret room and he strode forward, involuntarily drawn by the sheer effect of her delicate ethereal looks and all that beautiful trailing white-blonde hair. He stretched out a hand to clasp her smaller one, tugging her to him with an impatience he couldn't control even though his brain was warning him to go slow. There was so much hunger inside him for the bubbling warmth of her smile and the as yet undiscovered delights of her slender body and he wrapped his arms round her to capture her.

'Rashad…' Polly gasped, disconcerted by that sudden advance.

'You're my wife now. In some ways, I don't really believe it yet,' he confided in a thickened undertone, slowly winding a brown hand into the fall of her silky hair, long brown fingers gently caressing her pale-skinned throat. 'I can't believe you're mine—'

'Yes, b-but…' Polly stammered, struggling to hold onto her wits that close to Rashad when she could feel the thump of his heartbeat through their clothing and the heat and strength of his big muscular body against hers. He was fully aroused and she could feel the hard thrust of him against her. In receipt of that very sexual message the kind of brutal need she had never had cause to feel before held her rigid with momentary indecision. In that instant she wanted *so* badly to let him touch her just as she urgently wished to touch him. She ached to smooth explorative fingers over that long bronzed muscular body and learn everything that had until now been denied her.

'And there is no fancy protocol that can keep us apart now,' Rashad continued with a raw-edged smile of satisfaction, his gorgeous black-lashed, dark golden eyes locked to her wide blue gaze as he lowered his head.

His sensual mouth came down on hers with a devastating hunger that travelled through her slight length as violently as a lightning bolt. His tongue plunged deep, electrifying her with sexual desire. He tasted so good she moaned into his mouth, helpless in the grip of her desire to deny herself, never mind him. Rashad pushed up the long trailing length of her dress and found her, fingers flirting with the silky panties she wore and then sliding beneath the elastic to find her feminine core. Something similar to spontaneous combustion detonated at the heart of Polly's quivering body. She was so eager to be touched, she felt scarily out of control and that shocked her, reminding her that she *had* to pull back if she was to have any hope of defusing a difficult situation with honesty. Feeling as she did, it was wrong to be submerging herself in wholly physical sensation, she reminded herself fiercely, and she yanked herself back out of his arms with so much force that she stumbled back against the footboard of the huge bed, her hair tumbling across her face.

Taken aback by that vehement withdrawal, Rashad stayed where he was, a bemused frown forming between his black brows, dark yet bright as stars eyes glittering and narrowing. He had never looked more beautiful to her disconcerted gaze. 'What's wrong?' he asked levelly.

'I can't do this with you tonight,' Polly muttered hoarsely, still struggling to control the inner quaking of need that had momentarily burned right through her defences. Even as she stood there she was alarmingly aware of the pained ache between her thighs, the high of her excitement abating with painful slowness. 'I'm sorry, I can't. I'm not ready to go to bed with you… er…yet…'

'We are married.' Rashad framed the words with pronounced care, without inflexion, without expression. 'We are man and wife. What possible objection could you have?'

'Probably nothing that you will really understand,'

Polly countered in a discomfited tone. 'I hardly know you, Rashad. I haven't really even seen you since I agreed to marry you and today you were weird—'

His extreme stillness remained eerily unchanged. 'Weird?' he repeated darkly. 'In what way?'

'How can you ask me that when you wouldn't speak to me or look at me or even touch me if you could avoid it throughout the wedding festivities?' Polly demanded emotionally. 'I would have settled for friendliness if that was the best you could do.'

'Polly…it was a state wedding with television cameras and an army of onlookers. *Friendly?*' An ebony brow elevated in apparent wonderment and his entire attitude made her feel small and stupid and childish. 'I don't have the acting ability to relax to that extent in that kind of public display—'

Polly had turned very pale. 'It was more than that. You acted like…like you were *hating* having to marry me!'

Rashad lost colour below his bronzed skin, his strong facial bones tightening, because in truth he was in deep shock at what was unfolding. He was a very private man. Even as a child he had been forced by circumstance to keep his thoughts and feelings absolutely to himself. And in all his life nobody had ever been able to read him as accurately as *she* just had and it made him feel exposed as the fraud he sometimes feared that he was. He had done his duty, he conceded bitterly, but clearly he had not done it well enough to convince his bride. 'Why would you think such a thing of me?'

'If you lie to me now, it will be the last straw!' Polly warned him shakily. 'I deserve the truth.'

Rashad angled his proud dark head back in the smouldering silence that had engulfed them. Somewhere in the background Polly could hear the timeless surge of the sea hitting the shore outside and, inside her own body, she could feel the quickened apprehensive beat of her heart.

'For me, the last straw would be that you have married me today and now, quite independent of any reason or discussion, have decided that you will *refuse* to consummate our marriage!' he bit out rawly. 'That, by any standards, is unacceptable.'

His roughened intonation made Polly flinch at the standoff she had hoped to avoid by explaining her feelings. 'Trust a man to bring it all down to sex!' she shot back bitterly. 'Of course you can't get me pregnant if we don't have sex, so I suppose that has to be your main grounds for complaint—'

'I've had enough of this,' Rashad ground out abruptly, too many damaging memories tearing at him to allow him the calm and patience required to deal with an emotionally distraught bride. 'I'm going out.'

Polly was stunned by the idea that he would simply walk out on a row. 'You can't just walk out… Where are you going to go, for goodness' sake? We're on a beach surrounded by desert in the middle of nowhere! And what will people *think*?' she exclaimed in sudden consternation.

'Let me see…' Rashad inclined his handsome dark head to one side in a way that made her want to slap him, the slashing derision in his gaze unhidden. 'They will think that a honeymoon baby is unlikely,' he breathed curtly. 'But thankfully they will not know that my bride refused me!'

He strode through a connecting door she hadn't noticed until that precise moment and the door thudded shut in his wake. The silence that spread around Polly then felt claustrophobic and, her throat tight and dry, she collapsed down on the side of the bed, her lower limbs limp as noodles. What had she done? she asked herself in belated consternation. What on earth had she done? The right thing? Or the *wrong* thing?

In the room next door, Rashad paced the floor, smouldering with a rage so emotionally powerful it disturbed even him. But he never ever lost his temper with anyone because the need to regulate any potentially dangerous outburst had been beaten into him at an early age. He had taught himself to master his volatile nature, he had taught himself to quell the passion that fired him and…and walk away. But the look on his bride's face when he'd walked away had been frankly incredulous. Too late he was discovering the downside to marrying a woman unafraid to fight and argue with him.

As he paced, on several occasions he strode back towards the door that separated their rooms, eager to defend himself, but each time he stopped himself and backed off again. What, after all, *could* he say to her? That the knowledge he was on show in front of cameras invariably paralysed him with unease? That such intense attention had never been welcome to him and that her ability to behave with cool normality had astounded him? A man, particularly a king, was supposed to be stronger than that, more disciplined, more able to perform the essential duty of public appearances. A king was not supposed to be introspective or emotional, he was supposed to be a powerful figurehead, a flawless role model and a very strong leader. While Rashad reiterated his stringent uncle's most frequent directives inside his own head, he continued to pace in raging frustration.

He had married a foreigner with a different set of values. A foreigner who had fired an erotic hunger in him that was stronger than anything he had ever expected or even *wanted* to feel. In such a situation, it was downright unnerving and absolutely outrageous to positively *crave* another opportunity to argue with her. Tearing his attention from the door between them, he ripped off his ceremonial robes and donned more comfortable clothing. He had stayed long enough out of view not to rouse household comment at his abandonment of his new bride, he reasoned grimly as he left the room and strode down to the stables.

At least his horse wasn't going to ask him unanswerable questions and pick up on his deficiencies, he reflected with bitter humour. He wasn't sure of his ground with Polly, he acknowledged, furious at that demeaning reality. In truth his previous experience with Western women had been purely sexual and casual and nothing more than that. But he did have considerable experience of being denied sex. That Polly should do that to him when he recognised that she felt the same chemistry he did had enraged and frustrated him beyond bearing.

What did she want from him? What the hell did she expect from him? So, he had acted *weird*?

Possibly a bit stiff and silent, he interpreted as he directed his stallion, Raza, across the desert sands at a pace that his guards were stretched to match. But then Rashad had been born to the saddle and raised from the age of six within a nomadic tribe, who ranged freely across the vast desert landscape that spanned several countries and recognised no boundaries. That same innate yearning for complete freedom had been bred into his bones but the sleeker, more sophisticated man he had inevitably become wished he had paused to take a cold, invigorating shower before his departure.

He didn't get women, he reflected, recalling Rio once admitting the very same thing. And if Rio, an incurable playboy with vast experience of the opposite sex, didn't understand women, how was Rashad ever to understand the woman he had married?

Ironically he had been brought up to believe that he would own his wife's body and soul much as he owned his horse. Maybe he should've thrown that at her to show how far he had travelled from the narrow-minded indoctrination of his youth. So backward had his ancestors been that they would have taken such a refusal as a justification for forcing the issue. He was fairly certain Polly would not have been impressed by that admission and he could not imagine ever wanting to physically hurt a woman. But there were other ways of harming and hurting a wife. Even by the tender age of six he had heard and seen enough in the palace of his childhood to grasp that his mother was pitied by some and blamed by others for his father's relentless debauchery. That was why when Polly had banished him from the marital bed he had wanted to protect her reputation by waiting in the room next door.

But, in spite of that concession, Rashad remained blazingly, scorchingly angry with his bride. What a way to embark on a new marriage! This was not what *he* had wanted. Separation was not a way forward and sex was not a reward for good behaviour. And what was Polly's idea of good behaviour? Rashad hadn't a clue. He was right back to where he had started out, utterly in the dark as to what way he had somehow contrived to fall short…

Eventually, and only once Polly had surrendered all hope that Rashad would reappear and discuss their quarrel, she removed her jewellery and undressed and got into the giant bed. She felt curiously overwhelmed and deflated by the reality that she was *alone* on her wedding night. She couldn't even understand her own reaction, because she had *asked* him to leave her alone and now to feel dissatisfied on that score seemed perverse.

In truth, she recognised ruefully, on some level inside herself she had expected Rashad to reason, persuade or even seduce her into changing her mind. But Rashad hadn't done anything so predictable. Instead he had walked out on her. Angry? Bemused? Hurt? She discovered that she didn't like to think that he was either hurt or confused by her behaviour. But she *must* have hurt his pride, she finally acknowledged unhappily, wondering why she had not foreseen that very obvious consequence.

The next morning, she came awake with the sunlight. At some stage while she still slept her luggage had been unpacked. Her grandparents had insisted on equipping her with a new and more appropriate wardrobe to wear after the wedding. She had picked out styles she liked with a trio of Dharian designers and had been concerned by the likely cost of such exclusivity even after Hakim assured her that he was well able to afford such a generous gesture.

Polly extracted a comfortable dress and smilingly dismissed the maid kneeling at the door ready to assist her into her clothing. The blue sundress was light and airy and, with canvas shoes on her feet, she sat down to breakfast on the terrace on the floor below, to enjoy the view of the sea while telling herself repeatedly that she was not one whit bothered by Rashad's vanishing act. At some stage of the night that had passed, however, she *had* reached new conclusions about what she had done.

When she had been getting so wound up before the wedding, Rashad had been completely absent and unable to answer or soothe any of her concerns. Her sister's dire fear that she was making a mistake had encouraged her own insecurities, which in turn had exploded when Rashad had appeared to act differently throughout their wedding day. Had she imagined that he was different? Had she been looking for trouble, seeking a fatal flaw that would give her the excuse to step back and take stock of her new marriage? After all, what did she want from Rashad when she already knew that he didn't love her?

Honesty, respect, trust, caring, affection, she listed anxiously, her lovely face clouding as she acknowledged the unrealistic level of desired perfection inherent in making such a list about a man, particularly on the very first day of a brand-new marriage.

When Rashad in person appeared out of seemingly nowhere and joined her without fanfare and with a seemingly relaxed smile to bid her a good morning, Polly was so disconcerted she almost fell off her chair in shock.

'My goodness, I was wondering where you were!' she exclaimed helplessly.

Her attention involuntarily welded to the impressive physique outlined by a white tee shirt that hugged his muscular chest and biceps and faded jeans that outlined his narrow waist and long powerful thighs. In fact, although the sun hadn't at so early an hour been bothering her, she heated up so much she began to perspire. 'Last night—'

'We will not discuss last night,' Rashad broke in decisively. 'We were both overtired after the wedding.'

'Seriously...we're sweeping the dust under the carpet?' Polly muttered in astonishment.

Rashad answered her in Arabic, and then with an affirmative yes, the sculpted full line of his eloquent mouth firming, his devastating dark eyes cloaked by his lashes.

A fair brow lifted in growing disbelief. 'And you think that's *all right*?'

'I think it is better than the alternative,' Rashad told her truthfully, heaping sugar into his mint tea.

Polly stared down blindly at her own tea. 'What happened to the man who said dissension could be stimulating?'

'He learned that that brand of stimulation can be treacherous,' Rashad countered with level cool.

And that fast, Polly wanted to scream at him again and so powerful was that urge that her teeth chattered together behind her murderously compressed lips. He could set off a seething emotional chain reaction inside her and make her madder than anyone else had ever done and it seriously unsettled her. She sipped at her tea with a stiff-fingered hold on the tiny glass cup and looked out to sea in angry silence, her mouth tightly compressed.

'You see now we have nothing to talk about because you can't gloss over a major row and simply pretend it never happened,' she then pointed out, not feeling the smallest bit generous, especially not after having lain awake for half of the night wondering where he was, how he felt and what he was doing. Evidently if he simply moved on past the dissension without requiring any contribution from her, he had done no such wondering.

'We did not have a row, we had different opinions.' Rashad persisted in his peace-keeping mission much as he persisted against all odds to direct challenging meetings staged between enemies and rivals.

Polly almost lunged across the table as she leant abruptly forward, silvery blonde hair rolling across her slim shoulders like a swathe of heavy silk. 'I *want* a row!'

Rashad levelled resolute dark eyes on her, raw tension gripping him because he only had to look at that rosy soft mouth of hers to want to back her down on the nearest horizontal surface. Hell, it didn't even have to be horizontal, he acknowledged, his inventive mind rushing to supply every erotic possibility imaginable. His jeans uncomfortably tight around the groin, he flexed his broad shoulders. 'You're not getting one.'

'Even if I say please?' Polly pressed helplessly, because she genuinely believed that they had to discuss what had happened to move beyond it.

'With regret…not even if you beg,' Rashad spelt out a tinge more harshly. 'Rows are divisive and risky and we will not have them—'

'Says the King. But we still need to clear the air,' she muttered, shaken by an increasing fear that he really did believe such an approach could work.

'As far as I am concerned the air is already clear and further discussion would be overkill,' Rashad concluded in a tone of finality as he began to peel a piece of fruit, waving away the manservant who immediately approached him in a keen attempt to save him from the labour of such a petty task.

'Well, then you can *listen*,' Polly told him in desperation.

Rashad tensed at that seemingly new threat, dark eyes flashing gold below lush black velvet lashes as he focused on her. Why was she trying to destroy his calm and enrage him again? He had behaved honourably the night before. He had not argued. He had not threatened. He had walked away. This morning he had not uttered one word of reproach. If he had told her how he *really* felt about what she had done his anger would've blown the roof of the castle off and scared her. Whether he liked it or not, he was what he was, the heir to a ruthless lineage, and his belief that his wife belonged to him ran like a thread of steel through his every reaction even while his intelligence told him that life didn't work like that any more.

She looked so innocent and so very beautiful and yet she was totally off-the-wall crazy in Rio's parlance, Rashad acknowledged ruefully. Yet why did he continue to find that strange trait so incredibly attractive? Why, when he was in the worst possible mood, did that trait make him want to smile? He concentrated on his tea, which was less likely to unnerve him than the odd thoughts assailing him without warning. He told himself that he didn't want to listen, didn't want further criticism or a greater burden of guilt. After all, he knew who was ultimately at fault. Somehow he had screwed up. If his brand-new bride wasn't happy, he had to be to blame.

'And perhaps now that you've eaten you could dismiss the staff?' she added in a disturbing indication that she was likely to become loudly vocal once again.

Rashad signalled the two hovering servants to dismiss them before springing upright with fluid agility and sitting back down on the low wall bounding the castle ramparts.

Polly immediately froze in her seat. 'No, don't do that,' she said anxiously, blue eyes fixed to him in dismay.

'Don't do...*what*?'

'Don't sit there with your back turned to a dangerous drop,' Polly urged.

Rashad studied her in disbelief and then glanced round in a sudden movement that made her gasp to scrutinise the dangerous drop she had complained about. A couple of hundred feet of scrub and rocks sloped gently down towards the beach and he had climbed it many times with a blindfold as a little boy on a dare.

'Please get up and move away from it,' Polly whispered unsteadily.

Rashad studied her again, noticing how pale and stiff she had become. 'It's *not* a dangerous drop—'

'Well, it is to me because I'm terrified of heights and just looking at you sitting there is making me feel sick!' Polly launched at him at vastly raised volume with only a hint of a frightened squeak, her annoyance at his obstinacy having risen higher still.

Rashad raised calming hands as though he were dealing with a fractious child and rose with exaggerated care to move to the castle wall. OK...point taken.'

Polly flushed to the roots of her hair and slowly breathed again. 'I just don't like heights—'

'I think I've got that,' Rashad confided straight-faced.

'So, you're planning to listen now to me?' Polly enquired stiffly.

Impatience flashed through Rashad and no small amount of frustration at her persistence. Water dripping on stone had a lot in common with his new wife. But he was clever enough to know that listening was an important skill in negotiation and experienced enough to know that marriage encompassed an endless string of compromises and negotiations. 'I'll listen but not here. I'll show you round the castle and you can talk… quietly,' he added softly, but the dark-eyed imperious appraisal that accompanied it was a visual demand for that audible level. 'No shouting, no crying, no dramatic gestures.'

'I don't do crying and dramatic gestures,' Polly told him in exasperation.

By nature, Rashad recognised the ironic fact that, of the two of them, *he* was more volatile and more likely to be dramatic and his handsome mouth quirked at that sardonic acknowledgement. The night before, Polly had been very understated but a rejection was a rejection, no matter how it was delivered, and not a pattern Rashad wanted to find in his wife. He looked at her; in truth he never tired of looking at her and the plea in her shadowed blue eyes would have softened the heart of a killer.

'OK,' he agreed grudgingly. 'But if you embark on another argument—'

'You'll lock me up and throw away the key,' Polly joked.

'Considering that that is exactly what my ancestors

did with their wives, you could be walking a dangerous line with that invitation,' Rashad murmured, teasing on the surface but fleetingly appalled by how much that concept attracted him when it came to the woman smiling back at him.

## CHAPTER SEVEN

'EVERYTHING HERE IS unfamiliar to me. Your lifestyle, the customs, the language,' Polly murmured quietly as they walked along the battlements past stationed guards to take advantage of the aerial views. 'When you add you and a new marriage into that, it can occasionally be overwhelming.'

That made remarkably good sense to Rashad, who had been braced to receive a quiet emotional outpouring of regrets and accusations. Relief rising uppermost, he squared his broad shoulders and breathed in deep. 'I can understand that.'

'And I've barely seen you since the day I agreed to marry you. I realise that with your schedule you had no choice but it made me feel insecure.'

Rashad was downright impressed by what he was hearing, it never having occurred to him that a woman in a relationship with him could speak her mind so plainly and unemotionally. In silence he jerked his chin in acknowledgement of the second point.

'Yesterday was a very challenging day for both of us.' Polly's voice shook a little when Rashad settled an arm to her back to steady her on the uneven stones beneath their feet, long fingers spreading against her spine to send a ridiculous little frisson of physical awareness travelling through her all too susceptible body.

'It was…'

'I've never been in a serious relationship before…'

Rashad stopped dead. *'Never?'* he questioned in disbelief. 'But you are twenty-five years old.'

Polly explained about her grandmother's long, slow decline into full-blown dementia and the heavy cost that had extracted from her freedom while her sister was away at university. 'So, if I'm a little inexperienced in relationships, you'll have to make allowances on that score,' she told him tautly.

A frown line was slowly building between Rashad's ebony brows. His fingers smoothed lightly up and down her spine as if to encourage her to keep on talking as he stared down at the top of her pale blonde head, far more engaged in what she was telling him than she would have believed.

Polly could feel the heat of embarrassment rising into her cheeks in a wave. Gooseflesh was forming on her arms, the hairs at the back of her neck prickling while the warm hand at her spine had tensed and stilled. 'And I think that may be why I sort of freaked out last night because I was a bit nervous…*of course* I was…and you hadn't made me feel safe or special or anything really!' Conscious her voice was rising in spite of her efforts to control it, Polly looked up at Rashad in dismay and discomfiture.

And for the very first time, Rashad understood his bride without words and he felt like the biggest idiot ever born because he had been guilty of making sweeping assumptions without any grounds on which to do so. It had not once crossed his mind that Polly might be less experienced than he was. Indeed he had even worried just a little that he might not be adventurous enough or sophisticated enough to please her. With a sidewise glance at the guards studiously staring out at the desert and the beach, Rashad bent down, scooped his surprised bride up into his arms and carried her indoors. Doors were helpfully wrenched open ahead of him by the staff as he strode back to their bedroom.

'What on earth are you doing?' Polly exclaimed when he had finally tumbled her down in a heap on the giant bed in which she had slept alone the night before.

'Giving us privacy,' Rashad advanced with a sudden smile of amusement that sent her heart racing. 'I don't wish to offend you but I had made the assumption that you would have enjoyed at least a few lovers before me—'

'And why the heck would you assume that?' Polly demanded with spirit.

'Your values are more liberal. Here, although young adults now tend to choose their own partners, it is still the norm for women to be virgins when they marry. That would be more unusual in your society.'

'I suppose so,' Polly conceded reluctantly because she knew her sister fell into the same 'unusual' category, Ellie having admitted that she had yet to meet a man who could tempt her into wanting to cross that sexual boundary. 'But my sister and I were both brought up in a very strict home. My grandmother believed that both I and Ellie were illegitimate and until she fell ill she policed our every move because she was afraid that we would repeat what she saw as our mother's mistakes and come home pregnant and unmarried.'

'I know very little about your background.' Rashad settled fluidly down on the edge of the bed in a relaxed movement. 'Even your grandfather warned me against having unrealistic expectations of you—'

Polly flushed scarlet. 'My...*grandfather*? Please tell me you're joking—'

'There was no discussion, Polly, but I guessed what he meant. He merely wished to protect you from the risk of me being naïve in that line. I am *not* naïve,' Rashad completed with wry emphasis. 'But Hakim and I have naturally never discussed anything that intimate, so he could have formed no idea of my attitude in advance.'

In receipt of that explanation, her mortification ebbed. It was evident that her grandparents had made the same assumption and she couldn't find it in her heart to fault her grandfather for trying to shield her from the threat of Rashad's disappointment.

'You're not that old-fashioned,' she commented with a helpless little giggle. 'But obviously Grandad is.'

'I spent several years studying at Oxford University and that was an enlightening experience being a mature student,' he told her wryly.

'Must've been,' Polly conceded, picturing Rashad with his film-star good looks and wealth let loose to enjoy a student's freedom. 'Was that after your wife passed away?'

His lean, strong face tensed. 'Of course. I could not have left her behind here to be oppressed by her father.'

Polly frowned. 'How...*oppressed*?'

'In essence my late uncle was a good man but he was also a bully. I say that with respect because without his intervention I would not be alive,' Rashad admitted levelly. 'On several occasions during Arak's dictatorship rumours of my continuing existence put a price on my head. I could have been hunted down and killed like an animal but the tribe took me in as one of their own and protected me because my uncle was their sheikh.'

It was the first time he had given her a little window into the sheer turmoil of his formative years and it sobered Polly as nothing else could have done. Certainly it could not have been all rainbows and roses being brought up by a bully, most particularly not if he owed his very life to that same bully, who had coolly married the putative future King of Dharia off to his own daughter at the age of sixteen. Her heart was touched and she pressed her hand briefly against a lean masculine thigh in silent empathy.

'It seems we do, in spite of all that has happened, have something in common,' Rashad remarked with a flashing smile of such intense charisma that she couldn't drag her attention from his lean, darkly handsome features. 'We were both raised by strict guardians.'

'Yes,' Polly conceded feverishly, encountering the dark golden depths of his eyes with a mouth that was running dry and a stomach awash with butterflies as awareness of their proximity kicked in with electrifying effect.

'I do not want you to be nervous of me, *habibti,*' Rashad confided huskily. 'I promise you that I will never do anything that you do not want.'

'I...I pretty much want everything!' Polly confided with a strangled little laugh of self-consciousness because she didn't feel it was fair to go on acting as if she were a terrified virgin because she was not.

*'Everything...'* Rashad savoured the word and she flushed. 'I love your honesty.'

And he kissed her, slowly, carefully, nibbling at her lower lip, then tracing it with the tip of his tongue. In fact he turned up the temperature so gradually she was barely aware that one of her hands had crept up to spear into his thick black hair and the other to tighten on a strong shoulder. She wanted more, much more, she acknowledged, her whole body turning warm and languorous in response while the little prickles and tingles of desire were already pinching at her nipples and warming her pelvis.

'I will make it special,' Rashad intoned into the scented depths of her tumbling hair, his dark deep drawl roughened by the knowledge that she was giving him her trust.

'You can't promise that,' Polly felt forced to tell him prosaically. 'If it hurts, it's not your fault. I'm not *that* ignorant—'

'Hush...' Rashad groaned.

'No, you stop setting standards,' Polly warned him

playfully, tracing his hard jawline with a gentle forefinger, marvelling at how much closer she felt to him as he pressed her back against the pillows and leant back to flip off her shoes, letting them fall to the tiled floor.

'I've done that all my life—'

'But not here, *now*…when it's only the two of us,' Polly persisted helplessly.

And for a split second, Rashad contemplated the strangeness of not seeing everything in the light of passing or failing and shouldering the blame, but it was too engrained a habit for him to even imagine. He shook off that alien concept and homed in on his bride instead, studying that ripe rosebud mouth with an amount of hunger that threatened his control.

He kissed her again and the passion he couldn't conceal burned in that kiss and it thrilled her as much as the hungry thrust of his tongue melding with her own. He was *so* intense, she thought tenderly, no matter how hard he tried to hide it. He took far too many things far too seriously. Maybe she would be able to make him lighten up a little and relax more. But that solemn thought was quickly engulfed by the intoxicating delight of his demanding mouth crushing hers beneath his own. Little noises she didn't recognise escaped her throat.

He slid her out of her dress with admirable ease, so deft at the challenge that she was a little surprised to find herself lying there clad only in her lace underwear. All of a sudden she was worried about what he would think of her body, which she knew was kind of average. Breasts neither large nor small but somewhere in between. Hips a little larger than she would have liked, legs and ankles reasonably shapely, she reflected ruefully, shutting her eyes, just lying there, not wanting to beat herself up with such foolish thoughts.

'*Ant jamilat jiddaan…* You are so beautiful,' Rashad told her with fervour, and she dared to open her eyes again.

And yes, it *was* her body he was scrutinising much as if she were the seventh wonder of the world. Emboldened, Polly arched her spine to make the most of her assets, relishing his admiration while thinking no more about her physical imperfections. Her blue eyes settled on him and she murmured shyly but with determination, 'You're still wearing too many clothes.'

His dark golden eyes gleamed with appreciation and he pulled off his tee shirt to reveal a bronzed and indented muscular torso worthy of a centrefold. The tip of her tongue crept out to moisten her dry lips as her gaze crept inexorably down to the revealing bulge at his groin. Apprehension was the last thing on her mind as he unzipped his jeans, showing her the intriguing little dark furrow of hair snaking down over his taut flat stomach. She stopped breathing altogether as he came back to her and fastened his mouth hungrily to hers again, the warmth of his big body against her an unexpected source of pleasure.

He unclasped her bra and cupped a pale pouting breast, long fingers toying with the taut pink tip, rolling it, gently squeezing the distended bud before sucking it into his mouth and teaching her that that part of her body was much more sensitive than she would ever have believed. The tug of his lips on the straining tips of her breasts sent a pulling sensation arrowing down into the heat rising between her thighs. Lying still became a challenge while her hips dug into the mattress beneath her. The hollowed ache at the heart of her increased, making her restless and stoking her craving for more.

'You're not letting me touch you,' Polly muttered in a rush, gripped by the fear that she wasn't being much of an equal partner. 'Isn't this supposed to be a two-way thing?'

'It is but it would please me most if this first time between us is for you, not for me,' Rashad countered with assurance.

A little red in the cheeks, Polly abandoned her objections, particularly when he made a point of pinning her flat with another passionate driving kiss and her temperature rocketed up the scale. He tugged off her panties and finally touched her where she most longed to be touched, tracing the delicate skin at the apex of her thighs and concentrating on the tiny nub that seemed to control her every nerve ending.

The pleasure was the most irresistible sensation she had ever known. In an impatient movement Rashad disposed of his jeans and glided down the bed to part her trembling legs. She felt like a sacrifice spread out before him and it heightened her arousal. Before very long he contrived to teach her that what she had deemed to be irresistible pleasure could grow exponentially to an almost unbearable level. And she had never felt her body rage out of her control before until those frantic feverish moments when Rashad thoroughly controlled her with his carnal mouth and skilful fingers. Almost immediately he transformed her keen curiosity into an overpowering demanding need. Her spine arched, her hips rose and jerked and her heart thumped as madly as though she were sprinting. And then stars detonated behind her eyelids and the whole world went into free fall along with her body.

He slid over her and ran his mouth down the sensitive slope of her neck to her shoulder. A compulsive little shiver racked her languorous length. Her lashes lifted on his lean, darkly handsome features and she smiled, a little giddily, a little shyly, recalling how much noise she had made in climax and the way she had clawed at his hair and his shoulders. He brought out the bad girl hiding inside her and she rather thought she liked that, and the shimmering gold satisfaction in his eyes suggested that he did as well.

He nudged against her tender cleft and she tensed, feeling him there, hard and ready. He pushed into her with greater ease than she had expected but then he had prepared her well. Her delicate inner walls stretched to accommodate him and then he shifted his hips and sank deeper, sending a sharp little pang of pain through her that made her grit her teeth.

'Do you want me to stop?' Rashad asked thickly.

'No...' she wailed in shocked protest as in answer to his movement an exquisite little shimmy of internal friction eddied through her pelvis.

Rashad was fighting to stay in control, struggling to think about anything other than what he was doing. He shifted again, gathering her legs up over his arms, and drove into her hard and fast, rewarded by the gasp of pleasure she emitted. She was very vocal and he loved her lack of inhibition. He gripped her hips and pounded into the hot, wet grip of her glorious body with a growl of savage pleasure.

Polly could only compare the experience to a wild and thrilling roller-coaster ride. A tightening band of tension formed low in her body and the crazy rush of intense sensation heightened as he quickened his pace, changing angle, hammering into her receptive body with delicious confident force. Excitement flooded her as another climax beckoned and she could feel her body surging up to reach it, gloriously out of her control. She hit that peak with a wondering cry and then dropped her head back against the pillows, drained but wonderfully relaxed. Rashad groaned and shuddered and buried his face in her tangled hair.

'That was amazing,' she told him cheerfully as soon as she had enough breath to speak, one hand smoothing possessively over his long, sweat-dampened back.

Rashad's dark head reared up, a startled look in his dark eyes as he searched her flushed and smiling face. And then he threw back his head and laughed. 'Polly... only you would tell me that!' he said appreciatively, dropping a kiss on her brow. 'I thank you. It was even more amazing for me, *aziz*.'

'Do you think it would have been like this for us last night?' she asked, suffering a belated attack of regret.

'No, we were both too tired and irritable and I had no idea I would be your first lover,' Rashad replied, letting her off that hook with newly learned generosity as he freed her from his weight and rolled over.

Her hand sought and found his below the sheet. Had she had the energy she would have turned cartwheels because she felt happy and too laid-back to guard her words. Succumbing to her curiosity, she said lightly, 'Your first marriage was arranged, wasn't it?'

His fingers flexed and tensed beneath the light cover of hers. 'Yes.'

'Did you love her?' Polly pressed helplessly, desperate to know even though she didn't understand why she should have such a craving to know that information.

'Yes,' Rashad replied, stifling his unease at being forced to think back to his miserably unhappy first marriage. 'How could I not? We were childhood playmates.'

And somewhere within Polly a little hurt sensation sprang up like a claw that had the power to scratch her deep where it didn't show. She didn't understand it because it was surely good news that he had contrived to love Ferah, regardless of the reality that it had been an arranged marriage. But perhaps she had not been quite prepared to hear that he had known Ferah so well, a young woman who would have understood so much more about Rashad than Polly probably ever would. Her predecessor, she acknowledged unhappily, would be a tough act to follow.

# CHAPTER EIGHT

'YOU'RE DOING VERY WELL,' Rashad assured Polly seven weeks later. 'Your posture is much improved.'

With the ease of practice, Polly ignored the audience of grooms and guards gathered round the palace horse paddock. When Rashad had first informed her that he planned to teach her to ride she had laughed out loud in disbelief and outright denial of the idea because Polly had never been into anything even remotely athletic. Unfortunately, Rashad considered the ability to ride a horse an essential skill and from the instant she was put aboard a four-legged monster and then panicked at the height she was from the ground, the lessons had begun. If you had a weakness, you worked hard to conquer it: that was how Rashad expected her to operate. And backsliding and excuses weren't allowed.

If Rashad knew the actual meaning of the word 'honeymoon' he was hiding the fact very well, Polly conceded with rueful amusement while her mount trotted obediently round the paddock, her own body moving easily now in the saddle as Rashad had taught her to move. When she had pleaded her fear of falling as an excuse to avoid the activity, Rashad had borrowed a mechanical horse from somewhere and set it up with crash mats in the basement gym and she had spent two ghastly days learning how to fall as safely as possible. At no stage had she required Dr Wasem's attention but she had certainly picked up a few bruises before she'd learned the technique of tucking in her arms and her head and rolling to lessen the impact of a fall. When the doctor had cautiously suggested to Rashad that learning to ride could be considered a rather risky activity for a woman hoping to conceive, Rashad had scoffed.

'That will probably take at least a year to achieve!' Rashad had remarked dismissively to Polly, releasing her from the fear that her ability to conceive would be under constant scrutiny.

In fact, on that score, she had worried unnecessarily, she conceded with relief. Rashad appeared to have neither a sense of urgency nor indeed any level of expectation when it came to the question of his bride falling pregnant. Of course they weren't taking any precautions either, so she supposed that over time the odds of conception would naturally increase. It could hardly have escaped her notice that his first marriage had been childless but, when taxed on that question, Rashad had quietly admitted that Ferah had had a medical condition that made her infertile.

Rashad lifted Polly down off the mare and stared down at her with brilliant dark eyes of satisfaction. 'I'm really proud of you,' he admitted huskily. 'You've conquered your fear.'

Polly grinned. 'I'm going for a shower,' she told him cheerfully.

Their audience had vanished back to their duties when she trudged into the building at the rear of the stables that housed luxury changing and washing facilities. They had stayed at the castle by the sea for only two weeks before Rashad's necessary attendance at an important meeting of his council had interrupted their seclusion. They had returned to the palace, where it was much easier for Rashad to oversee the progress of various projects and still take time off.

But Polly still retained tantalising memories of the sea and the castle. They had picnicked on the beach and gone swimming, for both of them were proficient in the water. They had talked late into the night on the terrace and rumpled the bed sheets until dawn lit the skies. By the end of that stay at the castle Polly had admitted to herself that she had fallen head over heels in love with her husband. He could charm her with a smile and seduce her with the smallest touch but his greatest skill was that he made her feel wonderfully happy and content.

Rashad had reached the shower block ahead of her. She started in surprise when she saw him: a lithe, dark, electrifyingly sexy figure sheathed in a polo shirt, tight riding breeches and riding boots. As soon as she appeared he shut the door and locked it behind her, towering over her as she relaxed languorously back against the stone wall. He ran a calloused fingertip lightly over her pouting pink lips and breathed thickly. 'I can't keep my hands off you when I think of you getting naked in the shower, *aziz*.'

A shiver of excitement as stimulating as a storm warning snaked through Polly's slender body. While formal in so many other ways, Rashad was wonderfully earthy about sex. Over the past weeks they had probably had sex virtually everywhere they were left alone together in the palace. In his office, in the stables, in unoccupied rooms he showed her round and once, thrillingly, over the dining-room table. Polly was equally challenged to keep her hands off Rashad's gloriously masculine body. And as many of their unplanned encounters had proved to be the most sensational she literally stopped breathing when a certain smouldering look appeared in Rashad's dark golden eyes. It made her feel like the most seductive and beautiful woman in the world. And it was a level of intimacy with a man that she had never dreamt of experiencing.

Polly leant back against the wall, almost boneless with anticipation of his touch, her blue eyes starry. She was intensely aware of her own body, already screaming a welcome as her gaze slid down his body to the desire outlined by his breeches and impossible to hide.

'Getting naked, Your Highness,' she murmured playfully, 'would appear to be a sensible idea.'

Rashad planted his hands beside her head and pushed his lean strong body into hers, letting her feel the urgency of his need. 'Sensible is the very last thing you make me feel—'

Polly gazed up at him, loving every proud line and hollow of his lean, hard face and the stunning black-fringed dark eyes that often made her breath hitch in her dry throat. 'Well, if I have to suffer, why shouldn't you?' she teased.

Challenged, Rashad dug his hands into the silky swathe of hair she had unbraided and brought his mouth crashing down in hungry demand on hers. The very taste of her was an aphrodisiac. He was wound up tight as a spring and Polly was the only woman who had ever had that much power over him. He craved her body like a drug and revelled unashamedly in her responsiveness. At first, his extreme need for her had disturbed him and he had tried to restrain that need, but a willing Polly in his bed every night, and most unforgettably a Polly wantonly bending over the dining-room table while offering him a cheeky smile of challenge, had demolished his resistance entirely. They had a scorchingly sexual and satisfying connection he had never thought to find in marriage.

Polly's clothes came off long before they made it into the shower. He tormented her swollen nipples with his mouth while his lean fingers probed the receptive wetness between her thighs and expertly fuelled her hunger. He hauled her up to him and brought her down on him, bracing her hips against the wall to take her with hard, forceful thrusts that made her cry out in excitement and blissful pleasure. Barely able to stand in the aftermath, she rested up against him for support and let him carry her into the shower.

'How useful are you finding Hayat?' he asked curiously as he switched on the multi-jets of water.

'She's indispensable,' Polly admitted, for she was

making her first official appearance as Rashad's wife that evening at a diplomatic dinner in the capital, Kashan. 'She's explaining everything I need to know. She's like a walking book on faces, etiquette, clothes. I couldn't do without her.'

'That's good,' Rashad responded, hiding his surprise at the news. Polly's grandfather had suggested Hayat for the role of supporting Polly and it seemed the older man must also have seen a side to the waspish brunette that Rashad had failed to appreciate. At the same time, however, as his sister-in-law, he acknowledged that Hayat deserved superior status and recognition.

Having shampooed her hair, Polly surveyed Rashad as he lounged back against the tiled wall, slumberous and relaxed and all male to her appreciative gaze. She padded forward and rested her hands down on his wide shoulders before slowly tracing them down over his washboard abs, watching his lush black lashes shift upward, his dark golden eyes shimmer tawny with renewed desire.

'You are so predictable,' she scolded. 'Do you ever say no?'

At that sally, Rashad grinned with unabashed enjoyment, slashing cheekbones taut below his bronzed skin. 'Do you want me to?'

And no, she didn't, she acknowledged as her hands went travelling down over his lean, powerful physique in confident reacquaintance. She turned him on and she liked that power very much, adored the way he closed his eyes and simply let her do as she liked with him, the evidence of his arousal hard and smooth and pulsing between her fingers. She stroked, cupped, knelt at his bare brown feet and used her mouth on him until he groaned and shuddered and lifted her up to him with impatient hands and brought her down on him again with all the explosive demanding passion he couldn't control. Afterwards she was limp with satiation and drowsy as he washed her down, showering away the proof of their intimacy and roughly rubbing her dry with fleecy towels. Having to get dressed again was a trial, she reflected.

'I'm so sleepy,' she complained as he walked her back through the palace, his hand engulfing hers and maintaining a physical link with her that she appreciated.

'Take a nap before this evening. You'll be standing around a lot meeting people before the meal,' he warned.

'Do you need a nap?' his bride asked him winsomely.

'We will neither of us sleep if I join you in our bed, *habibti*,' Rashad parried with highly amused dark eyes and a flashing smile of acknowledgement. 'I'll catch up on some work in my office until it's time to get ready for the dinner.'

Screening a yawn and wondering why she was so very tired when she slept like a log most nights, Polly stripped in their bedroom. She pulled on a nightie rather than shock her maid, who seemed to think that sleeping in the nude was scandalous, and she slid into bed. Her sore breasts ached beneath the fabric and she put her hands over them, momentarily questioning why she was getting all the usual symptoms of her period arriving but nothing was actually happening.

She was wakened with a light snack and tea and warned that Hayat was waiting to see her. Hayat was in charge of her wardrobe and her itinerary. Reluctant to keep the other woman waiting, Polly ate and dressed in haste to join her. As she pulled on her jeans and teetered on one leg a wave of giddiness attacked her and she lurched and fell back against the bed. Her maid started forward in dismay while Polly waved her back and breathed in slow and deep, remaining where she was until the sensation ebbed. Maybe she should've eaten a little more after so much physical activity, she thought ruefully.

'Nabila said you were unwell,' Hayat commented, moving forward. 'Should I call Dr Wasem?'

'A spot of dizziness, nothing more,' Polly dismissed, knowing that the smallest hint of illness was sufficient to send the whole household into a state of either panic or premature celebration on her behalf and, as she was well aware that it was simply 'that time of the month' when she never felt that great, she didn't want to cause a fuss. Hayat had educated her about the Dharian attitude to her health and Rashad's, admitting that concern on their behalf was easily awakened by rumour and speculation and generally overexcitable in nature. Rashad's bout of tonsillitis the year before had had the leading newspaper questioning why their King had not been hospitalised and had accused the royal household of risking his health with an old-fashioned hands-off approach to medicine. Dr Wasem had been mortally offended.

'You are sure you are feeling all right?' Hayat prompted. 'Your devoted husband would never forgive me if anything happened to you.'

'I'm fine,' Polly said, wondering why that word, 'devoted', had seemed to acquire a sarcastic edge on Hayat's lips. 'It's just that time of the month, that's all. I always feel a little run-down.'

The brunette gave her a tiny smile. 'I am sorry your hopes have been disappointed…'

Polly bent her head and rolled her eyes. Hayat and the rest of the household might be eagerly awaiting the announcement that she was pregnant but neither Polly nor Rashad were concerned, both of them believing that at the very least actually conceiving would take several months. Moreover such close scrutiny on such a score was seriously embarrassing. 'I'm not disappointed, Hayat. We're only newly married.'

'I watched my sister break her heart over her inability to conceive,' Hayat told her. 'It is very hard for a woman to be in that situation—'

'But I'm not in *that* situation,' Polly broke in, hoping to shut down the too personal conversation for, while she found Hayat very efficient, she maintained careful boundaries with her and never quite relaxed in her company. The brunette was unpopular with the other staff and Polly had taken heed of that warning to stay on her guard.

'Soon enough, as time goes on, you will be,' Hayat

forecast with a look of exaggerated sympathy on her pretty face. 'How could you not be concerned?'

Polly shrugged a stiff shoulder in dismissal of the topic. 'You wanted to see me?' she prompted, keen to push the conversation in a less personal direction.

'Oh, yes. I brought the royal jewellery for you to choose from,' Hayat pointed out, indicating the large wooden box on the table. 'But I left the amber set out for you because it will exactly match the dress you're wearing.'

Polly studied the very ornate gold and amber collaret and suspected her neck might break under the sheer weight of it. 'It looks very heavy—'

'It's a favourite of Rashad's. The set first belonged to his mother,' Hayat told her quietly.

Hayat was a fund of such information about Rashad and the royal family and Polly invariably took the brunette's advice. Well, if Rashad liked it… she thought ruefully, although she was challenged to imagine him even noticing what she was wearing. He wasn't that kind of man. He didn't notice much in the way of feminine detail, having once tried to describe a dress she'd worn and he'd admired as 'that blue drapey thing'.

When it came to more practical matters, however, Rashad was a roaring success, she thought fondly. She loved Rashad so much more than she had ever thought she could love any man and, while as yet he might not love her, he was definitely attached to her. In a crowded room, his attention continually sought her out. Her favourite British foods now magically made regular appearances at mealtimes. Flowers arrived for her every day. Furthermore, he had insisted that they should settle Ellie's student loans, Polly thought with pleasure as she went into the bedroom to phone her sister in privacy.

'Ellie is part of *our* family now,' Rashad had pointed out. 'In the same way as your other sister will be when we eventually find her.'

Rashad had hired a London investigation agency to search for her missing sister the very day after she told him about her existence. Indeed Rashad took on Polly's deepest concerns as if they were his own and she loved that trait because for the first time ever she felt cared for and looked after without being made to feel like a burden or a nuisance. In the dark of the night she wakened to find him wrapped round her and, even though she got far too hot sleeping that close to him, she rejoiced in their closeness and kicked off the bedding instead of pushing him away.

'Polly!' Ellie exclaimed with satisfaction. 'I've got news about Penelope.'

'Oh, my goodness,' Polly muttered in shock, dropping down on the edge of the bed.

'Don't get too excited,' Ellie warned her. 'We haven't found our sibling yet but that investigation agency Rashad's London lawyer suggested certainly seem to know what they're doing—'

'Money talks,' Polly said wryly.

'Don't I just know it.' Ellie sighed guiltily. 'Here I am free of all my student debt thanks to the two of you.

I can't ever thank you enough for that. I've got all sorts of choices now that I didn't have before—'

'Penelope?' Polly prompted, uncomfortable with her sister's gratitude.

'Well, for a start, our sister doesn't go by that name. She is called Gemma Foster now. You'll be getting the agency report as well,' Ellie pointed out. 'Gemma was adopted but her parents, the Fosters, died and that landed her back into the foster system. She's twenty now and we just have to track her down.'

'Right.' Polly swallowed her disappointment that that was as far as the agency had got in their search for their sister and returned to an issue that was currently more on her mind. 'Remember you said that it usually takes at least six months to conceive—'

'That is *not* what I said!' Ellie sliced in, sounding infuriatingly like the newly qualified doctor she now was, having recently passed her finals. 'I said that was the average but obviously a woman *could* get pregnant the very first time she has sex without precautions. Nothing about conception is etched in stone. Why are you asking me about this again?'

'Just curious, that's all.'

'Don't be putting pressure on yourself in that department,' Ellie advised sagely. 'You're both young and healthy and you'll likely conceive sooner rather than later.'

The evening dress Polly was planning to wear was in autumnal shades of brown and gold with muted hints of tangerine. Her maid brought the amber set to her and she donned it with a frown because the necklace was every bit as weighty as she had feared and the exotic earrings were almost as bad. Fully dressed, her maid having bundled up her hair into an elaborate updo that gave her the height she lacked, she scrutinised her appearance, ready to admit that once again Hayat's advice had proved indispensable. The amber jewellery and the more mature hairstyle lent an impressive note of glamorous dignity to what might otherwise have been a rather plain outfit.

She did not see Rashad until she climbed into the limousine in which he awaited her and quite predictably, because he was never ever anything other than punctual to the minute, he was complaining that she had cut her timing too fine. As she turned towards him with a mischievous smile his attention settled on the collaret encircling her white throat and his lean, strong face snapped taut, sudden pallor accentuating his superb bone structure.

'You look stunning,' he murmured almost woodenly, turning his handsome face away, his jawline rigid.

'Is there something wrong?' Polly pressed uncertainly.

'No,' he asserted but not very convincingly.

The dinner was Polly's first public appearance at Rashad's side since the wedding and she was keen to get everything right. Hayat had prepared her well with a key sheet of useful information, listing names and faces and functions to ease her into the social evening.

Rashad, holding himself in rigid check, was temporarily drowning in his own memories. He could not see that amber necklace without also seeing Ferah wearing it. It had been her favourite, the colour of the semi-precious stones reflecting her brown eyes. During the drive to the embassy, he was steeped in the memories he had locked into a little box at the back of his head. He saw Ferah, laughing and smiling, full of energy and happiness at the outset of their marriage. Ferah before life had scarred her and fatally wounded her and *he* had let her down. Fierce discomfiture and guilt gripped him.

'Why did you choose that jewellery?' he asked with as much nonchalance as he could contrive.

'The amber gems match the dress perfectly,' Polly replied in some surprise.

'I prefer you in brighter colours,' Rashad imparted flatly, making a nonsense of the compliment he had initially paid her.

Polly squared her slim shoulders and gave a very slight shrug. 'I can't wear blue all the time. I have to ring the changes.'

Her soft mouth had settled into a surprisingly defiant line because she was annoyed with him. Didn't he realise how nervous she was at attending her first official function as the new Queen of Dharia? Didn't he appreciate that she needed support and encouragement rather than criticism? All right, he didn't like the dress, but he should have kept his opinion to himself, she reflected angrily.

Instead of clinging to his side as Rashad had expected, Polly vanished into the crush. It was obvious that she did not feel a need for his presence. Once or twice he heard her musical laughter and wondered what she was laughing at and, indeed, *who* she was laughing with. He told himself that he was grateful that she had found her own feet but, as a man whose first wife had never strayed more than a foot from him at such occasions and at all times followed his lead, he was perplexed and a shade threatened by Polly's independence.

'You've made a real find in the wife stakes with Polly,' a familiar voice drawled and Rashad's dark head spun.

*'Rio?'* he said in surprise. 'What are you doing back in Dharia?'

Rio Benedetti dealt him an amused smile. 'The Italian Ambassador knows we're friends and, as I had to check out a location for one of our hotels here, I volunteered to do my patriotic best to oil the wheels of diplomacy for him—'

'You mentioned Polly,' Rashad reminded him, unsettled to hear his wife's name on Rio's lips and at the same time to recognise Rio's admiration for her, because Rio was a notorious womaniser.

'Yes. She's lively and intelligent, a positive asset rather than the encumbrance you once feared a wife would be,' his old friend pointed out.

The faintest tinge of colour highlighted Rashad's hard cheekbones, for when he had been studying at Oxford with the younger man he had confided in him in a manner which, now that he was older and wiser, he would not risk repeating. 'I no longer fear that prospect,' he parried. 'In fact I am discovering that marriage suits me surprisingly well—'

Boldly impervious to hints, Rio laughed. 'Why are you surprised? She's gorgeous!'

'You seemed to be finding her sister equally attractive at our wedding,' Rashad commented, firmly moving the exchange away from his wife, whom he refused to discuss even with a close friend.

Rio grimaced. 'No, that went to hell in a handbasket for reasons I won't share. I'm afraid I landed the sister with the temperament of a shrew. By the looks of it, you got the sweet-natured one so be grateful for that reality,' he advised.

Rashad glanced across heads to where Polly stood engaged in animated dialogue with the British Ambassador. 'I'm very grateful,' he said grimly.

'Then why do you look anything but grateful?' Rio asked very drily.

Rashad truly didn't know how to answer that direct question. He shrugged a broad shoulder in smouldering silence. His brilliant dark eyes were hooded, his teeming thoughts full of conflict. He was well aware that he was being unreasonable. He had wanted a confident, independent woman as a wife and he had got one. Why was he now wishing that she would cling just a little? Seek him out for advice and guidance? Flash her eyes restively round the room, looking anxiously for him as if she needed and missed him? Why was he being so perverse? So illogical?

He invited Rio to dine with him at the palace and without hesitation chose the same evening that Polly invariably spent with her grandparents, Hakim and his wife. The less Polly was exposed to Rio, the better, he decided with pious resolve.

* * *

'You did incredibly well tonight,' Rashad told Polly on the drive back to the palace. 'You didn't once look to me for backup either.'

A sensation of unease niggled at the base of Polly's skull. Why did he make that sound more like a negative than a plus? Why had he kept his distance throughout the evening? Was she ever going to understand the man she had married? The minute she believed she had solved the mystery of Rashad he would do something she wasn't expecting and confuse her again.

'I thought you wanted me to be independent—'

'I do,' Rashad confirmed. 'I can't always be by your side and sometimes you will have to attend such events alone.'

'So why am I *still* getting a mixed message here?' Polly queried a shade tartly.

Rashad shrugged a broad shoulder as he sprang out of the limo, relieved to be back on palace ground. He knew he was being difficult, he knew he was being too emotional but he was a seething tangle of conflicting feelings inside himself and struggling to hide the fact. In truth, Polly had shone like the brightest of stars at the dinner and without the smallest help from him. He had been very impressed by the natural warmth she exuded. Yet she had still somehow managed to maintain a certain amount of royal distance and formality, a formality which in no way came naturally to her for she was one of the most unstudied personalities he had ever met. In short she had contrived to be the public success that Ferah had always longed to be but had never managed to be. That cruel comparison stopped Rashad in his tracks and yet another surge of guilt and regret bit into him.

Polly sped after Rashad into the palace, wondering what the heck was wrong with him. By the time she actually caught up with him he was poised by the window in their bedroom. He flashed night-dark brooding eyes over her lovely face as she entered. Brilliant dark golden eyes screened by ridiculously long black lashes. Her heart skipped a sudden beat, her breath catching in her throat. Her hand flew up to her constricted throat and rested on the weight of the amber necklace. With a sigh she stretched her fingers round to the clasp at her nape to undo it.

'Let me,' Rashad urged, taking her by surprise as he strode forward.

The ornate collaret lifted and he settled it down in a careless heap on a tall dresser. 'Don't wear it again,' he urged her in a roughened voice.

'Wear what?' Polly queried as she reached up and unhooked each earring in swift succession before looking at him in the mirror for further clarification.

'The ambers. I'll buy you another set,' he promised curtly, his lean dark face shuttered.

Her violet eyes kindled with curiosity. 'What's wrong with this set?' she asked bluntly.

Rashad tensed, dark lashes sweeping down to screen his expression. 'It was Ferah's favourite.'

*'Oh...'* Polly gasped as if he had punched her and deprived her lungs of breath, and in a way that was exactly what he had done. He didn't like seeing her wear-

ing his first wife's much-loved jewellery? What was she supposed to take from that admission?

'It awakens unfortunate memories,' Rashad declared abruptly.

He had loved his first wife and clearly he couldn't bear any reminder of her, Polly assumed, thoroughly discomfited by that awareness. 'I'm your wife now,' she reminded him flatly, wishing that that timely reminder didn't sound quite so childish.

'I'm well aware of that,' Rashad said drily.

'And maybe I don't brush up as nicely as Ferah did in the ambers but you've just made me want to wear them every darned day!' Polly admitted in a helplessly aggressive tone. 'After all, she is gone and I'm here and I have feelings too!'

'This is a crazy conversation.' A questioning black brow elevated, doubtless urging her to think more carefully about what she was saying.

But Polly had had enough and she didn't feel like pretending or indeed lying to save face. 'No, I'm a possessive woman. Either you're mine or you're *still* hers!' Polly fired at him in angry challenge.

'Ferah is my past as you are my present and my future,' Rashad countered in exasperation.

Polly's violet eyes widened and glittered and she planted her hand truculently on one slender jutting hip. 'But your past is raining on my present so I'm not getting a fair deal,' she told him accusingly.

Rashad groaned out loud, frustration gripping him. 'What am I supposed to do about that? I cannot help my past. I cannot forget my memories—'

'No…' Polly conceded. 'But you could share them.'

'*Share* them?' Rashad exclaimed, an expression of appalled fascination stamping his lean, darkly handsome face. 'What man would do that?'

'A man who wants a normal relationship with his wife. If your memories are coming between us, you need to share them,' Polly told him abruptly, for in actuality she was none too sure of the worth of what she was proposing. After all, she didn't really *want* to think about Ferah. She preferred to forget that his first wife had ever existed, which was probably distinctly mean and ungenerous of her. Would it be worse for her to have Ferah fleshed out as a person? Ferah, the woman he had loved who must have loved him too?

'My memories are *not* coming between us,' Rashad assured her with brooding ferocity. 'And I prefer to keep my memories to myself—'

'Oh, tell me something I don't already know,' Polly scoffed in a helpless rush of bitterness. 'It's like when you were made someone locked you up internally and threw away the key!'

'I am what I am—'

'Too set in your ways to change?' Polly skimmed back thinly.

'We have only been married for a couple of months. What sort of miraculous transformation were you expecting this soon?' Rashad derided.

Polly paled at that sardonic recap and intonation and turned away. 'I'm going to bed.'

'I'm going for a ride,' Rashad told her between gritted teeth.

'No, you're walking out on me again because I've said things you don't want to deal with!' Polly condemned angrily.

Rashad settled stormy dark golden eyes on her and froze. 'Very well. I will stay.'

To talk? To share? Or to prove her wrong in her contention that he'd walk away sooner than deal with difficult issues? With a determined little wriggle, Polly unzipped her dress while watching Rashad shed his clothing. Watching him made her mouth run dry, all that sleek bronzed flesh overlying lean, hard muscle being exposed. Flushing at her thoughts, she pulled on a robe and went into the bathroom to remove her makeup.

Now he was furious with her, she ruminated wryly. Golden fury had blazed like the heat of the sun in his beautiful eyes. But he wouldn't admit that he was angry. Nor would he raise his voice or lose his temper. His absolute control of his emotions mocked her trembling hands because she was so wound up she felt as though she might explode with the powerful anxious feelings racing round inside her.

Seeing her in his first wife's jewellery roused 'unfortunate memories'. It made him angry too. Had he watched her tonight in that wretched amber necklace and wished she were Ferah? What else was she supposed to think?

Rashad studied Polly's slender figure. The silk of the robe outlined the rounded curve of her derriere and delicately shaped her pouting breasts, hinting at her prominent nipples. His reaction was instantaneous and it infuriated him but there it was: the lust to take, the lust to possess gripped him almost every time he looked at his wife. The strength of that craving disturbed him as much as his loss of self-discipline. Hard as a rock, he stepped into the shower and put the jets on cold but it didn't help because all that out-of-control emotion washing about inside him like a dangerous rip tide threatening to drag him down only heightened his arousal, exacerbating his need to be close to Polly in the only way he knew.

Share his memories? Was Polly crazy to suggest such a thing? He did not want to relive his unhappy marriage to Ferah. The two women could not have been more different, he conceded heavily. Polly wanted to talk about sensitive issues but Ferah had refused to talk and had brooded on her disappointments until she was overflowing with the bitterness and self-pity that had eventually plunged her into long depressive episodes. How could he even consider sharing that unlovely truth with Polly?

Polly undid the robe and wondered if it would be a little ridiculous for her to put on a nightdress because they had had a disagreement. When she normally wore nothing to bed but her own skin a nightdress would be like making a statement, wouldn't it be? Ultra-sensitive and on edge, she glanced uncertainly at Rashad as he strode out of the bathroom. The air positively crackled when she collided with burning dark golden eyes and she noticed, really couldn't help noticing, his condition.

'Yes, I want you,' Rashad intoned thickly. 'But then...I *always* want you.'

'Don't say it like you wish you didn't!' Polly exclaimed, her mouth running dry, her heartbeat speeding up.

'It can be inconvenient—'

'What's a little inconvenience?' she whispered, achingly aware of him, struggling to remind herself that he hadn't dealt with her demand for more information and that she should be light on understanding while playing it cool and offended.

'I couldn't be gentle in the mood I'm in—'

Polly tried and failed to swallow. There was a wildness in his eyes, a gritty roughened edge to his dark deep drawl and, in the strangest way imaginable, she welcomed that hint that he was not as much in control as he usually was. It was almost as though a barrier had come down inside him, one of several barriers that kept her at a determined distance. 'I might not necessarily *need* gentle right now...'

Without the smallest hesitation, Rashad crossed the space between them in one stride, both arms snaking round her to bring her crashing up against his hot, muscular body. His sensual mouth feasted on hers with a ferocity that suggested she could be the only thing standing between him and insanity and she gloried in a fervour that empowered her at a moment when her self-esteem had taken a battering. After all, it was hard to be proud of being Rashad's consolation prize in the bride stakes, the replacement wife virtually forced on him by the Dharian people.

'I *burn* to be with you,' Rashad growled, erotic energy radiating from him as he brought her down on the bed, his hunger unleashed and sizzling with unashamed intensity. 'Every minute of the day. My appetite for you consumes me.'

She would have told him that that cut both ways but his mouth crushed hers again and the taste of him was like an aphrodisiac, the plunge of his tongue making her body arch up in a wave of shivering delight that shot a fire storm of response through her veins. There was a ripping sound as he extracted her impatiently from the entangling folds of the silk robe. Long, knowing fingers zeroed straight in on the slick pink flesh at the heart of her and she jerked and moaned out loud, on the edge of spontaneously combusting with excitement.

Rashad flipped her over and drew her up on her knees. With a heartfelt growl of satisfaction he sank into her in a single compelling thrust. She was stretched almost to the point of pain but simultaneously the raw pleasure stormed through her nerve endings like a healing drug. He took her hard and fast and that sense of being on an edge flung her up onto an endless high of breathless excitement. Carnal pleasure gripped her bone and sinew. His lack of control thrilled her because she knew that she wasn't in control either. In any case, this was Rashad and she loved him, trusted him, *needed* him, and that his savage hunger for her should be even stronger when he was angry and troubled comforted her. After all that same primal need to connect with him at such times was just as powerful and driving for her.

She was riding a ravishing surge of excitement when a skilled hand rubbed against her throbbing bud of pleasure and the world burst into Technicolor fireworks behind her eyelids. She jerked and cried out, caught up in a rolling climax that detonated deep in her pelvis and totally wiped her out. When she collapsed back down on the bed, Rashad rolled her into his arms and lay there with her, struggling for breath, his heart still thundering against her.

'I'm sorry,' Rashad gritted unevenly. 'I was rough, selfish. I am truly sorry—'

'No…I liked it…'

Long fingers pushed up her chin to force her eyes to meet his, his concern evaporating to be replaced by the beginnings of sheer masculine awe. 'You *liked* it?' he whispered wonderingly.

'Uh-huh,' Polly confirmed, her colour rising inexorably beneath that stunned appraisal.

'Sometimes I feel as though there's a crazy storm rising inside me—'

'Tension, emotion…'

'That I've failed to get under control,' Rashad pronounced, his beautiful mouth tightening with dissatisfaction.

'But you don't need to control it, not with me. With me, you don't have to put up a front, you don't have to impress.' Polly wrapped a possessive arm round his lean, damp body, small fingers smoothing down soothingly over his ribcage. 'I want you to be yourself.'

'Be careful what you wish for.' Rashad turned his tousled dark head away from her. 'Ferah chose to die sooner than remain with me,' he said flatly, no emotion whatsoever in the statement.

Completely taken aback by that shockingly sudden change of topic, Polly tensed. *'Chose?'* she queried with a frown.

'A few weeks before she was bitten by the snake she took an overdose. Fortunately she was found in time and I arranged for her to have treatment and therapy but sadly it wasn't enough. When she was bitten she concealed the bite until it was too late for the antidote to work,' Rashad revealed. 'She died in my arms. She told me that she was setting me free…'

Polly was appalled, belatedly grasping why any memory of Ferah was liable to upset him. She almost spoke her mind to say that she thought that that was a dreadfully cruel and martyred thing to have said to him in such circumstances but common sense made her bite her lip rather than speak in insensitive haste. 'Setting you free?' she whispered instead.

'Free to marry another woman, one who could give me a child as she could not,' Rashad extended curtly. 'She knew her father had been trying to persuade me to divorce her and take another wife and that I had refused—'

'Her own *father* was willing to do that to her?' Polly pressed in disgust.

'All my uncle saw was the end game and that was the restoration of the monarchy. He saw a king with an heir in tow as a safer bet than one with a barren wife,' Rashad advanced bitterly. 'Ferah knew how he felt because he told her that it was her duty to let me go. She was already depressed. All she ever wanted was to be a mother and when that was denied her she felt worthless. Being made to feel like a burden as well was too much for her. She wasn't a strong person.'

'I'm so sorry,' Polly muttered, feeling inadequate because he had told her a much more unhappy story than she had expected and for the first time she understood that Rashad had been as much wounded by his first marriage as he had been by the traumatic changes and injuries inflicted on him by his dysfunctional childhood. The sheer extent of the losses he had endured turned her stomach over sickly, making her feel outrageously naïve.

'I should've given her more support. It's my fault that she died,' Rashad murmured with grave simplicity.

'It *wasn't* your fault!' Polly argued vehemently. 'She was depressed. You got her professional help. What more could you have done? By the sound of it, her own family did nothing to help her recover!'

Rashad stretched out with a heavy sigh. 'It's in the past and can't be changed, *aziz*. Let us leave it there.'

But although Polly sealed her lips on further comment she couldn't leave it there because she felt ashamed that she had come over all jealous and possessive about his attachment to Ferah and his memories of his first marriage. Her sister had tried to warn her that Rashad had been through the emotional grinder in the past and she hadn't really listened. He had also trained himself to control his emotions and keep his secrets and in his position that was hardly surprising. That he had let the barriers down just for a few minutes with her was a promising sign, she told herself with determined positivity.

# CHAPTER NINE

POLLY SHIFTED IN the early hours, partially wakening to the sound of Rashad having a terse conversation with someone on the phone. Blinking, she turned over, eyes drowsy in the half-light before dawn as he put the phone down again and sat up.

'There was an incident on the border during the night.' He sighed, raking long brown fingers through his sleep-tousled jet-black hair. 'A man was shot but mercifully *not* killed. I'll be in meetings all day trying to calm this down, but first I have to fly out there and get the facts.'

He dropped a kiss on her brow and urged her to go back to sleep. A few hours later, Polly rolled out of bed with her usual energy and then stopped dead as a roiling wave of sick dizziness assailed her. There was nothing she could do but rush for the bathroom where she knelt on the cold tiled floor to be ignominiously sick. In the aftermath, she felt weak and shaky and it was a few minutes before she took the risk of standing up again.

She couldn't have fallen pregnant so quickly, she reasoned with herself as she stepped into the shower, needing to feel clean from head to toe. Ellie had said the average conception took around six months but that it could just as easily take longer. No, it was much more likely that she had caught some bug or eaten something at dinner that had disagreed with her digestion. Even so, she thought that it would be sensible to consult the palace doctor.

She dried her hair and got dressed, wondering if Rashad would be gone as long as he had feared. No matter what was on his agenda he generally managed to share breakfast with her and she had learned to cherish their quiet moments together. Her period was a week overdue, she recalled with sudden reluctance, but she hadn't paid any heed to that because she'd suspected that the radical change of diet and climate was playing havoc with her system. After all, last month she had been early so possibly this month her cycle would be late to compensate for that.

Hayat awaited her in the reception room next door with a list of Polly's phone calls and her emails, each starred in terms of what Hayat deemed important. That her sister, Ellie's call only rated the bottom of the list was telling. She learned that she had received an invitation to open the new wing of the hospital in Kashan and asked Hayat if she would arrange an appointment for her with Dr Wasem.

'You are unwell?' Hayat questioned, studying her with a frown.

'No. I simply wish to consult the doctor,' Polly replied.

After a busy half-hour of tests and an examination

with Dr Wasem Polly discovered that she *was* pregnant. Her idle musings to that effect were proven when she had least expected it. In truth she was stunned because Rashad's admission about Ferah's sterility and his laid-back assumption allied to her own that it would take months for her to conceive had all combined to make her look on motherhood as a distinctly distant possibility. Instead it had suddenly become her new reality.

'I am honoured beyond words to break this news to you,' Dr Wasem informed her, his huge smile warm with genuine pleasure on her behalf.

'I'll tell Rashad tonight so I would be grateful if this remains confidential,' Polly responded tactfully, well aware that in the claustrophobic gossip mill of the royal household the good doctor probably wanted to shout her announcement from the rooftops.

'Of course.'

Polly positively floated out of his ultra-modern surgery on the ground floor of the palace. A baby, Rashad's baby. He would be so happy, so *relieved*, she reflected ruefully. He had lived through the pressure of a childless first marriage and all the fertility testing that had gone with it, and she knew that he considered the entire process stressful and potentially disastrous. Now he would be able to relax and forget about worrying, she thought tenderly.

A radiant smile lit Polly's face as she began to formulate plans for the rest of the day. She phoned her sister first and beamed at Ellie's shout of delighted anticipation. Afterwards she called her grandfather's home to speak to her grandmother and ask if she could visit them on another evening. She held back her pregnancy news, wanting to share that with Rashad first.

'That would be best,' Dursa told her granddaughter in her halting English. 'Hakim is travelling with the King and will be away until late and your grandfather would not like to miss your visit.'

Her single social engagement cancelled, Polly decided to spend the rest of the day painting. She had her regular language lesson first, of course, and then spent another hour studying Dharian history and culture. The more she learned about every aspect of Dharian life, the easier she found it to understand Rashad's concerns and share them. It was particularly interesting to learn about the heroine of the legend, the saintly Queen Zariyah. Why *had* her mother named her Zariyah at birth? Her grandfather, Hakim, thought it might have been because the name was revered in Dharia and her mother had wanted to give her that link to her father's heritage, but Polly thought it was just as likely that her mother had simply thought the name was pretty. Evidently she had not appreciated or had possibly not cared that the name was almost never used out of respect for the original Zariyah. Now the world had turned full circle, Polly acknowledged, for while it was known that she was called Polly the media routinely referred to her as Queen Zariyah.

'You're going to paint,' Hayat said unnecessarily when Polly appeared in the loose sundress she usually wore for her sessions.

Polly nodded, wondering why Hayat was staring at

her, her dark eyes cool, her face stiff. Had she offended the other woman in some way? Polly pushed the concern to the back of her mind because she was not in the mood to tackle what would be a difficult conversation. In fact she kept on wanting to smile in the most stupid inane way because she was so happy about the baby she carried. As she relaxed into that startling concept she was finally allowing herself to think about what it would mean to have a child and become a parent.

Certainly, she hoped that she would manage to be a better parent than her own mother had contrived to be. Although she felt guilty feeling judgemental like that, she had had a great deal more compassion for her late mother since she had learned the tragic circumstances of her own birth. Yet Annabel Dixon had moved on from the loss of her husband by very quickly conceiving another child and once again landing the responsibility for that child onto her own mother's shoulders. Polly sighed with regret. It seemed that her mother had led a tumultuous, lonely and unhappy life, for she had never managed to sustain a lasting relationship with any one of her daughters' fathers. She wanted something very different for her own life and her own child, she conceded ruefully. She wanted love and stability and two parents for her baby, so that her child could feel safe and supported as he or she grew up.

The air-conditioned cool of the room set aside for her to use as a studio was welcome. There were two unfinished canvases on easels, one a painstaking watercolour in Polly's signature dreamy pastels of the star-shaped pool on the ground floor, the second a sunset in oils of the desert landscape. The second painting was a new departure for Polly. The colours were more adventurous, the brush strokes bolder, possibly expressing the many changes that had engulfed her since she first came to Dharia, she acknowledged thoughtfully.

And yet had she had a choice there was nothing she would change, she reflected while she painted. Rashad had transformed her life. Her gaze flickered to the ring on her wedding finger, the miniaturised fire-opal ring, and she smiled giddily, marvelling that her mother's legacy, inapt as it might have been, had nonetheless reunited her with her grandparents and allowed her to meet Rashad. Gorgeous but often unfathomable Rashad. He was passionate, clever and driven, sexy beyond words, everything she had not even known she wanted in a man until she met him. But he was also a multifaceted challenge with hidden and dangerous depths and that worried her, for she herself was not introspective and pretty much wore her feelings on the surface.

As the heat of day began to fade Polly went off to shower and change into the blue dress Rashad particularly admired. If he made it back in time she would tell him about the baby over dinner, otherwise over a late supper. In fact it didn't matter how late he got back, she would wait up.

When she reappeared, Hayat was waiting for her again. 'I'm afraid there has been an oversight. The King's friend, Mr Benedetti, is about to arrive to join him for dinner and the King is not here—'

Polly frowned, knowing how important the art of

hospitality was to Rashad and how very rude a last-minute cancellation would be. 'I'll dine with him and explain.'

Hayat gave her a bright admiring smile. 'You are daring—'

Polly raised a brow. 'How?'

'To dine alone with a man who is not your husband.'

Polly laughed. 'Neither my husband nor I are that old-fashioned,' she asserted with confidence.

Rio Benedetti was charm personified, soothing her concern that he might be offended by Rashad's absence with an easy flow of entertaining conversation stamped with an occasional subtle query about Ellie, which made Polly's sisterly antenna prickle with curiosity. After all, Ellie had evinced no similar desire to discuss Rio with Polly, claiming that she had only appeared to enjoy Rio's company at the wedding out of politeness and hadn't actually liked him at all. In fact she had dismissed him as a player with sleazy chat-up lines. Somehow, Rio had got entirely on the wrong side of her spirited sister.

The Italian billionaire did not keep her late and Polly was curled up in a corner couch on her own with a book by the time Rashad strode through the door after eleven that evening. The instant that she saw his stormy dark face, she knew that he was in a temper and concern indented her brow.

'What's happened?' she exclaimed, coming upright in her bare feet, noting that lines of strain bracketed his mouth.

Rashad regarded her in astonishment. She had spent

an entire evening alone with an infamous womaniser, utterly disregarding Hayat's advice. The minute Rashad had received that news he had assumed that his wife found Rio so compellingly attractive that she had decided to throw away the rule book and that thought, that *fear* had simply spawned an ungovernable rage that far outran any emotion Rashad had ever felt. Exhausted as he already was by an endless day of repetitive diplomacy and incessant meetings, Hayat's phone call had incensed him.

'Why didn't you listen to Hayat when she advised you not to dine alone with Rio?'

Polly tilted her chin. 'She didn't advise me *not* to do it, she just said it was daring. I thought that was nonsense when I was only trying to be polite and considerate. Telling him you were unavailable when he was literally on the way here would have been very rude and as he is a close friend of yours I thought you wouldn't want that—'

'Or perhaps the temptation of having Rio all to yourself was too great!' Rashad flung at her rawly. 'He is notoriously sought after by women.'

'Not by my sister,' Polly remarked abstractedly, suddenly recognising that Rashad, whether he knew it or not, was consumed by jealousy. 'You really don't have to be jealous—'

*'Jealous?'* The word hit Rashad like a brick thrown on glass, shattering what little control he retained. 'I have never been jealous over a woman in my life!'

'Sleep on it and then think about it,' Polly advised, losing patience and angry with him because she had been eager to tell him about their baby and now he had wrecked the mood with his temper. He was so volatile, so possessive. On what planet did he live that he believed she could be so eager to make love with him while planning to betray him with his closest friend? Had she been too eager? Was that the problem? Did he think she was some sort of natural-born wanton who could not be trusted in the radius of any attractive man? A dark flush of fuming humiliation reddened Polly's face and chest and she turned her head away from him to walk past him.

Long, lean fingers closed round her wrist to intercept her. 'Where are you going?'

'I've got nothing more to say to you.' Polly yanked her arm free and, feeling the prickle of angry, hurt tears stinging her eyes, she fled past him into the corridor. How could Rashad talk to her like that? How could he even see her in such a light? Was this her reward for matching that dark, passionate intensity of his?

'Polly…'

'I *hate* you!' Polly flung over her shoulder as she started down the stairs that led to their bedroom.

And it was that twisting round to make that final response that unbalanced her. She missed a step and lurched. Her feverish grab at the stone bannister failed and she fell, instinctively turning her body into herself as she had been taught to fall from a horse. Her hip hit stone and she cried out in pain and then the back of her head struck a step and she knew no more…

# CHAPTER TEN

A FAINT MOAN parted Polly's lips because her head was aching and she came awake with a sense of frightened confusion. Her eyes opened on an unfamiliar room. She saw a bewildering number of faces, blinked and registered that she was in a hospital bed with the side bars raised.

'Polly?' Rashad breathed tautly, springing out of the chair beside her.

'What?' she mumbled because moving her lips felt like too much effort. 'My head's sore…my hip.'

As she focused blearily on him he stepped back to allow the medical staff to attend to her and she wondered why he looked so tired and why the sun was shining into the room when only minutes ago it had been dark. A nurse checked her blood pressure and gave her a drink while a doctor asked her a series of questions. Her attention, however, stayed squarely on Rashad while she struggled to recall what had happened to her. Black stubble accentuated his stubborn passionate mouth, his luxuriant hair was dishevelled, his eyes shadowed, his powerful anxiety unconcealed.

Recalling her fall on the stairs and the argument that had preceded it taxed her concentration and then, with a sudden whoosh of awareness, all that fell away on the shocking surge of apprehension that shot through her. She pressed a stricken hand against her stomach.

'My baby?' she gasped fearfully.

Rashad strode forward and rested a hand over hers in a soothing gesture. 'Our baby is fine—'

'For the moment. There has been no bleeding but you must rest. The next twenty-four hours are crucial to your recovery,' the grey-haired doctor told her firmly as he urged her to lie still.

Rashad's hand was trembling over hers and just as she noticed that he withdrew it in a sudden gesture and dug it into the pocket of his trousers. He *knew* that she was pregnant; he knew about the baby. She assumed that Dr Wasem had told him after she fell and knocked herself out. Polly closed her eyes, guessing just how guilty Rashad would be feeling. She was still furious with him but she knew his habit of blaming himself for everything bad that happened around him. If she lost their baby he would never forgive himself for upsetting her. How could she be furious with him and yet aching inside herself for what he was feeling at the same time? It was that crazy conundrum called love, she decided ruefully.

While the doctor talked to her about the concussion she had sustained, Polly tried to think clearly and focus but it was no use, she simply *couldn't*. Both her head and her body ached. The mental confusion and the extreme fatigue the doctor had warned her about were steadily closing in on her because there was far too much to think about and it was infinitely easier to close it all out just then and drift. She still had her baby, she reflected with passionate relief, and that was the last clear thought she had.

Rashad paced the silent room. He had tidied himself up in response to Hakim's pleas but he had not eaten, he had not slept. How could he? His temper, that wild surging rage he couldn't always control, could have killed Polly. He looked at her, lying so still in the bed, white-blonde hair tumbling across the pillow, her face showing a little colour now, no longer that wan grey that had terrified him. She was so fragile, so precious…

And the baby? Rashad was still stunned by that development, that incredulous realisation that, if there was nothing medically amiss to prevent it, a pregnancy could happen so quickly, so easily, so…so *normally*, he recognised. He hadn't expected that, hadn't prepared for it either. In fact he had pessimistically assumed that although they might conceive a child eventually it would undoubtedly take a long time. Once again he had made the mistake of allowing past disappointment and disillusionment to influence his expectations in the present. And how could she ever forgive him for that?

He was fatally flawed, almost programmed to disappoint Polly. He had even failed to protect her from Hayat's malice. *'Either you're mine or you're still hers,'* Polly had flung at him, referring to Ferah, and he could see that now—could see that he had failed to make peace with the past and move on to embrace a wife far superior in every way to his first. And if it was wrong and disrespectful to think that then it was better to be wrong but at least rational enough to recognise that truth. Fate had rained gold on him when he least deserved it and he had virtually thrown away the opportunity he had been given, he conceded grimly.

'You *must* eat and rest, Your Majesty,' Hakim whispered fiercely from the doorway. 'How can you support your wife if you are exhausted?'

'As always, the voice of reason,' Rashad conceded wearily, but his every instinct still warred against leaving Polly alone. At least while he watched over her he could actually feel as though he was *doing* something to help, but in reality, while she was under medical supervision, he could only be an onlooker.

Polly wakened and slowly savoured the strength returning to her body. She pushed down the bedding and tugged up her gown to squint at the horrid blue-black bruising covering her hip and stretching down her thigh. Better her hip than her stomach, she decided as a nurse came in and gently scolded her for sitting up in bed without help. Suddenly she was surrounded by staff again and she was changed and the bed was changed and then breakfast was ushered in.

An hour later, Rashad arrived, sleek and shaven in a beautifully cut dark suit. He looked fantastically handsome and considerably more groomed and calm than he had the day before. His stunning dark golden eyes immediately sought hers and instinctively she evaded his gaze, too full of conflict to meet it. He had revealed his lack of trust in her. He had believed that even though they were married she could still be tempted by another man and that she could be unfaithful. How could she overlook or forgive that?

'I have a lot to say to you,' Rashad murmured tautly. 'But first your grandparents are waiting to see you and you should see them now to reassure them.'

'Of course,' she muttered uncertainly, wondering what he had to say to her, wondering what she would say to him.

'If your medical team agree, I can take you home later.'

Polly compressed her lips in silence.

'Hayat has now gone home to her mother. She won't be returning to the palace staff,' he told her in a harsh clipped undertone. 'I was foolish to trust her near you—'

Polly studied him directly for the first time. 'What on earth are you talking about?'

His lean, strong face went rigid. 'Apparently Hayat was angry and jealous that I had married you and she decided to cause trouble between us…and in that she succeeded,' he divulged grudgingly. 'I told her to cancel that dinner with Rio before I left the palace the day before yesterday. But she didn't cancel it. She set you up instead, set us *both* up…challenging you to dine alone with him, knowing that I am *not*—at heart—the liberated male I must strive to be for your sake…'

Polly was shaken by that explanation. 'But why would Hayat be angry and jealous? Were you involved with her before I came into your life?'

Rashad frowned. 'Of course not…she is Ferah's kid sister. I found it hard to warm to her personality, though—'

'Hayat's your sister-in-law?' Polly exclaimed in disbelief. 'Why did nobody tell *me* that?'

'It wasn't a secret. I didn't think it was important. I didn't want to discriminate against her either because she is, or *was*, very efficient.' Rashad lifted his handsome dark head high and expelled his breath in an audible rush, frustration and regret tensing his lean dark face. 'I made a mistake in allowing her access to you and I'm afraid you paid for my lack of judgement.'

Long lashes fluttering down, Polly cloaked her eyes to conceal her incredulity. How could he not have warned her about his familial relationship with the other woman? She remembered Hayat admitting that she had watched her sister break her heart over her inability to conceive and, remembering her own unease around the attractive brunette, she swallowed back angry words of condemnation. His first wife's little sister, someone who would be challenged to wish Rashad's second wife a long and happy life after Ferah's tragic fate.

'Hayat admitted that she resented my remarriage and our happiness,' Rashad volunteered tautly. 'I should have foreseen that likelihood and her spite.'

'Well, it's done and dusted now,' Polly pointed out curtly, because she was annoyed at what she had learnt. 'She's left the staff and as it happens I'm all right—'

*'Inshallah,'* Rashad breathed, rising to leave as her grandparents bustled in, all smiles and concern, to

present her with a very large basket of fruit. Their caring and affectionate presence was exactly what she needed to soothe her ruffled feelings at that moment. She received a hail of anxious words and a hug from her grandmother and a quiet squeeze on the shoulder from Hakim, who wasn't given to drama.

Rashad came to collect her from the hospital. He explained that there were crowds waiting for a glimpse of her outside the hospital and they left by a rear entrance.

'Why won't you look at me?' Rashad pressed on the drive back to the palace.

'I'm angry with you,' Polly admitted curtly.

Rashad released his breath on a slow hiss. 'Of course you are. I spoiled what should have been a special moment—'

She assumed he meant that she had missed the chance to tell him privately about their baby.

'Not only that,' she broke in jaggedly. 'You behaved as if I was some kind of harlot who couldn't be trusted alone in a room with a man!'

'I deeply regret the way in which I behaved,' Rashad admitted levelly. 'If I could go back and eradicate what I said I would…but I cannot.'

Colour scoring her cheekbones, Polly chewed the soft underside of her lower lip and made no response. What could she say? She *knew* he regretted it.

'I didn't like being confronted with the reality that you could think of me like that.'

'We will talk when we get home. I don't want to be interrupted,' Rashad murmured tautly.

A tense silence fell and Polly did nothing to break

it. In truth she was as annoyed with herself as she was with him. Wasn't she usually a forgiving person? But what Rashad had said had struck at the very heart of their relationship and had deeply wounded her because she loved him. He didn't know that she loved him. He hadn't asked her to love him. And she wouldn't tell him because he would assume that she craved some kind of matching response from him when she did not. She didn't want Rashad to feel that he had to pretend to feel more for her than he actually did. It would make him uncomfortable and he would be hopeless at faking it. Over the long term, honesty and common sense would be safer than emotional outpourings that would only muddy the water between them.

Tearful staff greeted her on their knees in the entrance hall. She was deeply touched by that demonstration of affection. Rashad's people were very emotional and unafraid to show it. She marvelled that they had a king who worked so hard at concealing every emotion he experienced as if emotion were something to be ashamed of.

'The doctors advised that you rest now,' Rashad reminded her as they entered the private wing of the palace.

Flowers were everywhere in the airy drawing room and piles of gifts cluttered every surface. 'What on earth…?' Polly began to ask.

'As soon as it was known that you had suffered an accident the flowers and the presents came flooding in,' Rashad explained. 'There has been no official announcement of your pregnancy, nor will there be for some time, but I suspect rumours are already on the streets. There were too many servants and guards hovering after your accident and Dr Wasem's anxiety on your behalf was unmistakeable.'

'And what about you?' Polly whispered. 'How did you react?'

'It was the worst moment of my life,' Rashad declared without hesitation, his strong jaw clenching hard. 'Until I realised you were still breathing I was afraid you were dead—'

'Or that I would lose the baby,' she slotted in wryly.

'I could have borne that better than the loss of you,' Rashad parried harshly. 'There could always be another baby…but there is only one *you*. And you are irreplaceable.'

There was a little red devil in Polly's brain because somehow she was not in the mood to listen while he made such comforting complimentary statements. 'No, I'm not,' she disagreed, turning her violet eyes onto his lean, perfect profile. 'You would still have women queuing up to marry you and become your Queen and the mother of your children.'

'Two dead predecessors in the role would limit my appeal somewhat. I would seem like a regular Bluebeard.'

A startled laugh was wrenched from Polly. 'There is that,' she conceded, turning away to hesitantly finger a tiny velvet soft frog toy that had been unwrapped.

It was undeniably a toy intended for their unborn child. Her eyes prickled with tears. Her most private secret had become public and she had been deprived of the right to share the news of her first pregnancy with her husband. She dashed the tears away with an angry hand, scolding herself for getting upset by gifts intended to express heartfelt good wishes.

'I wanted to tell you myself,' she framed gruffly.

'I know…I screwed it up,' Rashad bit out jerkily.

'Maybe we both did,' Polly muttered heavily. 'In a marriage it takes two to screw up. Whatever way you look at it, it's a partnership.'

'No,' Rashad disagreed. 'I didn't allow us to be a partnership. I have no experience of a marriage of equals. I have no experience of sharing feelings or memories. I have always had to keep such things to myself but with you…' He hesitated, shooting a look at her from shimmering dark golden eyes. 'With you, my control breaks down and things escape.'

Polly studied him and her heart felt as though he were crushing it because she bled for him at that moment, seeing him boy and man, rigorously disciplined to hold every feeling in, never allowed to be natural. 'That's not necessarily a bad thing,' she whispered shakily.

'It *was* a bad thing when I confronted you about your dinner with Rio,' Rashad pointed out heavily. 'I was…irrational. Rage engulfed me. I could not bear to think of you enjoying his company or admiring him. You do not need to tell me that I'm too possessive of you…I *know* it. I have never known such jealousy before and it ate me alive—'

'Well,' Polly murmured, inching a little closer because his sheer emotional intensity drew her like a flame on an icy day, 'I understand a little better now. But it upset me a lot that you seemed to distrust me—'

Rashad swung back to her, his stunning eyes bright with regret. 'But that is what is so illogical about it. I *do* trust you and Rio is my best friend and I know he would not betray me but *still* those feelings overwhelmed me!'

Polly brushed his arm with hesitant fingers. 'Because you're not used to dealing with that kind of stuff. You're on a learning curve.'

'I *hurt* you. If it hurts you I do not want to be on that curve,' he breathed rawly.

'But not expressing what you feel makes you a powder keg, which is more dangerous,' Polly argued.

'It won't ever happen again,' Rashad intoned. 'I will be on my guard now.'

'But that's not what I want,' Polly admitted ruefully.

'I have kept too many secrets from you,' Rashad confessed, striding over to the window, deeply troubled by his sense of disloyalty to his first wife's memory but accepting that such honesty was necessary. 'My first marriage was very unhappy—'

'But you said you loved her,' Polly reminded him in complete surprise.

'At the outset when we were teenagers trying to behave like grown-ups, we clung to each other for that was all we had. She was my first love even though we had very little in common. I made the best of it that I could but I did not love Ferah as she loved me,' Rashad declared with strong regret etched in his lean, darkly handsome features. 'And she *knew* it. Her inability to conceive was a constant source of stress for both of us and she became a deeply troubled woman. Nothing I said or did comforted her. I tried many times to get through to her and I failed. What love there was died until by the end we were like two strangers forced to live together.'

Polly stared at him in shock, utterly unprepared for that revelation.

'Now you know the *real* truth,' Rashad completed grimly.

'But…' she began uncertainly, frowning in bewilderment.

'For the last five years of our marriage I was celibate. That side of our marriage ended the day Ferah learned that she could not have a child. She turned away from me,' he revealed curtly, his difficulty in making that admission etched in the strained lines of his lean dark features. 'I felt unwanted, rejected…'

'Of course you did,' Polly framed, still in shock from what he had just told her, her every belief about his first marriage violently turned on its head and her heart going out to him.

'And that is why you were right to accuse me of a lack of enthusiasm on the day we married.' Rashad surveyed her with anguished dark eyes, full of guilt and regret. 'You said you wanted it all so I am telling you everything. I knew it was my duty to remarry but I *dreaded* the thought of being a husband again. I had nothing but bad memories of the first experience and my expectations were very low—'

Polly unfroze with difficulty and sat down on legs

that felt weak, not quite sure she was strong enough to take the honesty she had asked him to give her because what he was now telling her was beginning to hurt. 'I can understand that,' she said limply.

'I was completely selfish in my behaviour. I was bitter and angry. I felt trapped. And then you *saved* me,' he framed harshly. 'I did nothing to deserve you, Polly. I am not worthy of the happiness you have brought into my life.'

Reeling from that 'trapped' word that had pierced her like a knife, Polly studied him in confusion. 'You're talking about the baby?' she pressed. 'That's made you happy?'

His black brows drew together. 'No, I'm talking about you. Our baby is a wonderful gift and I am very grateful to be so blessed but my happiness is entirely based on having you in my life...'

'Oh,' Polly mumbled in surprise.

Rashad crossed the rug between them and dropped down on his knees at her feet to look levelly at her with insistent dark golden eyes. 'I think I probably fell in love with you the first time I saw you. It was like an electric shock. I had never felt anything like it before and of course I didn't recognise it for what it was. It was love but I thought it was lust because I didn't know any better...'

'Love?' Polly almost whispered. 'You *love* me?'

'Madly, insanely,' Rashad extended raggedly. 'I can't bear to have you out of my sight. I think about you all the time. The thought of losing you terrifies me.

And yet I have made mistake after mistake with you and done nothing to earn your regard—'

Polly grinned at him, the happiness he insisted she had brought him bubbling up through her in receipt of such an impassioned declaration. She definitely loved him and loved him all the more for abandoning his reserve and his formality and his pride to convince her of the sincerity of his feelings for her. 'I felt that electric shock thing too,' she told him teasingly. 'Every time I laid eyes on you, I felt like an infatuated schoolgirl. Why do you think I married you? I married you because I fell in love with you…'

*'Truly?'* Rashad exclaimed in ego-boosting amazement as he sprang upright and stepped back for an instant simply to savour her beautiful glowing face.

'Truly,' Polly confirmed with a helpless beaming smile of encouragement.

Rashad scooped her up very, very gently, being mindful of her sore hip, and carried her into their bedroom to lay her down on the bed. He shed his jacket and tie and settled down beside her to ease her fully into his arms. 'I love you so much, *habibti.* But I am forbidden to do anything more than hold you close for a few days,' he admitted in a roughened voice. 'Yet it is enough to still have that right, believe me.'

Ignoring the hint of soreness from her stiff hip, Polly squirmed round in the circle of his arms to face him. She ran wondering fingers across a high masculine cheekbone and marvelled at the silky black lashes semi-veiling his adoring eyes. 'I think a kiss is in order…and I'm expecting a real award winner of a kiss,' she warned him cheekily.

'I will try to deliver,' Rashad groaned, gazing down at her clear blue eyes with fervent appreciation. 'I always try to deliver—'

'Well, you were pretty nifty in the baby stakes,' she conceded.

'Nifty together…' He nibbled at her full lower lip and she closed her eyes, literally so happy she felt that she should be floating on high, but then she wouldn't have let go of Rashad for anything because his lean, powerful body felt so very good against hers. And they might be different and he might be much more old-fashioned than he was willing to admit, but she knew that they complemented each other beautifully.

# EPILOGUE

'I CAN'T BELIEVE that after all this time we still haven't found Gemma.' Polly sighed and shot a pained glance at her sister, Ellie. 'I mean, it's been months and we still know next to nothing about our long-lost sibling!'

'Well, we know that she had a tough childhood and she has no roots to cling to,' Ellie argued in a more measured tone. 'We can also assume that she moves around a lot because we never seem to catch up with her and we know she works in *really* dead-end jobs. That's a lot more than we knew about Gemma starting out.'

Polly nodded reluctantly. 'True...but what if she doesn't *want* to know about us?' she asked worriedly. 'We've advertised in the papers, notified social services that we're looking, informed everyone who has known her in the past that we want to find her—'

'We have to be patient,' Ellie cut in firmly. 'And that's not a trait you possess although, heaven knows, you possess everything else.'

'What's that supposed to mean?' Polly prompted.

Ellie rolled her eyes. 'Movie-star-handsome King as

husband—check. An adoring population who think you can walk on water—check. Constant sunshine overhead, royal palace—check. Loving grandparents—check. An adorable baby son… Yes, I'm talking about you, you little darling!' She stopped to speak to Karim, who crawled across the rug to his aunt to grab the toy she was extending. 'I suppose you're already planning on extending the family?'

Polly flushed. 'Not just yet. I'd like Karim to be a little older before we try again. I'm not a baby machine, Ellie. I mean, look at you, you don't even date—'

'I'm too busy working. Between my shifts and the hospital and the exams I don't have time for a man. Anyway, most of them are a waste of space,' her redheaded sister contended. 'No, I like my life just the way it is. I eat what I like, go where I like, do as I like and that's important to me. The minute a man enters the equation, all your choices start disappearing—'

'And you still have no plans to look into your background?' Polly pressed.

Ellie sighed. 'Actually I'm taking a couple of months off once I complete my residency and I'm planning on heading to Italy and doing a little discreet detective work—'

'Oh, that's great!' Polly gushed approvingly. 'Will you tell me your father's name now?'

Ellie groaned. 'The reason I didn't tell you the name before is that I got given two names—'

Polly's eyes widened. *'Two?'*

'Yes,' Ellie confirmed drily. 'Two names. Obviously our mother didn't know which man fathered me and, sleaziest of all, the men were *brothers*. I've done some research. One of the men is alive, the other dead. The living one is a wealthy retired art collector who lives in a *palazzo* outside Florence—his brother passed away years ago.'

Polly stared at her sister in consternation, belatedly grasping why the younger woman had been so silent on the topic of her own unknown father and background. 'Oh, dear…I'm so sorry—'

'No, you got the fairy tale…the military hero father who married our mother…and I got a pair of dead-beat dads,' Ellie mocked with wry humour. 'I'm glad it worked out that way. I can handle messy reality better than you can.'

'I could come to Italy with you!' Polly proffered in dismay. 'Be your support.'

'No, you'd wilt like a flower out of water deprived of Rashad and Karim,' Ellie forecast drily. 'And that's if your husband would even *let* you go—'

'Rashad doesn't tell me what to do—'

'No, but he hates it when you're away even for a couple of days,' Ellie reminded her wryly. 'You came over to see me at Christmas and Rashad was on the phone every five minutes. You actually fell asleep talking to him one night. Having you to stay was like separating a pair of lovelorn teenagers. It's unhealthy to be so attached to each other…'

Polly simply laughed, knowing that Ellie had never been in love. Nothing came between Ellie and the medical career she adored. But Polly had never had that burning ambition for a career and her wants and needs were satisfied by her family circle and her public role as the Queen of Dharia. She was always very busy, particularly since the birth of their son a year earlier. They had a nanny to help with Karim's care but both Polly and Rashad spent a great deal of time with their son. Polly wanted Karim to know how much he was loved and Rashad was determined to play a daily part in his child's routine.

'It's so beautiful here,' Ellie remarked dreamily, contemplating the star-shaped pool into which water flowed endlessly. Lush trees and luxuriant foliage softened the carved stone arches and pillars of the palace walls that surrounded the courtyard. 'You saw this place first, didn't you? Maybe that's why you fell for Rashad.'

'You are such a cynic, Ellie,' Rashad declared with amusement as he joined them.

Karim loosed a yell and crawled at speed across the tiles to greet his father. Rashad chuckled and bent down to scoop up the little boy and kiss him with an unashamed love that touched Polly's heart. The man she had married had slowly learned to loosen up and show his true colours. His passion in bed was now equally matched by the depth of his affection. He said that she had changed him but Polly believed he had changed himself. He was happy now and it showed in the ease of his brilliant smile and the burnished glow of his dark eyes.

'Well, was it the palace that cast a spell over you… or me?' Rashad teased, gazing down at his wife as she moved to his side.

'If you two are going to turn all lovey-dovey, I'm going upstairs for a shower,' Ellie announced in a deflating tone.

'Lovey-dovey?' Rashad queried, walking Polly out of the courtyard with an arm draped round her shoulder and Karim tucked below the other.

'Drippy…mushy,' she translated. 'Ellie hates that stuff.'

'Are we…drippy?' Rashad enquired with a pained look.

'Probably sometimes,' she said fondly. 'Who cares as long as we're happy?'

'I am not drippy,' Rashad proclaimed with distaste as Polly removed Karim from his arms and settled their son in his cot for his nap.

Karim howled as if he had been abandoned in the street and Rashad hovered worriedly.

'He's fine. He always does that. He's just like you, very resilient and he tries it on sometimes. Don't let him think you're going to lift him again,' Polly warned as she dragged Rashad out of the nursery again.

'Tough love…right?' Rashad guessed, wincing as Karim kept on crying.

'Wait,' Polly instructed in the corridor.

When he was deprived of an audience, the crying stopped and their son began to talk to himself quite happily.

Rashad smiled, much relieved by the development.

'Yeah, you're really drippy!' Polly teased with satisfaction, walking into their bedroom.

'I'm not. I'm a concerned parent who doesn't like to hear my child cry,' Rashad argued.

'And I'm what? The evil mother who left him to cry?'

'No, you're the wonderful wife who is giving me an hour of alone time with you before dinner,' Rashad said with a wicked grin as he began stripping off his clothes with alacrity. 'This is yet another reason why I love you so much.'

Polly ran appreciative fingers up over his rock-hard abdomen and watched his muscles ripple, dry-mouthed with admiration. 'I'm greedy… I always make time for you.'

He crushed her lips beneath his with a heady moan of pleasure. 'You taste so good, *habibti*.'

Her body was sparking like a fizzing firework, eager for the ignition point of his. No, they hadn't lost their passion for each other. Admittedly her pregnancy had slowed them down a bit in the final months but she had rediscovered her energy after Karim's birth and the nanny had helped by doing the night feeds. They rolled across the bed kissing and exchanging sounds of mutual love and longing and, as always, it was amazing. They lay together afterwards, wrapped in each other and temporary satiety.

Rashad ran his fingers through her hair, stared down at her peaceful face with true devotion in his gaze. 'You really are the best thing that ever happened to me,' he told her gruffly. 'When I wake up in the morning and see you beside me, my heart lifts and I feel that I can cope with anything.'

'I love you too,' Polly whispered with shining eyes.

And he kissed her again and dinner was served late and Ellie gave her sister a withering glance.

'And you looked at me when I said you were like teenagers?' she quipped.

'Wait until you fall in love,' Polly urged.

'Not going to happen. I'm too sensible,' her sister assured her confidently.

*****

# THE ITALIAN'S ONE-NIGHT BABY

My husband, Michael for his constant support and kindness over the years.

# CHAPTER ONE

RIO BENEDETTI SET his even, white teeth together hard and suppressed a very rude word as his godfather cheerfully chatted on about his plans to entertain his unexpected guest. Beppe Sorrentino was a naïve man, trusting and generous to a fault, not at all the sort of man to suspect his self-invited guest of a hidden agenda. Luckily he had a godson like Rio, determined to shield the older man from anyone trying to take him for a ride.

Rio, the billionaire veteran of many triumphant wins in the business world and a man cynically unimpressed by women, knew he had to proceed with discretion because Ellie Dixon had powerful, wealthy friends, and most important, she was the sister of Polly, the current queen of Dharia—a country which rejoiced in oil wealth. Even worse, on paper at least, Ellie was impressive. Nobody knew that better than Rio, who had met her at his friend Rashad's wedding to her sister Polly. She was a beautiful, intelligent and hard-working doctor. But saintly Dr Ellie's profile took a fast nosedive if you had her past history exhaustively checked. At best Rio knew her to be a thief and a gold-digger, at worst she could be the kind of doctor who befriended the elderly to persuade them to change their wills in her favour.

Ellie had had a disciplinary action brought against her at work after an elderly patient had died endowing Ellie with all her worldly goods. Not surprisingly, the old lady's nephew had filed a complaint. But then there had been indications that Ellie might have an unseemly lust for money earlier than that, Rio acknowledged, thinking of the section in the investigative report relating to her grandmother's diamond brooch. The valuable brooch should've gone to Ellie's uncle but Ellie had somehow acquired it instead, causing much family bitterness.

No, nothing about Ellie Dixon was straightforward, not least her surprising approach to his godfather in a letter in which she had asked to visit because Beppe had apparently once known her late mother.

Of course, it was equally possible that Rio himself was the actual target in Dr Ellie's sights, he conceded with a certain amount of cynical satisfaction at that idea. Perhaps Ellie hadn't realised just how very rich he was at the wedding and, knowing where he lived, had come up with this vague connection as an excuse to visit his godfather, Beppe. Women, after all, had often gone to quite extraordinary lengths to try to reel him in, and he was as slick as an eel when it came to avoiding commitment.

He refused to think about what had happened with Ellie at Rashad's wedding because Rio did not believe in reconstructing unpleasant past events. With women he was very much a 'hit it and quit it' kind of guy. He didn't do serious and he didn't do long-term. Why would he? He was thirty years old, rich as sin and very good-looking and his female options were so many and varied that, had he wanted to and without effort, he could have slept with a different woman every night of the year. So, if he was Dr Ellie's target she was in for a severe disillusionment. In any case, the woman was an absolute shrew with a streak of violence, he recalled sardonically.

'You're very quiet, Rio…' Beppe remarked. 'You don't approve of Annabel's daughter visiting, do you?'

'Why would you think that?' Rio parried, surprised that the older man had seen through his tolerant front.

Beppe simply grinned. He was a small man with greying hair and rather round in shape. Perched in his favourite armchair, he had the cheerful air of a playful gnome and Rio's shrewd dark eyes softened the instant they settled on him because Beppe Sorrentino was as dear to Rio as any father could have been.

'I saw you wince when I mentioned how disappointed I was that Ellie wouldn't agree to stay here in my home as my guest. She's a very frank young lady. She said she wouldn't be comfortable because she doesn't know me and would prefer to stay at the hotel.'

'It wouldn't be comfortable for you either to have her here. You're not used to having guests,' Rio pointed out, for Beppe had been a childless widower for almost twenty years and lived a very quiet and peaceful life in his family *palazzo* a few miles outside Florence.

'I know but I get bored,' Beppe admitted abruptly. 'Bored and lonely. No, don't look at me like that, Rio. You visit plenty. But, Ellie's visit will be stimulating. A fresh face, different company.'

*'Dio mio…'* Rio rhymed thoughtfully. 'Why are you

so reluctant to tell me anything about Ellie's mother and yet so excited about her daughter coming here?'

Beppe's rounded face locked down so fast it was like a vault sliding shut and his dark eyes evaded his godson's. 'It's not something I can discuss with you, Rio. Please don't take that the wrong way.'

Rio's even, white teeth gritted again. He had even considered the idea that in some way Ellie could be engaged in an attempt to blackmail his godfather about some dark secret, but even optimistic Beppe would hardly look forward so happily to the visit of a blackmailer. Furthermore Rio couldn't imagine that Beppe *had* any dark secrets because he was the most open, transparent personality Rio had ever known. Yet Beppe had known great unhappiness and loss in his private life. His delightful wife, Amalia, had given birth to a stillborn son and had then suffered a severe stroke. From then on right up until her death, Beppe's wife had endured precarious health and the confinement of a wheelchair. Beppe, however, had remained utterly devoted to his beloved Amalia and, although now pushing sixty, had evinced not the smallest desire to meet another woman.

Rio, in strong comparison, had never been open or trusting with other human beings. He was naturally suspicious and naturally complex. He had been abandoned in a dumpster at birth, born to a heroin-addicted mother and an unknown father and he had spent his formative years in an orphanage until Amalia Sorrentino took an interest in him. Through Amalia he had met her kindly husband, his benefactor. He knew very well that he owed almost everything he had become and everything he had achieved to the man seated by the fireside who had first recognised his intelligence and there was little he would not have done to protect Beppe from any potential harm. And Rio was absolutely convinced that in some way Ellie Dixon was a harmful threat.

Evil temptress? Gold-digging harpy? Hard-nosed feminist? Thief? Scam artist with the elderly? At Rashad's wedding, he had been treated to giggly, amusing Ellie and enraged Ellie. He had also been led down the garden path right to the door of his hotel room and then assaulted. He hadn't forgotten the experience. He hadn't forgiven it either. Insults lingered with Rio. For too many years of his life he had been a nameless orphan, bullied and abused and dismissed as unimportant. And Ellie Dixon had cut him down to size as effectively as the most terrifying nun at the orphanage, Sister Teresa, who had struggled to overcome Rio's stormy and essentially vengeful temperament.

No, Rio wasn't the forgiving and forgetting sort. He still occasionally dreamt about Ellie twirling on the dance floor in her diaphanous green dress, her glorious mane of red curls tumbling round her animated face, and he would remember how he had felt and it stung him like salt in an open wound. He had felt that night that he would die if he didn't have her. Lust multiplied by wine and wedding fervour, he dismissed now with still-gritted teeth. Now all he had to do was sit back and wait for Ellie and her character of many divergent colours to emerge into the unforgiving glare of daylight…

So, would she be the temptress, the prim doctor, the clever academic or the friendly, casual tourist? And just how long would it take for Rio to find out what her game was?

Whatever, it was still game on…

* * *

Ellie surveyed the vast cache of clothing in sheer wonderment.

'Yes, your pressie has arrived,' she confirmed to her sister Polly, with the phone tucked in her nape. 'What on earth were you thinking of?'

'I know you don't do shopping, so I did it for you,' Polly responded cheerfully. 'You need a holiday wardrobe for Italy and I bet you haven't had the time to buy anything… Am I right?'

On that score, Polly was right but Ellie, picking up a floaty white sundress with a designer label, was gobsmacked by her sister's generosity. Correction, her sister's embarrassingly *endless* generosity. 'Well, I'm really more of a "jeans and tee" sort of girl,' she reminded her sibling. 'In fact, I think the last time I put on a sundress was when I was visiting you. You know I'm very, very grateful, Polly, but I wish you wouldn't spend so much money on me. I'm a junior doctor, I'm not living on the breadline—'

'I'm your big sister and it gives me a lot of pleasure to buy you things,' Polly told her unanswerably. 'Come on, Ellie… Don't be stiff and stuffy about this. We never got much in the way of pressies and treats growing up and I want to share my good fortune with you. It's only money. Don't make it change things between us—'

But it *was* changing things, Ellie thought, suppressing a sigh. She might always have been the kid sister in their duo but she had also always been the leader and she couldn't help missing that familiarity and her sister, who now lived half the world away in Dharia. Polly didn't turn to her for advice any more. Polly no longer needed her in the same way. Polly had Rashad now, and a gorgeous little son, and unless Ellie was very much mistaken there would soon be another little royal prince or princess on the horizon. Her sister also had a pair of adoring grandparents in Dharia, who had welcomed her into her late father's side of the family with loving enthusiasm.

And that was why Ellie was travelling out to Italy clutching the emerald ring gifted to their by her late mother, Annabel, whom she had never known. Annabel had died in a hospice after a long illness while her daughters were raised by their grandmother. Ellie's mother had left behind three rings in separate envelopes for her daughters.

That there were *three* envelopes had been the first shock because until that moment Ellie and Polly had not realised that they had another sister, younger than they were, raised apart from them and most probably in council care. A sister, Lucy, completely unknown to them. In each envelope their mother had written the name of each girl's father.

Polly had flown out to Dharia to research her background in the hope of finding her father, only to discover that he had died before she was even born, but she had been compensated for that loss by the existence of welcoming, loving grandparents. In the midst of that family reunion, Polly had married Rashad, the king of Dharia, and become a queen. As soon as she had married she and Rashad had hired a private detective to try to locate Lucy but the search had been hampered by officialdom's rules of confidentiality.

Ellie had received an emerald ring along with two male names on a scrap of writing paper… Beppe and Vincenzo Sorrentino. She assumed that one of those men was her father and she already knew that one of them was dead. She knew absolutely nothing else and wasn't even sure she really *wanted* to know what kind of entanglement her mother had contrived to have with two men, who were brothers. If that made her a prude, too bad, she thought ruefully. She couldn't help her own nature, could she? And she didn't have unrealistic expectations about what she might discover about her paternity in Italy. Neither man might have been her father, in which case she would simply have to accept living with her ignorance. But the discovery of *any* kind of relative would be welcome, she conceded sadly, because since Polly's marriage she had missed having a family within reach.

At the same time she asked herself why she still cherished that idealistic image of 'family,' because the grandmother who had raised her and Polly had not been a warm or loving person and her mother's brother, her uncle Jim, had been downright horrible even when they were children. In fact, recalling how the older man had treated her in the aftermath of his own mother's death made Ellie flame up with angry resentment, which made her wonder if she would *ever* share that sad story with Polly. Probably not, because Polly preferred only to see the good in people.

In the same way Polly had blithely declared that her marriage would change nothing between the sisters but, in fact, it had changed *everything*. Ellie didn't even like to phone her sister too often because she was very aware that Polly had far more pressing and important commitments as a wife, a mother and a queen. Ellie loved to visit Dharia, as well, but the long flights would eat up a weekend off and she often spent her leave simply catching up on sleep because junior doctors routinely had to work very long hours. At her most recent training rotation she had been working at a hospice and her duties and her patients had drained her both mentally and emotionally.

Indeed as she packed the new wardrobe Polly had had delivered to her into a pair of suitcases Ellie was too weary even to examine the garments and belatedly very grateful that her sister had saved her from an exhaustive shopping trip. No doubt she would look a lot fancier and more feminine in clothing Polly had picked than she would in anything she would have chosen for herself, she thought ruefully, because she had never been interested in fashion.

Far more importantly, Ellie was much more excited about even the slight prospect that she might find her father in Italy. Even Polly, with whom Ellie had played it very cool and cynical on that topic, had no real idea how much Ellie longed to find a father at the end of the Italian trail.

Two days later, Ellie walked down the stairs of the small rural hotel she had chosen and was shown out to a delightful three-sided patio, which was festooned with flowers and overlooked a rolling section of the green, vine-covered Tuscan landscape. She breathed in the fresh air with a smile of pure pleasure and relaxed for the first time in many weeks.

Tomorrow she had an appointment to meet Beppe Sorrentino at his home, but today she was free to explore her surroundings and that lack of an actual to-do list was an unadulterated luxury. She settled down at her solo table, smoothing down the light cotton skirt and top she wore in mint green, only momentarily thinking that the uneven handkerchief hems Polly loved were very impractical. Fashion isn't about practicality, she could hear her sister telling her squarely, and she smiled fondly as a brimming cup of cappuccino coffee arrived along with a basket of pastries.

Ellie powered through her usual work schedule on snatched coffee pick-me-ups and the fresh cappuccino was glorious, as was the croissant, which melted in her appreciative mouth. Indeed it was as she was brushing tiny flakes of pastry from her lips that a tall, dark silhouette blotted out her wonderful view. She blinked behind her sunglasses, supposing it was too much to have hoped that she would be allowed to have the patio and the view all to herself. After all, it was a very small hotel but still a hotel and naturally there would be other guests.

A liquid burst of Italian greeted the new arrival, whom Ellie could not yet see because of the sunlight. The waiter seemed to be falling over himself in his eagerness to greet the man, which probably meant he was a regular or a local, she thought idly. He responded in equally fast and fluent Italian and there was something about that voice, that dark chocolate honeyed drawl, that struck a dauntingly familiar note with Ellie and she paled, dismissing that jolt of familiarity with brisk common sense. After all, it couldn't be the same man, simply couldn't be! *He* lived in the city of Florence and she was miles outside the city, staying in a village hotel convenient to Beppe Sorrentino's home. No, it absolutely couldn't be the male who had totally destroyed her enjoyment of her sister's wedding festivities and left her filled with self-loathing and regret.

Even fate couldn't be cruel enough to sentence her to a second meeting with Rio Benedetti, her worst nightmare cloaked in male flesh.

'*Buongiorno*, Ellie…' Rio murmured silkily as he yanked out the vacant chair at her table and sat down.

Shock, mortification and anger seized Ellie all at once. 'What the heck are you doing here?' she demanded baldly before she could think better of such revealing aggression.

Rio Benedetti angled his handsome dark head back, his dazzling dark golden eyes veiled by his ridiculously long black lashes. He had blue-black hair that he wore cropped short but the strands still revealed a striking tendency to curl, which gave him a tousled, sexy aspect. He had beautiful eyes, a lean straight nose and bone structure that belonged in an oil painting of a dark angel. He smiled back at her in complete silence.

That fast, Ellie wanted to slap Rio all over again and tell him what she thought of him even though she had already done that two years earlier. He was gorgeous and he *knew* it, a hanging offence in her list of the attributes of a decent man. In reality she had never met such a stunningly good-looking male as Rio and when she had, she had caved as fast as a brick shed built on sand foundations, she recalled with an inner shudder of revulsion.

*Why?* she still asked herself occasionally, because that kind of impulsive recklessness was not Ellie, not her way with men, not her style, nor even how she was prepared to behave. Unfortunately she hadn't counted on meeting a Rio Benedetti blessed with such extreme magnetism, intelligence and charm. At least that was how she had excused herself for having very nearly succumbed to a one-night stand that had no prospect of any future but she was still ashamed of her misjudgement, still unable to forget that awful moment when that hotel bedroom door opened and she saw what was already waiting on his bed for him…

Rio didn't want to smile. He didn't want to fake it, he wanted to glower at her, and he hadn't planned to sit down either. No, standing over her, intimidating her with his much greater height had been his intention. But then he had seen her and all bets were suddenly off. Watching the tip of that little pink tongue chase stray flakes of pastry from her full pink lips had been more than his libido could bear. And his libido rode him like a runaway express train around Ellie Dixon, his arousal enforcing the necessity of sitting down to conceal his condition. What was he? An uncontrollably horny fifteen-year-old again? Dark colour lined his hard cheekbones. Regardless of the fact that he disliked and distrusted Ellie, she was a real beauty with skin as translucent as creamy porcelain, luminous eyes as green as any emerald and a wealth of tumbling Titian curls. Although smaller than average height, she had stupendous sexy curves matched with a tiny waist. Her proportions were truly breathtaking.

Rio had been sexually entranced with Ellie Dixon from the instant he'd laid eyes on her and when he had been rejected for the first time in his adult life the bite of that experience had stayed with him. Ellie had returned to his hotel with him the night of her sister's wedding but, on the very brink of intimacy, it had all gone wrong. In departing, Ellie had slapped him and insulted him. Rio gritted his teeth at the recollection of that experience. Far too many people had treated Rio with contempt when he was younger for him to easily overlook that kind of slur.

'What do you think I'm doing here?' Rio enquired smoothly, turning her own question back on her.

Ellie shrugged a shoulder and concentrated on her cappuccino. She didn't even want to speak to him but could she be *that* rude? After all, he was her brother-in-law's best friend and she liked Polly's husband. 'Did Rashad tell you I was going to be here and ask you to check up on me?' she asked abruptly, thinking that that was just the sort of protective thing Rashad would do, believing that he was doing her a favour when she was staying in an unfamiliar place.

'No. I don't think Rashad knows you're in Italy,' Rio admitted.

'So, I don't need to be polite, then,' Ellie assumed with satisfaction, reaching out for another pastry.

A sizzling smile slashed Rio's wide, sensual mouth. 'No, neither of us need be polite.'

That smile of his engulfed Ellie like a blast of sun on a wintry day and she wanted to turn into it and smile back in reward. Suppressing that reaction took the exercising of several seconds of strained self-control. But Rio had still won in one sense because although she didn't return the smile her whole body was reacting to him in the most unnerving manner. Her teeth gritted as she recognised the stinging tightness of her nipples and the warm liquid feeling between her thighs. He could tempt her wretched hormones with just a glance and she hated him for having that much power over her treacherous body. Had she no pride? And after what he had done to her, had he not a single honourable streak in his character?

'So, if we don't need to be polite...' Ellie hesitated only for a second before giving him a very honest response. 'Go away, Rio.'

A very faint stab of bewilderment penetrated Rio's sharp-as-a-tack brain. He had decided in the absence of any other evidence that Ellie had most probably dreamt up some vague link between her late mother and his godfather purely to gain fresh access to *him*. And either she was now playing ridiculously hard to get in the hope of stoking his interest...*or*, he was actually nothing whatsoever to do with her reasons for visiting Tuscany.

'I don't believe in coincidences,' Rio asserted, his sculpted lips compressing as his coffee arrived along with the hotel owner, who lingered to exchange greetings both with Rio and Ellie.

'I don't believe in coincidences either,' Ellie told Rio with a freezing smile once they were alone again. 'I mean, it was bad enough meeting you at Polly's wedding...but *this*—this is overkill of the worst kind—'

'Is it really?' Rio was fearful of getting frostbite from that smile, marvelling that Ellie could dare to treat him with such disdain, and his strong and aggressive jawline clenched hard.

'Yes, I do appreciate that this is your home country but I can't believe we're running into each other again... accidentally,' she admitted.

'And you would be correct. My presence here is no accident,' Rio confirmed softly as he sipped his espresso, contriving to look relaxed.

But Ellie knew he wasn't relaxed. Rio had certain tells. She had picked up on them at Polly's wedding. His eyes were veiled, his jawline tight, his fingers too braced round the tiny cup he held. Rio was tense, *very* tense, and she wondered why and then she wondered why she would even care. He was the man whore she had almost slept with, and she was very grateful that she had found him out for what he was *before* she shared a bed with him. Having carefully ensured that she'd never visited Dharia when he was also visiting, there was no reason for her to waste further words or time on him.

'So, why are you calling on me? And how did you know where I was staying?'

'I want to know what you're doing here in Tuscany,' Rio informed her flatly without answering her questions.

'I'm on holiday,' Ellie told him with a roll of her fine eyes.

'I don't think that is the complete truth, Ellie,' Rio scoffed with a sardonic smile.

'Well, it's the only truth you're likely to get out of me,' Ellie responded as she stood up, her fine-boned features stiff with restraint and annoyance. 'It's not as though we're friends.'

Rio sprang upright with fluid grace. At her sister's wedding, his grace of movement had been one of the first things she'd noticed about him: he stalked like an animal on the hunt, all power and strength and purpose. 'Would you like to be friends?' he asked lethally.

Ellie stiffened where she stood, quick to pick up on the husky erotic note edging his enquiry. 'No. I'm very choosy about the men I call friends,' she declared with deliberate cool, not caring whether Rio assumed that she meant friends with benefits or not.

Heat flared like a storm warning in Rio's dark golden eyes. 'You chose me in Dharia,' he reminded her with satisfaction.

Ellie's hand tingled as she remembered slapping him hard that night. It occurred to her that a fist would have been better and less forgettable on his terms. She was outraged that he could remind her of that night when in her opinion, had he had any morals at all, he should've been thoroughly ashamed of how their short-lived flirtation had ended. But then Rio Benedetti was a shameless sort of guy, arrogant and selfish and promiscuous. That he should also be as hot as hellfire enraged her sense of justice.

'But I wouldn't touch you even with gloves on now,' Ellie traded without skipping a beat and, turning on her heel, she walked back into the hotel.

'Ellie… We will have this conversation whether you like it or not,' Rio ground out with a low-pitched derision that nonetheless cut through the sunlit silence like a knife. 'Walking away won't save you from it.'

'And you coming over all caveman and beating your chest won't get you anywhere,' Ellie murmured cuttingly over a slim shoulder. 'I've never been one of those women whose heart beats a little faster when a man turns domineering.'

'But then you hadn't met me,' Rio imparted in a raw undertone.

'And once met, never forgotten,' Ellie traded, saccharine sweet laced with acid. 'I live and learn, Rio… *Don't you?*'

With that final scornful comment, Ellie vanished into the cool gloom of the hotel. Rio wanted to smash something, break something, *shout*. It reminded him that that was yet another trait he loathed in his quarry. She got under his skin, set his teeth on edge, made him feel *violent*. And that wasn't him, had never been him around women, where he was usually the essence of complete cool and sophistication in his approach. At the same time Ellie sent disturbing cascades of sexual imagery tumbling through his brain. He would picture Ellie in his bed, all spread out and satisfied, Ellie on her knees, Ellie across the bonnet of his favourite sports car. *Troppa fantasia*...too much imagination, again a trait that only she awakened, and annoying. After all, he wasn't sex-starved, anything but. Possibly he had become a little bored with easily available women, who clung and flattered and pawed him like a trophy to be shown off, he reasoned impatiently.

But he didn't want Ellie Dixon except in the most basic male way and he had no intention of doing anything about the effect she had on him. And she might live and learn but she had still to learn that he didn't let *anyone* walk away from him before he had finished speaking. Without further hesitation, Rio strode indoors.

Ellie closed the door of her room behind her and leant back against it in a panic that nobody who knew her would ever have credited. Her heart was racing and she was sweating. She straightened her slim shoulders and stomped into the en-suite to wash her hands and put herself back into her usual calm, collected state of mind. She did not allow men to rattle her. She had never allowed men to rattle her.

But two years back, Rio Benedetti had pierced her shell and hurt her, she acknowledged grudgingly. He had contrived what no man before him had contrived and she had almost made a fool of herself over him. Wouldn't he just love to know that? Ellie grimaced. A man she had known for only a few hours had deprived her of her wits and defences and come close to ridding her of her virginity with her full collusion. And then he had unlocked his bedroom door and she had seen that his hotel bed was already occupied by not one, no, not one but *two* giggling naked women, twin sisters she had noticed at the wedding. Appalled, she had stepped back.

And Rio had smirked and laughed as if it was of no consequence that two other women were already waiting to entertain him. Even in retrospect she marvelled that she had slapped him instead of kicking him somewhere unforgivable because she had been devastated by that revealing glimpse of his lifestyle, his habits, his lack of scruple when it came to sex. The rose-tinted glasses had been cruelly wrenched off when she was least able to cope and vulnerable, forced to see with her own eyes how sleazy her chosen partner was. Awash with disgust, she had called him a man whore and stalked away with her head held high, concealing her agonised hurt. And it had been *agonised*, she conceded painfully. Rio Benedetti had knocked her for six and unravelled her emotionally for months after that night.

It had been too sordid a story to share with Polly, who would have been even more shocked to the extent that her sister might have discussed Ellie's experience with Rashad, and Ellie had not been able to bear the prospect of her humiliation being more widely known. At least what had happened had happened more or less in private.

Someone rapped on her bedroom door and she opened it, expecting it to be the maid because she had said she was going out after breakfast and the room would be free. She didn't use the peephole and was sharply disconcerted when she realised that Rio had followed her upstairs to her room.

Fixing her attention doggedly on his red silk tie, she said curtly, 'I don't want to speak to you… Leave me alone—'

'No can do, *principessa.* If only this living and learning life were so simple,' Rio intoned mockingly.

'Don't call me that!' she snapped. 'And you're not coming in—'

A brown lean-fingered hand curved round the door in silent threat and he moved forward but Ellie stood her ground. She had faced drunks in A & E, dealt with drug addicts and violent people, and she wasn't about to be intimidated by Rio Benedetti.

'I don't think you want me to say what I have to say out here where I could be overheard,' Rio murmured sibilantly. 'It won't embarrass me—'

'*Nothing* embarrasses you!' Ellie snapped with very real loathing.

'It's about Beppe… Beppe Sorrentino,' Rio extended, watching her face like a hawk.

And Ellie surprised herself by stepping back to let him into the room because she absolutely *had* to know what he had to say on that subject. She knew he didn't know the mission she was on in Italy and that she wanted to try to establish her father's identity. She was convinced that Rashad was far too reserved and protective of his own wife's privacy to have shared anything but the sketchiest details about Ellie and Polly's background. But that Rio should even know Beppe's name disturbed her.

'You can come in for five minutes…five minutes

only,' Ellie negotiated thinly. 'And then I want you to go away and forget you ever knew me.'

Rio's beautiful mouth curled, his whole carriage screaming that he wasn't convinced by that claim.

'And I warn you… If you smirk, I will slap you again.'

# CHAPTER TWO

'I DO NOT SMIRK,' Rio retorted very drily.

'Oh, yes, you do… You always look awfully pleased with yourself!' Ellie snapped back, her nerves all of a quiver and her brain no longer in control of her tongue because Rio in a confined space was too much for her.

It wasn't a large room. She had gone for cheap and cheerful in the accommodation stakes because she was planning to stay for an entire month in Italy and a classier room would have swallowed her budget within two weeks. But in a room already crowded with a double bed and a big wardrobe, Rio stole all the available space because he was very tall, at least six foot three and large from his broad shoulders to his lean hips and long, powerful legs. Her momentarily distracted gaze ran over the entirety of his sculpted physique, outlined as it was by a wickedly tailored suit that was sufficiently sophisticated to strike a formal note, but which also sensually delineated his muscular strength with fidelity. Colour flared in her pale face as she suddenly realised what she was doing and glanced away, her mouth running dry, her breathing disrupted and her thoughts overpowered by the stricken fear that he could somehow guess what she felt by the way she looked at him. Guess that she hated him but *still* thought he was gorgeous and incredibly tempting and incredibly bad for her like too much ice cream…

'Let's cut to the chase. What are you *doing* in Tuscany?' Rio demanded and it was a demand as only Rio could make it, every accented vowel laced with command and hostility.

'That's none of your business,' Ellie told him flatly.

'Beppe's my business… He's my godfather.' Lustrous dark eyes landed on her like laser beams, watching her face, keen to construe her expression.

Ellie froze in receipt of the very bad news he had just dropped on her from a height and in a defensive move she lowered her eyes. Rio actually *knew* Beppe Sorrentino and, even worse, had a familial relationship with the older man.

'You wrote to him looking for information about some woman he met well over twenty years ago,' he prompted doggedly, his dismissal of the likelihood of such a request clear in every word.

'Not some woman, my mother,' Ellie corrected, seeing no harm in confirming a truth he was already acquainted with. It was quite probable that Rio had already read her very carefully constructed letter to his godfather. Naturally she had mentioned nothing about boyfriends, pregnancies or putative fathers in it. She had been discreet, fearful of ruffling feathers and causing offence, but she did plan to question the older man to establish whether or not he knew anything about her paternity. It might be a long shot but it was the *only* shot she had. Beppe's friendly response to her letter had encouraged her and lightened her heart but the discovery that Rio Benedetti could be involved in any way in her very private quest for information infuriated her. Was she never to escape the shadow of that misguided night in Dharia?

'A mother whom you somehow know nothing about?' Rio pressed in a disbelieving tone.

'I was a newborn when my mother placed me in my grandmother's care. I never knew her,' Ellie admitted grudgingly, throwing him a look of hatred because she deeply resented being forced to tell him anything personal.

'Don't look at me like that when it's a lie,' Rio urged with staggering abruptness, fiery sparks illuminating his stunning eyes to smouldering gold.

The sudden apparent change of subject disconcerted Ellie. 'What's a lie?'

'You looking at me with dislike when you would really much prefer to rip my clothes off me!' Rio contended without an ounce of doubt in his dark deep drawl.

'Is that how you get women?' Ellie asked drily even while the betraying colour of mortification was creeping up her throat in a hot, seething tide. 'You tell *them* that they want you?'

'No, I only need to see you blush like a tomato to know I've hit pay dirt,' Rio countered with satisfaction. 'I don't do pretences, *principessa*.'

Even while betraying red climbed her face, the absolute curse of her fair colouring, Ellie stared back at him in genuine fascination. 'You honestly think I'm here for you and that my letter to your godfather is just some silly excuse to see you again? Oh, my word, Rio, how did you get through the door with an ego that big?'

'I hate the way you beat all around the bush instead

of just coming to the point. It is a very *simple* point, after all,' Rio told her impatiently, wondering how the hell his dialogue with her had suddenly turned personal but somehow unable to stop it in its tracks.

'We're not having this conversation,' Ellie responded icily.

'You're not my teacher or my doctor, so you can drop the haughty chilling tone,' Rio advised, lounging back against the bedroom door, his sudden slumberous relaxation screaming sex and the kind of bad-boy attitude that set Ellie on fire with fury and curled her fingers into claws.

'We were talking about Beppe,' she reminded him in desperation.

'No. I was talking about us having angry sex—'

Ellie reddened again, her green eyes luminous with disbelief. 'You did *not* just say that to me—'

Rio laughed with unholy amusement. 'I did. Why wrap it up like a dirty secret? We may not like each other but, *per meraviglia*, with the chemistry we've got we would set the bed on fire—'

Ellie focussed on him because she refused to let her gaze drop, lest he take it as a coy invitation. But it *was* a mistake to meet those stunning dark golden eyes of his, a mistake to be close enough to note the luxuriant curling length of his black lashes and the hint of stubble accentuating the shape of his full-modelled mouth. Rio Benedetti made her think of sex. It was instinctual, utterly brazen and when she collided with his eyes it was as if he were operating a gravitational pull on her. Ellie's body turned so rigid that her muscles hurt but even that reality couldn't block the tide of physical awareness flooding her every skin cell. With deep bitter chagrin, she felt the pulse at the aching heart of her thighs and the swollen sensitivity of her breasts.

'Angry sex could be a lot of fun, *principessa.* It would loosen you up. You are very, *very* tense and I know exactly how to take care of that,' Rio purred, cool as ice water, his pride soothed by her dilated pupils and revealing flush. After all, if he had to tolerate being constantly aroused around her, why shouldn't she have to suffer the same? But in contrast to him why couldn't she be practical and honest about it? Did she still expect and demand the fake flowers-and-diamonds approach from the men in her life?

'That's enough.' Ellie lifted her chin and closed a hand into his sleeve to yank him off the door so that she could reach for the handle, but it was like trying to move a very large and heavy boulder and he didn't budge an inch.

'You really do enjoy getting physical with me in other ways, don't you?' Rio derided huskily, looking down at her from his intimidating height, wicked amusement dancing in his beautiful dark eyes. 'Is that a hint about your preferences? I'm not into bondage but I can definitely picture you in one of those dominatrix outfits, twirling a whip—'

And that was it for Ellie. He wouldn't move from the door and he wouldn't shut up and frustration made her temper spontaneously combust inside her and shoot up through her like a rocket. 'If you don't get out of here, I'm going to call the police!' she screamed at him.

Rio flicked an imaginary speck of fluff from the sleeve her tight grip had creased infinitesimally. 'Fortunately the *polizia locale* are unlikely to arrest a native for making a pass at a beautiful woman—'

'I don't care!' Ellie lashed back at him, all patience and restraint stripped from her. 'I hate you…I want you out of my room…*now*!'

'When you tell me what you *really* want from Beppe I'll leave,' Rio bargained softly. 'I want the truth.'

'It's private and it's none of your business and I won't allow you to bully me!' Ellie retorted angrily. 'Does your godfather even know that you're here tormenting me?'

Rio fell very still, reluctantly recognising that he was dealing with a quarry worthy of his mettle. Beppe was an old-fashioned gentleman and particularly protective of the female sex and he would be shocked by Rio's interference.

'I didn't think he did,' Ellie declared in the telling silence. 'The letter he sent me was kind and friendly. So back off, Rio, or I'll—'

'Or you'll what?' Rio growled in raw interruption. 'You think that you can threaten *me*?'

'Unlike you I'm not in the habit of threatening people,' Ellie countered, lifting her chin, her green eyes deeply troubled.

'Well, then let us reach an agreement here and now,' Rio suggested silkily. 'I could approach Beppe with the results of the investigative report I've had done on you and, if I did so, you would be turned away from the door tomorrow because there are enough dynamite allegations against you in that report to make him very wary.'

Ellie took an uncertain step backwards, hugely disconcerted by that accusation coming out of nowhere at her. 'I haven't done anything wrong, so I can't imagine what you're talking about—'

'Of course you're going to say that,' Rio parried, unimpressed. 'But the point is that serious allegations have been made against you and by more than one person.'

Ellie fell silent because, although she was innocent of any wrongdoing and had been cleared during an internal enquiry, a serious allegation *had* been lodged against her, which could have had a most negative impact on her career as a doctor. Fortunately for her, she was protected by National Health Service rules there to safeguard staff in such situations and the allegation had been withdrawn and the complaint dismissed. Tears stung the backs of her eyes because that same allegation had caused Ellie a great deal of stress and many sleepless nights before it had been settled and she had viewed her Italian holiday as a much-needed period of rest and recuperation. To have that unpleasant business, in which she had been truly blameless, flung in her teeth by Rio Benedetti was seriously offensive.

'Those allegations were dismissed a week before I flew out here,' she spelt out curtly, struggling to control the wobble in her voice. 'And what were you doing getting an investigative report done on me, for goodness' sake?'

'I will always protect Beppe from anyone who could take advantage of him and I don't trust you or the coincidence that brings you here,' Rio stated grimly, noting the sheen in her eyes, wondering if it was fake, deciding not to be impressed because tears in a woman's eyes were nothing new to his experience. Virtually every woman he had ever been with had done the crying thing at some stage and all it had ever done was chase him off faster.

'That's not my problem,' Ellie traded with an unapologetic little sniff that strangely enough impressed

Rio much more than the hint of tears. 'And why would it even occur to you that I would *try* to take advantage of Beppe? Obviously you don't believe it but I'm not a dishonest person—'

At that claim, Rio quirked a sardonic ebony brow and thought about the diamond brooch she had somehow prevented her uncle from inheriting. 'Aren't you? Even though you can't even bring yourself to admit that you want me—'

'You know why—because nothing is going to happen between us,' Ellie told him piously, superiority ringing in every syllable. 'Why acknowledge it?'

And there it was again, that intonation that made Rio want to do or say something totally outrageous. It shot him straight back to his misspent youth when he had been regularly carpeted for his sins in Sister Teresa's school office. There was something so incredibly frustrating about Ellie's blanket ban on normal sexual behaviour, he reasoned angrily. He could not understand why a woman with so much pent-up passion should repeatedly strive to ignore the sizzle in the air between them. As if attraction was a weakness? Or a risk she wasn't prepared to take?

His own convoluted and uncharacteristic thoughts on that score exasperated him as much as they had in Dharia. The evening of her sister's wedding had been a washout but that hadn't been his fault, had it been? Ellie had been totally unreasonable and unjust when she'd blamed him for that episode. He had been honest with her, as well, *too* honest, and where had that got him? A slap on the face and a shedload of insults. They would never have worked anyway, he told himself impatiently, not with a woman seemingly hardwired to be touchy, angry and super judgemental.

'*Non c'è problema...* Don't worry about it,' Rio advised drily as he swung round and pulled open the door. 'But when you fall, I'll still be the one to catch you.'

'I won't be falling. Can I hope this is the last I'll be seeing of you?' Ellie dared as he strode out into the corridor and involuntarily she too stepped over the threshold.

'You have nothing to fear from me unless you distress or damage Beppe in some way,' Rio warned, his voice roughening at the mere thought of any harm coming to the older man. 'I don't know why you're being so secretive anyway. Beppe will eventually tell me what this was all about.'

Pretending sublime indifference to that prospect, Ellie shrugged a slight shoulder. 'Why would I care?' she said breezily, keen to discourage his suspicions that she was hiding anything of a serious nature.

But she *did* care. Rio could see it in her unusually expressive and anxious gaze. He realised that there was definitely a secret of some sort that connected Ellie to his godfather and that disturbed him because for the life of him he could not imagine any likely connection. Beppe, for one thing, had never travelled outside Italy and was very much a home bird. It occurred to him for the first time that perhaps he should have investigated the mother rather than the daughter, but unwisely he had overlooked that option because Ellie inspired greater curiosity.

'You *do* care,' Rio traded softly, moving slightly closer.

In a skittish move, Ellie backed up against the door

of her room. 'I'm a very private person,' she stated in a stubborn refusal to admit even the smallest weakness, because Rio was 100 per cent shark and she knew the blood in the water would be hers if she gave so much as an inch.

'Not always,' Rio disagreed, suddenly right there in front of her, eating her alive with his black-lashed smouldering eyes. A lean brown forefinger trailed gently down the side of her hot face.

She felt every tiny second of that fleeting caress like a brand burning right through to the centre of her body. She wasn't used to being touched, she told herself bracingly, should've been dating more, should've been less of a perfectionist, should've been less sensible. His eyes above hers flamed gold and she recalled a moment exactly like that on the dance floor in Dharia, and in a clumsy movement she tried to peel herself off the door into her room and safety but it was too late, way too late when Rio's beautifully shaped mouth came crashing down on hers.

And that kiss was something between a car crash and a shot of adrenalin in her veins. Her body came alive with a great whoosh of physical response and her hands flew up into his hair, touching, shaping, *clutching* the springy strands. And she wanted him as a dehydrated woman wanted water, as if he were the only thing that stood between her and death. That ferocious, screaming shout of need that instantly controlled her absolutely terrified her. The spear of his tongue in her mouth electrified her beyond all thought and the flick against the roof of her mouth was pure licking temptation by a maestro of sensation. He knew how to kiss, he knew how to do all the stuff she didn't and that drew her helplessly, that and the merciless craving making her heart beat too fast, making her body tremble and her legs weak.

'*Inferno*, Ellie…' Rio growled against her swollen mouth, rocking his hips ever so slightly against her.

And she could feel him through their clothing, long and hard and urgent with the same need that had already overwhelmed her and she shuddered, fighting for control against all the odds and without words, knowing that no, whatever happened, she just couldn't do this with him.

But Rio, womaniser that he was, kissed her again and again; being Rio, he had upped his game. Slow and tormenting had become rawly passionate and demanding and every skin cell in her body lit up in neon as if she had met her perfect match. The pulsing damp heat between her thighs was coalescing into a generalised burning ache that tortured and tempted and screamed. The sound of a metal bucket scraping across tiles was almost deafening and Rio sprang back from her at the same instant that Ellie literally forced her hands down to his shoulders to push him away.

And for once, Rio didn't have anything super smart to say, she noted with only the smallest amount of satisfaction because she had nothing to boast about either. Rio dealt her a scorchingly angry glance and swung away.

'I'll be in touch,' he said grittily.

'Not if I see you coming first,' Ellie quipped weakly, ducking back into her room under the curious appraisal of the cleaner and closing the door on legs that felt as limp as cotton wool. But *no*, she was not going to do that thing she usually did when she did something wrong.

She wasn't going to dwell on it and go over it endlessly. She had made a mistake and it was already behind her and that was all the brooding Rio Benedetti deserved. No more self-loathing, no more regret, she told herself squarely. He was like a cup of poison that tasted sweet, created only to tempt and destroy. Paranoiac…much, she asked herself then.

# CHAPTER THREE

THAT MORNING, ELLIE explored the village, bought a small gift for a colleague and walked in the glorious sunshine through the *piazza* to the café to take a seat. She was beginning to enjoy herself, starting to recognise that beating herself up about Rio was counterproductive because it kept him in the forefront of her mind. One kiss… What was a kiss? *Nothing!* Well, unless it made your knees go weak and threw your brain into la-la land—then it was a threat.

While she sipped her coffee, crossly policing her thoughts, she watched an opulent cream sports car park. The driver, who had a little dog with him, hailed several locals seated outside the café and his attention lingered on Ellie before he strode across the *piazza* to enter the shop there. The dog, however, a bouncy little Yorkshire terrier, hurtled straight across to Ellie and bounced up against her legs, craving attention.

The dog's owner shouted what sounded like, 'Bambi!' in an exasperated voice but the dog wouldn't budge from Ellie's feet and, with an audible groan and a wave that promised his return, the young man went on ahead into the shop.

'You're not the most obedient dog,' Ellie scolded

softly a few minutes later as pleading little round eyes appealed to her from knee height. 'No, you can't get up on my lap. I'm not a doggy person—'

'You could've fooled me,' the owner remarked from beside her and she glanced up and laughed.

'Well, I suspect your dog's not very fussy,' she teased.

'Bambi belongs to my mother and I'm looking after the dog all week.' He rolled his eyes in speaking suffering. 'She hasn't been trained and prefers women.'

'But that's not her fault,' Ellie pointed out, scratching a blissed-out Bambi behind one flyaway ear.

'I'm Bruno Nigrelli.' He extended a friendly hand. 'Join me for a glass of wine—'

'A little early,' Ellie began before she recalled that she was on holiday and not on duty. 'No, that's a good idea,' she told him with a sudden smile. Loosen up, she told herself irritably.

Bruno stayed with her for about half an hour, making easy comfortable conversation, and it was so relaxing after the emotional angst of dealing with Rio, Ellie acknowledged ruefully. Bruno was a contracts lawyer based in Florence and he was currently staying at his mother's home to look after it while she was away. When he asked her to dine with him the following evening, Ellie agreed. Polly's voice was ringing loudly in her ears. 'Attractive man—tick. Employed—tick. Good manners—tick. Stop looking for what's wrong with every man you meet!' Polly had told her that the reason she rarely dated was that she was far too fussy. But Ellie didn't think that was fair because when it came to men, Polly had proved equally hard to impress.

The following morning, Ellie drove her little hire car

to Beppe's impressive *palazzo*. The huge gates stood wide in readiness for her arrival. She drove slowly through the elaborate gravelled gardens that fronted the big house and parked, climbing out, smoothing damp palms down over the casual white skirt she had teamed with a navy-and-white tee and canvas espadrilles. She walked up the shallow steps to the front door and a youthful manservant in a very correct black jacket opened it before she could even reach for the bell.

'Ellie Dixon for Mr Sorrentino,' she said helpfully.

'Yes,' he said gruffly in English. 'He waits for you.'

Ellie was a mass of nerves and trying not to show it. Could Beppe *be* her…? No, she refused to think about that because it wasn't very likely when Beppe had been married at the time. The more likely scenario would be Beppe telling her that he hadn't known her mother well enough to give her any useful information as to who her father might be.

'Miss Dixon…' A small man near her own height greeted her at the door of a book-lined room with a warm smile. 'Come in and sit down. Adriano will bring us morning coffee.'

With a soft sound of pleasure she sat down in the chair overlooking the beautiful garden. 'This is such a comfortable room,' she told him cheerfully. 'All these books and bits and pieces are fascinating and when you throw the view in, as well—'

'I'm a lifelong collector and passionate gardener,' Beppe admitted as he sat down opposite her.

'Thank you for being willing to see me like this,' Ellie said a little awkwardly. 'I can only hope that I'm not about to say anything that may make you regret it—'

'I don't take offence easily,' Beppe reassured her.

'But I confess that I'm very curious about your mother. What happened to her after she left Italy?'

'I didn't even know for sure that she *had* been in Italy, although it was a fairly obvious assumption,' Ellie admitted, opting for complete honesty as she dug into her bag and extracted the emerald ring. 'My mother left me this ring…'

Beppe paled, his easy smile slipping for an instant. He scooped up the ring at the same time as the door opened and Adriano brought in a tray. He spoke to the young man with a couple of hand signals. 'Adriano's deaf,' he muttered absently, his attention still fixedly focussed on the emerald.

'He's a great lip-reader,' Ellie remarked.

'He's had a lot of training over the years. Once he's acquired the necessary experience working here, he hopes to find a more exciting position abroad,' Beppe told her and he leant forward to deposit the ring back on the table beside her cup. '*I* gave your mother this ring. It once belonged to my mother,' he added heavily.

'Okay.' Taken aback by that admission, Ellie nodded acceptance. 'So you knew her well?'

'Better than I should have done in the circumstances,' Beppe confided in a weighted undertone of discomfiture. 'Annabel spent that summer working for an English family who had a holiday home not far from here. My brother, Vincenzo, met her first and they got engaged before I even met her. I think you would call it a whirlwind romance because they had only known each other for a few weeks.'

Ellie sighed, thinking of what she had learned about her mother from her sister Polly. 'What year was that?'

Beppe told her and the timing dovetailed in Ellie's

mind. Her older sister would only have been a toddler when Annabel came to work in Italy.

'How do I describe Annabel to you…her daughter?' Beppe sighed. 'She was full of life and tremendous fun to be with but she was a little impulsive when it came to love.'

'Yes,' Ellie agreed, wondering what was coming next.

'I was married to a wife who was disabled. That is *not* an excuse. There can be no excuse for what happened,' Beppe continued with unconcealed regret. 'I learned that I was not the man I believed I was. I fell head over heels in love with your mother and it was the same for her. I was thirty-five then, hardly an impressionable boy, and I fully believed that I loved my wife. Amalia was a wonderful wife. It was not an unhappy marriage yet I broke her heart and my brother's. But mercifully, *generously* my brother did not choose to publicly accuse me of what I had done and my wife was not humiliated. Together, Amalia and I concentrated on restoring our marriage, locked away that secret affair and moved on.'

'I honestly don't know what I can say to what you've just told me because I know none of the people involved,' Ellie said carefully. 'But I am sorry to hear that other people were injured by my mother's actions.'

'Annabel injured herself most of all. She could've had a good life with my brother but she gave him up because she met me,' Beppe admitted with remorse. 'Vincenzo was still estranged from me when he died. It was a horrible mess for all of us—'

'I'm very sorry,' Ellie breathed, feeling inadequate in the face of such honesty and a very personal story, which she had never expected to hear told.

'The last time I saw your mother she was very angry with me,' Beppe confessed unhappily. 'I had told her from the outset of our affair that I would not leave my wife but she refused to accept that. My love for my wife was a different kind of love but no less real to me. Although I was an unfaithful husband, Amalia forgave me and we stayed together and we were blessed by many more happy years before she passed away…'

'My goodness…I genuinely didn't come here to cause you distress, but I can see that I've done nothing but rake up disastrous memories!' Ellie exclaimed guiltily, seeing the tears that shone in Beppe's dark eyes. 'Unfortunately, I came here with a very different angle, Beppe. I'm trying to find out who my father is—'

'In Italy?' he cut in, his surprise unconcealed. 'Surely you are far too young to believe you were conceived *here*? When were you born?'

And she told him and his face became very sombre. 'I believed you were several years younger, but it is certainly a possibility that I could be the man you seek. *Dio mio*, that could explain why your mother told me that I would live to regret not leaving my wife for her.'

Ellie fell silent, disturbed by the harsh nature of what she was learning about the mother she had never known.

'*We* will have to look into this more. With tests? That is how it is done, is it not?'

'Are you willing to do that?'

'*Certamente...* Of course,' Beppe responded. 'Now perhaps we should discuss something less challenging while we consider what we have both learned.'

Ellie's hand shook a little as she lifted her cup because she was marvelling at his calm manner.

Beppe chuckled. 'I must be on my very best behaviour now in case you turn out to be a relative.'

And Ellie's hopes soared, that he was the man, that he would turn out to be her father and that a lifetime of frustrating speculation would be ended. They parted an hour later with Beppe promising to contact a doctor he was friendly with, who would advise them discreetly on their quest. Tears rolled down Ellie's cheeks as she drove back to her hotel. She was in a daze and she was praying that Beppe would be the man she sought because she had really, *really* liked him and it would be beyond wonderful to discover a father she could actually connect with as a person.

Rio, however, had a very different experience when he joined his godfather for lunch. After what transpired there, bitter anger consumed him and when he left he headed straight to Ellie's hotel, determined to confront her. Learning that she had gone for a walk to a local landmark, he set off to follow her in his car.

Ellie paused halfway up the very steep hill and wiped the perspiration from her brow, registering that in such sultry heat, she had tackled a challenge too great for her fitness level. Hearing the sound of an approaching vehicle, she stepped back onto the verge. She was disconcerted to see Rio at the wheel of a very racy scarlet sports car. He braked and leant across to open the passenger door. 'Get in!' he told her uninvitingly.

'No, thanks,' Ellie responded. Her day had been demanding enough without adding him into it.

Without a word, Rio shot her an intimidating glance from molten gold eyes and sprang out of the car, stalked round the bonnet, and before she could even guess his intention he had scooped her off her startled feet and dropped her into the passenger seat, slamming the door after her.

'What the heck do you think you're playing at?' Ellie yelled at him in disbelief as she struggled to open the door to get out again and failed because he had already engaged the child lock to prevent her from doing exactly that.

Rio shot back behind the wheel, his lean, darkly handsome face granite hard. 'We have to talk—'

'No, we don't. I have *nothing* to say to you!' Ellie proclaimed vehemently. 'Let me out of this car—'

'Put your seat belt on!' Rio growled at her as if she hadn't spoken.

'No, I won't. I refuse to go anywhere with you!' Ellie yelled back at him.

Rio leant across her to wrench the seat belt round her and she was so taken aback by the second act enforced against her wishes that she studied him in shock. 'This is kidnapping and assault,' she informed him furiously. 'I will go to the police and make an official complaint about you!'

'Go ahead!' Rio bit out rawly.

'You are out of control,' Ellie informed him. 'You're not thinking about what you're doing!'

'*Sì*... If I'd thought about it, I would have come armed with a gag!' Rio slung at her wrathfully.

'Much good that would do you. I'm a judo black belt,' Ellie countered. 'Had I known you were planning to kidnap me, I would have defended myself to stop you grabbing me.'

'Don't kid yourself,' Rio practically spat at her as he raked the car on up the hill she had been struggling to climb. 'If you were assaulted, you would be far too busy assessing the pros and cons of acting aggressively to take action quickly enough to defend yourself!'

And Ellie was stunned by that eerily accurate reading of her character. Rio was the single exception to her abhorrence of violence in all its forms and even when it came to him she didn't want to actually *hurt* him, just hold him at bay or make him go away. 'Where are you taking me?'

'Somewhere we can talk in peace,' he grated.

Ellie skimmed an infuriated glance at his set profile, noting the classic slope of his nose, the definition lent by his perfect cheekbones, the outrageous sweep of his black lashes. 'You're driving too fast—'

'I am within the speed limit.'

Ellie flung her head back with a sigh of frustration, her wild mane of hair blowing in the wind. She would look like a rag doll with corkscrew curls by the time she got out of the car but what did that matter? The breeze against her overheated skin was wonderfully cooling. Kidnapping and assault? Rio had a temper worse than her own and that was a revelation that had a surprisingly cooling effect on Ellie's own temper. She had learned young that she had to learn to control and contain the ferocity of her feelings. Rio, evidently, had not. The oddest sense of compassion flooded her because she had not a doubt that he would be very embarrassed when he looked back and fully thought through what he had done to her.

Rio, however, was in a rage to surpass all rages and he was well aware of it. Beppe's distress had provoked a visceral reaction in him that he could not deny or fight. He *loved* that man, would have done anything for him! That he had failed to shield Beppe from whatever nasty business Ellie had somehow involved him in slashed Rio's proud protective spirit to the bone. He was going to get the truth out of Ellie if it killed him. *Inferno...* This mysterious nonsense everybody was refusing to discuss had to end right now because his patience was at an end!

Rio turned the car off the road down a long track. Dense clusters of ancient oak trees prevented Ellie from seeing more than a few yards ahead and when the car rounded the final bend she had no inkling that they were heading for a house until she saw it right there in front of her. It was a breathtaking *palazzo*, with a remarkable resemblance to an elaborate dolls' house, and it fitted into the landscape where it had clearly held its commanding position for centuries. It was built on a hill and undoubtedly had views that stretched for miles. She unclasped her seat belt and climbed out with a look of exasperated tolerance in Rio's direction once the child lock was finally disengaged.

'You can apologise now,' Ellie said.

'Apologise?' Rio practically roared at her in disbelief. 'Beppe was in *tears* over lunch! I haven't seen him in such a state since his wife died. What did you do to him?'

Ellie froze beside the car, her fine-boned features locking tight, her pallor noticeable. Clearly she had upset Beppe Sorrentino and yet she had never wanted to do that. Had she ever truly considered what her quest to discover her father would do to the man involved? No, she hadn't, she conceded guiltily. In fact, she had believed that it would be *safe* to approach Beppe because he was a childless widower who seemed to have no close relatives. Of course, she hadn't known about

Rio's connection to the older man then and, seeing the intensity of Rio's fury, she instantly recognised that he was attached to Beppe and it hit her hard. Rio might not be a blood relative but the way he was reacting he might as well have been.

'I didn't do anything to Beppe. I simply gave him some information he wasn't expecting to hear,' Ellie countered uncomfortably, because what on earth was she supposed to say to Rio?

If Beppe hadn't told his godson the truth, it was certainly not her place to do so. And she quite understood the older man's reasoning. He had had an affair while he was married, an affair that more than twenty years on he still obviously regretted. He was ashamed of his affair with her mother and Ellie had to respect that reality. It hurt to appreciate that, even if tests were done and Beppe did prove to be her father, he might well want the existence of an illegitimate daughter to remain a secret. She couldn't fairly complain about that, couldn't possibly resent it because Beppe had the right to guard his privacy and make his own choices. That he had agreed to DNA testing was more than enough, she told herself doggedly, scolding herself for the fantasy of having a *real* father, which she had rather naively begun to entertain. Really, how likely was it that Beppe would seek an ongoing relationship with her now that she was an adult and fully independent?

*'Ellie!'* Rio raked back impatiently at her as he stalked back from the front door he had unlocked. She had once watched a tiger pace a cage in the same way and it was distinctly unnerving. For the first time it dawned on her that so volatile a personality should have frightened her and she was even more surprised to ac-

knowledge that, not only was she unafraid, but also ridiculously attracted by Rio's sheer sizzling intensity. Even so, she wished that like a difficult piece of technology Rio came with a useful book of instructions because she didn't know how she was supposed to calm him down when she wasn't in a position to give him the explanation he so plainly wanted.

'The raised voice is getting really *old*,' Ellie told him drily instead.

Dark colour scored his razor-sharp cheekbones. 'Come inside—'

'Said the kidnapper to his victim,' Ellie added.

Rio swore in a flood of Italian.

'Yes, I give as good as I get,' Ellie pointed out, moving out of the sunshine into the shadow of the building because calling Rio's bluff was one thing, but baking alive while doing it would be foolish.

'I brought you to my home because I desired privacy in which to speak to you,' Rio framed with obvious difficulty in being that polite.

Ellie pondered her options, which were few. She had neither her phone nor any money on her person. Rio had stranded her in the Tuscan countryside. 'I'll come inside but there will be no more shouting and you will not put your hands on me again,' she warned him.

'I can't promise that I won't shout because I am very angry with you,' Rio admitted in a low-pitched growl as he watched her move towards him, her skirt fluttering above her slender knees, making him very aware of the long shapely legs beneath. His gaze filtered involuntarily upward, lingering on the soft fullness of her pink lips, and shifted with a jerk as she moved, the luscious sway of her full breasts below her top making his mouth run dry. 'And I wouldn't promise to keep my hands off you because I'm not sure I could ever deliver on that one, *principessa*.'

That honest response and possibly the reuse of that mocking label worked for Ellie and released a little of her nervous tension. In fact, she went pink while inwardly admitting that she wasn't that much better at keeping her hands off him, regardless of whether she was slapping him or kissing him. Rio awakened very strong reactions inside her. The usual barriers that she employed to keep a careful distance from people were shockingly absent with Rio Benedetti and that awareness rattled her nerves.

Ellie followed Rio into a cool, tiled hallway that was strikingly contemporary and into a vast reception room furnished with pale leather sofas and several dramatic modern paintings. The gorgeous house might be ancient but the cool interior decor and modern furnishings were in stark contrast.

Rio spun round to face her again, a dark shadow of stubble accentuating his beautifully shaped mouth and the raw tension etched in the hard line of his lips. And she found herself wondering for the first time if he was ever gentle or tender, traits that seemed far removed from his aggressive, competitive nature. And did it even matter, another voice mocked, when he looked the way he did? That mocking inner voice shocked her because it steamrollered over everything she believed she knew about herself, for since when had she been impressed by appearances? Yet when she looked at Rio, everything sane and sensible vanished from her brain as if it had been wiped. And then there was only room for glorying in his tempestuous male magnificence, room to marvel at the precise arrangement of his lean, darkly charismatic features and the stunning clarity of his smouldering golden eyes. She sucked in a startled breath to fill her deprived lungs.

'All I'm asking you to do is come clean with me,' Rio murmured lightly, as though what he was asking should be easy for her to do. 'Tell me what's going on…'

Ellie's slim figure tensed. 'It's not that simple, Rio.'

An ebony brow quirked in disagreement. 'It is a very simple matter that you are making difficult out of sheer stubbornness.'

'No, it is a private matter between Beppe and me,' she countered. 'Ask *him* to explain things.'

His intent gaze narrowed. 'You must know that I will not do anything more to upset him.'

'And I will not break his confidence without his permission, so we're at an impasse—'

'Have some wine,' Rio suggested wryly, strolling over to the drinks cabinet and giving her a choice.

'Rosé, but it won't loosen my tongue,' she warned him doggedly, but the extreme tension in her knees holding her stiff gave way a tad, reminding her that her meeting with Beppe and the walk had exhausted her.

'Help me out here… I am *trying* to be civilised,' Rio informed her.

'There was nothing civilised about the way you stuffed me in your car,' Ellie reminded him drily as she settled down on a sofa.

'*Per l'amor di Dio*, I never said I was perfect, *principessa*.'

'Why do you call me that?' she demanded abruptly as he settled a moisture-beaded wine glass into her hand, momentarily standing so close to her that the scent of him assailed her: hot, musky male laced with a hint of spicy cologne. A very faint shiver ricocheted through her.

Rio grinned and it was an unexpectedly boyish grin of keen amusement. 'Because the way you walk with your little superior nose in the air gives you that look. You remind me of the rich girls I used to watch when I was a penniless teenager. Oh, they looked at me, but they wouldn't have dirtied their lily-white hands by *touching* me.'

'I was never a rich girl,' Ellie parried uncomfortably, studying him with grass-green eyes that were luminous in the filtered sunshine and alive with curiosity. 'I grew up in my grandmother's working-class home and there were no airs or graces there.'

'*Cio nonostante...* Nonetheless you ooze that rich-girl quality of disdain,' Rio told her with assurance. 'And it sets my teeth on edge—'

'Everything about me sets your teeth on edge,' Ellie pointed out wryly while she wondered about his background, because she was surprised that he had ever been penniless and on the outside looking in at the more prosperous. '*We* annoy each other.'

'Beppe,' he reminded her darkly. 'Talk.'

In a sudden movement, Ellie stood up again because he was making her feel trapped. She understood exactly where he was coming from but she couldn't answer his questions. His godfather *could* have enlightened him and had chosen not to. Beppe's silence spoke for him. Clearly he had no desire to admit to Rio that he had had an extramarital affair or that that liaison could have led to the conception of a child.

'I don't back down, Ellie,' Rio murmured from close

by and every skin cell in her body jumped at the knock-on effect of that deep accented drawl of his, goose-bumps rising on her bare arms. 'I won't let you go until you fill in the blanks—'

'Well, then, you're going to be stuck with me!' Ellie exclaimed in growing frustration. 'Because I'm not going to talk—'

Rio removed the glass from her fingers and set it aside. 'Maybe talking's a total waste of time for us, *principessa.*'

'And what's that supposed to mean?' Ellie demanded thinly even though she had a very good idea.

Rio scored a light forefinger across her compressed lower lip. 'You're pushing it defying me. I don't have your patience—'

Ellie threw her head back, corkscrew curls tumbling across her pale brow, green eyes sharp with frustration and defensiveness. 'Don't touch me!' she warned him curtly.

'No, not a shred of patience,' Rio asserted with hypnotic quietness, reaching for her with scorching dark golden eyes of sensual threat.

# CHAPTER FOUR

'I CAME INTO this house with you because I trusted you,' Ellie declared starkly, twisting away.

'No, you don't. You don't trust me,' Rio assured her with grim amusement. 'You most probably came into the house because you don't like arguments in public and you are nervous of how far I would go to win.'

'Well, doesn't that just say it all about you?' Ellie quipped.

'You know nothing about me yet you still judge,' Rio condemned.

Ellie stilled, disconcerted by that criticism, and Rio took advantage of her momentary abstraction. His arm curved to her spine and he yanked her close, bringing her up against the hard, unyielding strength of his lean, powerful body, and her hormones leapt as though he had electrified her. His mouth nibbled along the plump fullness of her lower lip and all of a sudden she couldn't breathe for anticipation. Her lips parted for him, letting his tongue plunge deep, and an aching sweetness that drowned every thought rose from the very heart of her. Something in the furthest reaches of her brain was saying no, no, *no*, but all the rest of her was in open rebellion.

It was the kiss to end all kisses, fit to eradicate any previous kiss because no man had ever made Ellie's head swim with a kiss before. She felt dizzy and delirious, utterly unlike herself, adrenalin charging through her veins and lighting her up as though she had crossed the finishing line of a race. Her fingers delved freely into his springy black hair, sheer delight at the freedom to touch him consuming her.

Overwhelmed by her response, Rio tensed, wondering when it would end and abandoning any plan to stage a slow seduction scene. He had never wanted any woman as he wanted Ellie Dixon. Need was already flaming through him like a burning torch. One hand at the shallow indentation of her spine, he ground against her, so hard, so ready, so overpoweringly hungry for the damp release of her body that he trembled. It didn't make sense to him. Yes, she was a challenge, but no woman had ever come between Rio and his wits. He was in control, he was always in control, but this one time, he *wasn't*. Shouldn't that worry him? He shelved the question, too much lost in the moment to waste time considering the drawbacks and inconsistencies. He brought Ellie down on the sofa and kissed her with unashamed passion.

'What are we...doing?' Ellie mumbled through swollen lips as Rio whipped off her top, exposing the heavy-duty white lace confection she wore to confine the breasts that she considered to be too large. It was a stupid question and she knew it and the sight of her own almost bare flesh unnerved her and filled her with discomfiture.

'*Sta' zitto*... Shut up!' Rio urged, burying his face between those utterly magnificent breasts while wrestling with a bra that had more restrictive hooks than a corset. If she talked, she would talk herself out of it, he thought in consternation, and he looked down into her beautiful eyes, emerald as the most precious of jewels, and told her to close them.

'You are incredible' was wrenched from him, breaking his self-imposed silence as he studied the lush creamy swell of her glorious breasts. An awed fingertip brushed a large pink nipple already pouting for his attention. He wanted to carry her up to his bedroom, spread her out and enjoy her as she should be enjoyed but he didn't want to break the spell.

Instead he bent his dark head and succumbed to the considerable allure of her breasts. He whisked his tongue over a rigid bud the colour of a tea rose and teased the tortured peak, loving the way she shifted under him, instantly responsive to his every caress.

Ellie had fallen so deep that she was drowning in the world of sensation she had always denied herself. The hunger in her for *more* was unbearable. Her breasts throbbed, sending messages to the lush damp place between her shifting thighs. Her hips lifted in frustration. She wanted Rio everywhere at once. She wanted the impossible. She also wanted his clothes off with a strength of craving that shook her because it was not as though she was a stranger to the male anatomy. In frustration, she hauled at the shoulders of his jacket and he reared back from her with a sudden surprised laugh and peeled it off to pitch it on the floor.

'And the shirt,' Ellie instructed him shakily, scarcely believing what she was doing, what she was participating in, and unable to dwell on it lest her caution yank her back from the edge. And she wanted Rio, she wanted him so much that she was weak from the wanting and the never-ending wondering and longing that had dogged her since the day they had first met.

A couple of shirt buttons came loose of their stitching as Rio ripped off the shirt with an almost joyful air of abandonment. He was all lean muscle sheathed in sleek bronzed skin from his wide shoulders to his narrow waist and she stared helplessly entranced and surprised at her visceral reaction to his masculinity. As the shirt dropped, he smiled at her in a way he had never smiled before and that slanting, teasing grin was purebred enticement on his darkly beautiful face. Indeed that smile had so much appeal that she sat up and hauled him down towards her to claim his devastating mouth for herself again.

He lay on his side, kissing her breathless and she revelled in every kiss and the brush of his skilled fingers over her wildly sensitised breasts. He pushed up her skirt and traced the edges of her panties, teasing, tormenting, making her agonisingly aware of just how desperate she was to be touched. A finger slid beneath the lace and stroked her swollen folds. She was wet, so wet she was embarrassed by her body and its screaming eagerness. A fingertip circled her and suddenly there was no room for embarrassment, no room for anything but her own gasping, jerking response. He took away that final barrier and explored her.

He shimmied down the sofa and used his mouth on that tender place between her thighs and if lying still had been a challenge before it soon became an impossible challenge for Ellie. Her fingers clawed into his luxuriant black hair, her body dancing and twisting to the powerful drumbeat of desire. The sensations he evoked were excruciatingly intense and only heightened the tormenting ache of need building deep in her pelvis. Heat gathered and mounted uncontrollably at the heart of her and then, taking her entirely by surprise, exploded outwards in a violent climax of sweet, shattering pleasure.

'*Madre di Dio...* I can't wait to be inside you, *bella mia*,' Rio said huskily, rearranging her and sliding fluidly between her parted thighs. 'I am so hungry for you.'

*Do I want this?* Ellie asked herself and she knew she didn't need to ask that question because when she looked up into Rio's gorgeous dark eyes she was ready to agree to do anything he wanted to do. It was as though she were in a dream without a past or a future or even a present. She felt as though there was nothing but that moment and she liked it that way.

Rio tilted her back and drove into her with a single powerful thrust. And Ellie twisted her head to one side and bit her lip because it hurt, it hurt much more than she had expected, and that burning sting of pain wrenched a muffled little moan of discomfort from between her gritted teeth.

'Something wrong?' Rio rasped, lifting his tousled dark head. '*Dio mio*, you are so tight you feel like a virgin!'

'I *am*!' Ellie gasped before she could think better of making that admission.

Rio had already sunk as deep as he could get into her tiny body and he froze in shock to gaze down at her. 'A virgin?' he echoed in ringing disbelief. 'How can you be a virgin?'

Ellie wrinkled her nose. 'Oh, just get it over with, for goodness' sake,' she told him in desperation.

Stunned by that irreverent urging, Rio took several seconds to absorb what had happened. She was a virgin? How was that possible? And why hadn't he noticed anything different about her? He shifted position, withdrawing and then slowly gliding back. *Get it over with?* What was he? An ordeal to be endured?

The friction of his movement created a little hum of pulsing sensation low in Ellie's body. She shut her eyes tight, refusing to think, indeed terrified to allow herself to think about what she had just done, what she had just allowed him to do. And while she was battening down her mental hatches, Rio was putting every atom of skill he possessed into rescuing the situation. But he was hugely aroused and working alone because Ellie lay there under him like a little felled tree.

He pushed her knees up and ground down into her, delving deeper, setting an insistent rhythm that she couldn't ignore. Her hips lifted but much against her will because she was set on simply tolerating him. A frenzied heat began to build and she fought it off as though it were a forest fire. Her hips rose involuntarily and he slammed down into her, sending a startling pulse of pleasure through her. Her heart thumped like crazy, the ability to breathe stolen from her as he picked up speed and force and dominated her. Wild excitement surged and gripped her but much against her will. Her hands bit into his shoulders and then slid caressingly down his muscular back as this time she sensed the peak she was reaching towards.

A chain reaction of convulsions claimed her and she cried out as the ripples of ecstasy spread in a blinding moment of release that consumed her. Rio shuddered and held her tight and bit out something raw and rough in Italian, his powerful body surging into hers. Within seconds, however, she was free again, watching in a daze as Rio sprang off the sofa to fix his trousers and reach for his shirt.

'You were a virgin?' Rio repeated incredulously, because innocence and Ellie were a combination that refused to compute in his brain.

Wincing, Ellie sat up and pushed down her skirt. Her panties were lying on the tiles but she had no intention of trying to reclaim them in front of him. She was shell-shocked and shattered by what had taken place. She couldn't believe she had had sex with Rio. Just then in the aftermath it looked like the worst decision ever after a lifetime of vigilant caution.

'A virgin?' Rio prompted again as if a virgin were as improbable as a glimpse of a unicorn. 'So, why give it up to me?'

'Maybe I wanted to lose it with someone who would put me off further experimentation,' Ellie suggested with honeyed derision. 'Stop acting as if you've been grievously assaulted by a virgin, Rio. I can't be the first you've been with—'

'You *are*!' Rio contradicted accusingly, taken aback by her gutsy attitude.

Ellie stood up, very discreetly retrieved her underwear and, quite deliberately ignoring him, went off in search of a cloakroom. It actually hurt to walk, she acknowledged in shock. She ached as though they had had sex for hours. The experience felt less like an introduction and more like a lesson. Be careful of what you wish for, she told herself unhappily. He had leapt off that sofa as though he had been electrocuted. Innocence was clearly a hanging offence in Rio's book.

Another much more worrying fact was screaming along the edge of Rio's ragged nerves while he paced the hall, waiting impatiently for Ellie to reappear. He had never met a woman like Ellie and he was very certain that he never wanted to meet another. She drove him crazy. She made him do and say things he never did or said with anyone else. She screwed with his brain, unleashed his temper and sent him racing off the edge of sanity. She had the seductive powers of a temptress and yet how could that be when she had self-evidently had no sexual experience whatsoever? He was terrific in bed and he knew that but she had behaved as though he were useless. So, why did he want her to stay the night? Simply to rescue his ego? And what about Beppe? *And what about the lack of a condom?* He groaned out loud in frustration and raked his fingers through his cropped black curls. Rio felt *raw*.

Only innate courage persuaded Ellie out of the sanctuary of the cloakroom because in reality she wanted to curl up and die somewhere well out of Rio's sight and reach. She didn't want to see him again; she didn't want to have to speak to him again either. She simply wanted to forget what had happened and continue her holiday.

'Please drive me back to my hotel,' she said woodenly, refusing to look directly at him.

'Are you on the pill? Or any other form of contraception?' Rio asked her with startling abruptness.

Ellie almost flinched. She had spent a year taking contraceptive pills after her sobering experience with Rio at her sister's wedding. She had feared meeting that level of temptation again and as a result had taken sensible precautions to protect herself in the future. Sadly, however, she had suffered side effects from the medication and had stopped taking the pills.

'No. I'm not.' Ellie shook her head slowly and walked back into the reception room to sit down again, because she felt literally weak with shock and anxiety. 'How could we both be so stupid?'

'There are still…options,' Rio selected in a grim undertone.

Ellie's head reared up, fiery corkscrew curls tumbling back from her white forehead, accentuating her bright green eyes. 'Don't you dare suggest options to me! I'm a doctor, sworn to protect life,' she shot back at him.

'I didn't say that *that* was what I wanted. *Accidenti!* We are not reckless teenagers but we behaved as though we were,' Rio intoned in open exasperation. 'When we get together it is as though we are cursed. Let us hope there are no consequences…'

# CHAPTER FIVE

ELLIE BREATHED IN deeply and slowly released her breath in the hope of chasing away the brain fog afflicting her ability to think. She was struggling to perform little mental calculations around her menstrual cycle, very quickly realising that their timing had been little short of catastrophic. She had chosen the worst possible moment to abandon her usual caution, she recognised in steadily deepening dismay.

What if Rio made her pregnant? The consequences of unprotected sex were not something she wanted to contemplate, particularly when she had a very poor relationship with the potential father. She suppressed a fearful shudder and told herself to be strong. Whatever happened, it would happen and she couldn't change that. In the meantime it would be best to go on as though nothing had changed.

'Please take me back to my hotel or call me a taxi or something,' Ellie muttered in desperation.

'You still haven't told me what you've done to Beppe—'

'I haven't done anything to him!' Ellie proclaimed in a sudden fury roused by the stabbing of her conscience. After all, if Beppe Sorrentino was troubled, it *was* her fault because she had told him something that had upset him. She had been selfish and thoughtless, dwelling only on her right to know who her father was without ever considering the cost that that information might inflict on anyone else. Even worse, Rio was Beppe's godson and Beppe had no idea that Ellie had already met Rio and was currently involved with the younger man. But *was* she involved with him?

Ellie grimaced at the concept because that word, *involved*, lent a gravitas to their entanglement that it didn't deserve. They had engaged in a foolish and irresponsible sexual encounter, nothing more. They weren't in a relationship, nor were they likely to be. And how did she feel about that reality? And the answer was that that reality saddened and wounded her heart and her pride. With Rio, she was slowly and painfully learning that she was more vulnerable than she had ever appreciated. She had made a mistake with him two years earlier and almost unbelievably had made an even bigger mistake this time around. Sex might be a field that Rio played in but Ellie didn't play at anything she did. She didn't do casual either.

'Ellie…' Rio breathed impatiently.

Ellie rose from her seat to move back out to the hall. 'I can't discuss Beppe with you. I'm sorry but that's how it is—'

'What are you hiding from me?' Glittering dark eyes full of suspicion locked to the pale triangle of Ellie's face.

Ellie lifted her chin. 'People have secrets, Rio. Secrets they don't want to share. Dragging them out into the light of day isn't always the right thing to do,' she reasoned uneasily.

'Beppe has no secrets… He's not that kind of man,' Rio argued with sublime assurance. 'So, if you're not judging, you're preaching. Are you so perfect?'

'No, I know I'm far from perfect and I wasn't preaching. I was just speaking my thoughts out loud. I'm a little confused right now,' Ellie admitted tightly, her eyes suddenly stinging while she wondered if her entire trip to Italy had been an outsize blunder. Maybe she should have left the past buried, maybe she should've tried harder to suppress her curiosity. All she knew was that she felt very guilty at the knowledge that Beppe had been distressed by her visit. He had dealt with her kindly but perhaps she hadn't deserved that kindness.

'I'll take you back to the hotel,' Rio murmured without any expression at all. He had reached the conclusion that it would take a hacksaw to extract anything from Ellie that she did not want to share. What secrets was she concealing? What he had read in that investigative report? Or was there more?

'Yes, thank you. I have a da—' Ellie bit off the word before it could reach the tip of her tongue but she saw Rio's dark gaze switch fast to her face and she felt her cheeks burn.

'You have a date?' Rio pressed in growling disbelief, staring at her as she stood there in the comparative dimness of the hall, a glowing beauty with a sexily tousled mane of vibrant coppery curls, translucent skin and a mouth that would've tempted a saint. And he had never been a saint. Even less was he known as a possessive lover, because he didn't allow himself to become attached: once bitten, twice shy. So why did the very thought of Ellie becoming intimate with another man infuriate him? Disconcerted by that rush of anger, he tamped it down hard and gritted his teeth.

'A guy I met in the village invited me out to dinner tonight,' Ellie confided in a rush.

'His name?' Rio demanded.

'Bruno Nigrelli.'

Rio's nostrils flared. 'I think he did some work for Beppe once. Lawyer?'

Ellie nodded uncomfortably.

Rio gritted his teeth even harder in the smouldering silence. Was she expecting him to object? Even waiting for him to do so? Wasn't that how women sucked a man in, by assigning strings and conditions and making him want and demand more?

'I'm not much in the mood for dinner now, but I don't like letting people down—'

Rio's dark eyes flared golden as the sunset. 'Then cancel him and spend the night here with me instead.'

Ellie froze in bewilderment, green eyes flying over his lean, darkly handsome features. 'Spend the night?' she repeated shakily.

'It would make more sense—'

Ellie dropped her gaze defensively. 'Nothing about us makes sense—'

'We make perfect sense. You decided I was a *bastardo* two years ago and even if I saved the world you wouldn't budge an inch from that conviction,' Rio derided.

'I think a lot of women would think the same after that night at the wedding, but let's not get into that,' Ellie counselled heavily as she yanked open the hefty front door. 'We have enough differences without raking up the past. I can't stay, Rio—'

'Ellie... When will you know?'

Ellie dropped her head as she settled into the passenger seat of his sports car. 'In ten days to two weeks,' she framed jaggedly. 'I'll do a test as soon as I can.'

In the sunlight, Rio stood very still. What would he do if Ellie conceived his child? He recalled his own sordid origins with an inner shudder of recoil, knowing in that instant that there would be no sacrifice too great were it to mean that his child could look back with pride and contentment on his or her early years. Only when Beppe and Amalia took an interest in him had Rio learned what it was to have self-respect. Being cleverer than everyone around him had only attracted the bullies. Being prettier as a boy had also drawn the abusers. His lean, strong face was stamped by the grim lines and hollows of bitter recollection and experience. As an adult, Rio Benedetti might be as rich as the fabled Croesus but he had never forgotten his humble beginnings in that dumpster.

Ellie glanced up to see what was preventing Rio from joining her in the car and ended up staring, because it was a revelation to see that Rio, all lean, mean and magnificent six-foot-plus of him, could look haunted and almost vulnerable. She scolded herself for that imaginative flight as soon as he started up the car but his rebuke about her tendency to judge was still nagging at the back of her mind. Sometimes she was kind of black-and-white about situations, she acknowledged uneasily, but just as she had learned all her life to follow rules she *had* learned to compromise and understand what motivated people to do the things they did, as well. She supposed she *was* still holding the events of two years earlier against Rio because his colourful sex life had shocked her. As someone who had never pushed against conventional boundaries, possibly she *was* a little too conservative for a passionate free spirit like Rio.

Rio pulled the car to a halt in the hotel car park. He shot Ellie a glance, noting the fineness of her delicate bone structure and how clearly it showed beneath her pale skin. She was exhausted and he could see it and he compressed his mouth on the urge to make another comment about Beppe. He refused to think about the dinner date she had. He refused to admit that the idea annoyed him. After all, he wasn't possessive and he wasn't jealous. He didn't *ever* get attached to a woman—well, at least he hadn't in almost ten years.

And when Rio *had* got attached—to Franca—it had been a disaster, he recalled grimly. Treachery laced with infidelity and a woman's greed. Rio had learned the hard way that loving could be a one-way ticket to hell.

No, he definitely wasn't jealous. He already knew that Ellie was a gold-digger, he reminded himself resolutely. He would only care about Ellie Dixon's future if she became pregnant with his child. In the short term his *sole* interest in her lay in uncovering her mysterious connection to Beppe.

Rio sprang out of the car and strode round to open the passenger door. Disconcerted by that unexpected attention, Ellie climbed out and as she looked up warily into his glitteringly beautiful dark golden eyes, the sunlight hot on her skin, her conscience screamed like a fire alarm. She had been downright nasty about the sex even though he had been considerate and concerned and, bearing in mind that he had given her two climaxes, she had been unjust. Her skin flushed beet red.

'*Che cosa...* What?' Rio pressed in the strained silence.

'I shouldn't have said what I said back at your house,' Ellie gabbled before she could lose her nerve. 'It was a train wreck… Us, I mean, and me being…well, you know what. But you were good, I mean—'

Rio wanted to laugh but he fought the urge because she was so embarrassed, so utterly different from him in her attitude to sex. 'Okay…'

'I'm sorry,' Ellie said curtly. 'I was… I was upset.'

And with that apology she spun on her heel and walked into the hotel. Her head had a natural tilt, her hips a shapely sway, the skirt dancing above her long slender legs and, that fast, Rio was hard as a rock again, his hands clenching into fists by his sides. She drove him crazy, he reminded himself unnecessarily. But he had had her now and that should be that, game over. Hit it and quit it, he repeated to himself. He didn't *still* want her. Of course he didn't, so walk away, a little voice in his brain instructed.

Rio swung back into his car. The sound of Ellie moaning as he kissed her engulfed him, the surprised look of ecstasy on her face when she came, the exquisite feel of her soft, satiny skin. He swore vehemently, emptied his mind and dug out his phone. He needed a woman, *any* woman just as long as she wasn't Ellie.

In a daze, Ellie went for a shower. She still ached. There would be no forgetting what she had done. And the incredulous way Rio had looked at her in the car park would stay with her until the day she died. Her face burned afresh. She should have kept quiet, she shouldn't have said anything, should have left that short-lived intimacy and all memory of it back in his house in the hills where it belonged. A mistaken moment and not an important one in her scheme of things. Only sex. Although it would not be *only* sex if she fell pregnant, she conceded wretchedly, and refused to think about that angle on the grounds that it was stupid to worry before she knew she actually had something to worry about.

Although for the first time ever, Ellie desperately wanted to confide in someone and she thought about phoning Polly. She didn't think Polly would tell her husband, Rashad, about *that*. But how did she know for sure? She covered her face with wet hands, all the stress of the past forty-eight hours piling up on her along with every doubt and insecurity she possessed. She still didn't know how she had ended up having sex with Rio, but she knew she had wanted it to happen as much as he had. Being unable to put the blame on him stung, as well. He hadn't sweet-talked her, filled her up with booze or seduced her—*my goodness, anything but*, she conceded ruefully.

Beppe called her on her mobile and asked her to meet him at a doctor's surgery on the outskirts of Florence the next day. She refused the lift he offered her and assured him that she had satellite navigation and was happy to drive herself there. He invited her to dine at his home in the evening and she agreed, keen to take the opportunity to get to know him a little better, regardless of how Rio might feel about it. Should she tell Beppe that she knew Rio? Or would it be wiser to remain tactfully silent? She brooded about that while she got dressed to dine with Bruno.

It was a long evening. Bruno might have ticked all

the basic boxes in the tally of what made a man attractive but he bored on about his work ambitions while asking little about Ellie. He kissed her on the cheek outside her hotel. He invited her out again and she made a polite excuse and she didn't linger, speeding indoors, keen to get to bed.

Opening the door of her hotel room, she drew back with a sound of consternation when she saw the light burning beside her bed and the male reclining there. 'How on earth did you get in here?' she demanded.

Rio uncoiled fluidly off the bed and stretched with lazy assurance, not one whit perturbed by her attitude. 'It wasn't difficult. The staff know we're…close,' he selected with precision and the angry flush on her cheeks bloomed hotter still with chagrin. 'I also own a large stake in the hotel.'

'We are *not* close!' Ellie contradicted, tossing her bag down on the chair in the corner.

Rio shrugged a broad shoulder, gracefully and silently evasive. He was as effortlessly beautiful as a dark angel sent to tempt even with his black hair tousled, his jawline shadowed and his tie missing. Her heartbeat had picked up speed. Her tiredness had taken a mysterious step back and she was already breathing as if she had run up a hill. And there was the craziest melting sensation in that place where she still ached from his sheer sexual energy. Yet she didn't want *that* again, did she? It was a badly timed thought to have in Rio's presence because her entire body quickened as if she had punched a button to switch it on to supersensitivity. Her nipples stung and her thighs pressed together as if to silence the squirming readiness low in her pelvis.

'Are you planning to tell me what you're doing here?' Ellie enquired stiffly, tamping down all those disobedient thoughts and responses.

'I wanted to be sure you came back alone,' Rio told her.

'And how is that your business?'

'You were with me today,' Rio murmured.

Ellie tilted her chin, emerald eyes gleaming like chips of ice. 'Doesn't mean you own me.'

Rio shrugged again. 'I'd still have beaten the hell out of him had you brought him upstairs.'

Ellie's lips parted and then closed again because there really wasn't much she could say to that. 'You do a lot of that sort of thing?' she prompted a split second later, honest curiosity gripping her.

'Get physical? Once it was a regular activity.' Dark eyes spilling a glittering gleam of gold from below lush curling black lashes, Rio strode past her to the door. 'I had to, to protect myself. I grew up in a tough environment.'

'You're leaving?' Ellie framed in disconcertion and then could have bitten her tongue out because she was making it sound as though she wanted him to stay. And she didn't.

*'Sì...'* Rio treated her to a slow burning appraisal. 'Somehow I doubt that you'd be up for anything else tonight, *principessa*.'

Fury splintered through Ellie. Leave it to Rio to tell it as it is. He would stay for sex but not to chat or share a drink or supper or anything more civilised. The claustrophobic silence of the room enclosed her, increasing her nervous tension. The tip of her tongue stole out to moisten her dry lower lip.

'I *love* your mouth,' Rio husked soft and low, his attention locking to the sultry fullness of her pink lips.

Gooseflesh pebbled Ellie's arms and a wicked little quiver snaked down her taut spinal cord. She was so aware of him that her very skin prickled and tingled with it. For an insane moment she imagined pushing him backwards down on the bed and teaching him that he didn't know everything about her. And then she blinked, sane Ellie swimming back to the fore, and she spun and opened the door for him so that he would leave more quickly.

'Sometimes you crack me up, *bella mia*,' Rio confided with unholy amusement, recognising her defensiveness in that almost desperate pulling open of the door to hasten his departure. 'When you're thinking about me in bed tonight, will you be kissing me or thumping me?'

Ellie breathed in so deep she almost spontaneously combusted while she watched Rio clatter down the stairs without an ounce of discomfiture in his bearing. She had never met anyone quite like Rio Benedetti before and that was probably why he knocked her for six every time she saw him, she told herself soothingly. He was bad, he was brash, he was incredibly sexy and insolent and he had the kind of charismatic confidence that burned like a solar flare. She was too polite and inhibited to deal with him as he *should* be dealt with. Her hands clenched into fists.

He embarrassed her too. The staff had seen her going out with Bruno Nigrelli and now knew she had returned to find Rio waiting in her bedroom. Ought she to complain about that invasion? Or, having already been seen in Rio's company and kissing him, perhaps it was wiser to ignore the situation lest she end up even more embarrassed. Had Rio made her look slutty? Or like a femme fatale? She went to bed on that thought, deciding that Rio's pursuit, if she could label it with that word, made her look like a much more exciting woman than she actually was. But she still wanted to kill him for being so careless of appearances, so arrogant and incomprehensible.

Why would he have beaten up Bruno had she brought the other man back to her room? Presumably that had been a joke, although she had not seen the humour in it. She could not credit that Rio could be jealous or staking some sort of male claim to her. He wasn't the type. And instead of finding the sleep she badly needed the riddle of his complex personality ensured that she couldn't stop her brain running on and actually relax enough to drift off.

The following morning she met up with Beppe outside a smart suburban surgery near Florence. The older man looked perfectly calm and collected and there was no sign of strain or distress in either his expression or his friendly, easy manner. Had Rio exaggerated? Overreacted? They went inside the surgery and swabs were taken. Beppe passed over a tiny gold locket, which he quietly admitted contained a lock of his brother's hair. Ellie flushed and made no comment. After all, her mother, Annabel, had named both brothers as her daughter's possible father, and to do so, she had presumably been uncertain as to which had fathered her child.

'We will know within twenty-four hours,' Beppe assured her with quiet satisfaction. 'And now that I have you here in my beloved Firenze, I will play tourist with you and show you the sights as they should be seen.'

Relieved by his mood and the welcome offer of his company, Ellie relaxed and over a cup of coffee and a pastry in a sun-drenched square found herself admitting that she knew Rio and had first met him at her sister's wedding.

The older man did not hide his astonishment. 'He should've told me that—'

'To be honest,' Ellie added hurriedly, 'Rio and I didn't get on very well, so it wasn't an acquaintance either of us was likely to pursue.'

Beppe sighed. 'You surprise me. Women are drawn to my godson. Obviously you've seen him since your arrival—'

'He called in at the hotel on my first day. I didn't tell him anything,' Ellie assured him, her cheeks colouring when she was forced to think of what else she had done with Rio since that day, but it was a major relief for her to admit simply that she knew Rio.

'Rio put me on a pedestal a very long time ago,' Beppe confided wryly. 'If you and I discover that we are related by blood, it will be a huge shock for him and that is why I have told him nothing as yet.'

'Were you friends with his parents? I know he's your godson.'

'No, my wife and I never knew his parents,' Beppe admitted dismissively and changed the subject to ask her to choose where she would like to go first with him.

Beppe took her to see Michelangelo's sculptures in the Galleria dell'Academia before showing her his favourite paintings in the Uffizi. Her frank admission that she knew nothing whatsoever about art did her no disservice in his eyes and when she liked something he asked her *why* she liked it, evidently set on forming her taste. He also told her a little about his own family background. The *palazzo* had been in his family for several generations and the Sorrentino prosperity had originally been built on the production of internationally acclaimed wines. His younger brother, Vincenzo, had once managed the vineyards. Beppe had always been academic and had worked as a university professor before his wife's ill health had forced him to take a step back from his career. From that point on, he had become more involved in his wife's charitable endeavours, which had been very much focussed on the needs of disabled and disadvantaged children.

'What time is dinner this evening?' Ellie asked when Beppe had finally returned her to her car. She noted that he was out of breath and perspiring and she scolded herself for letting him do so much on a hot day when he was clearly by his girth and indoor habits not usually a physically active man.

'Nine o'clock. And it will be formal,' Beppe warned her. 'But don't worry about that if you have no formal wear with you. Everyone will understand that you are on holiday.'

Ellie smiled at that recollection as she returned to her hotel. Thanks to Polly's holiday shop, Ellie had a dream of a dress hanging in the wardrobe. In fact, uninterested though she had always been in fashion, it was the sort of dress that brought stars to her eyes because it was wonderfully feminine and flowing. Fashioned of peach lace, it was a daring colour for a redhead, but remarkably flattering against her pale skin and bright hair. She showered and paid more heed than usual to the minimal make-up she wore while wondering if Rio would be at the dinner. Would he be annoyed that she had gone ahead and told his godfather that they already knew each other? Staying silent on that score had become impossible for her because Beppe was so very straightforward and plain-spoken and she did not want to risk losing his good opinion by keeping secrets from him.

The gravel in front of Beppe's home was a sea of luxury-model cars, which disconcerted Ellie because evidently the dinner party was a much bigger, fancier event than she had assumed it would be. Her fear that she would prove to be overdressed receded as soon as she was shown into a crowded salon filled with clusters of very elegant laughing and chattering guests. Beppe hurried straight over to welcome her and tucked her hand over his arm protectively as he took her to join the group he was with. Within a few minutes, Ellie had relaxed.

And then the door opened again and she glanced across the room to see the new arrivals and saw Rio entering with a tall willowy blonde clinging to his arm. Her heart sank and she couldn't stop it from doing that. Her pleasant smile lurched and her tummy flipped and all of a sudden she felt ridiculously sick and shaky. What the heck was the matter with her? She was not in a relationship with Rio, was she? Why should it bother her that he was already showing off another woman? After all, she had known from the outset that he was a notorious womaniser with few moral scruples.

Rio was taken aback by Ellie's presence because Beppe hadn't mentioned that his visitor would be attending. Nor did it help that Ellie looked stupendous in an apricot dress that smoothly shaped her lush curves at breast and hip while highlighting her porcelain-pale skin and the sheer vibrancy of her coppery tumbling mane of hair. His physical response was swift and urgent, the swelling at his groin an unwelcome reminder that 'hit it and quit it' hadn't worked for him where she was concerned. Above her breast, she had fastened a diamond brooch in the shape of a star and it was the only jewellery she wore. So, she *did* have the diamond brooch her uncle had accused her of stealing, Rio recognised in sudden disgust, the brooch she had denied all knowledge of after her grandmother's death. For Rio, it was a timely reminder of the kind of woman he was dealing with in Ellie Dixon. At heart she had to be a greedy, gold-digging liar who had learned how to put on a good show as a caring, compassionate doctor.

Rio strode straight up to Beppe and introduced his gorgeous companion, who seemed unable to take her eyes off Ellie's dress. The blonde's name was Carmela and she was unquestionably beautiful and very different in style from Ellie. She was taller, thinner, blue-eyed and possessed enviably straight, long silky blond hair. Her dress was much more revealing than Ellie's but then she had a perfect body to reveal. A long slender leg showed through the side slit in the dress while the plunging neckline showed a great deal of her improbably large, high breasts. Gorgeous but kind of slutty, Ellie decided, discomfited by the speed with which that shrewish opinion came to her mind.

'Of course, Ellie needs no introduction to you, Rio,' his godfather, Beppe, pointed out smoothly as an opening salvo. 'Since you first met at her sister's wedding.'

Rio was transfixed by that bombshell reminder coming at him out of nowhere and unadulterated rage roared through his big powerful frame as his attention shot to Ellie, who evaded his gaze while slowly turning as red as a tomato, her guilt writ large in her face. Ellie had chosen to come clean with Beppe and had dropped him in it without conscience, Rio registered grimly. A power play? Or was it a warning? What else might she choose to tell his godfather about him? Shot through with anger and frustration at his inability to respond with the truth, Rio was incapable of even forcing a smile.

'We didn't hit it off,' Ellie said abruptly. 'That's why he didn't mention it.'

Shot from rage to wonderment at that apparent intervention on his behalf, Rio dealt Ellie a suspicious look from glittering dark-as-jet eyes semiveiled by his lush lashes and shrugged. 'First impressions are rarely reliable,' he quipped as he turned away to address someone else who had spoken to him.

Ellie was appalled that something she had revealed had caused tension between Rio and Beppe. Her trip to Italy and her search for her father were definitely beginning to feel like a minefield she was trying to pick her way across.

As Rio moved to grasp a glass from a tray and pass it to her, Carmela hissed, 'That redhead's wearing a Lavroff!'

Rio shot the fashion model on his arm a blank appraisal.

'That dress was the star of the Lavroff show I walked for in the spring.'

A designer gown, surely a little rich for a junior doctor's salary? Although perhaps not too expensive for a doctor whose dying patient had left her everything she possessed, Rio reflected sombrely. It was starting to occur to him that he had underestimated Ellie and how much trouble she was capable of causing. He could see at a glance that she already had Beppe wrapped round her little finger. In fact, her hand was resting comfortably on the older man's arm. Rio dragged in a sudden breath, his lean, darkly handsome features tensing into tough lines of restraint. Was *that* what he had to fear?

Ironically that risk hadn't even crossed his mind because Beppe lived a celibate life and had never been known to seek out female companionship. But Beppe had been acquainted with Ellie's mother, and if Ellie's mother had been even half as beautiful as her daughter, she would hardly have been forgettable. Back then, however, Beppe had been safely married and now he was not and he was making no attempt to hide his delight in Ellie's company. Rio stationed himself where he could watch his godfather and he was sharply disconcerted by the level of familiarity he could already see developing between the pair. Ellie whispered something in Beppe's ear and he chuckled and patted her hand fondly. He moved her on with him to another group of guests, giving her no opportunity to stray.

At his elbow, Carmela was still whinging on enviously about the Lavroff gown. Rio wasn't interested. He often paid for the designer clothes his lovers wore but he took no interest in the names or the cost, writing the expenses off as the cost of maintaining a reasonable sex life. His entire focus remained on Ellie. He listened to her making intelligent conversation, heard her laugh several times and learned that she had toured the Uffizi gallery with Beppe. *Inferno*, she certainly didn't need to be taught how to best please a much older, lonely man with a lifelong love of art. But she would soon learn her mistake if she persisted on her current ambitious trajectory. Rio would destroy her before he would allow her to hurt Beppe Sorrentino.

*And what if she's pregnant?* Rio backed away a step as Carmela tried to get closer to him. He studied Ellie as they were seated at the dining table and strove to imagine that shapely body swollen with his child. The idea unnerved him but it also excited him in a peculiar way, which only had the effect of unnerving him even more.

Ellie barely touched the food on her plate. She eavesdropped on Carmela's airheaded views on suntans as affected by climate change. She noticed that Rio didn't listen to a word his companion said and appeared to be tuning her out like an irritating noise. She watched him, as well, catching the downward slant of his beautifully shaped mouth, the tension in his exquisite bone structure that hardened his exotic cheekbones and placed hollows beneath them. He was furious with her, she *knew* he was. Rio had a temper like a flamethrower and he was boiling like a cauldron of oil.

But Ellie was angry too. Only the day before he had been with her and last night he had been waiting for her in her hotel room. And now he was with a beautiful blonde model, who operated off one very talkative brain cell. Why was she hurt? Why the hell was she hurting over his rejection of her as a woman? Time after time over the years Ellie had learned that men didn't really want career-driven, independent women. She wasn't feminine enough, she wasn't *soft* enough, she could deal with a spider just fine but a mouse sent her screaming. She was stubborn and contrary and choosy and he didn't fit the bill for her either, so why was she agonising? Why would she want a gorgeous, arrogant, shameless man whore in her life anyway? She was far too sensible and strait-laced for a male of his ilk. Sheer lust had put her in his arms and she had got what she deserved, she told herself repressively.

Beppe took her and several other guests to admire his latest painting acquisition in the hall. Rio and Carmela joined them. Carmela wondered out loud if the seventeenth-century subject of the portrait was wearing hair extensions. Ellie whispered a polite, 'Excuse me...' in Beppe's ear as he guided the group into his library to show them something else and she walked down the corridor to the cloakroom instead. Freshening up, she grimaced at her anxious reflection in the mirror. Why was it that when Rio was around he dominated everything? Including her thoughts?

When she emerged, Rio was standing waiting for her, his lean, dark face stormy and tense. 'I want a word,' he told her grimly.

'But I *don't*,' Ellie told him as he snapped a hand round her wrist and pulled her outdoors onto the cool, formal *loggia* with pillars that ran along that side of the house.

'You're such a bully, Rio!' Ellie objected, rubbing her wrist the instant he released it as though he had bruised her.

Rio backed her up against the stone wall behind her by the simple expedient of moving forward, shutting out any view of the gardens and forcing her to tip her head back to look up at him. 'What did you tell Beppe about us?' he demanded in a raw undertone.

'Very little. That we met at the wedding and that you called on me at the hotel the day I arrived,' Ellie proffered. 'I didn't tell him what you said or threatened or anything of that nature. I simply wanted to clear the air. Pretending we were strangers…I mean, why would I mislead Beppe like that? I've got nothing to hide—'

'Not according to the report I had done on you,' Rio reminded her darkly.

Ellie bridled at that reference, fully convinced that any close and proper check on her background would reveal that she was innocent of any wrongdoing. 'I didn't intend to cause friction between you and Beppe. I didn't think of that angle,' she admitted guiltily. 'But I'm sorry that I embarrassed you like that—'

'Are you really?' Rio lifted a sardonic ebony brow, staring down at her, noting the mere hint at her neckline of the pale valley between her full breasts and entranced by the new discovery that showing so little could actually be sexier than showing a lot. As he tensed, inescapably recalling his own response to those luscious curves the day before, he whipped his gaze up to her face in the hope of lowering his temperature. 'I think you dropped me in it deliberately to cause trouble,' he contended.

'But then you would think that because you always think the worst of me,' Ellie shot back at him in exasperation. 'Exactly what is your problem, Rio?'

Rio ran his fingertip along the succulent curve of her lower lip and watched a tiny pulse flicker fast at the base of her elegant white throat. 'You're my only problem, *principessa*,' he told her huskily. 'We had our moment and that was supposed to be it—'

'It *is* it!' Ellie seethed, furious that he was cornering her when he had brought another woman to dinner.

'Not for me,' Rio confided, letting a coppery corkscrew curl coil round his finger like a vine, his stunning dark golden eyes hot and hungrily gripping hers by sheer force of will. 'I'm not done yet—'

'But I *am*,' Ellie spelled out thinly. 'You're ruining my holiday—'

'When we're done, I'll *tell* you,' Rio asserted, bending down to nip at her full lower lip with the edge of his teeth.

A violent shiver ran down through her taut body, that tiny sting of pain somehow setting off a chain reaction of electrified awareness and sensitivity. He lowered his head and he took her mouth with a raw sexual demand that momentarily stole Ellie's wits. She fell back against the wall, knees weak, melting heat surging in her pelvis.

*'Rio!'* a voice interposed curtly, and both of them froze.

Rio lifted his dark head and stepped back to study his godfather, keen to interpret his expression. Beppe looked angry and protective. Ellie straightened, her face flushing as mortification consumed her.

'Carmela's looking for you,' Beppe murmured flatly. 'I suggest that you take her home. I would also suggest that you stay away from Ellie.'

Rio released his breath in an audible hiss. 'Although I'm always ready to listen to suggestions, Beppe,' he conceded, 'I've always forged my own path.'

With a nod of acknowledgement to Ellie and the older man, Rio strode back indoors, not one whit perturbed by the scene Beppe had interrupted. Or, at least, if he was bothered, he wasn't showing it, Ellie acknowledged.

'I have no right to interfere,' Beppe said uncomfortably to Ellie. 'I love Rio like a son but I also know him.

He had some unfortunate experiences with women in his youth and I would advise you to keep your distance. He plays with women. He doesn't take them seriously. He would hurt you and I would hate to see that happen. Furthermore, if you prove to be either my niece or even my daughter, you will often meet Rio and that—'

'Could get very awkward,' Ellie filled in ruefully for herself. 'It's all right, Beppe. I kind of worked out that stuff about Rio anyway, so don't worry about me. I'm a big girl and I can look after myself.'

Rio and Carmela were nowhere to be seen when they rejoined the rest of the guests. Ellie stayed quite late but insisted on returning to her hotel when Beppe offered her the use of a guest room. She drove back in a contemplative state of mind and wondered if she would find Rio in her room again. Not this time however.

Soberly she lay in bed, wondering about the results of the DNA test. Would she prove to be half-Sorrentino? Or was she in for a shock on that score? It was perfectly possible, after all, that some time after Beppe's rejection her mother had spent a night with some other man. Well, at least she would soon know one way or another, even if she didn't actually manage to identify her father, she told herself soothingly.

But how would Rio react if she was a Sorrentino? Ironically she didn't want to upset him but nor was she willing to apologise for an act of fate. She was already wondering what Beppe's mention of Rio's 'unfortunate youthful experiences' with women had entailed. But then surely no intelligent male could be so innately distrustful and cynical about her sex without cause?

And what did it matter? She relived the teasing sting of his teeth on her lip and a forbidden little quiver snaked through her. With a groan she rolled over and pressed her offending mouth into the pillow. Rio was as potent as poison and equally toxic and Beppe was right, she *needed* to keep her distance. To do anything else would be to court disaster because Rio had no off switch, no respect for boundaries…and probably even less respect for her, she conceded unhappily.

# CHAPTER SIX

BEPPE CALLED ELLIE bright and early and asked her to come to his home. Ellie surmised that he had bad news and she took her time over her breakfast in the hotel courtyard, trying not to stress over what could not be changed. Beppe had been wonderfully approachable and kind and helpful and she wanted to thank him for that. He could've denied any knowledge of her late mother but instead he had told her the unvarnished truth, even though doing so had raked up guilty memories and regrets.

Ellie drove over to the *palazzo* and Adriano showed her out to the shaded *loggia*, quickly reappearing with a tray of coffee and biscuits. Beppe appeared then, rather flushed in appearance and with eyes that were a little shiny.

He studied her and he then smiled widely, a smile brimming with happiness and appreciation. 'Ellie,' he began emotively as he handed her a sheet of paper to study. 'You *are* my daughter and I cannot begin to describe how much that discovery means to me.'

Lively with excitement, Beppe could hardly be persuaded to drink his coffee as he ignored her medical training to explain rather unnecessarily the 99.99 recurring percentage of accuracy established by the successful DNA test. 'I would've been delighted to discover that you were my niece but to discover a daughter, a first child after all these years, is an unimaginable joy!'

Ellie reached across the small circular table and grasped his hand to squeeze it. 'Thank you for saying that.'

'It comes from the centre of my heart,' Beppe told her warmly. 'Amalia give birth to a stillborn son just weeks before she suffered her stroke. We were devastated. I don't believe, though, that I could have told her about you were she still alive. It would have hurt her too much and my affair had already caused her enormous grief.'

'How do you think Rio will take this news?' Ellie asked, dry-mouthed.

Beppe emitted a heavy sigh. 'He will be here for lunch and I will tell him then. He will be happy that I am happy but very disappointed to hear that I once betrayed Amalia. If only we had adopted him as I wished, he would have been more certain of his place in the family.'

Ellie sat forward, brow furrowed, her curiosity engaged. 'You wanted to *adopt* Rio?'

'*Sì.* I will respect his privacy by not giving you details but he had neither parents nor a home and I wanted to take him in, but Amalia refused to set another child in what she always viewed as our stillborn son's place,' he confided heavily. 'There were also elements of Rio's background which disturbed her and she could not be persuaded to change her mind. He never knew that I wanted to adopt him though. Our contribution to his life became less direct as he grew up. We advised him, ensured he got a good education and supported him when he needed us but we could have protected him a great deal more had we adopted him and brought him up here.'

'That's unfortunate but Rio has still done very well for himself, hasn't he?'

'If you measure success by prosperity, his wealth reached stratospheric proportions after he won the oil contracts in Dharia. He is very much a self-made man,' Beppe declared with pride. 'But he is also a man damaged by a traumatic childhood and a tough adolescence. I should've done more for him.'

'By the sound of it, you did the best you could in the circumstances,' Ellie remarked soothingly, troubled more than she liked by the reference to Rio's traumatic childhood and troubled adolescence. Yes, she could imagine how such experiences would have hardened him and what a difference a loving, supportive home background could have made. After all, she knew that she too was marked by the lack of love in her childhood. Her grandmother hadn't wanted to raise her daughter's two illegitimate children and had only done so because Annabel had paid her handsomely to take on that responsibility. When that flow of money had stopped, presumably because Annabel had suffered bankruptcy and ill health, her grandmother had complained bitterly about how much of a burden her granddaughters were. Polly's affection had provided the only love Ellie had experienced during those years.

'I think I'll go back to the hotel now,' Ellie announced, hardening herself to Beppe's look of disappointment. 'Rio will be arriving soon and we both need some time to think. This is a lot to take on board and so much more than I ever expected to learn.'

'I hope you will pack and come here to stay with me for what remains of your holiday,' Beppe admitted. 'And perhaps someday you will feel comfortable enough to call me *Papà*.'

Ellie's eyes prickled with tears as she left. She felt ridiculously emotional and when Beppe gave her a small, almost daring hug on the doorstep it almost made the pent-up tears spill down her cheeks. He was willing to be her father and she was in a daze of shock and happiness. It bothered her to appreciate that Rio was unlikely to celebrate the same news. Rio didn't like her and didn't trust her and the revelation that she was his precious godfather's daughter would hit him hard. Would it hurt him that she had the blood tie with Beppe that he had been denied? She flinched from the thought, marvelling at how oversensitive she was to any thought of Rio being hurt.

It was so ridiculous, she thought ruefully. Big, tough, angry, hostile Rio would not be so easily hurt. Why was she even considering how he would feel about her parentage? What business was it of his? After all, the scene had been set before she was even born by Beppe's affair with her unhappy mother. By the sound of it that extramarital affair had caused tremendous unhappiness for all the parties involved, but surely after so many years Beppe could begin to forgive himself and both of them could now concentrate on forming a relationship? That conviction at the forefront of her mind, Ellie packed her case and then walked down to the village to kill some time and allow Beppe to speak to Rio in peace.

Rio departed from Beppe's home reeling from what his godfather had dropped on him. An adulterous affair and a daughter? No, he had certainly not seen that possibility on the horizon and it changed everything, his own position most of all. Ellie had played a blinder of a game by concealing her true motivation for being in Italy right to the very end, Rio acknowledged bitterly. In fact, she had trussed him up like a chicken ready for the roasting pot. Beppe had openly voiced his concern that Rio nourished dishonourable intentions towards his newfound daughter. Beppe had no idea that Rio had already gone much further than that and if he found out it would destroy his relationship with Rio. Worse still, if she was pregnant, Beppe would be digging out a shotgun.

It was time to take the initiative, not a time to sit back and vacillate over what-ifs and maybes, Rio reflected sardonically. Left in ignorance, he had dug himself into a deep hole and he had to dig himself out of it again and to do that he needed Ellie's help whether he liked it or not. Raging resentment surged up through the cracks inside him and there was no healing balm of acceptance to soothe it. Beppe was, after all, the only true family Rio had ever had, the only adult who had ever shown him love, consideration and understanding while he was still a child. And now Beppe had a daughter, whom Rio had wronged. That she could well be a money-grabbing young woman keen to feather her own nest scarcely counted now that she was about to become Beppe's heir. Furthermore, Beppe would never believe the allegations made against Ellie for there was virtually no proof of misconduct on her part.

Rio had hired a second agency to check and update the evidence he had originally been given. The hospice enquiry *had* cleared Ellie of any wrongdoing and she *had* refused the inheritance left to her by one of her patients. The only dirt left in the first investigative report relied heavily on her embittered uncle's tale about the diamond brooch and, as the police had refused to prosecute, the whole story could easily be written off as being more rumour and backstabbing than actual fact. And furthermore, if Ellie *was* a gold-digger, Rio was about to make her feel as if she'd won the lottery.

When he learned that she had checked out of the hotel he was taken aback until he noticed that her hire car was still parked outside. The receptionist told him that Ellie had walked down into the village. He found her in the cool of the ancient stone church, studying a much-admired triptych of the Madonna and Child.

When he spoke her name, she whirled round, a figure of light and movement in the dim, dark interior. Her dress was the ice blue of diamonds and the sunlight cascading through a stained-glass window high up the wall showered her in a dancing rainbow of colour that only emphasised the vibrant copper of her tumbling hair. She wasn't quick enough to hide the dismay and anxiety that crossed her face when she saw him and the tense expression and attitude that took over to stiffen her into stillness was no more welcoming.

*Welcome to your biggest challenge yet*, Rio thought grimly, trying not to notice how beautiful she was in that naturally beautiful way that so many women tried and failed to achieve. He froze there, suppressing his body's equally natural instincts, none of which felt appropriate in the House of God.

'Rio…' Ellie whispered uncertainly, mortified by the nerves that had stolen the volume from her voice.

He could have been carved from stone as he stood

there, still and quiet as a predator, sheathed in a light grey designer suit. He resembled a stone angel with cutting cheekbones, a hard-hewn jawline and a mouth as wilful, stubborn and passionate as sin. His eyes were a pure dazzling gold in the light and she blinked rapidly, striving to shut the sheer intensity of him out and to be polite but distant, treating him the same way she usually treated men. But how could she achieve that when she knew in her heart that he had sought her out because he was shocked and agitated by what Beppe had shared with him?

'Are you a believer?' he prompted lightly.

'Yes. Are you?'

'I was raised by nuns in an orphanage and spent more time on my knees than in school. Of course I am,' Rio told her wryly.

And it was as though he had squeezed her heart at the same time as he filled in some of the blanks in her repeated attempts to understand what made him what he was. An orphanage, she thought sadly.

'I bet you were always in trouble,' Ellie remarked without thinking.

'Pretty much. Beppe and his wife raised funds for the home and did a lot to help the children, particularly the disabled ones amongst us,' Rio admitted. 'Although that home is closed now and conditions are greatly improved in its replacement. Beppe is still very much involved in finding employment and educational opportunities for the less fortunate. He is a good man.'

'Yes,' Ellie agreed tightly.

'And you are his daughter,' Rio declared without any perceptible emotion at all. 'I must assume you take after your mother since you don't look much like your father.'

'She was tall, red-haired and pale-skinned like me. I think I get my lack of height from Beppe,' Ellie breathed uncomfortably. 'You're angry that I didn't tell you why I so particularly wanted to meet Beppe.'

'It wasn't your secret to share,' Rio conceded, surprising her. 'But I must confess that I was completely unprepared for what he admitted to me. I shouldn't have been. There must have been times when he felt trapped in his marriage. He is only human.'

'Let's not talk about that,' Ellie advised. 'I don't think we can ever understand that sort of situation unless we've actually lived the same experience—'

'*Porca miseria!* That's a very compassionate comment from judgemental Ellie!' Rio commented, an ebony brow slanting up in apparent wonderment.

'Let's also try not to argue.' Ellie sent him a rueful look of appeal. 'You're shocked right now, of course you're shocked. You thought you knew everything there was to know about Beppe—'

'I don't want judgemental Ellie *or* Dr Ellie right at this moment,' Rio interposed.

The pale triangle of her face flushed as though he had slapped her. 'I'm not sure I know how to be anything else—'

'We'll have coffee…and talk,' Rio framed, extending a lean, long-fingered hand to her in invitation.

Ellie hesitated as if a shark had bared its teeth at her. And then she forced her arm to lift and she grasped his hand, a frisson of quivering awareness shimmying down her spine. He was trying to accept her and because he was making the effort, she had to make it too. His attitude thoroughly disconcerted her because she had expected only anger, condemnation and suspicion from Rio and he had just as swiftly proven her expectations wrong.

She had expected Rio to walk her across the square to the local café but instead he tucked her into the car illegally parked outside. Belatedly it occurred to her that the busy little café would scarcely be a good choice for a private chat.

'Where are we going?' she asked.

'My home. Have you had lunch?'

'No, but I'm not really hungry… Too much excitement today,' she extended wryly.

His long brown fingers flexed smoothly round the steering wheel and she remembered those fingers skimming across her body, expert and deliberate. She dragged in a short sustaining breath but she could still feel the tingling in her swelling breasts and the pulse of damp heat between her thighs. He had stripped her bare of every conviction she had once had about herself, she acknowledged reluctantly. She was a much more sexual being than she had ever dreamt but it had taken Rio to awaken and set free that side of her nature. It was terrifying to feel so vulnerable and yet Rio was currently on his very best behaviour, she recognised suddenly. Why was that? What was he planning? Why had he not yet said a single angry or insulting word to her?

'Who did this house belong to before you bought it?' she asked to break the silence as he steered the Ferrari down the long drive.

'An ancestor of Beppe's, who kept his mistress here—'

'How novel,' Ellie said drily.

'Yes, he was considered the rotten apple in the very respectable family barrel and after he died the house was left to go to rack and ruin because no one in the family thought it acceptable to live in what had once been the mistress's home. I bought it at auction and restored it. It's convenient to have somewhere close when I visit...*your father*.'

He voiced the designation with cool clarity. *Your father*. It shook her to accept that she finally had a father and that the ancestor who had kept a mistress had actually been one of her ancestors, as well. It was as though a family tree had suddenly unfolded in front of her and she smiled at the wonderful sense of security that gave her. 'I thought you would've stayed with Beppe when you visited—'

'Not if I wanted female companionship. You may not have noticed it but Beppe is rather old-fashioned in spite of his liaison with your mother,' Rio commented. 'It's simply easier to keep that side of my life away from him.'

Ellie climbed out of the car in the sunlight, grateful to have movement to distract her from thoughts of Rio's chequered past. None of her business, she reminded herself doggedly as he led the way into the big house. A housekeeper greeted them at the door and Rio addressed her in Italian.

'I ordered a light lunch for you,' Rio told her. 'You shouldn't be skipping meals.'

Ellie compressed her lips on a hasty reply.

'And you know I'm right,' Rio added with unblemished assurance.

He guided her out to a shaded terrace and pulled out a comfortable padded chair for her. 'Sit down...'

'You're so bossy,' Ellie complained, settling down and kicking off her canvas shoes to flex her overheated bare feet on the cold stone.

His housekeeper arrived with freshly squeezed orange juice for her and a glass of wine for Rio. She wondered if she was being deprived of the alcohol option because she could be pregnant but said nothing because she had been avoiding alcohol since their moment of madness. She liked that label. A moment of madness suggested a crazy once-only impulse that was out of character, but then everything that had happened with Rio had been out of character.

'What did you want us to talk about?' she pressed boldly, not wanting him to think she was tongue-tied in his presence.

'I brought you here to propose to you but I'm not quite sure how to go about it,' Rio murmured lazily. 'If I got down on one knee, you would laugh. If I told you how much I'm worth, you would accuse me of being boorish—'

Her lashes lifted high on her bright green eyes as she stared at him fixedly. His lean, darkly handsome features were sardonic and she frowned in bewilderment. 'Propose…propose what exactly?'

Rio gazed steadily back at her, dark eyes glittering like black diamonds. 'Marriage…obviously.'

'Are you out of your mind?' Ellie gasped sharply.

'No, possibly I'm foreseeing Beppe's reaction if he discovers that I've got his wonderful new daughter pregnant,' Rio extended quietly. 'And, yes, I'm aware that we don't know as yet whether you have conceived but it would be much worse to wait and see in the current climate.'

'You *are* insane,' Ellie exclaimed, gulping down a reviving swallow of orange juice.

'Not at all. I know that Beppe will never forgive

me if I've got you pregnant. He will blame me entirely for it because I have a rather raunchy reputation with women—'

*'Raunchy?'* Ellie rested her head to one side as if she was considering that word. 'Do you think rumours of your three-in-a-bed sexcapades have spread?'

Rio groaned out loud and sprang upright while shooting her a reproachful look. 'Can't you please put judgemental Ellie away for a while and have a serious conversation with me?'

Ellie winced. 'Not really. I can't take a marriage proposal from you seriously.'

Rio backed up against a stone pillar like a cornered lion and studied her with scorching golden eyes. 'That night in Dharia, I did not invite those women to my hotel room. They bribed their way in—'

Ellie pushed her stiff shoulders back into her comfortable seat and inclined her head. 'Oh, I guessed that,' she admitted. 'I assumed you wouldn't have double-booked yourself.'

The faintest colour scored Rio's hard cheekbones. 'You can't blame me for what *they* chose to do—'

'No, but what they did and what they assumed was acceptable said a great deal about the nature of your prior relationship with them,' Ellie pointed out with hot cheeks.

Rio swore long and low in Italian and finished his wine to set the glass down with a jarring snap on the table. 'I didn't have a *relationship* with either of them!' he fired back. 'I had sex with them on one drunken night years before the wedding. I admit that I did stuff when I was younger that I wouldn't do now—'

Her face stiff as she struggled not to betray any reaction, Ellie nodded.

'Just because you never felt the urge to experiment doesn't mean we're all the same…or that you're better than me!' Rio raked back at her.

'I don't think I'm better than you in any way. But that kind of experimentation doesn't appeal to me,' she confided.

'I can't lie and say I'm surprised,' Rio breathed, watching her like a hawk. 'Now we've got that out of the way and I can disclose that I have no plans to involve you in any form of sexual deviancy, can we concentrate on the marriage proposal?'

Ellie stiffened. 'Why would you want me to marry you?'

'If you do turn out to be pregnant I would have been asking you anyway,' Rio advanced. 'There is no way I would allow any woman to raise my child without me—'

'Rio… These days, single and separated parents are common—'

'I want my child to have everything I *didn't* have. A home, a solid background, two caring parents, security,' Rio extended almost argumentatively. 'It's only when you don't have those advantages that you realise how very important they are.'

'I understand that and I understand how you feel,' Ellie assured him, relieved that she knew more about his background than she had. 'But there's a reasonable chance that I *won't* be pregnant—'

'I don't want to wait and take the risk that you are because Beppe will judge me for that, as well, and regard me as an unwilling husband and a very bad bet.

It would be much easier just to tell him that we have fallen in love and wish to get married as soon as possible,' Rio argued. 'He will understand that and he will see nothing wrong with it.'

'I'm here on holiday,' Ellie reminded him helplessly. 'In a little over three weeks, I have to go home and return to work—'

'I will not come between you and your medical career. I own property in England and if you have to be there to complete your training, I will make that possible, whether you are pregnant or not,' he asserted.

That argument taken from her, Ellie slowly shook her buzzing head because he had taken her so much by surprise that she could barely think straight. 'So, you want to marry me to help take care of any child we might have and to keep Beppe content… Am I correct?'

'Sometimes you have the tongue of a viper,' Rio condemned in a harsh undertone. 'I want you for myself and for my own reasons and you know that! You know it every time you see me look at you, every time I touch you and struggle to *stop* touching you…'

Her pale skin flamed red at the dark liquid intensity of his deep voice. She lowered her head, finally acknowledging that she was equally out of control around him. In that they were equals. One kiss, one touch, one moment of madness wasn't enough to sate the craving. But marriage, marriage was something else entirely, wasn't it? It was forging a future together as partners, trusting each other.

'You don't trust me,' she reminded him. 'How can you marry a woman you don't trust?'

'With care,' Rio fielded. 'You don't trust me either. Time and better understanding would take care of that.

I'm sure we would both try to make the marriage a success—'

'People try that all the time with marriage and fail.'

'But there is honour in the trying,' Rio declared without hesitation. 'At least we would be doing the best we could to give our child a brighter future.'

'What if there is no child?'

'Then we eventually divorce and blame your long hours as a doctor and my business trips for keeping us apart too much,' Rio told her smoothly. 'Getting married now is a precaution for our potential child's benefit. The right start, the right environment—'

Ellie held up a hand to silence him. 'Yes, I get it but living with you would be a little like living on the side of a volcano waiting on the next eruption. You're very volatile—'

'And you're *not*?' Rio tossed back, watching her closely as her fine-boned hand closed round her orange juice to raise it to her peach-coloured mouth. 'If I had you in my bed every night I would be a lot less volatile—'

Ellie almost choked on her drink and, spluttering, set it down, her face flushing.

Rio shrugged and dealt her an amused look. 'Well, it's true. Having Beppe warn me off you doesn't improve my mood and makes it almost impossible for me to be with you.'

'We don't even have a relationship—'

'Then what *do* we have? You're splitting hairs, being too cautious. Take a risk on me,' Rio invited.

And she so *wanted* to do that, Ellie realised in astonishment. She had never done a reckless thing in her life but Rio tempted her to the edge of foolishness. What if she *was* pregnant? It would upset Beppe and mess up his relationship with Rio. It would be virtually impossible for her to manage to work and care properly for a child without a partner and a settled home. But to make that decision now when she had no idea whether or not she had conceived? She glanced up at him, at the strong face that sent her heart racing and turned her resolve to mush. Was it wise to give into that side of herself? Or would she live to regret it?

'Ellie…' Rio prodded impatiently.

'I don't rush major decisions!' Ellie responded.

Rio shot her a wicked smile. 'We could go to bed and think about it—'

'Another version of angry sex?'

'But you're not angry with me right now. You're attempting to work me out,' Rio surmised, uncoiling with fluid grace from the pillar he had been lounging back up against. 'But I'm really quite basic. If I didn't want you I wouldn't be suggesting this.'

The silence smouldered with unspoken undertones. In the interim, Rio's housekeeper reappeared with a tray. A plate of delicate and ridiculously enticing little sandwiches and a pot of tea were set down in front of Ellie.

'Think of how simple all this could be…if we do it my way,' Rio urged silkily. 'We say we're in love. We marry in haste. Beppe tries to dissuade us but is secretly delighted… And a baby, if there is one…would be the icing on the cake for him.'

Ellie snatched up another sandwich, registering that listening to Rio weave his arguments with such panache and conviction improved her appetite. He had drawn an attractive picture. If she didn't marry him and then discovered she was pregnant, how much damage would she do to her new relationship with Beppe? And could she really stand by while Rio took the blame when she knew she was just as much to blame? In addition, if she was pregnant, she would definitely be seriously considering Rio's marriage proposal because no one knew better than Ellie that raising a child alone was hard. In the course of her work she had met a lot of exhausted single parents struggling to keep work and family afloat. Her grandmother had struggled with that burden, as well, and both Polly and Ellie had been made thoroughly aware of that fact.

'I'm thinking about it,' she told Rio, who was emanating a wave of silent impatience. 'I won't give up work, you know. I'll never be a trophy wife. I don't like shopping or fussing with my appearance either,' she warned him.

'I'll shop for you,' Rio countered smoothly.

'Stop being so reasonable!' Ellie exclaimed in frustration. 'I'm not used to it—'

Rio stole the last sandwich and grinned at her. 'Stop being so sensible and so negative in your outlook.'

Ellie breathed in slow and deep. 'All right… I'll do it. I'll marry you. Are you happy now?'

Rio treated her to an approving appraisal. '*Finally*. We'll go and tell Beppe straight away and I'll get my staff on to organising the wedding—'

'I have to phone my sister first…and I want to do it in private,' Ellie told him squarely, sounding a great deal more sure of herself than she actually felt.

'And then we go and buy a ring,' Rio informed her. 'We'll go the traditional route—'

'Will we?' Ellie looked at him uncertainly, for she

certainly hadn't expected to be offered what she assumed to be the equivalent of an engagement ring.

Was the ring to impress Beppe with the reality of them as a couple? Or was it supposed to please her? And what was she going to say to Beppe? And how was she going to explain to Polly that she was suddenly rushing into marriage with a guy she had said she loathed?

# CHAPTER SEVEN

'I JUST NEVER thought I'd see the day,' Polly carolled with a misty smile as she stepped back to scrutinise Ellie's appearance. 'You're getting married. I thought you were all set to be a spinster with a string of important letters after your name and a cat.'

Ellie had thought that too but she didn't admit it. She had never compromised on what she wanted from a man until Rio had literally crashed into her life at Polly's wedding. And that encounter had altered her image of herself and softened her rigid views. She had gradually begun to appreciate that she was lonely and that there was something hollow about achievements and more painful about trials when she had nobody to share those experiences with. Only now she was putting herself out there in a way she never had before, taking a risk on getting attached to a male who against all the odds appealed to her more than any other for no sane reason that she could find.

For Rio, she had lied for the first time in her life. She had told her father that she loved Rio but in actuality she had no idea what she felt for him. At first she had thought it was a mad infatuation but her thirst for information about him and her craving when he was absent had not faded. Surely an infatuation would have long since died from lack of fuel? All she really knew for certain was that Rio absolutely fascinated her, drew her and compelled her. And he made her feel more with him than she had felt in a lifetime of sensibly repressing strong emotions that unsettled her. And Rio had always specialised in seriously unsettling her.

She had been impressed even more when Rio had accurately forecast her father's every reaction to their marital plans and the stages of it. Beppe had initially been taken aback and had urged her not to rush into anything, but then Beppe had also confided that had he been free when he had met Ellie's mother he would have rushed to marry her. He had also admitted that he thoroughly understood the powerful life-enhancing effect of falling madly in love. And ultimately he had decided that as far as family growth went he could wish for no more than to see his daughter married to a young man he had always valued.

'Rio will grow with you by his side,' Beppe had forecast loftily. 'You make him think, you make him question what he truly wants from life. And what he has always wanted most of all is a family.'

Ellie gazed into the mirror and wondered if she was pregnant, if she could give Rio what he supposedly most wanted. But *was* that what Rio most wanted? Cavorting with all those women seemed a funny way of going about attaining a stable family life. Tomorrow morning, however, she would carry out the pregnancy test she had already purchased. She was both excited and scared by the idea. But most of all she was wondering how Rio would feel, regardless of what the result was.

She had naively assumed that she would see a great

deal more of Rio once their relationship was out in the open, but Rio had flown out to Dharia to settle some complicated dispute about oil well rights and although he had urged her to accompany him and she would've loved to see her sister sooner, she had refused. Why? Girly though it was, she had wanted to work with the wedding planner Beppe had hired and make her individual choices while also being available to ensure her gown fitted perfectly. After all, she was only planning to marry once.

And her dress fitted like a dream. The corset top had been chosen with Rio in mind. She just knew Rio would revel in hooks and laces and cleavage. The long skirt skimmed down in a flattering cut over her curvy hips and fanned out below the knee. Her feet were shod in Polly's gift, a pair of enchanting high-heeled sandals studded with pearls.

'Rashad really likes Rio and the men will be able to go off together when you visit and give us peace to gossip,' Polly remarked happily.

Ellie hid a smile because Polly was sometimes so innocent. The very last thing Ellie could imagine wanting just then was to be deprived of Rio's company. After all, he had been more absent than present since the wedding fervour kicked off. Beppe had held a series of social evenings to introduce his long-lost daughter to friends and relatives. Rio had dutifully attended those evenings before he flew out to Dharia, but Ellie's need to respect Beppe's boundaries had ensured that the bridal couple had little time alone together. Predictably, Rio had been much less accepting about the simple reality that she did not feel free to leave the *palazzo* to spend the night with him and possibly Ellie's insistence on restraint had kept him from hurrying back to Tuscany.

'When you have me wondering if we could contrive to have sex in my car without being picked up on a charge of public indecency, we have a problem, *principessa*,' Rio had complained the night before when he had joined them with Polly and Rashad for a quiet prewedding dinner. 'You need to learn to be more selfish and put us first.'

'No,' she had said. 'You need to learn that anticipation can act as an aphrodisiac.'

'But I don't need one of those,' Rio had responded with sardonic bite.

An abstracted smile tilted Ellie's lips now.

'You're nuts about him. I don't know how I didn't spot it at my wedding—'

'Your attention was elsewhere...on your bridegroom? And I'm not what you call "nuts" about him—'

'Oh, you so *are*,' Polly contradicted. 'Everything you've done just screams it, Ellie. You are not the sort of woman who meets a man and marries him within a couple of weeks unless he rocks your world...'

'People change,' Ellie argued and, eager to change the subject, added, 'isn't it really sad that we still haven't managed to find our missing sister? She could have been with us here today...'

Tracking down Lucy had so far proved difficult because she lived a travelling life, moving around a lot and surviving on casual jobs.

'We'll find her eventually,' Polly said soothingly. 'And it'll be very exciting when we do. Haven't you been tempted to look in her envelope and see what ring she was left and what name is attached to it? It could possibly help us to locate her.'

'No, I was trusted with that envelope and I wouldn't open it,' Ellie swore. 'How would you ever explain that to her when we finally met?'

'We could use steam to open it,' Polly suggested, colouring lightly at Ellie's raised brows.

'No, we should respect her privacy,' Ellie decreed.

Ellie descended the stairs smiling at her father, who stood at the foot beaming with pride. Beppe could not compliment her on her appearance enough. They travelled to the church in a limousine. She paused on the steps in the morning sunshine and she breathed in deep and slow, recognising that the elation she was feeling was happiness and marvelling at it while also fearing the undeniable storms ahead. She knew that she and Rio would argue and tussle and that there would be many times when she wanted to strangle him. That was normal life, she told herself prosaically, but true happiness was so rare a sensation for her that she wanted to make the most of it while she was feeling it.

Rio turned from the altar to get the full effect of his bride. And Ellie was stunning with her coppery hair swept up and her green eyes gleaming with intelligence above her sultry mouth. As for the dress, well, he was extremely impressed by that surprisingly sexy corset, which defined his bride's splendid curves to perfection. No, getting married didn't feel half as bad as he had dimly expected. He had thought he might feel trapped but the prospect of peeling Ellie out of that corset was more than equal to the challenge of surrendering his freedom.

Her hand trembled in his when he grasped it to

thread on the wedding ring. She had worn her engagement ring on her other hand. And like Beppe's family emerald, which she had brought out to Italy with her, it was another emerald to reflect the colour of her eyes, an emerald teamed with white diamonds but not over large because Ellie didn't like flashy jewellery and had wanted something she could occasionally wear to work. So sensible, his Ellie, Rio thought wryly, wondering just when he had started thinking of her as *his*. When he'd imagined her pregnant with his child and liked the idea? When he saw her walking down the aisle towards him? Or when he realised that he was her first lover and strangely determined to be her *last*?

Of course, he knew why he was marrying her. With Ellie, the sex was on another level even though it had gone wrong the one and only time it had happened. She stood up to him, she talked back, she was his equal in every way. But more importantly she had signed a pre-nup contract ringed with so many iron hoops of protection that an escape artist couldn't have undermined it. If Ellie liked money, he had plenty of it and there were worse weaknesses for a woman to have, he reasoned. She could have been the unfaithful type, forever in search of the next big thrill. She could've been the uncaring, uncommitted type but he'd already seen her bonding happily with Beppe and witnessed just how close she was to her sister. And if there was to be a baby Rio was convinced that she would always and without hesitation do right by their child. The ability and the desire to be a good mother was the most imperative trait of all that a woman could have, he reflected with sombre conviction.

Ellie emerged from the church on Rio's arm. A crowd

of people were crushed into the street outside. Fleeting introductions were made while the photographer fluttered around. They were congratulated and showered with rice.

In the midst of the noise and excitement, Ellie suddenly noticed two blondes wielding their camera phones and giggling like drains as they urged Rio to look at them and smile. And it was *them*, unmistakably the identical twins who had gambolled naked on Rio's bed in that Dharian hotel two years earlier. Ellie's throat convulsed. She couldn't have been mistaken, she thought angrily. They were highly noticeable women, blonde, beautiful twins, whippet thin and impossibly sparkly and effervescent in a way that was seen as ultrafeminine. Rio had actually *invited* the twins to their wedding. Ellie paled and compressed bloodless lips while the perplexed photographer urged her to smile.

She settled almost dizzily into the limousine beside Rio and looked at him. How could he do this to her? How could he be so insensitive to her feelings? Those blondes reminded her of the most humiliating moment of her life. Before Rio had opened the door to that hotel room she had been on a high, feeling like a sexy, attractive woman for the first time ever and ready to move forward, no longer feeling like the drab, clever redhead whom few men approached. And her first glimpse of the giggly twins on his bed had cut her like a knife, making her feel ridiculous and pathetic and useless.

'*Cosa c'e di sbagliato?* What's wrong?' Rio asked as the car moved off to whisk them back to the *palazzo* where the reception was being held.

And Ellie didn't know what to say. After all, he was

entitled to a sexual past and in marrying him she had accepted that past. Exes at a wedding, well, not exactly what you wanted but not always avoidable either. But did the twins recognise her as the shocked woman in that doorway two years back? And would they mention that to anyone? Have a good giggle about it? She cringed inside herself and said nothing.

'Nothing's wrong,' she assured him quietly. 'It's just all the wedding hullabaloo. When it comes all together, it leaves you feeling shell-shocked.'

'I didn't invite Becky and Roz,' Rio breathed impatiently, cutting through her pretence.

So, he had noticed the twins. Well, really, how could he have missed them bouncing up and down with excitement only a few feet from him, determined to be noticed by him? Yet he had somehow contrived not to look once in their direction, nor had he shown the smallest hint of self-consciousness. But then why would he?

'Is that their names?' Ellie queried with a wooden lack of expression.

'I told the wedding planner to contact Rashad for the list of our university friends because I haven't kept up with their addresses,' Rio explained. 'They were invited to your sister's wedding and that's probably how they ended up at ours. If I'd taken a greater personal interest, I would've left them off the list.'

If anything, Ellie had grown even stiffer. 'Of course, if they're uni friends, why would you leave them out?'

'Ellie, you're putting out more sub-zero chills than a freezer,' Rio said with sardonic bite. 'But I can't change the past and neither can you.'

'I didn't realise the twins had ever been actual friends of yours,' Ellie admitted stonily, not best pleased to hear that information. 'Probably because I've never slept with any of my male friends.'

'Sadly, I wasn't quite so particular,' Rio countered in the same measured tone. 'And neither were they. In those days I could only cope with casual—'

Her smooth brow indented. 'And why was that?'

Rio squared his broad shoulders and settled back with a sigh. 'I set up a property venture when I was nineteen. Beppe was pressuring me to go to university to study business but I thought I could take a shortcut to success,' he admitted wryly. 'My business partner, Jax, had the security of a wealthy background. The property market was booming and we were doing very well, which is when I met a gorgeous brunette. I fell in love with Franca, asked her to marry me and we moved in together.'

Ellie dragged in a startled breath, for what he had just admitted was the very last thing she had expected to hear from him. After all, she had simply assumed that Rio had *always* played the field without ever pausing to settle on one particular woman. Learning different shook her up, learning that he had found that one particular woman years earlier and presumably lost her again filled her with insecurity.

Rio skimmed narrowed dark eyes over the pale, still triangle of her face and his shapely mouth twisted. 'The property market stalled and I was overstretched. I still believe I could have made it through but Jax pulled out and hung me out to dry…and Franca, who had been screwing him behind my back and who very much liked the luxuries of life, ran off with him.'

Ellie winced and dropped her gaze, imagining the sting of that double blow of financial loss and treachery. 'I'm really sorry that that happened to you,' she murmured ruefully. 'It must've been very hard to pick yourself up after that experience.'

'It taught me a valuable lesson. At university I learned enough to ensure that I would never leave myself that vulnerable in business again,' he confided. 'I succeeded but after Franca, I avoided any kind of serious involvement with women. What the twins offered suited me at the time. No strings.'

'I can understand that,' she conceded reluctantly. 'You know…er…that night at Polly's wedding, after we parted…I've always wondered what happened—'

'You don't want to know,' Rio cut in succinctly, his tone cold as ice water.

And in telling her that he had told her everything there *was* to know, she acknowledged in consternation, just as suddenly furious with him. She had rejected him that night and had raced back to her room at the palace to take refuge in time-honoured tears and self-recriminations. But Rio had taken solace where he could find it and what right had she to object? Finding that out annoyed and disturbed her though. Rio could divide sex from emotion and treat sex like an athletic pursuit and he had done so for years before he met her. Could Rio really change? Could he switch back to the young, optimistic male he must once have been when he fell in love with Franca? And what exactly did it take to make Rio fall in love?

Rio was watching Ellie as the limo drove through the *palazzo* gates. Her delicate little profile was set, her brain running at a mile a minute on thoughts he didn't want to share. Maybe he should have lied. But lies would catch up with him sooner or later. Did she realise that she really wanted him to be perfect? Prince Charming straight out of a fairy story? And that he could never be perfect? Frustration and growing anger raged through his lean, powerful frame. He could not pretend to be something he was not in an attempt to impress her. And why would he want to anyway? Ellie would smell a rat sooner than most women because she was always looking below the surface, weighing pros and cons, picking up on inconsistencies, seeking out flaws. And he had still to confess his biggest flaw of all to a woman who had chattered animatedly about how her discovery of Beppe would now enable her to chart the previously unknown paternal half of her medical history.

In the greeting line, Becky and Roz made much of Rio and their previous acquaintance while acting as if they had never laid eyes on Ellie before. They didn't recognise her, she registered with relief, didn't remember her at all from that fleeting glimpse of her in the hotel doorway that night. But instead of being relieved at that realisation, Ellie was angry with Rio and angry with herself. She had agonised so much over that night and she had been so hurt but their backfired encounter had not had a similar effect on Rio's tough hide. She needed to guard herself from being too emotional and vulnerable around him. She had to toughen up, she told herself urgently.

Polly whisked her off after the meal. 'What on earth's wrong between you and Rio?' she demanded.

'There's nothing wrong—'

'Even Rashad's noticed the atmosphere and to be honest he's not usually that quick to notice that sort of stuff,' her sister admitted.

And Ellie spilled the whole story from its start two years earlier to the presence of the twins at the wedding. She was too upset to hold it all in any longer and Polly's shocked face spoke for her. It was several minutes before she could even move her sister on from repeatedly saying '*Both* of them?' as if she had never heard or dreamt of such behaviour before. Her attitude did nothing to improve Ellie's mood.

'And that night you met…?' Polly pressed. 'He told you that?'

'Yes, Polly,' Ellie confirmed wearily. 'I've married an unashamed man whore.'

'If Rashad had ever done anything like that, nothing would persuade him to admit it to me,' Polly declared wryly. 'But at least Rio is honest, well, brutally so.'

'I think he was just thoroughly fed up with me asking awkward questions.'

'I suspect he's already heard more than enough about that night and you shot him down in flames, which is not the sort of treatment he's used to receiving from women,' Polly pointed out grudgingly in Rio's defence. 'Let it go, Ellie. It's in the past and you weren't dating him or anything, so you can't fairly hold it against him. He didn't cheat on you. As for those blondes, ignore them, forget they're here!'

Ellie knew that was sensible advice but something stubborn in her refused to back down. Hard reality was steadily taking the bloom off her wedding day.

Rio tugged her stiff, resisting body close as he swept her out onto the floor to open the dancing. He bent his arrogant dark head and whispered, 'Do you know just how annoyed I'm getting with you?'

'Do you know how annoyed I am with you?' Ellie whispered back, unimpressed.

'Are you always going to be this jealous and possessive of me?' Rio enquired silkily.

A current of rage travelled through Ellie as hotly as a flame. 'Are you? I seem to remember you threatening to beat up Bruno for buying me dinner—'

'That was different,' Rio asserted without hesitation. 'We were already involved.'

Angry tears prickled behind Ellie's lowered eyelids and she finally knew what was really wrong with her. She had got involved with Rio on an emotional level the very first night she met him. But he hadn't got involved with her until she entered Beppe's life and became what he initially saw as a threat to someone he cared about. Was he even involved with her now that he had married her? Or had he only married her to please Beppe and because she might be pregnant? And why was she only asking herself that now and worrying about the answer?

Rio caught her hand firmly in his as they left the floor, deftly weaving them through the clusters of guests addressing them, never pausing longer than a few polite seconds. Only when they reached the foot of the main staircase did Ellie question where he was taking her and she tried to wrench her hand free.

'We're going to sort this out in private,' Rio delivered in a driven undertone.

'There's nothing to be sorted out,' Ellie protested, trying once again and failing to free her fingers from his.

Determined not to be sidetracked, Rio headed for the opulent guest suite where Ellie had dressed for the wedding. He thrust the door shut behind him in a movement that sent dismay skimming through Ellie. She had not expected Rio to turn confrontational because she had assumed that the presence of their guests would control and inhibit him. The message she was getting now was that Rio's temper was rarely repressed.

He dropped her hand and Ellie immediately made for the door. 'We can't do this in the middle of our wedding,' she argued.

Rio cut off her escape by stepping in front of the door, which in turn sent Ellie stalking and rustling angrily in all her finery across the room towards the window. She flipped round, colour accentuating her cheekbones, green eyes very bright and defiant.

'It's our wedding and it's almost over and we can do whatever we like,' he told her grittily.

'Do you have an off button?' Ellie asked helplessly. 'Because I think it's time to hit it. Yes, this is our wedding and we have had a slight difference of opinion but I have done and said nothing anyone could criticise—'

*'I'm criticising you!'* Rio bit out harshly.

Ellie stared at him in shock, her lips falling open, because once again, Rio was blindsiding her and catching her unprepared. He had the most amazing eyes, stunning dark gold fringed with black curling lashes, and for a split second she was held fast by them while noting the aggressive angle of his strong jaw line, the faint black stubble already shadowing his bronzed skin and, finally, the ferocious determination stamped into his amazing bone structure.

'I'm not perfect, Ellie, and I'm never going to be but I was prepared to give this my best shot—'

'I never expected you to be perfect, for goodness' sake!' Ellie spluttered uncertainly as she moved warily back towards him. 'Look, maybe I was a bit oversensitive but there's absolutely no need for us to start having this out now! Let me go back downstairs before anyone notices we're missing—'

'No,' Rio breathed with finality.

'You don't just tell me no like that and expect me to take it!' Ellie argued furiously, trying to push him away from the door.

'I keep on hoping that you'll learn from experience,' Rio growled, scooping her up, nudging a giant vase of flowers out of his path and planting her down squarely on the marble-topped side table behind her. 'But you never do.'

'This is getting ridiculous. Let me down,' Ellie told him forcefully.

Rio pinned her in place even more effectively by pushing her knees apart and stepping between them to wedge himself even closer.

'You may be physically stronger but you can't bully me,' Ellie informed him tartly.

'I don't want to bully you, *principessa*. I want you to start using your brain,' Rio bit out impatiently, settling his big hands down on her bare shoulders. 'It's time to put sulky, moody Ellie away, ditch the negativity and look forward.'

'I am neither sulky nor moody,' Ellie pronounced with as much dignity as she could summon while seated as she was on a table, being held still. His hands were hot on her bare skin, sending odd little prickles of awareness travelling through her.

'Bear in mind the fact that I'm not sulking about having had to marry a woman who *could* be a scheming little gold-digger,' Rio urged, stunning her with that statement as his long fingers flexed expressively over her shoulders.

Her lips opened. 'A…a *gold—*'

'But I gave *you* the benefit of the doubt. When do you extend the same privilege to me?' he demanded grimly.

Ellie tried to slide off the table but he forestalled her. Flushed by the undignified struggle and enraged by the label of gold-digger, she snapped, 'Let me go!'

'No. I'm keeping you right where I can see you and we're having this out right now,' Rio decreed.

'How *dare* you call me a gold-digger?' Ellie slung at him an octave higher.

'What else am I going to call you when you still haven't explained yourself? You see, I may not be perfect, Ellie but the news is that *you're* not perfect either. You've had serious allegations made against you and although I'm now aware that an enquiry dismissed one set, there are still others in your background made by a family member,' Rio reminded her caustically. 'But I was prepared to overlook that history to marry you and give you a fair chance.'

Ellie had frozen where she sat and she didn't know what to say or even where to begin. 'You said you'd *had* to marry me,' she said, instead of tackling his accusations head-on. 'But you didn't have to. I didn't demand it. I wouldn't have allowed my father to demand it either. It wasn't necessary—'

'It was necessary to me,' Rio cut in ruthlessly. 'I could not live with the chance that you could be pregnant. I had to ensure that we were a couple and that if there is a child, he or she will not grow up without me.'

'So, this really is a shotgun marriage,' Ellie breathed painfully.

'No, it's what we make of it and so far you're doing your best to undermine us,' Rio condemned.

'You know the enquiry cleared my name,' Ellie reminded him sharply. 'How can you still think I could be a gold-digger?'

'It's all those shades of grey that lie between black and white,' Rio commented reflectively. 'What was your true intent when you befriended that old lady at the hospice where you were working?'

'I didn't befriend her. I was doing my job, acting as a sympathetic listener when there was nobody else available!' Ellie told him angrily.

'Maybe you would've got away with that inheritance had a complaint not been lodged against you and maybe you thought you could get away with it. Maybe you only looked up your father after you found out that he was a reasonably affluent man,' Rio murmured lethally. 'Who can tell? That's what I mean about shades of grey. How can I know either way? But I still took a chance on you—'

Ellie relived the stress and worry she had endured when quite out of the blue, one of the patients she had been tending had altered her will and left her estate to Ellie instead. It had been wholly unexpected and she had not felt in any way that she deserved that bequest. She had reported it immediately but naturally the old lady's nephew had lodged a complaint. It had been a nasty business and there had been nothing she could have done to avoid the ordeal. Rage and distress over Rio's suggestions roared through her taut body. 'I hate you!' she gasped chokily.

'No, you don't. You just don't like being questioned

and judged without a fair trial but it's exactly what you do to me,' Rio condemned levelly.

'I don't want to be married to you!' Ellie slung at him wildly.

'You don't mean that,' Rio assured her, the hands on her shoulders smoothing her delicate skin as he bent his head. 'You want me as much as I want you.'

'Stop telling me what I want, what I think!' Ellie exclaimed in seething frustration.

'Maybe I'm talking too much… Maybe I should be *showing* you,' Rio husked, tipping her back a little and burying his mouth hotly in the smooth slope of her neck while his hands delved beneath her skirt and swept up over her thighs.

*'Stop it!'* Ellie hissed, struggling against the great wave of quivering weakness that assailed her as the heat of his lips and the teasing nip of his teeth grazed her sensitised flesh. 'You're not allowed to do this when we're fighting!'

In answer, Rio crushed her angrily parted lips beneath his own, his tongue flicking the roof of her mouth and tangling with her own. The forbidden pulse at the heart of her pounded faster and hotter while honeyed liquidity pooled in her pelvis. His hands firm on her thighs, she squirmed on the table.

'Rio!' she cried in frustration.

He ripped the delicate panties out of his path and traced the damp wet folds between her parted thighs, and so much excitement surged up inside Ellie that she feared she might go up in flames. He had distracted her, she knew he had distracted her with sex and she knew she had to defend herself but in that instant nothing was more important to Ellie than the fierce, urgent demands of her own body.

'We *can't…*' she moaned for her own benefit as much as his.

Rio sank his hands below her hips and lifted her to him as though she were a doll. He sank into her hard and fast and the sudden fullness of him boldly stretching her made her shudder and gasp. And then he moved with brutal efficiency, hitting some magical spot inside her that knew no shame and the treacherous excitement came in a drowning, remorseless flood that overwhelmed her. Her teeth dug into the shoulder of his jacket, her hands clawed any part of him she could reach. The pleasure was unbearable, pushing her relentlessly to the edge. Her body careened into a teeth-clenching climax that left her bereft of breath and he freed her as the final convulsions trammelled through her weakened body.

He disappeared off to the bathroom leaving her sagging on the table. He had taken precautions this time around, she registered in surprise. So, he was no longer willing to take that risk of conception with her, even though they were now married. Did Rio *still* want an escape route? Was he hoping she wasn't pregnant? That he could still walk away?

And why wouldn't he when he was convinced that she was a shameless gold-digger? Anger sizzled through Ellie. She had lost another battle with Rio. She slid, almost limp with satiation, off the table and retrieved one of her shoes, which had fallen off. Her torn underwear was nowhere to be seen and she had no spare clothing in the room since her suitcase had already been removed. With a grimace she smoothed down her dress and staggered slightly on cotton-wool legs in front of a mirror to check her hair.

'You look fantastic, *principessa*,' Rio said huskily, lazily, catching her hand in his. 'And you're my wife now—'

'Not sure I want reminding of that right now—'

'I *like* reminding you,' Rio murmured, studying her with hungry dark golden eyes. 'Smile, Ellie—'

'No, Rio—'

'Smile,' Rio insisted. 'It's our wedding day and we should be making the most of it—'

'Oh, I think you've already done that,' Ellie told him before she could think better of that comment.

And Rio laughed with unholy amusement. 'You're mine. I needed the proof of it.'

All shaken up and fizzing with conflicting feelings and emotions, Ellie returned to the wedding festivities. Rio kept a hold of her, not letting her stray far from his side. Her body still felt hot and alien, the aftershock of forbidden pleasure and excitement still trapped inside her like a shameful secret. There was wanting and then there was wanting Rio, and he had just taught her that she was the one without the off switch when she needed it. That knowledge made her feel achingly vulnerable.

# CHAPTER EIGHT

RIO SCOOPED HER out of the helicopter with precision. The flight had taken less than an hour.

'Why won't you tell me where we're going?' Ellie demanded.

'In a few minutes you'll know exactly where we are—'

'I wouldn't bet on that. I haven't travelled much,' Ellie admitted as he walked her a few steps down a quay and assisted her into a motorboat.

But as he had forecast, Ellie recognised where she was even though it was a place she had only previously seen in pictures. The view of Venice as the boat sped across the lagoon was breathtakingly beautiful. 'It's just like the paintings Beppe showed me,' she whispered, entranced.

On the Grand Canal, the boat slowed amidst the busy water traffic and nosed in at a smartly decorated landing stage. Climbing out, she accompanied Rio into a magnificent foyer ornamented with huge Venetian glass chandeliers. 'Welcome to the Hotel Palazzo Sorrentino,' Rio murmured. 'The jewel in the crown of my hotel chain.'

'Sorrentino?' she queried in surprise.

'Yes, it once belonged to your family but it was last used as a home by your great-grandfather and even he only lived in a tiny corner of it. Beppe was quoted millions for the repairs that were needed and he sold it to me,' Rio explained. 'It was being used as a warehouse by then because it wasn't fit for habitation. Converting it into an exclusive hotel took years but it was a worthwhile investment. Now it's fully booked years in advance.'

Recognising that almost every eye in the reception area was on them, Ellie went pink, suddenly conscious of her wedding finery. A little man in a smart suit approached to welcome them and handed her a beautiful bouquet with the compliments of the staff. Rio accepted a key from him and guided her across the foyer and down a corridor.

'We're staying here?' she asked.

'Not in the hotel. The *palazzo* came with a couple of attached buildings and I retained one of them for personal use. Beppe uses it regularly. He loves Venice, particularly in the winter when it's quiet,' Rio told her, leading her outside and along a wisteria-clad walled alley to a narrow door flanked by Venetian gothic windows. 'It's very private here and the staff service it so we don't have to worry about housekeeping or cooking.'

Ellie walked into a charming wood-panelled reception room that overlooked a tiny lush green garden at the rear. Beyond the garden, a gondola sailed past on a narrow waterway. It was a magical scene.

Rio removed the bouquet from her hold. 'I'll stick the flowers in the sink.'

Ellie knew she should go with him and deal with

the flowers but the diverse traffic flowing past on the canal commanded her attention and she stayed where she was.

'I'll show you round now,' Rio said lightly, and in a great gilded antique mirror she caught a glimpse of her answering smile that softened her face, and looked away again, dismayed that she could look happy in the company of a man who had implied that she could be a gold-digger.

'I need to tell you about Violet… The lady in the hospice, who changed her will in my favour,' she said tightly.

'Not now, we've had enough stress. Leave it until later,' Rio urged as he opened the door on a dining room where food already awaited them on the table, fearful that any sudden revelations from Ellie would set them at odds again on a night that he very much wanted to be special and all about 'them.' 'We should eat first. You didn't have much earlier.'

'I wasn't hungry,' she admitted as he pulled out a chair for her. 'I didn't think you'd notice—'

'I notice everything about you,' Rio incised drily.

'If that was true, you'd know I'd never have sought out Beppe simply because he was well off,' Ellie contended uncomfortably. 'It didn't matter who or what he was. I just wanted to fill in the blank I've lived with all my life and know what happened between my parents. You couldn't possibly understand how much it means to me to know who my father is and to actually feel a sense of connection with him. It's so much more than I ever hoped to have.'

'I understand a lot more than you appreciate,' Rio countered, his lean dark face setting into grim lines. 'I will never know who my father is and, frankly, I don't *want* to know. I met my mother as an adult and that killed off any sentimental delusions I might have had. My mother and I didn't have a single thought or feeling in common.'

Ellie studied him in shock at that revelation.

'You were very lucky to find a man like Beppe waiting at the end of your identity trail,' Rio remarked wryly.

He had met his mother and it hadn't worked out? But he had grown up in an orphanage. Where had his mother been when he was a child? And why didn't he know who had fathered him? Consternation gripped Ellie and she veiled her eyes. Rio managed to be incredibly sanguine about realities that would have seriously disturbed her and it made her all the more aware of how very little she knew about him and how unwittingly tactless she must have been while she was happily rambling on about what finding Beppe had meant to her. Of course, what had she ever personally shared with Rio? Discomfiture filled her. As a rule, Ellie was reserved and she kept her secrets close. She didn't share personal stuff except with Polly but that had to change now that she was married. Didn't it? It wouldn't be fair to expect more from Rio than she was prepared to give herself.

'Yes, I was incredibly fortunate,' Ellie agreed ruefully as she took another appreciative bite of her delicious pasta salad. 'Can I ask you about something?'

'Anything…'

'Earlier when we were together, you…you used a condom,' Ellie reminded him.

'Isn't that what you wanted?' Rio responded, his

ebony brows drawing together in a frown. 'If you are pregnant, we'll make the best of it but if you're not, well…it gives us more options.'

'You mean, we wouldn't have to stay together,' Ellie framed, her heart suddenly beating with a dulled thunderous thud against her breastbone.

Rio lounged back in his chair with his wine glass and settled frowning dark golden eyes on her. 'Don't put words in my mouth. I said options and I *meant* options. I believe that babies should be planned and greeted with joy on their arrival.'

Ellie nodded woodenly, thinking about the pregnancy test waiting in her case. 'I agree. The circumstances weren't ideal.'

'Ideal isn't everything, *principessa*.' A slow-burning, wicked smile slanted Rio's beautiful mouth. 'But I did notice that day at my house that the idea of getting pregnant turned you as white as a sheet. It's not a risk I'll run with you unless you ask me to…'

And how likely was that? Yet that unexpected offer soothed her in some strange way. He wasn't slamming the door in her face. He had not said that if she wasn't pregnant they would eventually separate and divorce. His outlook wasn't that simple or that final. So why was she relieved? What had she feared? She searched his lean, darkly handsome features, her mouth running dry as she struggled to look beyond the sleek dark beauty of him into her appalled reaction to the threat of being parted from him. Polly had seen what she had hidden even from herself: she had got attached, dangerously attached to Rio Benedetti. Recognising that reality hollowed her out with fear. She was afraid of getting hurt and very reluctant to want more from Rio than he was likely to give.

She went upstairs to explore and discovered a dreamy spacious bedroom swathed in opulent fabrics and a divine four-poster bed. Their luggage had arrived in advance and had been unpacked for them. Off the bedroom there was a splendid marble bathroom with sumptuous heated towels and very fancy fittings. Champagne and flowers awaited them. She filched a chocolate off the silver dish beside the champagne flutes and bit into it with so much pleasure that she closed her eyes.

'You like chocolate,' Rio said huskily from the doorway.

'Correction—I would *kill* for chocolate,' Ellie admitted with a sudden laugh.

His amusement ebbed as he looked at her, the sheer stunning elegance of her in her gown, stray copper curls showing round her hairline now, the heavier make-up she had worn for the wedding faded, a faint streak of eyeliner at the side of one eye where she had rubbed. And yet she was still so beautiful with her clear green eyes and lush pink mouth. 'I think I would kill for you,' he breathed, stunned and unsettled both by the thought and the feeling.

Unfortunately Rio was being forced to work without a script. He was out of his comfort zone. Hit it and quit it was no blueprint for a marriage or a woman like Ellie. If she was pregnant, she would be with him for a long time, he reminded himself darkly. She would make demands, the sort of demands he had never had to deal with before. She would restrict him. She would also probably and regularly drive him nuts. But on the other hand, every pleasure came with a price tag and she was clever, amusing, passionate and ridiculously sexy.

Ellie plucked the pins from hair and let the thick mass fall to her shoulders. Then she spun round. 'I need your help to get out of this,' she admitted, turning and indicating the lace ties. 'It's beginning to feel very tight.'

Rio removed his jacket and cravat and unbuttoned his shirt. He was thinking about the curves inside that corset, the wondrous curves that bad timing had forced him to neglect that afternoon. Raw hunger roared through him afresh. 'I love corsets,' he confided.

'Thought you would,' Ellie murmured a tad smugly.

He released the ties and the hooks and let the garment drop to the floor while she exhaled in relief that the constriction had gone. He kept his arms round her, dipped his mouth to the smooth slope between her neck and shoulder and dallied there, lifting his head to nip teasingly at her earlobe at the same time as he raised his hands to cup her full breasts.

Ellie rested her head back against him, tiny flames of arousal dancing over her skin as long fingers tugged and teased at her swollen nipples. She was so sensitive there that she pressed her thighs together as if she could contain the rush of damp heat at her core. He backed her down on the bed but she demurred, pausing to unzip her skirt and let it fall, momentarily forgetting that she was bare beneath.

'Memories,' Rio teased with a wicked grin, disposing of his shirt to reveal a corrugated abdomen, hard with lean muscle.

'You work out,' Ellie guessed, studying him closely, faint colour feathering into her cheeks.

'Every day. I'm at a desk too much. Ah…is that a look of approval from Dr Ellie?'

Ellie scrambled onto the bed and beneath the smooth white linen sheet and immediately felt better about hiding her overlarge behind and sturdy thighs. She didn't think there was anything wrong with her body, she simply wished that when she had been blessed with curves she had also been blessed with more height to carry them. Rio undressed, dropping everything in a heap while Ellie watched him like a hawk, thinking that it had never occurred to her to wonder what it would be like to have her own male stripper. He had a really great body. Broad shoulders, lean hips, the inverted V of muscle running down to…*that*! Ellie stared, reddened, no longer marvelling that she had been sore in the aftermath of her introduction to sex. He wasn't small anywhere and, being Rio, he was already primed for action.

'We can do without this,' he told her, yanking the sheet back. 'I plan to make you very hot, *principessa*.'

Ellie rested back on the pillows. 'And I plan to make you equally hot,' she warned him.

Grinning, Rio came down on the bed beside her. 'You've already achieved that…or didn't you notice?'

Ellie stroked the velvet-smooth thrust of him with wondering fingers. 'I noticed—'

'A little less of that,' he censured as she explored him.

'No, you don't get to hand out orders in bed,' Ellie told him.

And Rio laughed with startled appreciation and looked at her, the humour slowly draining from his lean dark face to accentuate the black diamond glitter of his slumberous eyes and the feverish colour lacing his exotic cheekbones. 'Am I being treated to bossy Ellie now?'

'I have more than one setting. I can't have you getting bored,' Ellie murmured intently as her hand spread over his chest. 'My goodness, I'm so pale I must look like a milk bottle beside you—'

Rio rolled over and pinned her half beneath him. 'A very, very sexy, curvy milk bottle—'

'In the mood you're in you'd find anything female sexy,' Ellie protested.

'No, you really don't get it, do you? Growing up, you were probably too busy polishing your brain cells to look in the mirror,' Rio quipped, running a fingertip along the peach-soft curve of her lower lip. 'You have the body of a goddess and a very beautiful face. Did I mention the gorgeous hair…?'

'I hate the hair. I went through school being called "ginger,"' Ellie muttered. 'And "clever clogs."'

'But you still triumphed, *bella mia*. Passed all your exams, married me—'

'Marrying you counts as a triumph?' Ellie gasped.

'See how you feel about me in the morning,' Rio murmured with lashings of sexual assurance.

'That you're tiring me out?' Ellie teased, her fingers dancing over a smooth bronzed shoulder, enjoyment lighting her eyes for such intimacy was very new to her and unexpectedly wonderful to find.

And then he leant down and he kissed her and it was exactly what he had promised, hot and hungry and wildly intoxicating. The heat of his long, lean, powerful frame against hers sent a current of prickling awareness flying across her entire skin surface. The plunge of his tongue electrified her, sending tiny shivers darting through every pleasure receptor. Her breasts tingled and swelled, the tips straining.

His mouth roamed over her, tugging at the sensitive buds, seeking out delicate spots and lingering. He worked his way down her body to explore the most responsive place of all and her hips writhed and her lips parted on tiny cries. She had never felt so much pleasure or such a relentless drive for release. It was as if something deep within her were screaming impatiently for satisfaction. She twisted and turned, drowning in sensation, her body programmed to leap and rise to fever point at his every caress. Slowly she could feel her control being torn away from her but this time it didn't frighten her. She didn't fight, she let go, rejoicing in the strong waves of pleasure convulsing her and thrumming like a euphoric song through every skin cell.

'You're really, really good at that,' Ellie whispered, limp and breathless in the aftermath.

'I'm good at a lot of things,' Rio husked, all sexual promise and dominance as he rose over her, rearranging her singing body to his satisfaction.

And if he was set on proving the fact, he proved it as he plunged into her tender depths with passionate force, reawakening her to arousal. Her heart hammered, her adrenalin kicking in as she arched beneath him, deepening his penetration, and suddenly she was greedy to experience every thrilling sensation. He moved faster, lithe and potent. Her excitement climbed with every compelling thrust. Perspiration dampened her skin, a furnace-like heat rising from the heart of her as the desire for fulfilment clawed at her. And then she was there at the summit and the blinding surge of heart-stopping pleasure seized her body and soul. She jerked and shuddered and cried out, thrown over the boundary between reality and fantasy.

Afterwards, Ellie wrapped her arms tight round Rio, feeling madly affectionate and happy.

'What are you doing?' Rio asked, tensing.

# CHAPTER NINE

'I'M HUGGING YOU,' Ellie said witheringly.

'I don't do hugs.'

'I do a lot of hugging. You'll have to get used to it.' She sighed, blissfully unconcerned by his objection. She loved the hot, damp heaviness of him against her and smoothed her fingers gently down the long line of his spine. 'If I'm pregnant, you'll have a child to hug.'

She felt the charge of tension that stiffened him in her arms.

'That day…you went pale at the prospect too,' she pointed out sleepily, exhaustion weighing heavily on her.

'Of course I did. I haven't a clue how to be a parent,' Rio pointed out feelingly. 'How could I? I never had one—'

'Just like me. You'll learn as you go along,' Ellie told him drowsily, the words slurring slightly.

Rio lifted his tousled dark head. 'You can't go to sleep yet… It's our wedding night.'

But Ellie was already sound asleep. He went for a shower and eventually climbed back into bed.

Ellie wakened while it was still dark and suppressed a sigh. Her sleeping pattern had been disrupted by ever-changing shifts and a regular shortage of sufficient rest while she worked. Knowing that she was unlikely to drift off again, she got up and put on a comfy dress while scrutinising Rio as he lay sprawled in bed. He was taking up more than his share of the space, she noted without surprise. It was as well for him that he could look so good doing it, she acknowledged with tender amusement, noting the black hair curling against the pillow, the angular bone structure shaded in by stubble, the relaxed line of his mouth. Asleep he looked younger than his thirty years.

Dragging her attention from him, she went downstairs and the first thing she noticed in the sink of the elegant little kitchen was the bouquet of flowers, and guilt shot through her. A trawl through the cupboards produced a vase and she settled the blooms into water and put them on display in the sitting room. A search of the fridge revealed bottled water and savoury pastries and she ate standing up, watching the dawn light rise over the building on the other side of the canal and slowly illuminate the little garden.

'What are you thinking about?' Rio asked from behind her.

Ellie turned her head to take in Rio clad only in a pair of ripped blue jeans, his feet bare. 'Violet,' she mused wryly. 'The old lady who died in the hospice. She loved to see the dawn. If I was on duty I'd open the curtains early for her. I was thinking of how much she would have loved Venice but she never got to travel because her husband liked home best and in her day husbands ruled the roost—'

Rio grinned. 'Dare I hope it'll be the same for us?'

'Wouldn't hold my breath on that one,' Ellie advised.

'Why are you out of bed so early?'

'I've always been an early riser,' she confided. 'But then I'm not used to having the freedom to sleep in. If I wasn't working the past few years, I was studying for exams. The pressure is constant.'

Rio groaned out loud. 'Tell me about Violet while I order breakfast.'

'She was lonely. She'd outlived everyone who mattered to her,' Ellie told him. 'She had no visitors. Her nephew came once when she first entered the facility but he didn't come back. Some relatives can't handle the last stages of a terminal illness. You can't judge them for it. We're supposed to stay detached…and I never thought I'd have a problem with that.'

'Sometimes you get involved whether you want to or not.'

Ellie squared her slight shoulders. 'When I had a few minutes free I kept Violet company. That was all. She reminisced about her past and I would listen and it made her happy. Once she was asleep I would tiptoe out again. I knew nothing about her changing her will until her solicitor contacted me after her death,' she admitted. 'I couldn't have accepted anything from her anyway because it's against the rules of the trust that employed me for medical staff to make a financial gain from patients. Even though I'd turned it down, the nephew made an official complaint against me and the whole business dragged on for months before it got to the enquiry stage and I was officially cleared. Why would I have wanted her money anyway?'

'What do you mean?'

'Rashad and Polly insisted on paying off my student loans but they also tried to persuade me to accept a large lump sum off them to buy a property. It was very generous of them but I turned it down because, while I can deal with the extravagant gifts they insist on giving me, I don't want to be the family charity case,' Ellie admitted ruefully. 'Polly buys all my clothes as it is, but she's married to Rashad and I'm not. That's *her* life, not mine.'

'And now you've got a life with me,' Rio murmured, tugging her backwards into the circle of his arms.

'I'm not sure how much of a life I can have with a man who thinks I'm after his money.' Ellie sighed just as a loud knock sounded on the front door.

Without responding to that leading comment, Rio went to answer it.

It was a waiter with a covered trolley and at Ellie's instigation it was wheeled out to the small patio, which was now bathed in early morning sunshine. The screening shrubs in the garden gave it all the charm of a forest glade.

Ellie poured the coffee. 'So now you know about Violet. It was a storm in a teacup but it had long-lasting repercussions. Mud sticks. People I trusted made nasty comments. I was worried it would damage my career and I got very stressed.'

'Naturally,' Rio conceded, wondering why it hadn't occurred to him that, had she been mercenary, Ellie could have chosen to rely on her seriously rich brother-in-law for financial support. Rashad was very generous and very family-orientated. Had she so desired, Ellie could have given up work and lived the life of a rich socialite. Why had that very obvious fact never crossed his mind at any stage? Had he preferred to think of Ellie as a gold-digger? And if so, why was that?

'That's why this break in Italy was so important to me. I needed a holiday—'

'And instead you got me—'

A natural smile tilted Ellie's lips as she looked at him, lounging back shirtless in his seat, a beautiful, self-assured and ruthless work of art, who continually surprised her. 'Yes, I got you.'

'When do we find out whether or not you're pregnant?' he prompted without warning.

'I was planning to do a test now,' she confided.

'For *yourself*?' Rio queried in visible consternation. 'No, that won't do at all. We'll go and see a doctor, get it done properly—'

'I am a doctor—'

*'Sì...'* Rio gave a fluid, very Italian shrug '...but this is an occasion and it requires special treatment.'

Midmorning, following their visit to a very charming private doctor, they sat down to coffee and pastries in the atmospheric Piazza San Marco. Both of them were shell-shocked, Ellie most of all, because she had believed she would recognise some tiny sign and somehow *know*. But she hadn't known, hadn't recognised anything that different with the exception of being more tired than usual, and with all the fuss of the wedding that hadn't seemed worthy of note.

'So, now we know,' Rio pronounced without any expression at all.

And Ellie recognised the dazed light in his eyes and knew that he was just as stunned as she was to learn that he was going to become a parent in a few months.

'I just didn't really think it could happen that... *easily*,' he admitted in an almost embarrassed undertone.

'I've met a few distressed teenagers who made the same assumption,' Ellie admitted, smiling to herself, quietly pleased with the knowledge that she was carrying her first child. And no, their baby hadn't been planned and was likely to drive a horse and cart through her career choices, but neither of those facts mattered when set beside the wonder of conception, which she had watched give such great joy to Polly and Rashad. She would gladly make space in her life for her child, she acknowledged, recognising that in the blink of an eye after hearing that news that her goals had changed.

'Saying we would make the best of this development if it happened wasn't the most supportive or sensitive approach,' Rio conceded belatedly. 'I want to celebrate now but not only can you not drink, you've even been warned off coffee.'

There it was again, that ability to surprise her that made her love Rio all the more, Ellie reflected. In fact, loving Rio seemed to have been stamped into her genes like a no-escape clause because, of course, she loved him, didn't know quite when it had happened and certainly not *how*. She smiled, happiness bubbling through her that he was so flexible, so willing to happily embrace their unplanned baby. 'I'll drink decaf—'

Rio grimaced at the idea for he had a true Italian love of unadulterated coffee.

'There are other ways of celebrating,' Ellie pointed out, lashes screening her eyes as she covertly studied him, recognising that she would never tire of this particular view. Rio, hair blue-black and gleaming in the sunshine, stunning dark golden eyes welded to her with an intensity she could feel, sprawled back with indolent grace in his seat, his shirt pulled taut across his broad chest, his trousers straining over his powerful thighs. Her mouth ran dry.

'Eat your ice cream, Signora Benedetti. I love your curves—'

'Just as well. My curves will be expanding—'

A slashing grin curved his sculpted mouth. 'I can only look forward to it, *principessa*. But when it comes to celebrating—'

'You could take me out on a gondola,' Ellie suggested with enthusiasm.

Rio looked pained. 'Seriously uncool. That's a touristy thing—'

*'Please...'* Ellie urged.

And she got her gondola ride the whole length of the Grand Canal. Rio had caved and she was touched. He was much more comfortable sweeping her into a fancy jeweller's store afterwards, where he insisted on buying her an emerald pendant to mark the occasion. They lunched back at the house and he watched her smother a yawn.

'You should lie down for a while—'

'Only if you lie down with me,' Ellie murmured softly.

Disconcerted, Rio flashed her a glance as if he couldn't quite credit the invitation. But without hesitation he lifted her up out of her seat and crushed her ripe mouth under his own, all the seething passion of his intense sexuality rising to the fore.

He tumbled her down on the bed but he unwrapped her from her clothes like a precious parcel, pausing to admire and tease what he exposed, and she writhed like a wanton on top of the silk bedspread in the full glare of the Venetian sunlight, utterly lost in passion and equally lost to all shame. He took her from behind then, hands firm on her overheated body as he drove into her with a roughened growl of satisfaction. His urgent rhythm was wildly exciting. Heart pounding, breathing forgotten, Ellie reached a peak and her body detonated in an explosive charge of pleasure. She slumped down winded on the bed with Rio on top of her.

He released her from his weight and settled down beside her, reaching for her to pull her into his arms.

'Thought you didn't do hugs,' Ellie commented.

Rio splayed a large hand across her flat stomach and said piously, 'I'm hugging my child.'

Ellie laughed, feeling amazingly relaxed and at peace. Her fingers lifted and fiddled absently with the emerald she still wore round her neck.

'You can tell me about your uncle now,' Rio informed her in the tone of someone doing her a favour.

Ellie wrinkled her nose. 'Jim Dixon? My mother's brother? I guessed he would be the family member you mentioned. I take it he's still peddling his sob story about how I ripped him off?'

'You're not surprised?'

'Jim's vilified me everywhere and no matter what I said to him, he refused to listen. He doesn't *want* the truth. He didn't get on with my mother and he never liked Polly and me, but my grandmother was living on the poverty line when she agreed to raise us. Our mother gave her a lot of money to take care of us and the arrangement suited them both from that point of view. Unfortunately my uncle always resented us being there.'

'Tell me about the brooch,' Rio urged with typical impatience.

'Oh, the *famous* diamond brooch, the family heirloom for several generations and the only item of worth the Dixons ever owned,' Ellie recounted ruefully. 'My grandmother sent me a letter during my first term at medical school. In it she told me she wanted me to have the brooch because she was so proud that I was going to be a doctor. She gave it to me the first weekend I was home after that. I didn't tell Polly, well, I couldn't *bear* to—'

Rio had sat up, glorious dark eyes locked to her expressive face and narrowing. 'Why not? I thought you and your sister were really close.'

'Oh, come on, Rio, think about it! Polly was the eldest and the brooch should have gone to her if it had gone to anyone!' Ellie argued. 'Polly sacrificed her chance to go to art college to get a job and help out financially and when Gran developed dementia, it was Polly who looked after her. She deserved the brooch, *not* me, and I was astonished enough to get it because our grandmother wasn't a warm woman. She didn't neglect or abuse us but she didn't love us either. Polly would've been hurt by me getting the brooch, so I decided to sell it and split the proceeds with her and make up some story about where I got the money from.'

'Women… Why do you always complicate things?' Rio groaned. 'A man would just have told the truth. It wasn't your fault that your grandmother chose to give it to you.'

Ellie rolled her eyes, unimpressed. 'But when I tried to sell the brooch, I discovered it was only paste, not real diamonds, which made better sense to me. I mean, why *would* a poor family have held on to a valuable diamond brooch all those years? It was worth so little that I didn't bother selling it but I still haven't told Polly about it,' she completed guiltily.

'Where does your uncle come into this?'

'Our grandmother left her son the contents of her house when she died and, of course, he assumed that the brooch would be there and when I told him she'd given it to me a couple of years earlier, Jim accused me of being a thief. While Polly was out applying for the death certificate and making burial arrangements, I was wrangling with Jim. I told him the brooch was only a costume piece but he wouldn't believe me and he stomped off and wouldn't speak to us at the funeral. A few weeks later he got the police involved,' she revealed wryly. 'They came to see me at university. I showed them the letter. They were satisfied—'

'But your uncle wasn't?'

'No, he'll probably go to his grave convinced that I deprived him of his prized inheritance. I tried to sort it out with him and he wouldn't listen and by that stage I was past caring. I was sick and tired of the whole stupid business,' she confessed.

Rio traced a fingertip over the shadows below her eyes. 'You look tired, *principessa*. Have a nap.'

He owed her an apology for having entertained the ridiculous idea that she could be a gold-digger, Ellie thought in annoyance, but she was *still* waiting for that apology. He was far from perfect, she mused, and he was too strong to find it easy to own up to being in the wrong. On the other hand, he had wonderful taste in emeralds, had endured a gondola ride at her behest, was learning to hug and he was happy about the baby, she reasoned with sneaking contentment while swallowing another yawn.

Rio watched Ellie sleep and heaved a sigh. Had she noticed his moment of sheer panic when her pregnancy was confirmed? His blood had run cold. He had asked himself how he could possibly be a decent parent when his own parents had had more in common with the dregs of humanity. He didn't know what was in his genes, never would know, but that sort of stuff was important to Ellie. Was that why he *still* hadn't told her about the dumpster? Pride? He had always told himself that where he started out didn't matter; indeed that all that really mattered was where he ended up.

And where had he ended up? Married to a woman he had treated badly! His sins had come back to find him out and haunt him. So, he had to reinvent himself again, just as he had as a boy, as a young failed businessman, a student and, finally, a success story. He would change and adapt to his new lifestyle. He would be *the perfect husband.* That was what Ellie deserved. He owed her that. All her life, Ellie had only had her sister Polly to rely on but now she had him. He smoothed a corkscrew curl back from her pale brow, careful not to wake her, and abstractedly wondered if it would be too soon to visit a toy shop. Probably as uncool as that awful gondola ride, he conceded ruefully. But then wasn't he supposed to be reinventing himself?

'So how do you think my Italian is coming on?' Ellie enquired in the language.

'You are learning quickly and the accent, it is good,' Beppe told her cheerfully. 'Rio must be a better and more patient teacher than I expected.'

'He's been very patient but we only talk in Italian for a couple of hours a day. I find it exhausting,' she admitted. 'But I have a good memory. Outside of maths and science, languages were my best subject.'

'When will you be home?' Beppe asked plaintively. 'I miss you both.'

'Tomorrow. We'll join you for dinner,' Ellie promised and she finished the call because Polly had already texted her twice asking her to ring.

'What's happened?' she asked her sister worriedly minutes later.

'You *have* to open Lucy's envelope,' Polly told her and then she explained why and Ellie came off the phone again looking worried.

'What's wrong?' Rio pressed, lifting his handsome dark head from his laptop.

'Well, that kid sister we've been trying to find?' She sighed. 'It turns out that we didn't really think things through properly at the start. Because we didn't know who our fathers were, we assumed Lucy would be in the same boat. But Lucy's had access to her original birth certificate since she was eighteen and her father's name is probably on it. After all, he was living in London with our mother when she was conceived. All the investigator has been able to discover from enquiries is that Lucy's father is Greek and he thinks it's possible that the reason we can't trace her is that she could be in Greece.'

'That's reasonable, so stop fussing and open the envelope. It's only a name and a ring, nothing more important.'

'It just feels wrong,' Ellie muttered, going upstairs to extract the envelope from her case and clattering back down into the sitting room. She opened the envelope and extracted a ruby ring and read the name. 'Kreon Thiarkis,' she sounded out uncertainly.

'I think I've heard that surname before. I'll look into it. Text the name to Polly so that she can pass it straight on to the investigator,' he urged unnecessarily because she was already doing exactly that.

'Stop with the bossy stuff,' she warned him.

'Have you ever listened to yourself talking to Beppe? Telling him to eat more vegetables and drink less wine? Urging a man, who is physically very lazy, to go for walks? It's not going to kill him to be a little overweight at this stage of his life,' Rio opined. 'You climb on your healthy-living soapbox every time you're on the phone.'

Ellie winced. 'Have I been overdoing it?'

'No. Beppe enjoys being fussed over. He's never had that before. And if it's any consolation, you're giving him very good advice but he's very set in his ways.'

Afternoon tea was served to them out in the little garden and Ellie sat watching the canal traffic wend past in all its tremendous variety while she ate a divine slice of blackberry-limoncello tart. She was thinking about how very happy she was and that it seemed downright incredible to her that she had only been married for four short weeks.

After all, she had made some very major decisions during those four weeks. Finding Beppe, marrying Rio and discovering she was pregnant had forced her to have a serious rethink about her future. She had withdrawn at the last minute from her scheduled placement in London and was officially unemployed. But she was learning Italian as fast as she could and with Rio's assistance had already collected up the documents required for her to register as a doctor in Italy. Her career wasn't taking a back seat, she reasoned, she was simply on a go-slow diversion for a few months. Obviously, her priorities had changed.

She didn't want to leave Italy now that she had found her father. With Polly married to Rashad and living in Dharia, she had no family waiting for her back in London. She wanted the time and the space to get to know Beppe, as well. And she loved Italy and saw no reason to demand that Rio live in the UK when it was perfectly possible for her to work in Italy. That decision had removed much of the stress and the fear of the future weighing her down.

And she was so happy with Rio, even though he was the sort of near-workaholic who brought his tablet out even for afternoon tea in the sunshine. They had still contrived to enjoy the most incredible honeymoon exploring Venice. Well, she had explored and he had guided, occasionally complaining bitterly when she dragged him into old buildings or shot what she thought were interesting historical facts at him. They had wandered hand in hand off the beaten track and eaten wonderful food at little restaurants known only to the locals.

Many a morning had drifted long past noon before they got dressed. He was insatiable or maybe she was, she reflected ruefully, but they at least seemed well matched in that field. For the first time ever Ellie was learning what it was to have time to waste, to be indolent, to read a something that wasn't a textbook or a research paper.

And throughout every step of that most entertaining renaissance of hers, Rio had encouraged her and supported her. He made her happy: it was that simple and that was probably why she loved him. They still argued though. After she had told him the story of her grandmother's brooch, Rio had made the very extravagant gesture of buying her a star-shaped brooch studded with enough diamonds to sink the Titanic. 'You *deserve* it,' he had told her while she was trying to remonstrate with him over the expensive jewellery he kept on buying for her even though she rarely wore jewellery because she had never had much to wear. Stone Age man went hunting and dragged a carcass home to his cave to feed his woman. Rio's equivalent was inviting exclusive jewellers to visit the house to show her an array of fabulous gems worth a small fortune. And if she said no, he looked frustrated and hurt, and it was the hurt she couldn't bear to see.

If she made any sort of comment relating to gold-diggers, he froze and changed the subject. No, he still hadn't apologised but she was bright enough to know that the flood of expensive jewels was Rio's way of telling her that he no longer nourished such insulting suspicions about her. And the one thing he wouldn't talk about was his time in the orphanage and his dealings with his mother as an adult. For some reason the story of his early years was a complete conversation killer.

Ellie stirred that night soon after she heard the phone ring, for working in the medical field had wired her to take greater note of alarms and phone calls. Coming sleepily awake, she sat up and watched Rio pace the floor naked. He was speaking in Italian and far too fast for her to follow, shooting urgent questions to whoever was on the other end of the call. And he was upset, lines grooved into his lean dark features, mouth a thinned tense line. Disturbed by what she was seeing, Ellie breathed in deep, bracing herself for trouble of some kind.

Rio made another call and then looked across at her with unconcealed anxiety. 'We need to go home. Beppe's in hospital. He had a heart attack while one of his friends was dining with him. He received immediate attention…which is good. *Isn't it?*' he demanded jerkily, seeking reassurance.

Ellie braced herself, fighting the strong emotions tearing at her at the very thought of losing the father she had only recently found. 'Yes, it will greatly improve his chances of making a full recovery,' she muttered hollowly, striving and failing to be more upbeat.

# CHAPTER TEN

'SILLY FUSS,' BEPPE said again as Ellie gripped his hand. 'No reason to come back early.'

Even though Ellie was no stranger to the environment of an Intensive Care Unit, she was having a first-hand experience of how very intimidating it could be to see someone she loved lying in a railed bed, and Beppe looked so small and shrunken. She breathed in deep and slow, composing herself, because she was determined not to inflict more pressure on her father by overreacting.

Beppe had had an emergency angioplasty to clear a blocked artery soon after his arrival at the hospital and his prognosis was good if he followed the rules on how best to maximise his recuperation. But her father's heart attack had given him a terrible fright because he had not spent even a day in hospital before and had enjoyed excellent health.

Rio, however, had suffered an even worse fright, Ellie acknowledged. For during the flight that had whisked them back to Florence in time to see the dawn, Rio, sky-high on anxiety, had sat lost in his thoughts and barely speaking. Right at that moment he was poised at the foot of Beppe's hospital bed trying to act strong and optimistic for Beppe's benefit but Ellie could spot a pretence when she could see one. One of Rio's hands was clenching and repeatedly unclenching in a betrayal of stress that could not be hidden. And for the first time—and she scolded herself thoroughly for it being the first time—she finally recognised that Rio loved Beppe as much as she did, indeed probably more because Beppe Sorrentino had been a part of Rio's life since he was a child.

'Want to live to see grandchildren,' Beppe told them apologetically, his speech abbreviated and slurred by the medication. 'Never had family, want that now.'

'And you'll have that family,' Ellie assured him soothingly.

'Maybe sooner than you think,' Rio slotted in, ready, Ellie could see, to expose her there and then as a pregnant bride if it helped his godfather to look forward and raised his spirits.

'Hopefully we'll have news of that nature sometime soon,' Ellie delivered to silence Rio.

A nurse adjusted the machinery surrounding Beppe and a more senior nurse with a clipboard questioned her quietly from the doorway.

'Franca...' Beppe murmured with a weak smile in the direction of the woman in the doorway. 'Wondered when you'd visit.'

Ellie watched Rio freeze in patent disbelief and then slowly turn round. Her own brain, drained by the sleepless night and the stress, seemed to be refusing to function. The nurse in the doorway was Rio's ex? Or another Franca entirely? Could she possibly be the woman Rio had once planned to marry? The same one who had run off with his one-time business partner, Jax, when

Rio's property venture failed? It was a moment when Ellie would happily have given ten years of her life to be seated in the right place to actually see Rio's face and interpret his reaction.

'Franca…' he acknowledged after a noticeable pause and he addressed her in quiet Italian, moving forward and indeed stepping outside into the corridor to speak to her at length. She was a small, fragile brunette with big dark eyes and ridiculously pretty and right at that moment she was gazing soulfully up at Rio as though he had hung the moon for her.

Beppe squeezed Ellie's limp fingers to attract her attention and her shaken eyes darted back to him. 'She's been working here for years,' he whispered. 'I knew and never said. He didn't know.'

'They're old friends though,' Ellie pointed out with forced casualness, deliberately avoiding any hint of discomfiture for the older man's benefit.

Beppe patted her hand. 'Good girl,' he mumbled. 'Sensible girl.'

Ellie watched his eyes drift shut and slowly breathed in again, feeling almost giddy as the oxygen hit her lungs. Switching her attention back to Rio and Franca, she saw a doctor joining them and she rose from her chair quickly, keen to join the medical discussion clearly taking place in the corridor. But as she straightened she lurched and stumbled, a sudden wall of blackness closing in around her. And her last thought was, *How could you be so stupid?*

Rio scooped up Ellie at such speed that he almost tripped over Beppe's bed in his haste to reach his wife. 'She's pregnant,' he announced in a panic to anyone who cared to listen.

Guilt slashed at Rio as he carted Ellie out to the waiting limousine. He had dragged her out of bed in the middle of the night and she hadn't eaten in hours. That combined with the stress of Beppe's condition had been too much for a newly pregnant woman. Why hadn't he paid more attention to Ellie's needs? As Franca had explained, Ellie was probably experiencing low blood pressure and low blood sugar at this stage.

Ellie began to try to sit up in the car, saying limply, 'What are you doing? I don't want to leave the hospital—'

'Beppe is asleep. For the moment, the crisis is over and there's no reason for you to stay by his bedside,' Rio argued forcefully. 'Right now, you need to eat and rest. And *no*,' he instructed, actually daring to rest two long fingers against her parted lips in reproof. 'Don't bother reminding me that you're a doctor when you can't remember to look after yourself.'

A furious flush mantled Ellie's cheeks. She felt the sting of his censure all the more because it was warranted. But there had been no food on the private jet because there had not been time to restock it for the emergency flight from Venice, so eating had not been an option during the flight, and since their arrival she had only seen the inside of the ICU.

'Beppe didn't see me faint, did he?' she pressed worriedly.

'No, he was fast asleep—'

'What did his doctor tell you?'

'That he's on the mend but that he needs to make the changes you mentioned.' Rio swore under his breath in driven Italian. 'I feel guilty now. I should've tried to talk to him too—'

'At the end of the day, it's his life and his decision,' she said tiredly. 'I think he'll be practical, especially once he realises the next generation is on the way, although how he didn't guess from the way you were talking I'll never know!'

*'Dio mio...'* Rio growled out of patience. 'We *are* talking about a man who had an adulterous affair with your mother! Beppe wasn't perfect. Why would he expect us to be?'

Ellie sniffed, still reluctant to be exposed as the loose woman who had ended up on a sofa with Rio within days of her arrival in Italy. Not even in a bed, her censorious alter ego reminded her darkly. Rio made her reckless but he also made her happy…well, when he wasn't annoying her or worrying her.

'So was that the same Franca you once planned to marry?' she simply shot at him, going straight for the jugular, in no mood to contrive a subtle approach.

Rio flexed his broad shoulders and sprawled back in his corner. 'That was a surprise but I gather Beppe knew and never mentioned it.'

'I didn't know she worked in the medical field—'

'How would you?' Rio parried. 'It's not relevant in any way.'

Ellie pursed her lips. No, it might not be relevant on his terms, she was thinking grimly, but that one little fact of Franca's nursing profession and her treatment of him could certainly shed some light on Rio's reluctance to view medical staff as being 'caring' and the suspicious reception he had given Ellie.

'How did you feel seeing her again?' Ellie asked baldly, knowing it was intrusive but unable to kill the question before it leapt off her tongue. Because, in truth, the answer to that one little question was literally *all* she wanted to know.

Rio treated her to an incredulous appraisal. 'I'm not going to answer that. It's a stupid question.'

Ellie nodded, mouth compressing harder than ever.

And Rio thought quite spontaneously that Beppe would never have got the chance to stray from his marital vows with a wife like Ellie around. Ellie picked up on every nuance, dissected it, stressed about it and absolutely had to *talk* about it immediately. And sometimes it drove Rio crazy because his brain didn't work like hers. Why would he even *want* to talk about Franca? Aside from the reality that that liaison had happened what felt like half a lifetime ago? Women discussed feelings but he had never felt that need, had he? He very shrewdly kept that kind of nonsense to himself. Why did Ellie always want something from him that he couldn't deliver? Time and time again she showed him that he was failing to meet her expectations.

His jawline setting like granite, Rio brooded about yet another major flaw in his character. He didn't know how to talk about feelings, where even to begin, never mind end. He had had lots and lots of feelings when he was a boy, but he had learned through hard experience that it was wiser and safer to suppress them. He was resolutely practical and always had been. There was no point wanting what you couldn't have and even less point in wasting energy agonising over life's misfortunes. That creed had served him faithfully for thirty years. So, how *had* he felt seeing Franca without warning? Surprise and curiosity. Nothing wrong with those reactions, was there?

'You go to bed while I make you something to eat. What would you like?'

'You can cook?' Ellie gasped.

'Proficiently,' Rio assured her with satisfaction.

'Could you manage an omelette? Omelettes are kind of complicated, aren't they?' Ellie said in the tone of a woman who lived off salads and ready meals.

'Not that complicated,' Rio told her.

He led Ellie up to the master bedroom in his house and her luggage was brought up. She studied her surroundings with tired interest. Luxury fabrics and pale oak furniture lent the bedroom a traditional, almost feminine opulence that disconcerted her because it was very far from what she had expected to find in a rampant womaniser's intimate lair. Had she been less tired she might have noticed that Rio was scanning the bedroom, as well, in a manner that suggested he was equally unfamiliar with it.

And so he was, having hired a decorator to chuck out his man cave accoutrements and decor while they were in Venice. Everything was new, fresh and Ellie approved even though she didn't know it because he had made note of her favourite colours and the style of furniture she liked. She didn't like cutting-edge contemporary and she didn't like flashy and his former bedroom decor would have qualified in both categories. There had also been the serious risk of inadvertently encouraging Ellie to think about how many other women could have visited his home and slept in that bed. No, Rio was convinced that keeping Ellie happy meant acting as if that past of his didn't exist. He understood her passionate possessiveness, in fact, it warmed him as much as the hottest day, but he didn't want any element of his libidinous past coming between them.

And that included Franca. If he talked about Franca, he would be clumsy and he might well say the wrong thing. For that reason it was much better not to discuss Franca at all. Thinking that that was the troublesome topic of Franca now as done and dusted as a gravestone in a cemetery, Rio went downstairs to make an omelette worthy of a cordon bleu chef because he never missed out on an opportunity to impress Ellie and he had just realised that she couldn't cook.

As removed from the real world as a zombie, Ellie opened her case, extracted the necessities and went into the bathroom. She had a quick shower, discovered she had left her toothbrush behind in Venice and searched the drawers in the storage units. She found several new toothbrushes, a giant box of condoms, a choice of several different lipsticks and make-up containers and two unmatched earrings. All had clearly been left behind by previous visitors. Tomorrow she would dump them. Right at that moment, she was reminding herself that Rio was her husband, that, yes, he had had a past with other women, but that that was nothing to do with her, certainly not something she should be worrying about.

Rio presented her with a perfect golden omelette and she was undeniably as impressed as though he had owned up to being a rocket scientist. Washed and fed, she was taken over by exhaustion again and she slid down in the blissfully comfortable bed, quite unaware that Rio went for a shower and then slid in beside her.

When she wakened it was afternoon the next day and she was alone. She was shocked that she had slept so long and anxious to get to the hospital and see how her father was doing. When she came downstairs, Rio's housekeeper appeared, introduced herself as Sofia and brought her lunch on the terrace. Marooned without transport, she went into the large garage off the rear courtyard and discovered a stable of vehicles. Rio liked sports cars, she thought with amusement. *Boy*, did Rio like sports cars. Sofia showed her where the keys were and she picked a car in fire-engine red that appealed to her mood.

Navigating the many turns in the sweeping road that led down to the main route was more of a challenge than she had expected because she had never driven such a powerful car before but she made it to the hospital in good time and went straight to the ICU. Beppe, however, had been moved out of intensive care to his own room, a sign that he was making good progress, and she greeted him with a smile when she found him sitting up in bed and much more able to talk than he had been in the early hours of the morning.

'Rio's gone for coffee in the canteen,' he explained. 'You've just missed him.'

After she had been with him about thirty minutes, Beppe began to flag and she suggested he have a nap, reminding him when he argued that he was recovering from surgery and that it would take a few days for him to regain his strength. Ellie went straight down to the canteen in the basement to find Rio but it was very busy and she bought herself a cup of hot chocolate as a treat, while she queued and scanned the crowded tables.

When she finally located him, she stopped midway on her path to joining him because he was not alone, he was sitting with Franca. Reluctant to interrupt out of the fear that Rio would deem it jealous and possessive behaviour on her part, Ellie slid into a corner table nicely shielded by a tall fake potted plant and waited for his companion to leave. She barely sipped her hot chocolate while she watched the pair of them, former lovers, looking much more friendly than anyone would have expected in the circumstances as they sat opposite each other, both leaning forward to get closer and talking intently.

In not treating Franca like an enemy, Rio was acting like an adult, she told herself soothingly. It was downright nasty of her to think that Franca was looking at him with much more appreciation than the occasion could surely require. Slowly it sank in that they appeared to be having a quite emotional conversation and that unnerved her, but all the signs were there. Franca reached across the table and gripped one of Rio's hands at one point and then brushed away tears. Rio did not go into retreat. In fact, none of the barriers that most would expect to be present between lovers who had parted on very bad terms were to be seen.

Stop being so blasted jealous and suspicious, Ellie urged herself in exasperation. Obviously Rio and Franca were catching up on the past and had discovered that at heart they were still friends. But it really, *really* bothered Ellie that Rio was clearly having the sort of emotional chat with his ex-girlfriend that he refused to have with his wife. And for how long had he been chatting to Franca? All that time she had been upstairs sitting with Beppe? And he was *still* with her?

Ellie drank her hot chocolate, refusing to allow herself to watch Rio and Franca any more since she was obviously too susceptible to paranoia. She had fallen insanely in love with Rio, married him and turned into a maniac she didn't recognise. Every hour of the day she wanted Rio *so* much. It was frightening, mortifying, but she had to get control of her craving, her suspicions, her insecurity. One last look at them and then she would go and check on Beppe again, she bargained with herself.

And Ellie glanced, only allowed herself that one glance, and she saw Rio reach over the table to grip Franca's hand in a heartfelt gesture that felt like a knife plunging into her own heart. Franca put one of her hands on top of his and gave him a wobbly, tearful smile full of warmth and admiration. Ellie's glance became a stare and then she literally tore her gaze away at the same time as she stood up, abandoning her drink, and walked out of the canteen to wait for the lift.

Right, so, Rio had some weird new connection with his ex, not necessarily a sexual or romantic connection. Who was she trying to kid? She had sat watching a woman crying and smiling and holding hands with her husband. What was she supposed to think? A woman he had once loved enough to want to marry. But he had never loved or wanted to marry Ellie, had he? And now he was stuck in a marriage with a woman he didn't love, who was pregnant.

Ellie's eyes prickled like mad. She hardly ever cried and right at that moment she had a crazy urge to howl and sob, and holding all that pent-up emotion in was a challenge. Rio was so intense in everything he did and yet, unless he lost his temper, he didn't let that emotion escape, at least not around Ellie. But what had really seriously hurt was seeing Rio demonstrate unashamed emotion with Franca, Rio taking part in the kind of emotional exchange he had denied Ellie. So what had they been talking about?

Had they discovered that they both still had feelings for each other? Franca must have been Rio's first love and first loves, with all the memories involved, were notoriously hard attachments to shake. Ellie breathed in slow and deep to calm herself and checked on Beppe, but he was sound asleep and, according to the nurse she spoke to, likely to be for some time. There was no reason for Ellie to remain at the hospital, particularly not when she wanted to avoid Rio, who she knew very well wouldn't tell her anything about his encounter with Franca. If she taxed him he would think she was a jealous, suspicious cow and he would be right. She *was*...

As she drove off from the hospital she struggled to calm down. Only a couple of hours earlier, aside of her ongoing concern for her father, she had been blissfully happy and Beppe did seem to be improving. She was making a mountain out of a molehill, she told herself soothingly. She would say nothing, do nothing, wait and see how matters went.

But inside herself, Ellie felt as though her heart were breaking. She kept on getting a flashback of Rio holding hands with Franca, Franca staring back at him with so much brimming emotion. Was that love she had seen between them? Why not? Why shouldn't he love Franca? Seeing his former love in such a crisis as Beppe's illness had created when Rio had been in a very emotional state of mind, even though he wouldn't ever admit the fact? Had Franca and Rio recognised that they both still had feelings for each other?

And, yes, she had believed that Rio was happy with her in Venice, but what if all along from the very outset of their marriage Rio had only been making the best of things? The best of a bad job? He found her sexually attractive but was there any more to their connection on his side than that? Meeting Franca again could well have made Rio appreciate the difference between love and sex. Her stomach turned over sickly.

So *why* should she keep quiet about what she had seen? an angry voice inside her demanded.

After all, how would Rio have reacted to seeing her holding hands with another man? Rio would have gone up in flames, created a scene and demanded an immediate explanation. That was the truth of it. Rio was as hot-headed and impulsive as she was invariably sensible and cautious. So, if Rio wouldn't swallow that kind of behaviour, why should she?

Ellie drove back to the house, steadily getting more and more upset and tearful. Whatever she did, she had to make a statement. She had to make it clear that she would not tolerate any kind of flirtation because if she didn't Rio might go on doing it. He needed boundaries, no, he needed a giant wall built round him to keep him within acceptable behaviour limits, she decided furiously. So, it was better to overreact now in the hope that the fallout from her anger ensured that there would not be a *next* time, she reasoned in growing desperation.

A preventative gesture in mind, Ellie began to pack her cases again. She would move into Beppe's house for a few days and Rio would appreciate that she was seriously annoyed with him. But was that the right thing to do? What if Rio had realised he was still in love with Franca? A terrible frightening sensation of emptiness spread inside Ellie, because if she lost Rio, she felt as if she would lose everything.

And that was sad, really, *really* sad, she told herself bracingly. She loved him but that didn't mean that she intended to be a doormat or throw wild, volatile scenes whenever he did something she disliked. Walking out on him for a couple of days was a better, quieter option and he would realise that she was serious. Screaming at Rio would be unproductive because he was as stubborn as a mule.

Rio drove back to his house, still surprised that he had somehow missed Ellie at the hospital. He was in an extraordinarily good mood. Beppe was on the mend, Ellie was pregnant and certain misconceptions he had once held had been cleared up and had left him feeling more in tune with the world than he had felt in a long time. He was in the wrong place mentally to reach home and have a troubled Sofia indicate the envelope left on a coffee table while learning that his wife had departed with cases.

He tore open the envelope. It was an Ellie letter, very succinct and to the point. There was only one sentence, telling him that he had failed to demonstrate the commitment she required from a husband. What the hell was that supposed to mean? Rio swore and then he swore again. It was as if electric shocks were going off in his brain. Ellie had walked out on him and moved into Beppe's *palazzo*. Outrage roared through him. He had made a huge effort to meet Ellie's high standards and yet now she was trying to ditch him like an old shoe.

Rio reacted by doing something that Ellie had not foreseen. He phoned Rashad and asked to speak to Polly. But within a minute of speaking to Ellie's sister, he realised that she was as shocked as he was and had no idea what could have fired Ellie up to that extent.

'Ellie's really not the dramatic type,' Polly told him

unreassuringly, because that only suggested that he must have been guilty of some giant sin that had provoked sudden and uncharacteristic behaviour.

'But I haven't *done* anything!' Rio raged, pacing round the hall in sizzling frustration. 'Do you think it could be pregnancy hormones or something weird?'

Polly's astonishment at that news only convinced Rio that phoning your wife's sister for insight into an unfathomable development could be a seriously bad and undiplomatic move. But then it had never occurred to him that Ellie could have kept quiet about the baby even with her sibling. After all, she and Polly talked most days! It finally dawned on him that Ellie was a much more private person in nature than he had appreciated—someone who didn't share personal stuff unless forced, as he had had to almost force her to tell him about the diamond brooch and the old lady at the hospice. She held all her distress in, *hid* it, trying to stay strong. Until that moment he hadn't recognised just how similar they were in that category and he suppressed a groan because it only complicated his situation more. Maybe she was deeply unhappy living with him. How was he to know? She wasn't a talker or an emoter… *Per l'amor di Dio*, he was *so* grateful for her restraint in that line. After all, Franca had almost talked him into a trance.

Initially, powered on anger, fear and a desperate need to take a stance, Ellie had expected Rio to rush straight to Beppe's home to confront her, but as time wore on into the afternoon she started to worry that he wouldn't even *try* to get her back. In fact, maybe she had played right into his hands by leaving, maybe he had reached the conclusion that he didn't want to be married any longer. For a male as rich and gorgeous as Rio the grass always had to look greener on the *single* side of the fence.

What had she done in walking out like that? What way was that to save a marriage?

She *loved* him, for goodness' sake, even if it turned out that he was the biggest flirt imaginable!

Suddenly feeling distinctly nauseous for the first time in her pregnancy, and shaky and damp with nerves, Ellie went upstairs to lie down. She knew the stress was bad for her and her baby and she beat herself up more for the decision she had made. Since when had she been a drama queen? And walking out on the assumption that the man you were leaving would follow to beg you to return was almost suicidal if he didn't love you. Tears prickled and stung behind Ellie's lowered eyelids. What had persuaded her that she had to make such a theatrical challenge to Rio of all people? A fit of temporary insanity?

Rio walked through the bedroom door and surveyed his wife. She was fast asleep and his keen gaze could detect the faint redness round her eyes that suggested tears had been shed. His confidence rose. If his unemotional Ellie had been crying, that was a healthy sign. He sat down on the side of the bed and gently shook her shoulder.

Luminous green eyes flew open and settled on him in strained silence. Her lush lips parted and closed again as she regrouped and sat up to hug her knees. 'What are you doing here?' she asked coolly.

'You're here,' Rio said simply.

'You can't stay here,' Ellie argued, thoroughly disconcerted by that declaration. 'It's Beppe's house.'

'It's not. I bought it from him years ago when the upkeep was becoming too much for him. I begged him to stay on and look after it,' he explained with a casual shrug. 'It was a property investment for me—'

'You're such a liar!' Ellie told him helplessly. 'You did it because you love him!'

'That too.' Rio looked uncomfortable. 'Can we get to the point of what that stupid note you left behind meant? One sentence? I get *one* sentence of explanation?'

Ellie stiffened, more challenged than she had expected because Rio wasn't shouting or raging, giving her the fight she had subconsciously craved and yet feared with every atom of her being, lest it lead to the end of their relationship. She lowered her legs and slid off the other side of the bed. 'After the way you spent your morning, I should think the note was self-explanatory...'

'After the way I spent... Franca? You *saw* me with Franca?' Rio thundered without warning as he finally made the connection. 'Why the hell didn't you rescue me?'

Taken aback, Ellie froze. '*Rescue* you?'

'*Sì*... I'm sitting in a public place while a woman weeps and sobs and talks about the kind of stuff I really don't want to know and I can't *decently* escape!' Rio recounted wrathfully. 'You think I was enjoying that? Are you out of your mind?'

It began to sink in on Ellie that she could have made a huge error of judgement.

'I can't believe this is all about Franca!' Rio exclaimed with rampant incredulity.

'You were holding hands. I thought you were flirting with her—'

'You need to learn what flirting entails, *principessa*. I assure you that there was no flirting whatsoever. Franca lost her eldest daughter to leukaemia only weeks ago and has only recently returned to work after compassionate leave.'

'Oh, my goodness…' Ellie whispered in shock. 'That poor, poor woman.'

'Yes, even Rio with the heart of a stone was not going to get up and walk away from that!' Rio grated. 'And that was only a part of the doom and gloom rehash of the previous nine years that took place. She said it did her good to get it off her conscience but it only made me realise that my sense of moral superiority over events back then was entirely unmerited.'

Ellie nodded. 'Okay. You contributed to the breakup and her going off with your business partner. I assumed that some of it must've been your fault.'

Rio dealt her an exasperated look. 'I *didn't*. I blamed Franca and Jax, but then I didn't know what was going on behind the scenes. Her fling with Jax only lasted about five minutes, and at her lowest ebb she ended up homeless.'

Feeling guiltier than ever for her wrong assumptions, Ellie backed down into a corner armchair and sighed. 'That can't have been easy for you to hear—'

Rio's gaze was sombre. 'No, even at the time I never wished harm on her, but then she lived with me and I didn't even realise I was living with an alcoholic—'

Ellie's brows lifted in wonderment.

Rio grimaced. 'That tells you how much attention I gave Franca. My sole interest back then was really the business of making money. But to some extent that wasn't *all* my fault. I was driven by the need to show

Franca's family that I could provide well for her. They had done everything they could to try to separate us—'

Ellie was now genuinely interested in what he was telling her and some of her stress had ebbed because she had recognised that her worst fears had been groundless. 'But why?'

'Primarily my background,' Rio divulged stiffly.

'That you grew up as an orphan?' Ellie exclaimed. 'But that's so unfair!'

Rio braced himself to tell the truth and he paled and gritted his teeth. 'It was more sordid than that. I was an abandoned baby, born addicted to heroin. I was left in a cardboard box in a dumpster and found by street cleaners,' he admitted very stiffly. 'The manufacturer's name on the box was Rio. The nuns christened me Jerome after St Jerome but I was always known as Rio.'

Ellie was so appalled that she couldn't speak. She glanced away to get herself back under control but her eyes shone with shocked tears. To think of Rio as a defenceless baby thrown out like so much rubbish absolutely broke her heart. 'Why…a dumpster? Why not somewhere safer?'

'I asked my mother when I met her. She said she didn't want to get in trouble or be asked questions. It was nothing to do with my safety—it was *all* to do with her. I meant nothing to her. She was an addict and a whore,' he confessed grimly. 'Franca's family were convinced that I had to have evil genes. Some people *do* think like that, Ellie, which is why I've always kept the circumstances of my birth a secret. It is not that I am ashamed but that I do not wish to be pitied or thought of as being a lesser person because of those circumstances.'

Fierce protectiveness slivered through Ellie as she looked back at him, all the love she had for him enveloping her. 'I love you no matter what you came from. I love you more than I've ever loved anyone or anything and I *like* Rio as a name. And only now understanding why it was so important for you to give our child a safer, happier start in life…well, it only makes me love you even more!'

Rio was transfixed. He had been prepared for Ellie to flinch and be repulsed by the sleazy facts of his birth and ancestry and then pretend that they didn't matter even when it was obvious that they did. He certainly hadn't expected her to tell him that she loved him without reservation.

'Don't you realise,' she murmured gruffly, her throat thickening, so great was her emotion, 'that you should be *proud* of what you've achieved from such a tough beginning in life? It genuinely makes me feel incredibly proud of you.'

Rio studied her, lustrous dark golden eyes with a suspicious shine, lean, darkly handsome face clenched hard. 'You mean…all that?'

Ellie rose from her seat, empowered by his stillness, his uncharacteristic uncertainty. Never had she loved him more or understood him better. Franca and her family had taught him to be ashamed of his birth and background and she marvelled at their unwitting cruelty over something that he could not have influenced as she crossed the room and wrapped both arms tightly round him.

'Hug time?' Rio interpreted shakily, hoping she didn't catch the break in his voice, because in his whole life he had never known such a relief as the moment when Ellie told him that she *loved* him no matter what. It was the unconditional love he had sought without ever knowing it and suddenly he didn't feel alone and pitched against the world any longer.

'Hug time,' Ellie confirmed unevenly, winding round him like a vine. 'I'm really sorry I misunderstood what I saw with you and Franca. I sort of went haywire. I knew she was your first love and I thought maybe—'

'No.' Rio shuddered at the thought. 'She's happily married to a radiographer at the hospital and has two other children. But she developed a guilt complex about me when she finally got into rehab and started to rebuild her life. She says part of the recovery therapy was the need to mend fences with those she had wronged while she was still drinking but she could never face getting in touch with me after what she had done.'

'So, when she met you again—'

'It all came spilling out.' Rio sighed heavily. 'And I *had* to listen. It would have been cruel to tell her that it was very old history for me and that I no longer cared. I kept on saying that we had both made mistakes and weren't suited in any case but she kept on and on and on talking and crying—'

'I'm glad I didn't interrupt. Listening was the right thing to do. That was kind because I'm sure you were very uncomfortable and if I could've seen your face, I would've known that, but I could only see *her* face. When did you become that sensitive without me noticing?' Ellie asked in honest surprise.

'Oh, that probably happened when I realised I was in love with you. I then decided that I wanted to be the perfect husband—'

'You are…but I'm a very imperfect, distrustful wife,'

Ellie mumbled in shame, burying her hot face in his shoulder, drinking in the familiar scent of him with an enormous sense of relief combined with sheer wonderment. He *loved* her? Her gorgeous, passion-filled, outrageously exciting husband loved her? He didn't find her too boring or sensible? Jealous and possessive? She was ecstatic with wondering happiness. 'So what happened with your mother when you did meet her?'

'There was a piece in the newspaper about me being found when I was abandoned and she always knew where I was. When I began to make money she looked me up,' he confided grimly. 'And that's all she wanted… Money. She told me a lot of lies. I found out that although she had weaned herself off her own addiction, she made a living by dealing drugs to others. I had nothing more to do with her—'

'That must have hurt.' Ellie sighed in sympathy.

'It is what it is. Getting off drugs didn't magically turn her into a nice or caring woman.' Rio shrugged. 'As to my potential father? I was an accident. Probably one of her customers. She had no idea.'

'It really doesn't matter to me,' Ellie emphasised. 'I wasn't only saying that. What matters to me is the man you are now and I love him. I even love you a little more for being kind to Franca, which you must've found trying.'

Rio tilted up her face, dark golden eyes adoring. 'There could never be another woman for me, Ellie. I've never loved like this. I didn't know I even *could* love like this but you're everything I ever wanted in a woman…even if I didn't realise that until I met you the second time.'

'We just fought,' Ellie groaned.

'And I got more of a kick out of fighting with you than I got out of any affair I've ever had,' Rio confessed. 'But the hunger for you was overwhelming...I couldn't fight that—'

Ellie lifted warm eyes to his lean, strong face, glorying in his scorching appraisal. 'I couldn't either. I always keep my feet firmly on the ground and then I met you and everything, including me, went crazy—'

'But we've had so much enjoyment out of each other,' Rio commented with appreciation. 'On levels I didn't even know there could be between a man and a woman. Before you, it was all about sex for me—'

'Oh, I know that.' Ellie flushed. 'In Dharia—'

Rio winced. 'I was a jerk...but I had never wanted any woman the way I wanted you that night and I was on a high and then it all went pear-shaped, thanks to the twins—'

'Perhaps we both needed another couple of years to be ready for something more serious,' Ellie suggested forgivingly.

'*Dio mio*, I love you!' Rio swore passionately in receipt of the face-saving, utterly unearned excuse she was giving him and appreciating her generosity. He gathered her into his arms and almost squeezed her with his enthusiasm into suffocation. 'Really, *really* love you and I can't wait for the baby now that I know for sure that I have you by my side...'

'Well, when you ordered that giant train set in Venice and told me there was no reason why a little girl shouldn't enjoy it as much as a little boy I kind of guessed that our baby would be welcomed,' Ellie confided as he smoothly edged her down onto the bed. 'Nap time for pregnant Ellie, is it?'

'No. No rest for the imperfect wife,' Rio teased with a charismatic slashing grin as he looked down at her flushed, smiling face. 'Adriano was so relieved when you and then I showed up. He hates the house being empty because he has nothing to do and he's been fretting about Beppe. He's making dinner for seven, which gives us a few hours to fill—'

Ellie's eyes widened at that implication. 'You mean, you were so sure of yourself when you arrived here that you just went ahead and ordered dinner?' she exclaimed in disbelief.

'I wasn't prepared to leave here without you and if you refused to leave I had a case out in the car to enable me to stay here with you,' Rio explained without hesitation. 'When I want something, *principessa*...I don't quit and I don't surrender and I do believe that I would fight to the death to keep you in my life.'

'At heart you're a romantic,' Ellie told him with satisfaction and approval. 'When I came here, I was fighting for you too—'

Rio interrupted her in Italian to tell her argumentatively that walking out of their marital home had been a dreadful, shocking action to take.

Ellie refused to apologise. 'I was trying to make a statement, draw a line for you. Maybe it was a little extreme but I was hurting so badly—'

'I don't need a damn line, woman...I've got you in the flesh!' Rio told her aggressively. 'And it was not only extreme but also forbidden. You are not allowed to walk out on me ever again in this lifetime!'

'Is that a fact?'

'*Sì*... You're my wife, the centre of my world, my everything. You don't walk out. You stay and *shout*.'

Ellie breathed in deep, helplessly touched by that instruction. 'I'll shout the next time,' she promised.

'There won't *be* a next time!' Rio spelled out feelingly. 'Promise me—'

'*Sì*... I can promise that,' Ellie whispered, running adoring fingers through his cropped black hair and down one proud cheekbone to rest against his wilful lower lip. 'You're mine. I'm never going to walk away from you again.'

'Or drive off in my sports car,' Rio instructed. 'It's far too fast and powerful on these roads when you're not used to it.'

'I liked it—'

'No. I want you safe, *bella mia*.'

And before Ellie could demand that she had the right to influence what *he* drove in the interests of *his* safety, Rio kissed her with all the passion of his relief, love and desire for her and her impressionable toes curled. *Take that, sensible Dr Ellie*, she thought in wonderment that he truly was hers after all her anxiety and distrust, and then a thought occurred and she wrenched her mouth free...

'You never apologised for calling me a gold-digger!' she reminded him hotly.

'Of course I didn't.' Rio slowly shook his handsome dark head in apparent amazement at that reminder. 'That would have been owning up to flawed judgement or stupidity and it would've made you think less of me, so I decided to tough it out because I was trying to win you over to wanting to keep me by that stage.'

'*Nothing* would make me think less of you, you stupid man,' Ellie mumbled before she locked her lips to his again, his instant forgiveness procured, and there was no further conversation or indeed argument for quite some time. The excitement of their reconciliation powered the passion and the promises with buoyant happiness and fresh appreciation of the love they had found where they least expected it.

# EPILOGUE

POLLY GROANED. 'I'M OUT of my depth here. What *do* we do about this situation?'

Ellie groaned too. 'Mind our own business for now. If the sister we haven't even met has a thoroughly wicked and dishonest father, it's not our place to tell her so. Lucy doesn't know us or trust us yet. She's found her dad and, at the very least, probably thinks very highly of him and, at worst, really loves him because he's been kind to her—'

'But what if he's just using her for some reason?' Polly proclaimed emotively. 'Doesn't she deserve to know he went to prison for fraud?'

'We need to establish a relationship with her as sisters first,' Ellie opined, crossing the terrace of her Italian home to prevent her fiery little daughter from striking the younger prince of Dharia, tall, sturdy Hassan, aged two, for taking one of her dolls and wheeling his toy tractor over the top of it with little-boy glee.

Across the terrace, his older brother, Karim, the crown prince of Dharia, shouted at his little brother in Arabic.

'He's telling him off,' Polly translated. 'He's so like Rashad, very well behaved.'

'That's never going to be my problem with Teresina,' Ellie whispered. 'She's always ready to fight for what she wants. It's a continual battle.'

'Well, you mix two pretty opinionated people like you and Rio and that's what you get,' Polly pointed out cheerfully. 'She's gorgeous with that hair though.'

Ellie smiled at her daughter, who was two years old now. Born of parents who both had curly hair, Teresina had miraculously straight shoulder-length black hair and eyes that were a lighter green than her mother's. She was small and slight in build and had learned to walk at nine months old. She was lively and quick-tempered and the greatest joy in Ellie's world, for she had never realised just how much she would love her child.

In the three years that Ellie had been married, her whole life had changed and she had not a single regret. She spoke fluent Italian and had secured her dream job in the hospital where Beppe had been treated and where she was now continuing her training as a doctor specialising in children's ailments. Beppe had made an excellent recovery and had, under considerable protest, begun walking to take exercise. She had grown very close to her father and was profoundly grateful to have found him in time to get to know him.

They had finally contrived to trace their long-lost sister to Greece, where she was living with her birth father, who appeared to be a most unsavoury man. But Ellie was convinced that considerable tact had to be utilised where their unknown sister was concerned and Polly and Ellie had yet to work out how to best approach Lucy without frightening her off. Ellie was in favour of sending the ruby ring with a letter introducing themselves and inviting contact. How that would go down was anyone's guess but at least it couldn't be seen as threatening or interfering.

Ellie had grown no keener on shopping in recent years, because if she wasn't at work she was exulting in precious *family* time and certainly didn't want to waste that time shopping and preening. Ellie had always dressed for comfort and she was still doing it. For that reason, Polly was still buying her clothes and now Rio was doing it too and her wardrobe was bursting at the seams with designer garments she only wore at the occasional swanky event Rio attended. On the jewellery front, however, her collection could almost have rivalled the jewellery of Dharia's royal family. Rio never went anywhere and came back without gifts for her and Teresina, and soon he would have a third little person to buy for, Ellie thought with quiet contentment. And she had finally told her sister the story of their grandmother's diamond brooch and Polly had simply laughed and dismissed the matter without concern, more worried that Ellie had had to deal with their uncle's spite without support.

The sound of a car coming down the drive sent Ellie leaping upright.

'I'll watch the kids,' Polly proffered. 'Go on…greet him and make his day! Rio's so romantic.'

Rashad climbed out of the passenger seat. The friendship he and Rio had formed while at university had only deepened when the men married sisters who liked to see each other regularly.

Rio's sizzling smile broke out as Ellie threw herself at him and wrapped her arms round his neck as if she hadn't seen him in a week. He was a little disconcerted because he had only left her early that morning and she wasn't usually given to any public displays of affection.

'You missed me?' he whispered, wondering if something was worrying her.

'A little. I've got news,' Ellie murmured soft and low. 'Let's go upstairs.'

'Is this about your sister Lucy?'

'No, nothing new there. Polly still wants to jump in the royal jet and land on Lucy's doorstep and explode into her life,' Ellie told him ruefully. 'But I think she's beginning to come round to a more diplomatic approach.'

As Rashad, the king of Dharia, strolled past them to join his wife and two sons Ellie gripped Rio's hand and practically dragged him up to their bedroom.

'You're beginning to worry me,' Rio confided, shooting a glance at Ellie's glowing face and registering that whatever had happened, it couldn't be anything bad.

'We're pregnant again!' Ellie announced with delight.

Rio blinked and nodded very slowly. 'I wasn't aware we were even *trying*...'

'I didn't want to put pressure on you so I didn't mention that I wasn't taking anything,' Ellie revealed cheerfully.

Rio almost laughed out loud. *Put pressure on him?* Nothing could keep him away from Ellie. He adored her. But he still compressed his lips and said, 'It might have been nice to be asked...to have discussed this as a couple,' he remarked, rather woodenly because he still wanted to laugh.

Ellie's face fell as if he'd slapped it. 'I didn't think of that. I know how much you love having Teresina and I want to have my family while I'm still young and I would like them close together in age.' She chewed uncomfortably at her lower lip. 'I suppose I should've said something—'

Rio grinned. 'I was only joking. I'm delighted,' he assured her with heartfelt enthusiasm. 'The more the merrier—'

'Polly's pregnant again too. She's very keen to have a daughter,' she confided. 'I'll tell her about me over dinner, so don't go breaking my news ahead of me like you did the last time with that phone call.'

Rio linked his arms round her slim waist. 'It's my news too, *principessa*. I did figure in the conception.'

Ellie beamed up at him approvingly. 'Yes, you're wonderfully fertile—'

'Good to know I'm useful for something—'

'*And* spectacularly good at the action part,' Ellie whispered lovingly, hands running below his jacket to skate possessively over his hard muscled chest and then lowering in a much more intimate caress.

Rio shed his jacket and his shirt in record time. 'I won't sulk about not being consulted on the extending-the-family issue,' he admitted huskily. 'I know Dr Ellie was in the driving seat worrying that I might suffer from performance anxiety in bed for the first time in my life. In short, I'm perfectly happy to be used and useful.'

'I know you are,' Ellie told him cheerfully, shimmying out of her dress even faster, her eyes full of love and appreciation as she fasted her gaze on his lean, bronzed body, the passion that always simmered below the surface of their marriage gripping both of them with its scorching intensity. 'Did I ever tell you how much I love you?'

'Not since last night.' Rio studied his wife with wondering admiration and marvelled that he had found her, that she had married him, learned to love him and overlooked his every flaw. Loving Ellie had brought him untold riches in the happiness stakes and he would never ever take it for granted because he had lived too long without that security. 'But if you want to be competitive, you couldn't possibly love me as much as I love you…'

* * * * *

# SOLD FOR THE GREEK'S HEIR

For Rachel and Michael for their
unswerving support and their ability to
consider my characters as seriously as I do.

# CHAPTER ONE

IN THE PIT, Jax Antonakos climbed out of the low-slung car, adrenalin still pumping fiercely from the excitement of the race. Only a show race for charity, though, he reminded himself wryly, bracing himself as he was engulfed by a large, noisy crowd of people.

He yanked off his helmet, revealing tousled black hair and eyes as strikingly green as emeralds, and the usual collective female gasp of appreciation sounded. While he stripped off his track regalia, photographers flashed cameras, journalists demanded quotes and shot questions at him and beautiful women tried to sidle closer to him, but then all of that was the norm in Jax's goldfish bowl of a world.

Jax, however, ignored all of them to stride over and congratulate the winner of the race and the reigning world champion.

'You gave me a good run for a man who hasn't been behind a wheel in years!' Dirk conceded cheerfully. 'Maybe you shouldn't be pushing numbers behind a desk, maybe you should still be racing.'

'No, Jax is a business genius,' a female voice crowed from Jax's other side, and before he could react the bubbly brunette wrapped her arms round him with enthusiasm. 'Thank you so much for stepping in last minute to do this when Stefan had to let me down. You know how grateful I am.'

'Kat,' Jax acknowledged, frowning as the photographers predictably went for a shot of them as a couple. But he and Kat Valtinos weren't a couple, no matter how much the media and their families wanted them to be, both of them being conveniently young, single and very rich.

Jax stepped back from Kat with a guarded smile. He liked Kat, he had *always* liked her but his father was in for a disappointment if he was still hoping for a dynastic marriage that would unite their parents' massive business empires. Unfortunately the photos would only encourage him in that delusion.

'Let's get you a drink,' Kat urged, closing a possessive arm round his spine. 'I really appreciate you flying out here and doing this for me today at such short notice—'

'It was for a good cause,' Jax pointed out. 'And you're a friend—'

'A friend who could be *so* much more,' Kat whispered with laden intent in his ear.

'I enjoyed the race,' Jax admitted, choosing to be tactful and sidestep her leading comment. After all, there was no kind way of telling her *why* she was wasting her time chasing him and, with his reputation for womanising, it would be sheer hypocrisy for him to do so. Even now he retained fond memories of Kat's raunchy wildness when they were teenagers and he had been on the outskirts of the same social set but he still wasn't willing to marry a woman who had slept with every one of his friends. If that was a double standard, so be it, he acknowledged grimly.

In any case, he didn't want a wife, *any* kind of wife. Nor was he prepared to deliver the grandchildren his father, Heracles Antonakos, was so eager to have. Parenting was a minefield: Jax knew that better than anyone because he had stumbled through his own very unhappy childhood, filled as it had been with constant change and even more constant emotional drama.

His parents had gone through a bitter divorce when he was only a toddler and for the following twenty-five years his father had pretty much ignored his younger son's existence. Heracles's elder son, Argo, had been born from his first marriage. Widowed, Heracles had plunged into his second marriage far too quickly and he had never forgiven his second wife, Jax's mother, for her subsequent infidelity. Jax had paid the price for his mother's extra-marital affair in more ways than one. He had had no safe harbour from which to escape the fallout of his mother's broken relationships, nor any paternal support. He had struggled alone through Mariana's divorces, suicide attempts and regular stays in rehabilitation facilities.

And one of his earliest memories was of hiding in terror in a cupboard from one of his mother's druggie meltdowns. He must have been about three years old, he mused, old enough and wise enough to know that he would be kicked and punched if she found him before the rage wore off. His mother, a gorgeous, much-adored film star on the public stage and a drug-addled monster behind closed doors. That was the woman whose tender mercies his father had left him to rely on as a defenceless child.

And then, when he was twenty-six years old, everything had suddenly and quite miraculously changed. His half-brother, Argo, had died in a bungled mugging in a city street and without the smallest warning Heracles Antonakos had moved on surprisingly fast from his grief and had begun to take a passionate interest in the younger son he had snubbed for years. Of course, Jax's mother had been gone by then, Jax reminded himself ruefully, but he still could not adequately explain or understand the very abruptness of his father's change in attitude. Even so, the paternal recognition and support he had craved from his earliest years had unexpectedly and finally become his. Naturally he still wondered if his father's change of heart would last and life being what it was, of course, he had discovered a whole new set of challenges because life as the Antonakos heir was not all peaches and cream.

As the only son of one of the richest men in the world Jax had more money than he knew what to do with. Everywhere he went in Europe he was photographed and treated like a celebrity. Bands of adoring, manipulative and rapacious women tracked and hunted him much as if he were big game. But in the business field, he reminded himself with determined positivity, he had countless stimulating projects to command his interest and engage his brilliant mind.

One of Jax's bodyguards brought a phone to him, his expression dour and apologetic. Jax compressed his lips and accepted the predictable call from his father. Heracles ranted and raved in a rage about the risk Jax had taken by going on the race track and driving at breakneck speeds. Jax said nothing because over the past two years he had learned that arguing or trying to soothe only extended such frenzied sermons. Since Argo's shocking death, Heracles had developed a morbid and excessive fear of Jax participating in any activity that could possibly harm him and if he could have got away with wrapping his only surviving son in cotton wool and packing him away safely in a box he would have done so. While Jax valued his father's new apparent attachment to him even if he didn't quite trust it, he loathed the restrictive and interfering trappings of expectation that came with it.

Only for the sake of peace had Jax accepted the five heavily armed bodyguards he didn't need and who accompanied him everywhere he went. But he remained every bit as stubborn and fiercely independent as he had always been and when he felt the need to relieve stress he still went deep-sea diving, mountain climbing and flying. He still slept with unsuitable women as well…the sort of women even his father couldn't expect him to marry.

And why not? He loved being single and free as the air because he hated anyone trying to tell him what to do. On the only occasions he had strayed from that practical stance he had ended up in disastrous relationships, so now he didn't *ever* do relationships, he only did sex and uncomplicated sex at that. Once he had run off with another man's fiancée and barely lived to tell the tale, he recalled darkly.

Franca had crept into his bed one night when he was drunk and the deed of betrayal had been done before he'd even recognised *who* he was doing it with. Franca, of course, had simply used him to escape a life that had no longer suited her but he hadn't grasped that little fact. He had fallen hook, line and sinker for her 'damsel in distress' vibe long before he'd appreciated that he was dealing with a highly manipulative and destructive alcoholic. He had betrayed his friendship with his former business partner, Rio, but in the end he had more than paid his dues sorting Franca out. But had he learned? Had he hell. After Franca had come his second biggest mistake...

Yet another female-shaped mistake. So, he didn't want a wife and he didn't want children either and *nothing*, certainly not any dormant desire to please his long-absent father, was going to change that, he reflected cynically as Kat Valtinos approached him bearing drinks and a winning smile...

'I hate you doing work like this,' Kreon Thiarkis hissed under his breath as his daughter brought him a drink. 'It's demeaning—'

'Hard work is never demeaning, Dad,' Lucy declared, her dimples flashing as she smiled down soothingly at him. 'Don't be a snob. I'm not half as posh as you are and I never will be.'

Kreon bit back tart words of disagreement because he didn't want to hurt his daughter's feelings, most particularly because she had only been in his life for the last six months and he was afraid of driving her away by acting like a heavy-handed parent. After all, Lucy had never had a proper parent to look out for her, he acknowledged guiltily. But fiercely independent and proud as she was at twenty-one years old, she had been very much down on her luck when she'd finally approached Kreon, toting his baby granddaughter in her arms, both of them shabbily dressed and half starved. The older man's heart softened at the thought of little Bella, who was the most adorable toddler and the light of his life and his wife, Iola's, for he and Iola had met and married too late in life to have a family. He loved having the two of them in his home but he was firmly convinced that his daughter and her child still very much needed a husband to look after them when he himself was no longer around.

And that would have been *so* easy to achieve if only Lucy weren't so defensive and insecure, Kreon reflected in frustration, because his daughter was an extraordinarily beautiful girl. In the bar where she worked men stopped in their tracks simply to stare at her. With a mane of strawberry-blonde curls reaching halfway down her back, creamy skin and big blue eyes, she was a classic beauty and dainty as a doll. She made more on tips than any other waitress in the hotel and was, he had been reliably assured by the owner, who was a friend, a terrific asset to business.

Lucy went about her work, ruefully aware that the job she had insisted on taking only annoyed her father. Unfortunately, being a single parent was an expensive challenge even with the wonderful support her father and stepmother had given her in recent months. She was very grateful that she had come to Greece to finally meet her long-lost father for he and his wife had freely given both her and her daughter love, kindness and acceptance. Her father was the son of a Greek who had married an Englishwoman and he had grown up in London. Kreon was a wonderfully supportive parent and grandparent. Without a word of protest or reproach he had taken in Lucy and her child even though she hadn't warned him about Bella when he'd first invited her out to Greece.

But while Lucy was willing to accept free accommodation as well as her stepmother Iola's help as a sitter with Bella, she was determined not to become a permanent burden or to take too much advantage of the older couple's generosity. She was willing to admit that she had desperately needed help when she'd first arrived in Athens but she was trying very hard now to stand on her own two feet. Her earnings might be small but that salary meant she could pay for the necessities like clothing for herself and her child and for the moment that was enough to ease her pride.

As she stepped away from a customer, her boss and the hotel owner, Andreus, signalled to her. 'We're hosting an important business meeting here in the rear conference room tomorrow morning at eleven,' he informed her. 'I'd like you to serve the drinks and snacks. I only need you for a couple of hours but I'll pay you for a full shift.'

'I'll check with Iola but that should be fine because she doesn't usually go out in the morning,' Lucy said, before taking off to serve a customer waving his hand in the air to get her attention.

The customer tried to chat her up and get her phone number but Lucy simply smiled politely and ignored his efforts because she wasn't even slightly interested in dating, or indeed in anything more physical, being well aware that the very fact she already had a child encouraged most men to assume that she would be a good bet for a casual encounter. She had been there, done that, lost the tee shirt and got a baby for her pains. Unhappily, as a green-as-grass nineteen-year-old virgin she hadn't grasped that she was involved in a casual fling until it was far too late to protect herself and she had been ditched. In fact, having been treated with such devastating contempt and dismissal by Bella's father, that final humiliation was still etched into her soul like a burn of shame that refused to heal whenever she thought about it...which was why she didn't allow herself to think about it *or* him very often.

In any case, what was the point in agonising over past mistakes and misjudgements, not to mention the most painful and cruel rejections she had suffered? Agonising never did change anything. Lucy had learned that the hard way time and time again when she was a vulnerable child growing up in care, subject to the whims of others and unable to control where she lived or even *who* she lived with. Now it meant that she found it hard to trust people and if she didn't have a certain amount of independence and choice she tended to feel horribly trapped and powerless.

But life, she reminded herself with dogged positivity, *was* getting better because for the first time in years she was daring to start putting down roots. She was happier than she had been in years and hoping to come up with a plan to improve her career prospects for Bella's sake. Very probably she would accept her father's offer to pay for some sort of job training or further education that would enable her to move out of low-paid employment. Perhaps it was finally time to start making some long-term decisions and think like a responsible adult, she told herself firmly.

*'You're worth so much more than this kind of grunt work...'* Bella's father had told Lucy two years earlier in Spain.

Well, look just how badly daring to have dreams and believe in them had turned out for her then, Lucy reflected, rigid with regret and pain as she stood at the bar to collect an order. Her friend at the time, another waitress called Tara, had been far more realistic about that relationship.

'He'll sleep with you and dump you and move on the minute he gets bored,' Tara had forecast, although the words she had used had been much earthier. 'Guys like that don't stick with girls like us. We're only good enough to party with for a few nights.'

Perspiration broke on Lucy's short upper lip and she wanted to punch herself hard for letting herself drift even momentarily down that bad memory lane, because hindsight only made her more ashamed of how stupid and naïve she had been. It was not as if she hadn't known what men were like, not as if she had grown up in some little princess castle, always protected and loved. She should have known better and she had yet to forgive herself for her rashness.

But at the end of her shift, when she got home to her father's very comfortable small town house and crept into the bedroom she shared with her daughter, she realised that nothing was quite that cut and dried. Bella slept nestled in her cot, curly black hair dark against the bedding, her olive skin flushed by sleep, long lashes screening her bright green eyes. Bella was gorgeous, like a little angel, Lucy thought with her eyes stinging and, although she could be sorry for everything else, she could not find it in her heart to regret Bella's existence in *any* way.

'Come with us to this dinner on Saturday night,' Iola urged over breakfast the next morning. She was a curvy brunette in her late forties with smiling dark eyes. 'It would please your father so much.'

Lucy went pink as she washed her daughter's face clean of breakfast debris. She knew that her dining out with them would please Kreon, but she also knew it would entail fending off the advances of at least two handpicked young men because her father's current main aim in life seemed to centre on finding her an eligible boyfriend. In that line Kreon was old-fashioned because he refused to credit that Lucy choosing to remain a single parent could be a viable plan for the future.

'Mum… Mum,' Bella carolled cheerfully as she was released from the high chair and set down to toddle somewhat clumsily round the room.

Lucy steadied her daughter as she almost fell over the toy box and ruffled her untidy curls. Curls, aside of the colour, just like her own, frizzy and ungovernable in humid weather, explosive when washed. Lucy looked back at her stepmother uncomfortably. She felt like an ungrateful brat for her reluctance to do what her father wanted her to do. 'I'm just not interested in meeting anyone at present…maybe in a few months I'll feel differently,' she added without much conviction.

'You had a bad breakup and you went through a lot alone afterwards,' Iola acknowledged gently. 'But your father's a man and he doesn't get it. I did try to explain to him that this is more of a healing time for you—'

'Yes, that's it, that's *exactly* it!' Lucy exclaimed, giving the older woman a sudden impulsive and appreciative hug. 'I'm not ready right now, not sure if I'll ever be though…'

'Not all men are like Bella's father. There *are* decent caring men out there,' Iola reminded her quietly.

'Nobody knows that better than me. I kissed a lot of frogs before I met Kreon.'

Lucy grinned and then laughed because her stepmother really did understand her viewpoint. A few minutes later, she left the town house and set out to walk to the small select Hotel Palati where she worked. Sited in an exclusive district in Athens, the hotel catered mainly to a business clientele.

Her father had met Iola when he'd engaged her as a PA in a property rental business that had eventually gone bust. But then Kreon had led a chequered 'boom to bust and back again' life and had been divorced once for infidelity. Lucy had respected his honesty with her. Even on the subject of her late mother, Kreon had proved to be painfully frank. Kreon hadn't once whitewashed his own failings or hidden the fact that he had gained a criminal record over some pyramid selling scheme he had got involved with as a younger man. Yet in spite of that honesty, Lucy still wasn't quite sure what actually funded her father's comfortable lifestyle.

She knew that Kreon gambled and took bets on a near professional basis and that he was always enthusiastically involved in some hopefully lucrative business scheme of one kind or another. Whatever he did, he seemed to be successful at it. Even so, she would not have been entirely surprised to learn that some of his ventures skated a little too close to the edge of breaking the law. But basically because he and Iola had given Lucy and her daughter both the home and the love Lucy had never known before, she closed her eyes to that suspicion and minded her own business the best she could.

After all, there truly *were* shades of grey between the black and white of absolute right and absolute wrong, she ruminated ruefully. Nothing and nobody was perfect. Even at the height of her passionate infatuation with Jax, she had recognised that he was flawed and all too human. He had been moody, controlling, domineering and arrogant and they had fought like cat and dog on a regular basis because, while Lucy might be only five feet tall and undersized, she was no pushover. At heart, she was stubborn and gutsy and quick-tempered. Even if Jax hadn't let her down so horribly, it would never have worked between them, she reasoned, feeling pleasantly philosophical on that score and firmly stifling the painful little push of heartache that still hollowed out her tummy. So, she'd had her heart broken just as Iola and thousands of other women *and* men had. It had only made her more resilient and less foolish and naïve, she told herself squarely.

The hotel manager showed her into the lofty-ceilinged back room, which had been comprehensively redecorated only weeks earlier with an opulence that was calculated to appeal to the more discerning customers.

Sometimes when Lucy daydreamed she wondered, if she had come from a more fortunate background, would she have become one of the elegant well-educated young businesswomen she saw round the hotel. Unfortunately she had been handicapped at the outset of life by her birth. Her parents' marriage had broken down after her mother had had an affair.

'Annabel always thought some better man was waiting for her round the next corner,' Kreon had said wryly of Lucy's mother. 'I wasn't rich and I lived by my wits and she had big ideas. We were living in London then where she was struggling to get the finance to set up her nursery business. But my father had returned to Greece after my mother died and he fell ill out here. I *had* to go to him. When I left London I had no idea Annabel was pregnant and when I contacted her to tell her that I was coming back she told me we were finished because she had met someone else. Now from what you're telling me, it seems she may have learned that she had this dreadful disease and she didn't want me around even though she had my child. I can't understand that, I will *never* understand that...'

And Lucy couldn't understand it either because, just listening to Kreon talking, she had recognised that he *had* loved her mother and had planned to return to London to be with her. But the more Kreon had spoken of her mother's beauty and her feverish love and need for fresh male attention, the more Lucy had suspected that there definitely *had* been another man and Annabel had burnt her boats for ever with Kreon shortly before illness had cruelly claimed her future.

Lucy had been two years old when Annabel was hospitalised and her daughter put into care. Her only memory of her mother was of a beautiful redhead lying in bed and shouting at her, so she wasn't sure that the mother who had surrendered her to the authorities had been that much of a loss in the parent stakes. Kreon had described a flighty, selfish personality, ill-suited to the kind of personal sacrifices a mother was often forced to make. And when, to Lucy's very great astonishment, Kreon had revealed that Annabel had actually had two other daughters being raised by her own mother somewhere in northern England, Lucy had been silenced by that shattering news.

Apparently she had two half-sisters somewhere, born from her mother's previous liaisons. Some day Lucy planned to look into that startling discovery but she didn't even know where you started in such a search because, not only had she no money to pursue enquiries, but also no names even to begin with. Naturally all these years on Kreon didn't recall such details about Annabel's background and history. After all, he had never met Annabel's mother and had been stonewalled by Annabel when he'd asked to do so. All he had remembered was that Annabel never went to visit the two little girls she had left behind her and he had said that even then he had recognised that as a warning sign that Annabel's attachments were of the shallow sort.

Lucy had counted herself lucky that she was not equally superficial because she adored Bella and would have laid down her life for her child, counting Bella as one of the few good developments in a life that had been far from easy or happy. On the other hand, had she cared less about Jax she would have been less devastated when he disappeared. My goodness, she had fallen apart at the seams and done stupid stuff, she recalled ruefully. She had been thrown off his father's yacht and warned never to show her face at the marina again while being marched off by security guards. She had been shouted at, called nasty names and utterly humiliated in her fruitless pursuit of Jax. All because she was fundamentally stupid, she conceded with regret.

After all, it had been crazy of her to believe that she meant anything more to Jax than an easily forgettable sexual fling, and when he was done with a woman, he was definitely *done*. The crewman on the yacht had called her a cheap whore as he'd bodily manhandled her off the polished deck and forced her down the gangway. She had fallen, been hurt and bruised by that brutality and she had been pregnant at the time. That was one reason she had never told her father the whole truth about Bella's parentage, preferring him to assume that Bella was the result of some one-night stand with a man in Spain. She knew Kreon would seek revenge and restitution if she ever told him the whole story.

So, in a way, staying silent was protecting her father from doing anything rash, she reasoned uneasily. Kreon was extremely protective. He would hit the roof if he realised that Lucy had been homeless even though Bella's father was a rich man, who could so easily have helped her and their child. A rich man, who was also Greek. That information wouldn't help either when Kreon was so immensely proud of his heritage.

But then Lucy had long since decided that rich people were pretty much untouchable, unlike the rest of humanity. The very rich had the power and the money to hold the rest of the world at bay and she saw the evidence of that galling fact every time she saw Jax in the media. Jax surrounded by bodyguards and beautiful women, never alone, never approachable, as protected and distanced from ordinary people as an exhibit in a locked museum case. Jax Antonakos, renowned entrepreneur and billionaire in his own right with a daddy who had billions also.

Her hands trembled as she set out china on the trolley awaiting her. She hated Jax now with the same passion she had once put into loving him. He had strung her along, faked so many things and she could never,

ever forgive the fact that he had quite deliberately left her stranded in Spain without a home or a job or any means of support. That she had been pregnant into the bargain was just her bad luck, but then Lucy had little experience of good luck.

A cluster of chattering businessmen entered and she served the coffee, standing back by the wall to dutifully await any further requests. Beyond the ajar door there was a burst of comment and then a sudden hush and the sound of many footsteps crossing the tiled hallway outside. The door whipped back noisily on its hinges and two men strode in, talking into ear pieces while checking the exit doors and all the windows, and that level of security warned Lucy that someone tremendously important was evidently about to arrive. The security men backed against the wall in silence and two more arrived to take up stances on the other side of the room. The almost militaristic security detail seemed so over the top for a small business meeting that Lucy almost laughed out loud.

And then Jax walked in and she stopped breathing and any desire to laugh died in her suddenly constricted lungs…

## CHAPTER TWO

THE INSTANT LUCY saw that untidy black hair and the gorgeous green eyes so arrestingly bright against his bronzed skin, she wanted to run and keep on running and only innate discipline kept her where she was while she questioned her reaction. Why should *she* want to run? What had she done to be ashamed of? She was not a coward, she had never been a coward, she reminded herself doggedly, unnerved by that craven desire to flee. Indeed if anyone should be embarrassed it should be Jax for the cruel way he had treated her.

Couples broke up all the time but the process didn't have to be downright nasty. She hadn't been a stalker. There had been no excuse for threats and no need whatsoever to run her out of the neighbourhood.

Recollecting that vicious goodbye, Lucy lifted her chin high. Seated centre stage at the circular table, the cynosure of all attention and conversation, Jax mercifully wasn't looking round the room enough to notice her. Lucy might have overcome the urge to run but it did annoy her to find herself in a subservient role in Jax's radius again. In a mad moment she had once fantasised about swanning through some swanky club some day looking like a million dollars and seeing Jax and totally ignoring him to demonstrate her disdain and overall superiority as a decent human being. But now that she was actually on the spot she discovered that she was indefensibly and horribly curious and could only stare at him.

He had kept his black hair short. Once he had worn it long but he had had it cropped not long after she'd first met him, hitting the more conventional note she had suspected his father preferred. In retrospect she found it hard to credit that they had once bonded over their absent fathers. Jax had admitted how recently his father had come back into his life and had shared his grief over the death of the half-brother he had loved, not to mention his mother's abuse and infidelities. None of those deep conversations had fitted into what she assumed could be described as a typical short-term fling. But then that was Jax, a tough individualist, unpredictable, fiery and mysterious...the archetypal brooding hero beloved of teenaged girls with an overly romantic disposition, she concluded sourly.

That he *was* startlingly handsome had undoubtedly influenced the fantasies she had woven, she acknowledged, chewing at her lower lip, fingernails biting painfully into her palms. High cheekbones, strong clean jaw line, stunning eyes set beneath well-shaped ebony brows. Of course his mother had been a very famous and stunningly beautiful Spanish movie star and he had inherited her looks. In a big magazine article she had once read about him, which had been accompanied by a close-up photo, the journalist had raved about those dazzling wild green eyes and the spiky length of his sooty lashes.

Bella had *his* eyes. Lucy swallowed hard, recalling her feelings as her daughter's blue eyes at birth had slowly transformed to an eerily familiar emerald in her innocent little face. Innocent, something Jax was not and had never been. And reading about his sexual exploits over the past two years had helped Lucy to understand that he had always been a selfish, ruthless womaniser but she had been too trusting and inexperienced to recognise his true nature. Her heart was fluttering a beat so fast behind her breastbone that she wanted to press a hand against it to slow it down.

And then the truth of her response hit her and she was aghast that in spite of everything her body could still react to the presence of his. He glanced up from the file he had been perusing and for a split second, a literal *single* heartbeat, she clashed in dismay with his fierce gaze. It was like an electric shock pulsing low in her pelvis, tightening bone and sinew, awakening sensations she had almost forgotten and had never felt since. Every pulse she possessed went crazy, her breath catching in her throat, her very skin as achingly sensitive as if he had actually *touched* her. And then that tiny moment was over and past as Jax blanked her and passed the file back to someone at the table while making some comment about profit margins.

Her Greek vocabulary was slowly growing but in unfamiliar scenarios she still got as lost as any non-Greek-speaking foreigner. And *of course* Jax was going to blank her, she told herself shakily. Had she really thought he would greet a worker bee as low on the proverbial food chain as a waitress? Her mouth compressed as she wondered anxiously how he would react to the news that he was a father were she to tell him. With furious hostility and denial, she reckoned, her skin turning clammy at the prospect. Jax had once been very upfront about the fact that he didn't ever want children. Bearing that in mind, Lucy ruminated grimly, he should have been more careful to ensure that he didn't get her pregnant.

Jax's lean, chiselled features were rigid. He refused to look back in Lucy's direction. He didn't need to. That momentary image was stamped into his brain like a punch. What the hell was she doing in Athens? And her sudden appearance in his presence? Some sort of a set-up? And if so, why? Jax never took anything at face value any more. After all, he had once accepted Lucy for what she appeared to be and learned his very great error.

Bile tinged his mouth as he briefly recalled what he had read in that investigation file on her background: a string of drug offences stretching back years and convictions for soliciting sex. He had felt like a complete idiot. He had rushed off to see her, *confront* her even though it was late at night and then he had seen who she really was for himself…down an alley with a man enthusiastically giving up what she had made him wait weeks to enjoy.

Disgust and distaste flooded Jax, bringing back even less welcome memories of his mother's rampant promiscuity and empty promises of fidelity. He had seen her cheating break more than one man who had adored her. His father didn't know it because he had never dared to ask what his son's life had been like with his mother but Heracles had not been the only man to be chewed up and spat out in pieces by Mariana, who had wilfully followed every stray sexual impulse. As for Lucy, she was a liar and a cheat and he did not forgive betrayal. The entire episode had been sordid in the extreme. So why was he remembering that she had given him the wildest, hottest sex he had ever had?

A stubborn push of raunchily sexual images infiltrated Jax's hind brain even while he fought to hold them at bay and kept on talking about the project on the table. Hard as a rock behind his zip, Jax went rigid with angry aggression. How dared Lucy even walk into a room that contained him? He had always told himself that he had not inherited his father's notorious temper and equally notorious ability to hold a grudge but just then he recognised that he had lied to himself. Had it been possible to bodily throw Lucy out, he would have done so!

One of the bodyguards nudged Lucy's elbow and she glanced up, dragged from her own bemused thoughts with a vengeance. The older man indicated the coffee on the trolley and angled his head in his employer's direction, clearly urging her to get on with her job.

Reddening all the way up to her hairline, Lucy unfroze in an effort to behave normally. Even so she had to fight a huge inner battle to force her legs over to the trolley and pour Jax a coffee when all she really wanted to do was empty the entire contents of the pot over his hateful, arrogant head. Without him looking once at her or indeed acknowledging her in any way, she settled the coffee at his elbow with a hand that trembled slightly. Next she laid out the snacks and topped up the cups, signalling the bar waiter at the door when one of the men requested a shot of ouzo to wash down his coffee.

From below screening lashes and the almost infinitesimal movements of his proud dark head, Jax tracked Lucy's every move like a predator planning an attack. A blinding flash of memory assailed him: skin as translucent as fine porcelain in the dawn light, his fingers knotted into tumbling golden ringlets spread across a pillow, glorious bright blue eyes holding his, a tiny slender body with surprisingly sexy little curves reaching up to his. A little curvier than she used to be, he estimated abstractedly, remembering for a few seconds and then suddenly emerging again from that uncharacteristic reverie to answer a question, angrier and hotter than he had been in years.

The louse could at least have thanked her for the coffee, Lucy reflected with growing annoyance. Even a nod would have been acceptable but then Jax had always been a law unto himself, ferociously uncompromising and challenging, driven to succeed, survive and flourish as if it was in his genes. And perhaps it was. Only in a fantasy could there ever have been a scenario in which she believed that Jax Antonakos would settle down with a humble waitress… Bitterness gripped her and resentment shot through her like a sheet of lightning flashing off all her exposed nerve endings with painful effect.

Who the hell did Jax Antonakos think he was to treat her with such derisive dismissal?

Jax summoned Zenas, his head security guard, with an almost imperceptible flicker of his gaze and passed him a note. Zenas stood back to read it and confusion gripped his features for an instant before discipline kicked in and he left the room to do his employer's bidding. Lucy paid little heed to the byplay and only tensed when her own boss appeared in the doorway and silently summoned her out into the hallway.

A frown line bisected the older man's brow as he studied her. 'Mr Antonakos wants to speak to you in private when he's finished. I'm not sure how your father would feel about that request—'

Comprehension gripped Lucy fast. Andreus had no idea that she already knew Jax. He simply thought that Jax was trying to get off with her.

'Please don't mention this to Dad,' she muttered unevenly, for that was not a connection she wanted made. Once a link of any kind was established, secrets could spill out.

Andreus cast open the door of a smaller room across the corridor. 'Wait in there…but only if you *want* to,' he added with deliberate meaning. 'This is nothing to do with your employment here or with me. I have only passed on his request because I am very reluctant to offend so powerful a man.'

Lucy turned a slow, painful red, rage mushrooming inside her again as she imagined what her employer must be thinking. Jax wouldn't care about appearances. Jax had never *had* to care about appearances. For an instant she almost walked away from the opportunity to tell Jax what she thought of him. But she was too nervous, too aware of what had happened the last time her very existence nearby had become objectionable to Jax Antonakos. He had paid her then boss in Spain to sack her and she had lost her job and the accommodation that went with it. That was the kind of power the super wealthy had. Her boss in those days had been outrageously frank with her, admitting that he couldn't afford to keep her on when so much money to do otherwise was on offer and that he had had a poor summer season.

She paced the floor in the small room that was normally used as an office by the hotel housekeeper, thinking herself lucky that Jax hadn't had a room in the hotel and called her there, which would have looked even worse. Why on earth after ignoring her would he have demanded a meeting? From his point of view that made no sense, she reasoned with a frown. After all, he had ditched her two years earlier without an explanation or even a text. He hadn't turned up for their last date, hadn't phoned, hadn't done anything and when she had tried to contact him he had blocked her calls. Either he had simply tired of her or she had done or said something that had offended.

It hurt to look back and recall how many weeks she had tormented herself by pathetically wondering what she had done to annoy Jax. But nothing could have justified his subsequent behaviour in having her sacked and forced to leave the area like some vagrant whose very presence was offensive. That more than anything was what she could not forgive.

'You literally have three minutes or you'll miss your flight,' Zenas warned Jax outside the door.

Jax strode into the room, absently wondering if there was actual truth in the idea that human beings needed closure following certain experiences because he could not imagine any other reason why he should still feel driven to confront Lucy. Two years ago, he had never wanted to see or speak to her again. But possibly curiosity provided more motivation than he was willing to admit, he reasoned impatiently, angry tension tightening his lean, darkly handsome features.

'What the hell are you doing in Athens?' Jax demanded.

Lucy spun round from the window to face him, inwardly reeling from the shock of Jax in the flesh standing close enough to touch. He was so tall and he radiated restive energy and dominant vibes in waves. Tensing, she lifted her head up but she still had to tip it back to actually see any part of him above chest level. Not for the first time her diminutive height struck her as an embarrassing flaw. Being almost child-sized often meant that people didn't take her seriously or treat her like an adult. 'What's that got to do with you?' she slung back sharply, her tone similar to his own.

Jax drew himself up to his full six-foot-three-inch height and glowered down at her, green eyes luminescent with rage because it had been two years since anyone but his father had challenged him. 'Answer me,' he ground out impatiently.

'I don't owe you any answers…I don't owe you the time of day,' Lucy traded with the kind of provocation that struck a deep and unwelcome note of familiarity with Jax.

'You *will* answer me,' Jax raked back at her in a raw undertone, watching as she angled her head back and struck an attitude, hand on hip. Strawberry golden curls slid round her shoulders, her hair falling round her heart-shaped face, accentuating the defiant blue of her eyes and the lush fullness of her rosy lips.

And that fast, that urgently, Jax wanted to throw her down on the desk and control her the only way he had ever really controlled her, with the seething passion that was the mainstay of his character. For the briefest of moments he allowed himself to imagine the hot, wet tightness of her and the pulse at his groin reacted with unbridled enthusiasm. He reminded himself that it had been a toxic relationship and that she had played him like a con artist with her stories, her fake innocence and her lies. A dizzy surge of rage ignited inside him like a threatening fireball.

'If you don't answer me you will live to regret it,' Jax threatened in a wrathful undertone, every drop of his merciless Antonakos blood burning through him and hungry for a fight.

An angry spurt of fear made Lucy's stomach turn over sickly. He was too influential to challenge as even her boss had reminded her. She knew Jax could cause trouble for her, maybe even for her father as well if she wasn't careful. She might hate Jax but it would be insane to risk such penalties. 'What am I doing in Athens?' she repeated flatly. 'I finally looked up my birth father and he lives here—'

'But that was all lies,' Jax breathed in momentary bewilderment. 'You don't *have* a Greek father.'

Her smooth brow furrowed with genuine confusion. 'Lies? I don't know what you're talking about. I believe my birth certificate is as accurate as anyone else's. At the moment I'm living with my father and his wife.'

'That's not possible,' Jax told her, stiffening as a light knock on the door warned him that their time was up if he planned to make it to the airport. His long, lean frame swivelled as he half turned towards the door to leave, common sense and practicality powering him.

'I just want you to know that I hate you and I'll never forgive you for what you did to me,' Lucy confided in a belated rush of angry frustration that she could not tell him what she really thought of him any more bluntly than that. In truth she wanted to scream at him, she wanted to throw herself at him and hammer him with angry fists for hurting her.

'I didn't *do* anything to you,' Jax parried with complete cool.

'It was vicious…what you did, unnecessary!' Lucy condemned chokily, bitterness almost overpowering her along with a very human need to hit back. 'Having me sacked? Leaving me penniless and homeless and forced to go back to the UK when I had nothing there!'

An ebony brow elevated at that improbable accusation of bullying behaviour on his part, Jax swung back to her just as another knock sounded on the door. Whatever else he might be, Jax prided himself on never having treated a woman badly. 'I don't have time for this and I shouldn't make time for it either,' he acknowledged grimly. 'You're a liar and a cheat—'

'Of course you're going to say stuff like that, rewrite history, because you're so up yourself now,' Lucy shot back at him in disgust as she thought about her innocent, trusting little daughter. 'But I never lied to you or cheated on you and you never once thought about consequences, did you?'

He wanted her phone number but he wouldn't ask for it, wouldn't allow himself to ask for it. He knew what she was. He didn't want anything to do with her. So, having reached that decision and feeling invigorated by it, he could not explain why he then turned back like a man with a split personality and told her to meet him for a drink the following evening at a little bar he patronised on the marina, a haunt of his for quiet moments, which the paparazzi had yet to discover. Even as he walked back out again, he was questioning the decision and regretting it, lean brown hands clenching into impatient fists. What the hell had he done that for?

But what had she meant by 'consequences'? And how come she *did* have a Greek father when according to that file she did not?

He was simply curious, nothing wrong or surprising about that. His libido was not in the driver's seat, he assured himself with solid conviction. Stray memories had briefly aroused him when he saw her again, nothing more meaningful. All men remembered incredibly good sex. Furthermore, he had a little black book of phonebook proportions to turn to when he felt like sex, hot and cold running women on tap wherever he travelled. *That* was the world he lived in. There was no way he could ever be tempted to revisit a manipulative little cheat like Lucy Dixon, he reflected with satisfaction.

Naturally, becoming the Antonakos heir had ensured that Jax became significantly more cynical about women. He didn't listen to sob stories any more, he didn't let his inherently dangerous streak of chivalry rule him. Indeed the sight of a woman in need of rescue was more like aversion therapy to him now. He knew from experience that that kind of woman was likely to be far more trouble than she was worth.

After all, how many times had he felt he had no choice but to race to his mother's rescue? When the men she betrayed became violent as her lies were exposed? When she needed another spell in some discreet rehabilitation facility before she could be seen in public again? When he was forced to lie to protect *her*?

And yet at heart he had always known that his

mother was a deeply disturbed and egocentric human being, undeserving of his care and respect. That was why his little sister, Tina, had died, he reminded himself bitterly. Mariana's self-centred neglect of her younger child had directly led to the incident in which the toddler had drowned. But he had only been fourteen, so what could he possibly have done when so many adults had witnessed the insanity of his mother's lifestyle and yet failed to act to protect either of her children?

Lucy walked home in a pensive mood. Of course she wouldn't meet him, she told herself firmly. What would be the point? *Bella!* Jax was a father whether he liked it or not but she knew he wouldn't like that news any more than he liked her. And why was her being in Greece such a big deal? What was it to him? It was not as though they were likely to bump into each other again in normal life. Jax lived against a backdrop of massive yachts, private jets and private islands. He didn't rub shoulders with ordinary working people.

Yet a giant ball of despair was threatening to swallow Lucy up and she didn't know why. Seeing Jax again, she recognised, had *hurt* and hurt much more than she had expected. It had brought back memories she didn't want. She had loved him and had given her trust to a man for the first time ever. His sudden volte-face had almost destroyed her because she had given him so much she had felt bare to the world without him.

And yet he *still* wasn't married. She had thought for sure that he would marry the wealthy heiress his father kept pushing in his direction, the very lovely but very bitchy Kat Valtinos. But then Jax was bone-deep stubborn. You could take a horse to water but you couldn't make it drink and getting Jax to do anything he didn't want to do was like trying to push a boulder up a steep hill.

Kat Valtinos had organised the party the night Lucy had met Jax on his father's enormous yacht. Lucy's memory wafted her back two years into the past. Back then, Jax had been in Spain setting up a new resort on the coast. When the caterers had mucked up with a double booking, Kat had personally trawled through the local bars seeking waitresses for the event.

'You two will do,' she had said to Lucy and Tara, looking them up and down as though they were auditioning as strippers. 'You're young and pretty and sexy. Just what men like. You put your make-up on with a trowel,' she had told Tara critically and to Lucy she had said, 'You need to show more leg and cleavage.'

If the money hadn't been so good, Lucy wouldn't have done it but back then she had lived on a budget where no tips meant stale bread and going hungry. Their boss didn't feed them for free and they had no cooking facilities in their mean little attic room, which had been hot as hell up under the eaves above the restaurant kitchen. Any extra cash was deeply welcome in those days.

The party had been full of blowhard bellicose men talking themselves up in Antonakos's company and drinking too much. One of them had cornered Lucy when she was sent to a lower deck to restock the bar from the supplies stored there. She had been trying to fight him off when Jax had intervened. Jax, blue-black glossy hair brushing his shoulders, green eyes glittering like shards of glass, who had dragged the guy off her with punishing hands and hit him hard without hesitation.

'Are you OK?' the most gorgeous guy she had ever seen had asked, pulling her off the wall she had slumped against, smoothing down the skirt the creep had been trying to wrench up. '*Diavolos*, you're so tiny. Did he hurt you?'

'Only a little,' she had said shakily, trembling like a leaf and in absolutely no doubt that Jax had saved her from a serious assault because, with the noisy party taking place on the deck above, the lower deck had been deserted and nobody would have heard her crying out.

'Take a moment to recover,' Jax had urged, guiding her into an opulent saloon to push her down into a seat where her cotton-wool legs had collapsed under her as if he had flipped a switch. 'What were you doing down here on this deck?'

He had issued instructions on the phone to a crew member to have the bar supplies refreshed. And the whole time she had just been staring at him like a brainless idiot, utterly intimidated by everything about him from the expensive quality of his lightweight grey suit and hand-stitched shoes to the sheer beauty of his perfect features from his edgy cheekbones to his sculpted mouth. It was the eyes that had got to her the most, the tender concern she'd seen there and then the budding all-male appreciation. He had the most stunning eyes and his rare smile had been like the sun coming out on a dark day.

'Are you OK?' he repeated.

Well, no, in fact from that moment she had never

been OK again. Something she'd needed to survive had lurched into strange territory and softened to let him in, no matter that it had gone against sense and practicality and her life experience. She had truly never been the same since.

# CHAPTER THREE

LUCY WAS RIVEN with extreme guilt by the time she finally climbed on the bus that would take her down to the marina.

She had had to lie to Iola simply to get out. She had pretended that she was joining a couple of the other waitresses for a few drinks. To weigh down her conscience even more, Iola had been delighted to believe that her stepdaughter was finally going out and about. Her stepmother had hovered helpfully, urging her to put on make-up and wear the pretty white sundress that Iola had bought for her a few weeks earlier. But how *could* Lucy have admitted that she was heading out to meet Bella's father? After all, she had already lied on that subject by declaring that she had no way of getting in touch with the man who had fathered her daughter. Kreon and Iola had averted their eyes in dismay and embarrassment at that claim, clearly assuming that she did not know the man's name.

Indeed, one lie only led to more lies, Lucy conceded shamefacedly, annoyed that she had found it impossible to be more honest. But Kreon would raise the roof if he discovered that Jax was Bella's father and she didn't want to put Kreon in the potential firing line of Antonakos displeasure.

And why was she off to meet Jax when she had sworn she would not do so?

Obviously she was thinking about her daughter's needs, wondering if there was any chance that Jax could have changed his outlook on children and could possibly be willing to embrace the news that he was a parent. It was definitely her duty to check out that possibility and finally tell him that he had a child, she told herself staunchly even while her heart hammered and her breath caught in her throat at the prospect of seeing Jax again.

You're pathetic, she scolded herself angrily as she marched past crowded bars, ignoring the men who called out to her. He's a very good-looking guy and of course you still notice that but that's all, leave it there. You are *not* a silly impulsive teenager any more, she coached herself, you know what he is and what he's like and *you know better.*

Jax lounged outside the bar with Zenas close by, the rest of his security detail settled within hailing distance. He didn't know why he had come until he saw Lucy, her dress flowing and dancing round her slender knees, the pristine white lighting up below the street lights, her strawberry-blonde ringlets a vivid fall round her narrow shoulders. And then he knew why he had come and he hated that surge of absolute primal lust, raw distaste flaming through him even as his jeans became uncomfortably tight. A wave of male heads slowly turned to check her out as she passed by. Jax gritted his even white teeth at that familiar display.

'The waitress...*really*?' Zenas teased from the shadows.

'I need to have this conversation in private,' Jax warned his old school friend quietly, relieved that Zenas had only joined the team the year before and had no idea of his prior acquaintance with Lucy.

Zenas strolled obediently across the street and plonked himself down on a bench. Jax lifted his newspaper, refusing to continue watching Lucy walk towards him, perturbed by the level of his own interest. He would get answers from her, satisfy his curiosity and leave. There would be nothing more personal and absolutely *no* sex.

Lucy saw Jax outside the bar, arrogant dark head bent, the bold cut of his chiselled profile golden beneath the lights, his black hair still long enough to tousle in the light breeze. And her heart bounced inside her like a rubber ball because she was helplessly reliving the excitement he had always induced in her. There were flutters in her tummy, crazy tingles pinching the tips of her breasts taut and a dangerous hot, liquid awareness pulsing into being between her legs. Just as quickly her entire body felt overheated and she was seriously embarrassed for herself.

As she took a seat Jax glanced up at her from below his ridiculously long lashes, crescents of uncompromising green running assessingly across her flushed face. 'At least you're on time for once...I assume you hurried.'

Lucy blinked and bit down on her tongue hard. Her poor timekeeping had always infuriated Jax because he hated being kept waiting and never, ever understood how time could sometimes run away from her.

He had always contended that being late was rude and indefensible. But then Jax, who was relentlessly practical and full of ferocious initiative in tough scenarios, had probably never had a weakness for daydreaming.

Daydreaming, however, had always been Lucy's escape from challenging experiences. When she didn't fit in at the many different schools she had attended she had floated away on a fluffy cloud inside her own mind. When life was especially difficult, fantasies had become her consolation and she would dream of a world in which she had love and security and happiness.

In the smouldering silence that had now fallen, Lucy forced herself out of her abstraction and registered that Jax was watching her with impatient green eyes as if he had guessed that she had momentarily drifted away with the fairies. In receipt of that aggravated look, she felt her mouth run dry as a bone. In desperation she spun his newspaper round, her attention falling on a recent custody case that had attracted a lot of media coverage. 'Oh, my goodness…' she muttered as she slowly traced the headline with a fingertip while she carefully translated it. 'The *father* got the kid? How could they take a child away from his mother?'

Jax shrugged an uninterested shoulder as he signalled the waiter. 'Why not? Life has moved on. Fathers are now equal to mothers—'

'Yes, but—'

'Read it and you'll see why the family court reached that decision,' Jax said drily.

'I can't read Greek well enough yet,' she admitted grudgingly.

'The father is willing to work at home to be with the child while the mother would be leaving him in a nursery all day. Why are we talking about this anyway?' Jax demanded impatiently.

'It's an interesting case,' Lucy proffered stiffly. 'The mother's a paramedic who doesn't have the option of working at home.'

'While the father wants his child and what's best for his child, which is as it should be,' Jax interposed as a bottle of wine and glasses arrived at the table.

A cold skitter of fear pierced Lucy's tense body as a glass of wine appeared in front of her. 'Is that how you would feel?'

'We're not talking about me. I won't be fathering any children,' Jax declared with a cynical twist of his expressive mouth. 'Don't need the hassle or the responsibility. But if I *did* have a child I certainly wouldn't sit back and allow a woman to take my child away from me…in fact that is the very last thing I would do.'

A quiver of sheer fright rippled down Lucy's taut spine as she reached for her wine. That risk, that particular fear of losing her child, had never once crossed her mind as a possibility. And why hadn't it? Jax might not want children but he *was* a very possessive guy. What was his was very much his, not to be shared or touched or even looked at by anyone else. Once he had treated Lucy like that, enraging her with his determination to own her body and soul and control her every move. Suppose she told him about Bella and he felt the same way about his daughter?

Sobered by that fear, Lucy decided there and then to continue keeping Bella a secret until she had, at least, taken legal advice. In fact maybe the legal route would be the best way to go when it came to breaking that news, she thought cravenly. It would be more impersonal and less likely to lead to confrontation and bad feeling. Just at that moment Lucy could not face telling Jax that he was the father of her child and that because of his behaviour after their breakup she had had no way of telling him that she was pregnant. That was not her fault, she reminded herself. That was unquestionably *his* fault.

'When did you move to Athens?' Jax prompted.

'Six months ago…I was struggling to make ends meet in London,' she confided, almost rolling her eyes at that severe understatement before taking several fortifying swallows of wine.

'When we talked in Spain, you had no plans to track your father down,' he reminded her with a frown. 'You thought he had deserted your mother and you *said*—'

'I was wrong. When I needed help, my father came through for me,' Lucy admitted. 'Why did you ask me to meet you?'

Jax watched her sip at the wine, one little finger rubbing back and forth over the stem of the glass, her lush mouth rosy and moist. Like a sex-starved adolescent, he remembered the feel of her mouth, the flick of her teasing little tongue and he went rigid.

*'Jax?'* she pressed, setting down the glass.

Lean, dark features taut, Jax topped up the wine. He had tried to teach her about wine once: how to select it, savour it, how to truly *taste* it, and she was still knocking it back as if it were cheap plonk. That had been another lesson that had inexplicably ended up between the sheets. But then nothing had ever gone to plan with Lucy. His self-discipline had vanished.

When he had taken her shopping he had taken her in the changing cubicle up against the wall, stifling her frantic cries with his hand. Yes, she had definitely *earned* that red dress he had later seen her wearing while she gave her body to another man.

'Why?' Lucy prompted in growing frustration at his brooding silence.

Jax inclined his head to Zenas and spoke to him soft and low when he approached. 'We'll go somewhere more private—'

Lucy collided with smouldering green eyes like highly polished emeralds and stiffened in instant rejection of that idea. 'No.'

'I don't know what I was thinking of. This is not the place to talk.' Or fight, Jax reflected, in no doubt that angry words were likely to be exchanged when he challenged her.

Lucy gulped down more wine in an effort to steady herself and think carefully before she spoke. 'I don't want to go anywhere else with you,' she argued.

'Don't lie,' Jax advised in the driest of tones. 'I could have you on your back in five minutes if that's what I wanted...but it's *not*.'

A tide of outraged colour slowly dappled Lucy's creamy skin as she gazed back at him, aghast at his crudity. 'I can't believe you said that.'

Jax shrugged again, a knowing look in his stunning eyes. 'It's only what we're both thinking about.'

Lucy bristled like a cat stroked the wrong way and threw her shoulders back. 'No, it's not. Speak for yourself.'

'I fell for the virgin ploy once. Don't push your luck, *koukla mou*,' Jax advised as he thrust back his chair and began to rise. 'Born-again virgins push the wrong buttons with me.'

'Don't call me that…I'm *not* anyone's doll!' Lucy protested, aware of the meaning of those words because her father used them around Bella.

'Don't push your luck, Tinker Bell,' Jax stabbed instead.

And the sound of that once familiar pet name hurt like the unexpected swipe of a knife across tender skin. It turned her pale because it took her back to a place she didn't want to go, to a period when she had fondly believed herself to be loved and safe and cherished. But it had all been a lie and a seriously cruel lie at that. It hurt even more that she had adored that lie and longed for it to last for ever and ever, just like in the fairy tales.

'You still haven't told me what this is about,' Lucy argued as she drank down her wine with desperate little swallows that pained her throat. 'I'm staying here.'

A long silver limousine purred along the kerb. They were in a pedestrian zone and the car shouldn't have been there but the two police officers lounging across the street did nothing to interfere with its progress.

'Get in the car or I'll throw you in it!' Jax bit out in a driven undertone, what little patience he had taxed by her obstinacy.

He had made a mistake, he thought furiously, turning his head and unexpectedly encountering Zenas's shocked appraisal, registering that the other man had heard that threat.

Incredulous, Lucy giggled. 'You wouldn't dare,' she told him.

And he *did*. He picked her up off the chair and

shoved her into the back seat of the limo as if she were a lost parcel he was retrieving, aware throughout that his bodyguards were watching him as if he had gone insane. But it was entirely Lucy's fault. She would never ever do as she was told. She would never ever accept that he knew best. And the whole situation was going to hell in a hand basket fast and he could blame himself for that because he should never have arranged to meet her in the first place. Why the hell did what had happened two years ago even *matter* to him?

So, she had lied to engage his sympathy and ensnare him, pretending to be younger and more innocent than she actually was. He already knew why she had done it. She had lied to impress him because he was rich and there was nothing more complex behind her behaviour back then than greed and a desire to rise in the world. He had been cunningly targeted and chased by hundreds of other women for the same reasons. Why was *her* deception still raw?

As he swung into the car, radiating blazing tension, his dazzling eyes splintered like green lightning with anger and Lucy stared at him.

'You still have a terrible temper,' she complained. 'And you just kidnapped me and the police did nothing—'

'Maybe you should've tried a little screaming and struggling to demonstrate fear,' Jax mocked, convinced that she was secretly delighted to be in his limo again and probably already planning a lucrative rehash of their Spanish fling.

*No way*, he swore to himself, black lashes almost hitting his cheekbones as he glanced studiously away from her, sitting there as she was watching him like a little spider planning an intricate web in which to capture him. On the other hand, *he* could play her the way she had once played him, he conceded grimly. And while he was doing that he could do whatever he wanted to do with her. That thought, that very idea took him aback because he didn't usually play games with women. But there was no denying that the concept of playing games with Lucy hugely turned him on.

Lucy breathed in slow and deep to calm herself. She focussed on the strong male thigh next to her own, the fine fabric of his trousers pulled taut across his powerful muscles and across his crotch. Her attention lingered there a split second longer and then hurriedly shifted because it was obvious that he was aroused. Why? Did he *ever* think of anything but sex? Colour warmed her cheeks because once they had had a very physical relationship. It had lasted six weeks, with them only becoming intimate in the last two, but during it she had realised that sex was unbelievably important to Jax and an unapologetic drive he made no attempt to restrain. Bella, after all, had been conceived in a brazen episode in a changing-room cubicle, she recalled in serious mortification. She had *tried* to say no but she had never been very good at denying Jax when her own body burned for his like a fire that couldn't be doused.

'I hate you,' she told him truthfully, still thinking about that changing-room cubicle in which the use of precautions hadn't figured.

'Because I found you out?' Jax drawled in a tone of boredom. 'Or because I dumped you?'

Lucy's nails bit crescents into the soft skin of her

palms. She had told him the truth: she *did* hate him. In fact the idea of wreaking revenge on Jax energised her. He was so unbearably confident, sure of his every move in a way she had never been. He was clever, successful and rich. He was also worshipped like the Greek god he resembled by women more akin to groupies than anything else.

'Where are you taking me?' she demanded curtly. 'Why do you even want to talk to me? It's a bit late in the day, isn't it?'

'Is it?' Jax traded unfathomably, leaning forward to press a button that opened a gleaming bar.

'I don't understand you!' Lucy bit out in frustration.

'Why would you?'

Jax thrust a foaming glass of champagne into her hand, thoroughly disconcerting her. Big blue eyes skimmed up to his in confusion and she looked so lost and bewildered that a momentary pang of conscience pierced his tough hide. Of course it wasn't real, he recognised angrily.

*Fool me once, shame on you, fool me twice, shame on me.*

He knew he could trust Lucy to put in an award-winning performance. He would get what he wanted. He would get answers and doubtless tears, self-justification and grovelling into the bargain. He positively warmed to an image of Lucy grovelling and a smile flashed across his forbidding mouth. Lucy on her knees poised to please...just what the doctor would order for a bored billionaire.

That was what lay at the root of his bizarre behaviour, he reasoned broodingly. He was bored. Bored with the flattery of too many far too eager to please women. Well, Lucy had never been into the art of hanging off his every word and complimenting him on his brilliance. Lucy had fought him and criticised him and driven him crazy on many occasions. Yet he had only been with her six short weeks interspersed with the business trips that had parted them. Six weeks. That was a sobering acknowledgement. Why did he remember so much about her when generally he was challenged to recall the name of a woman he had shared a bed with only a week ago?

She had hurt his pride. That was why. That was the only reason he still remembered her, Jax decided. Well, that and the supercharged, highly satisfying sex…

Lucy sipped the champagne, bubbles bursting under her nose and tickling, tiny beads of moisture cooling her too hot face. She felt out of control and she didn't like it. She was in Jax's car and she didn't know where he was taking her or why he would want to talk to her after so long. She crossed her legs, then re-crossed them, looking everywhere but at him.

'I want to go home,' she said abruptly.

'No, you don't.'

'I don't trust you. I don't want to be anywhere alone with you,' she told him sharply.

'My housekeeper lives in,' Jax murmured flatly.

'Like that's going to change my mind!' Lucy scoffed. 'Nobody you employ will go up against you. Do you think I'm stupid?'

'A little hysterical,' Jax confided. 'And it's undeserved. I've never harmed you in any way.'

'But your employees will if you tell them to. I was dragged off of *Sea Queen* two years ago and I got hurt,' Lucy told him reluctantly.

Jax turned his head to frown at her as the limousine coasted to a halt. 'What on earth are you talking about?' he demanded.

The door beside him clicked open and then the one beside her. She climbed out onto a well-lit driveway fronting an ultra-modern villa of quite astonishing size. The cool night air hit her hard and she felt slightly dizzy. A large glass of wine topped up by champagne had been too much for her system, she acknowledged heavily. Alcohol always hit her hard.

'We'll discuss this indoors,' Jax ground out impatiently. 'Come on...'

How had she got herself into this situation? Lucy asked herself with angry self-loathing. She didn't know where she was and had no idea how to get home again. She *should* have kicked up a major fuss when Jax had lifted her out of her chair at the bar but she had let him get away with it sooner than cause a public scene. In certain moods, Jax was as unstoppable as a juggernaut. He didn't care what anybody thought. The only opinion he cared for was his own.

'I want a taxi home,' she informed him. 'Right now...'

'I thought you were dying to tell me about the assault on the yacht,' Jax murmured, shooting her a politely enquiring appraisal that she immediately distrusted.

Lucy hovered uncertainly, noting the security team standing around and the older woman waiting to greet them at the front door. Compressing her lips, she forced herself to follow Jax, carefully picking her path up the steps into the contemporary hall. The preponderance of mirrors and multiple reflections confused her and she didn't object when Jax rested a light hand on her back to guide her into a huge reception room furnished with sofas and monochromatic modern art works.

'Assault…yacht,' Jax prodded expectantly. 'When did this happen?'

'About two weeks after I last saw you in Spain—'

'I had already left the country by then. Tell me what happened.'

'I went looking for you and I was told you weren't on board the *Sea Queen*—'

'Which was true.'

'The crew member that dealt with me was horrible. He called me names and manhandled me—'

Jax had fallen very still. 'In what way were you "manhandled"?'

'I said that I wasn't willing to leave until I was given a phone number or an address where I could contact you. Maybe that was foolish,' Lucy muttered ruefully. 'Anyway, this big bald guy got really aggressive and called me a whore and just dragged me across the deck and pushed me down the gangway. I fell at the foot, bloodied my knees and my elbows and nobody helped me. And someone had called the marina security to escort me away and they accused me of trespassing in a restricted area. It was hideous.'

A frown line had drawn his fine ebony brows together. 'I refuse to credit that any member of the crew would be so rough with a woman—'

Lucy bridled. 'Well, believe it…it happened!'

'Nor can I accept that there was verbal abuse. But I can confirm that you would not have been given my phone number or address because I left that instruction,' he admitted grimly.

'Why was that necessary? What did you think I was going to do?' Lucy framed in an angry rush. 'Spring a terrorist attack on you? Turn into a stalker?'

'I didn't want you making a nuisance of yourself,' Jax advanced flatly, turning away from her for an instant, memories interfering with his thoughts.

What she had made him feel had been too intense. In the aftermath of his discovery of her true nature, he had overreacted, he acknowledged with hindsight, stepping back and instinctively protecting himself from further exposure to her. It had seemed imperative that he neither speak to her nor see her again.

'I can't understand why you went to the yacht or why you tried to contact me again,' he said drily, swinging back to her with his brain fixed firmly in the present.

Bitter recriminations bubbled on Lucy's lips and she swallowed them back because she didn't want to make an announcement about Bella in the midst of a heated dispute. And Jax might be poised in front of her as ice cool and expressionless as a glacier but the atmosphere felt combustible and the tension was horrendous.

'Obviously I tried to contact you…but you simply vanished. I didn't hear from you again. Most people would seek an explanation—'

'There was a *very* obvious explanation. I'd grown bored,' Jax murmured with derision.

'Sometimes you are a very nasty piece of work,' Lucy mumbled shakily, appalled that he could throw that humiliating statement in her face.

'Put your cards on the table, *koukla mou.* And maybe I will too.'

'I don't know what you're getting at—'

'Stop acting like a poor little victim—stop faking it,' Jax urged with stark impatience. 'You told me a lot of lies back then—'

'No, I didn't!' Lucy broke in furiously.

Exasperation gripped Jax. She was moving agitatedly round the room, luminous blue eyes fixed intently to him. The floor lamp behind her turned that pale dress almost transparent, clearly delineating the rounded swell of her small, succulent breasts and the shadowy outline of her pink areolae. He went hard, his reaction instantaneous.

'*What* lies?' Lucy demanded hotly, watching the fluid movement of his long, lithe body as he paced the tiled floor in front of her.

He was so beautiful he still took her breath away. It wasn't merely his lean, strong face and stunning green eyes. Jax simply radiated masculine power from the aggressive angle of his arrogant head to the square swing of his wide shoulders and the decisive gait of his long, muscular legs. She was so busy staring, so busy drinking him in with greedy eyes that she couldn't concentrate. A prickling sensation assailed her nipples and tightened them into hard little nubs while a sliding, pulsing warmth began low in her pelvis.

'What lies?' she mumbled afresh, her brain in a fog.

Throbbing with arousal, Jax compressed his sculpted lips. He was done with conversation. Lucy would verbally twist and turn and prevaricate and embellish and evade until he was ready to strangle her. And why was he even bothering? He didn't ever travel an emotional road with women these days. He wasn't interested in their motivations and their deepest secrets. He kept it simple, straight. So, why wasn't he being straight with himself? He hadn't brought Lucy home to *talk* to her, had he? His mouth quirked into a flashing sardonic smile as he studied her.

It was the bad-boy smile Lucy had seen Jax wear a dozen times in glossy photos. It wasn't the smile that had once made her heart jump and fill to overflowing with love. It was a dark edgy smile with a sensual hint of threat in it.

A forbidden tingle of anticipation infiltrated what remained of her defences. She took a sudden step back, struggling to keep her distance and stay in control. But Jax reached out a hand and closed it round hers in a sudden movement, pulling her to him before she could back off. He wrapped both arms round her, lifting her easily off her feet to hoist her high against him.

It was a decisive moment and she knew it, knew she should push her hands down on his shoulders to force him to put her down and release her. But nothing was ever that simple for Lucy when it came to Jax. As he brought her down he nuzzled against her neck, dark stubble scratching her tender skin, and a shudder of awareness powerful enough to leave her dizzy enveloped her. The scent of his cologne laced with clean, husky male flared her nostrils; he smelled so unbelievably good she wanted to bury her nose in his hair. Her hands went round his neck and for a split second as he worked his erotic path towards her parted lips she clung like a limpet.

Just one kiss, she bargained with herself, just *one*, but the man who had once seduced her with kisses had no intention of breaking his perfect track record. He always knew what she wanted and he gave it to her, all the seething passion he had taught her to crave. He kissed her and she went up in flames. Her body flared into shocking awareness and suddenly burned back to almost painful life with every plunging thrust of his tongue. She gasped and quivered, filled with all the hunger she had suppressed.

He brought her down on a firm but yielding surface and her head fell back as he wrenched down her dress to squeeze a straining pink nipple between his fingertips, swiftly following it up as she arched up to him in response with the warm sucking pull of his mouth. It was as if a river of liquid fire ran down through her to engulf her feminine core. A strangled moan of excitement was torn from her as his mouth traced a fiery path down over her twisting body, long, lean fingers clenching on a slender thigh.

And just then she wondered how he had contrived that skin-to-skin contact and the answer shook her so much that she yanked herself violently free and rolled off the sofa, hitting her hip painfully hard in the fall. Her dress fell round her knees. Tears of pain and mortification in her eyes, she got onto her knees and, with great difficulty, clumsily and awkwardly hauled her dress back up over her exposed body, shame roaring through her in long agonising waves.

*'Thee mou...'* Jax began rawly.

'I want a taxi home. This is not going any further,' Lucy swore breathlessly, unable to even make herself look at him.

Jax wanted to break something. Instead he breathed in very deep. Lucy hadn't changed. She had to have all the ducks in line before she would fire. Two years ago, that simple process of withholding sex had worked on him but he was no longer that suggestible, Jax told himself with fierce conviction. Yet when he touched her, she *owned* him, he recognised, unnerved by that realisation.

As she struggled with a singular lack of dignity or cool to refasten the difficult ties on her slender shoulders, Lucy's hatred of Jax rose like a tide of poison inside her. Ten seconds and he had had her half naked, nothing but a pair of knickers standing between her and total nudity. She had been a pushover. Maybe she was so starved of sex she *did* need a man in her life, she decided, her eyes stinging with hot, angry tears. But that man would not be Jax Antonakos.

'The limo will take you back home,' Jax told her flatly. 'That is if you *really* want to leave.'

'It's my turn to do the walking away,' Lucy framed gruffly, loathing coursing through her slight body in such powerful waves that she trembled with it. 'I wish I'd done it two years ago. What were you planning on happening? Another session of unprotected sex? Haven't you ever had consequences from that?'

'What the hell are you trying to imply?' Jax demanded in a raw undertone.

Lucy flung her head back, all fired up on adrenalin and resentment and bitterness. 'When you got bored and dumped me,' she told him shakily, 'you left me pregnant—'

# CHAPTER FOUR

JAX HAD FALLEN very still. 'That's not possible—'

'Why? Are you infertile?' Lucy shot back at him, unimpressed. 'I don't think so because we have a *child*, Jax. A little girl, who's fifteen months old.'

Jax stared back at her in rampant disbelief, hard lines settling between his nose and mouth, his handsome bone structure drawn stark and taut. 'Impossible,' he said again, green eyes brilliant with outraged denial.

'That last week we were together you had sex with me in a changing-room cubicle and you didn't take precautions,' Lucy reminded him angrily. 'Why do you think I tried so hard to get in touch with you that I got thrown off the yacht? I needed help.'

Shock ensured that Jax's brain continued to rebel and tell him that what she was saying was totally and absolutely impossible but his memory was infinitely more accurate. He knew he had taken that risk and had thought nothing of it at the time, indeed revelling in the reality that not even the thin layer of a condom separated him from her. He also realised in that moment that if she was telling him the truth, he had very probably made the biggest, messiest mistake of his life.

Panic hurtled through Lucy when she saw the shrewd dawning of genuine concern in his glittering green eyes. What had she done? Throwing it at him like that? Oh, my goodness, what had she done? Dully she recognised that she had been hitting back at him the only way she knew how. Needing to shock and hurt him as he had once shocked and hurt her with his rejection. But she knew instantly that she should not have used Bella like a weapon against him.

'This has to be discussed,' Jax intoned in a driven undertone.

'Not tonight. I want to go home,' Lucy breathed tightly. 'Right now.'

'You can't tell me I could be a father and then—'

'Yes, I can,' Lucy incised fiercely. 'I can do whatever I like just as you do whatever you like. And it's not a question of "*could* be a father". Bella is yours because I've never been with anyone else!'

Jax knew that was a lie for he had seen her cheat on him with his own eyes but DNA testing would provide proof neither of them could refute. He was appalled by the idea that he could have unwittingly had a child with a woman who not only lied and cheated but also had a criminal record. Even his parents' numerous unsuccessful marriages and affairs paled beside such a development. And the existence of an illegitimate Antonakos heir would send his father through the roof.

'I want to see the child,' Jax told her doggedly.

Lucy lost all her hectic colour. 'No.'

'If that child is half mine, you don't get to say no. I'll call in the family legal team,' Jax warned her without skipping a beat. 'Who looks after her when you're at work?'

That reference to lawyers and the reality that she was a working mum made a cold, hollow sensation of fear spread inside Lucy's tummy. 'My stepmother,' she told him, struggling to suppress the defiance rising inside her because a mood of conciliation struck her as being far more sensible in the circumstances.

'I'll call in with you tomorrow and we'll take care of the necessities,' Jax breathed coldly as he strode out to the hall. 'I need your address—'

'No.' The sense of being trapped built up inside Lucy until she felt almost suffocated by it. She had told him about Bella. She had done it in a recklessly provocative way too, absolutely the worst way to give Jax bad news. As volatile as he was, he didn't need the encouragement. And she had no doubt at all that learning that he was a father was very bad news on his terms because from the instant the concept had set in, Jax had turned icy-cold and businesslike. Now, however, Lucy recognised that she had to deal with the fallout from her impulsive decision and that would entail finally telling Kreon and Iola the truth.

'If you come in the morning I'll be there,' Lucy conceded abruptly. 'I usually only work evenings. My father and stepmother have a funeral to attend, so they won't be at home.'

Jax demanded the address and then stood poised in the doorway of his home watching her clamber into the limousine outside. Lucy tore her gaze from his forbidding stance and told herself that she had only done what had had to be done. He had the right to know about Bella. It was his own fault that he hadn't found out about his daughter sooner. Maybe he wouldn't want anything to do with their child, Lucy reasoned with sudden hope that that might be the case. And then she felt horribly guilty because she knew how much it hurt not to have a father and she didn't want her daughter to suffer the same way.

Yet when she looked back to her affair with Jax she could never have believed that they would have ended up so bitterly opposed. That night after the yacht party, Jax had sought her out and insisted on seeing her back to her room at the bar.

'You *are* over twenty-one?' he had checked. 'I don't get involved with anyone younger than that.'

'I'm twenty-three,' Lucy had lied instantly, adding on four years to her age, determined to make that all important grade for him.

He had told her he would pick her up for dinner the following evening. She had told him she was working.

'Take a night off,' Jax had urged.

'I can't afford to,' she had argued.

'I'll cover the cost of it,' Jax had declared.

'But then you'd be paying for my time and I couldn't agree to that—'

'You're very difficult,' Jax had condemned.

'And you don't understand how to take no for an answer.'

'I want to see you again,' Jax had proclaimed impatiently.

'I'm free Thursday night.'

'I don't want to wait that long.'

'All right. You can see me at midnight tomorrow when I finish my shift…unless that's too late for you?'

'No, that will do.'

'But know upfront I'm not spending the night with

you, so if that's what you're expecting, just forget about me,' she had warned him staunchly.

Lucy had learned to be blunt with men. She thought of it as managing their expectations. She had gone out with so many men who had simply assumed that she would sleep with them at the end of the night and who had reacted badly to a refusal. But her body was the one element in her world that Lucy had always felt was truly hers and until she finally met someone who could make her want him enough to move beyond that she had no intention of sharing her body with anyone. She genuinely hadn't expected Jax to be any different and she had slowly learned her mistake until saying no to Jax had become painful because she hadn't been able to control her own hunger.

'You're too defensive. Not every guy is out to nail you—'

'You mean you're *not*?' Lucy had exclaimed in surprise.

'I can see that trying to be smooth and seductive with you will be a huge challenge,' Jax had laughed, flashing her a highly amused smile.

And she had started falling for him that very night because that glorious charismatic smile of his had stopped her in her tracks and left her short of breath. She had met him the following night, sharing tapas and a couple of drinks with him in an upmarket bar. But sadly, she had dropped off to sleep in the middle of the conversation, bone tired from being on her feet serving all day. He had shaken her awake and taken her home without even attempting to kiss her, confiding that yawns weren't sexy. He had put his phone number in her phone while she slept and the next day he began texting her, first letting her know that he would be out of the country for a couple of days, then arranging to see her on her next free night.

A day later Kat Valtinos had shown up at the bar and cornered her. 'Jax is the ultimate playboy and you're the British equivalent of trailer trash—'

'Probably,' Lucy had conceded, looking back on her troubled poverty-stricken past.

'Obviously Jax will get bored fast and you look like the clingy sort.'

'I haven't had a chance to cling yet but I'm a quick learner. Does he like clingy women?' Lucy had asked, wide-eyed. 'Is he your boyfriend?'

'No, a very good friend,' Kat had declared. 'But you're wasting your time. I intend to marry him.'

'Tell that to him, not to me,' Lucy had advised and got back to work, ignoring the bitchy brunette until she'd finally stalked out in a snit at not being taken seriously.

The following morning, Lucy rose early after a sleepless night of wandering painfully through her mortifyingly fresh memories of being with Jax two years earlier. She watched her father and stepmother leave to attend the funeral. Over breakfast they had been too preoccupied with a sad and affectionate exchange of stories about their now deceased friend to notice how heavy-eyed and silent Lucy was.

But Lucy was also restless with anxiety and operating on pure adrenalin. Now that Jax knew about Bella she had to worry about how he would act on that information. She winced at the knowledge that Jax had power over her again. Certainly he had rights as a father that she could not deny. But would he choose to exercise those rights and seek an active parenting role?

Barely an hour later, Lucy received her first taste of Jax choosing to exercise his rights. A smartly dressed, fast-speaking lawyer arrived and asked her to agree to DNA testing and no sooner had she given consent, her face burning at the humiliating suspicion that Jax could doubt that he had fathered her child, than a lab technician arrived and took samples. That matter dealt with, the lawyer then settled a confidentiality agreement down in front of her. It seemed to be what Lucy had seen referred to as a 'gagging order' in the media and she refused to sign it, sticking to her guns when the older man persisted in his persuasions.

'Mr Antonakos does not like what I shall describe as private matters broadcast in the public domain. If you sign this document, it will form a secure basis for good relations between you in the future.'

'I can assure you that I have no intention of speaking to the press but I'm not prepared to sign anything that says I cannot talk about my own daughter,' she told him quietly.

By the time the older man departed, Lucy fully understood that he had been engaged in a potential damage-limitation plan. And Lucy was utterly unnerved by Jax acting to protect himself and the reputation of the Antonakos family even before he had definitive proof that her child was his. She was appalled that he could distrust her so much that he suspected that she might sell nasty stories about him to the newspapers.

In truth she did have a very low opinion of Jax but she had every intention of keeping that low opinion to herself for her daughter's sake. Whatever else Jax was, he was and always would be her daughter's father and she didn't want to do anything to damage that relationship. That meant, she registered with a sinking heart, that she would have to keep her personal feelings very much to herself. Airing her anger, resentment and bitterness would be destructive and the situation they were in where they shared a child but nothing else would be difficult enough to deal with.

An hour after the lawyer departed, Jax arrived and, for once, not in a limousine. He roared up outside on a motorbike and it was only as he doffed his helmet on the way to the front door that she realised it was him and not someone making a delivery. He was trying to be discreet, endeavouring to ensure that he wasn't recognised, she realised. When she had first met Jax in Spain he had only recently stepped into his late brother's role and as he had been relatively unknown there had been no paparazzi following him around then. Now that a kind of celebrity madness erupted around Jax's every public appearance she was grateful that he was being careful because she did not want to see her face or her daughter's appearing in articles full of embarrassing speculations.

Lucy opened the front door and stepped back. Jax strode in, bringing with him the scent of fresh air, leather and masculinity. In the narrow hall, he towered over her and she thrust the door quickly shut to walk into the spacious front room, which was sprinkled with colourful toys and baby equipment.

Jax slung his motorbike helmet down on a chair and raked impatient fingers through his black hair. 'Where is she?' he demanded.

'Bella's having a nap. I'll get her up in ten minutes. She wakes very early in the morning and then she gets tired again…' Realising that she was gabbling, Lucy flushed, insanely conscious of Jax's stare.

Lucy sported cropped jeans, a pink tee shirt and bare feet. She looked very young and cute and definitely hadn't dressed up for his benefit. Jax was irritated that she had not made the effort. He hadn't slept much the night before. The cold shower hadn't worked any miracle and that sexual tension piled on top of the shocking announcement Lucy had made had done nothing to help. When he had a problem Jax liked a plan to work towards, a plan with firm boundaries. Unhappily there was no convenient plan available to tell him how a man behaved when he discovered he was a father even though he had never wanted that particular joy. But he *had* been reckless with Lucy in the birth-control department and in retrospect he could not forgive or excuse himself for that lack of responsibility. Of course, he reminded himself wryly, the kid might not be his, in which case he was dealing with nothing more than a storm in a teacup.

'Stop staring at me,' Lucy told him, cheeks burning from the intensity of his scrutiny.

'Of course I'm staring. You dropped a bomb on me last night. I'm still reeling,' Jax breathed in a raw undertone, green eyes glittering warily below curling ebony lashes.

'Well, I've been mentally reeling from the minute I discovered I was pregnant,' Lucy confided truthfully. 'With time you get used to the idea. I couldn't bear to imagine life without Bella now.'

Jax scanned the youthful glow of her unblemished

skin and the luxuriant tumble of strawberry-blonde ringlets that merely highlighted her bright blue eyes. He acknowledged her beauty for there was no denying what was right in front of him. As his body began to react he clenched his teeth together hard and wandered back towards the front door, determined not to let his libido take over when there would soon be a child in the room.

'Coffee?' Lucy pressed as the awkward silence stretched when he reappeared in the doorway.

'This is not a social visit,' Jax answered.

A cry sounded out somewhere above them and Lucy scurried upstairs, her face flushed by his deflating statement.

Jax plonked himself down on a sofa and struggled to relax but it had been more years than he cared to recall since he had been around a baby. He was godfather to several but his role had never been hands-on, nor would it ever have been more because nobody expected a single man, who was also erroneously known as his actress mother's only child, to be comfortable dealing with young children. Ironically Jax had learned the daily routine of how to look after a baby when he was only twelve years old. It had been the end of the summer before his mother had finally engaged a nanny because Jax was returning to boarding school.

He heard the creak of the stairs and vaulted upright. As he straightened his shoulders Lucy walked into the lounge and he immediately saw the child in her arms. He froze into a statue in the same moment that he saw the little girl's black curly hair and the green eyes. That fast, that dramatically, Jax knew he didn't need a DNA test to prove to anyone that the little girl was his. Lucy's child was the living image of his kid sister, Tina, and that uncanny resemblance hit him like an avalanche. His mother had had very strong genes, he reckoned ruefully, for both he and the little sister who had died as a toddler had looked far more like Mariana than the men who had fathered her two children. He knew too that his striking likeness to his mother had only been another nail in his coffin as far as his oversensitive father was concerned.

'This is Bella…' Lucy framed, kneeling down to settle the little girl gently on the floor.

A thumb planted in her rosebud mouth, Bella studied Jax fixedly, her green eyes full of curiosity.

Jax bent down and lifted a toy that broke straight into a catchy tune as soon as he pressed the right button. Bella grinned and came closer, steadying herself on one powerful thigh with a clutching little hand.

'She's not scared,' Jax remarked, marvelling that he could still speak normally after being plunged without warning into some of his darkest memories. The remnants of that guilt, anger and pain still resonated powerfully with him.

'No, she's quite confident and she likes men. My father makes a fuss of her and spoils her. I suppose we all spoil her a bit,' Lucy conceded, staring at the little tableau of Jax and his daughter as they each assessed the other. 'She looks very like you—'

Jax skated a teasing forefinger off Bella's determined little chin and swallowed thickly, struggling to master his almost overwhelming emotions. He should not cloud his first meeting with his daughter with such tragic memories, he censured himself fiercely. The past was the past and it would be wiser to leave the sad little ghost of Tina safely buried there.

'What is it?' Lucy prompted, troubled by the feverish glitter of Jax's stunning eyes, their brilliance enhanced by the surround of spiky black lashes. 'What's wrong?'

'Nothing,' Jax insisted, his wide sensual mouth slashing into a sudden forced smile, for he had shared far too much private stuff with Lucy in the past and he had no plans to make himself vulnerable in that way again 'But when she was born you should have moved heaven and earth to ensure that I knew I was a father.'

Unprepared for that criticism when she had tried every way she knew how to contact him, Lucy stiffened. 'That's not fair—'

'What isn't fair,' Jax fielded as he accepted the little plastic doll that Bella brought him, 'is that this little girl and I weren't able to be in each other's lives from the start.'

Lucy's bright blue eyes hardened. 'As you said though, when you dumped me, you didn't want me making a *nuisance* of myself,' she reminded him thinly. 'If you didn't want to hear from me ever again, how was I supposed to tell you?'

Not trusting himself to speak in the mood he was in, Jax shrugged a muscular shoulder in brooding silence.

'Didn't think you'd have an answer for that,' Lucy sniped, leaning down to clasp Bella's hand and guide her into the kitchen where she set about filling a toddler cup with milk.

Bella pushed against the back door, keen to get out onto the patio and play. Lucy opened it and watched her daughter toddle out into the sunlight to retrieve the little plastic pram she loved.

*His* child, *his* daughter, a new generation in the Antonakos family, Jax acknowledged, watching Bella swig her milk and then set down the cup with exaggerated care before pushing the little pram out onto the small lawn. Somehow, he didn't know how, he didn't care, Lucy *should* have contacted him, he thought angrily.

'I have missed out on over a year of my daughter's life,' Jax intoned grimly. 'That is not acceptable—'

Under sudden attack, Lucy spun. 'No, what was unacceptable back then was the way you treated me!' she condemned with spirit.

Jax thought about the contents of the investigative file he had been given. He saw no point in throwing the contents of that file in Lucy's face now. Likewise her little session in that alleyway. His reaction had been all too human. He had let his anger and aggression take over and dictate his moves. 'I'm afraid it never occurred to me that you could be pregnant,' he admitted in a harsh undertone. 'I should've acknowledged that possibility and made provision for it but I didn't. That was a serious oversight on my part.'

A little of the tension in Lucy's slender shoulders eased. 'Yes, it was.'

'Then let us not waste time stating the obvious and rehashing a past we both prefer to forget,' Jax countered impatiently.

'We can't forget it when Bella was born from it,' Lucy argued helplessly. 'We may not like each other but we'll just have to live with that. I'll make coffee, and not because this is a social occasion but because we need to learn how to act civilised.'

As Lucy left the doorway to switch on the kettle Jax strode out onto the patio, unable to let his newly discovered daughter out of his sight and reach. It crossed his mind that he had no intention of living with his distaste of Lucy and forging a civilised alliance with her as a co-parent. With what he knew about her past, he didn't, *couldn't* possibly trust her to be a caring decent mother. Bella's well-being came first and nobody would ever persuade him that his child could be safe with a mother who had once dealt in drugs and sold her body. It didn't matter that to all intents and purposes Lucy appeared to have turned over a new leaf.

Jax, after all, was the son of a drug addict. He had heard too many promises, seen all too many fresh starts *and* witnessed the subsequent falls from grace. Bella would always be at risk of harm if she remained with her mother, he decided cynically. He would have to fight Lucy through the courts for custody of their daughter. He was sure that she loved Bella to the best of her ability but with her fatal weakness for substance abuse he couldn't trust her to always put their daughter's needs first.

'Are we capable of behaving like friends?' Lucy asked Jax hopefully as she hovered in the doorway.

Jax glanced at her in astonishment, questioning how she contrived to still look so young and innocent in spite of her misspent past. Friends? Never, he conceded wryly. And once Lucy received the first official communication from the Antonakos legal team and realised what he planned to do friendship would be the last thing on her mind. But what other choice did he have?

'You have to stop blaming me for everything that's gone wrong,' Lucy told him squarely. 'In any relationship it takes two people to screw up. Remember that…'

As she spoke Bella fell flat on her face on the lawn and let out a yell, followed by frantic sobbing. Jax strode across a flower bed and snatched the little girl up into his arms, speaking softly to her, smoothing a lean brown hand gently over her shaking back to soothe her before getting down on his knees to show her something on the ground in the clear hope of distracting her from the fright she had sustained. Lucy stared at that seemingly effortless display of child management in sheer amazement, involuntarily impressed.

'Jax…' she muttered in a daze.

Once Bella was restored to calm again, Jax set her down. His lean, strong face taut, he glanced at Lucy, noting how the sunshine lit up the shades of red in her hair and illuminated her perfect skin. Lucy bent to pick up the pram and the shapely curve of her heart-shaped derriere pulled tight below the cropped jeans she wore. Jax remembered ripping her jeans off her, desperate to sink into the damp, welcoming heat of her, and fierce tension gripped him as he suppressed the hunger flaring through him like a dangerous burning brand. 'In a couple of days I'd like to take Bella out. I'll bring a nanny with me if that keeps you happy.'

'I assumed you would be waiting for the DNA results before you did anything official,' Lucy parried, thoroughly disconcerted by his request as she walked back to him.

'The DNA tests will only confirm what I already know,' Jax murmured. 'Are you going to make me fight for access to her?'

Lucy winced and set her teeth together. If in doubt, weigh in with the threats. That was Jax. He could afford the very best lawyers. Ultimately he would be entitled to time with his daughter whatever she did or said and trying to ignore that reality would be foolish. In any case, didn't she want Bella to have a father? Yes, she did, but she hadn't expected to have to share her time with her daughter quite so immediately.

'No, but I wouldn't want her away from me for more than a couple of hours at a time,' she admitted. 'She's still very young.'

'I can agree to that,' Jax traded. 'Give me your phone number and I'll be in touch.'

Bella cuddled to her, Lucy watched Jax swing back onto the motorbike, the lithe powerful lines of his big muscular body moulded by his designer jeans and leather jacket. Across the road a car started up and pulled out to follow him, his security team, she assumed.

When her father and stepmother returned from the funeral, Lucy sat them down and finally told them the truth.

Straight away her father erupted like a raging volcano. '*Jax Antonakos?* Are you serious?'

'Please don't get mad,' Lucy pleaded. 'It will only make this situation worse.'

'You were only nineteen, Lucy,' her father protested with pained condemnation. 'He must be nearly ten years older than you!'

'Well, he can't be blamed for that. When he said I had

to be over twenty-one to spend time with him I lied,' she admitted ruefully. 'I said I was twenty-three—'

'You *lied* to him?' Kreon repeated censoriously.

'Calm down, Kreon,' Iola interposed gently. 'She was a typical teenager and when a handsome young man approached her, she pretended to be older and more sophisticated than she was. A lot of girls that age would have done the same thing.'

'Yes,' Lucy admitted, her cheeks burning.

Iola dragged the rest of the story of those six weeks in Spain from Lucy while Kreon sat fuming, his anger unhidden. 'I knew his father, you know,' he told them abruptly. 'And he was a selfish, arrogant thug of a man too.'

'Jax's father? You *knew* him? *How?*' Lucy asked, astonished by that admission.

'My parents worked for the family of Heracles Antonakos's first wife, Sofia, in London. Sofia and I grew up together and we never lost that friendship even though she lived in a very different world. She was only thirty when she died,' Kreon revealed gruffly.

'I'm really sorry I didn't tell you the truth from the start,' Lucy confessed. 'I didn't want to upset you—'

'Never you mind about me being upset,' Kreon told her through compressed lips. 'Be grateful I'm here to support you. Antonakos sending in the lawyers straight off is your first warning of his plans—'

'What do you mean?' Iola interjected worriedly.

'Well, was what happened this morning a nice or considerate thing to do to the mother of your child? Demanding DNA testing? Trying to browbeat Lucy into signing a confidentiality agreement? As a first warning shot, it tells us all we need to know…'

'Jax is trying to protect himself. I can't blame him for that,' Lucy muttered ruefully, troubled by her father's angry gravity and all too conscious that she was the cause of the lines of stress that had appeared on his weathered face.

'He can protect himself all he likes but not at your expense or Bella's,' Kreon replied.

Lucy was anxious and preoccupied when she went into work that evening and she struggled to remember the drinks orders and deliver them back to the correct tables. Her father's genuine fear of what Jax might be planning had seriously scared her. Not for the first time she wished she had the ability to get inside Jax's head.

Earlier that day he had been strangely distant with her but very different in his wholehearted response to Bella. In retrospect it was hard to credit that he had been kissing her, *touching* her only the night before. Of course, that made sense, she told herself squarely. Everything had changed the minute she'd told Jax about their daughter. She recalled his glacier cool when she had first told him at his house and barely restrained a shiver of apprehension. Her father's concern had set off all her internal alarms and had left her on the edge of panic and thinking thoughts she had believed she would never think again…

What if she simply upped sticks and vanished? She had done it before and she could do it again. But it would be wrong, her inner voice warned her sternly. It would be wrong not to give Jax the opportunity to form a relationship with his daughter. It would be equally wrong for Lucy to run away from the life her father and stepmother had generously offered her. Running away from her problems would be the childish thing to do and she wasn't a child any more…

# CHAPTER FIVE

'SO, YOU ARE Lucy's father,' Jax commented, lounging back against his office desk with lethal cool, not a shade of what he was thinking revealed by his lean, darkly handsome features. 'Where were you all the years Lucy was growing up in the care system?'

Kreon straightened his shoulders. 'That's my business and Lucy's. She's welcome to tell you if she wants. But I'm here now to protect the welfare of my daughter and my granddaughter.'

'I don't understand how you plan to do that,' Jax remarked.

'Oh, that's very simple,' Kreon told him almost cheerfully. 'I have access to secrets that your father would kill to keep out of the newspapers—'

Taken aback, Jax laughed. 'My father fears nothing. Is this some sort of clumsy blackmail attempt? I advise you to back off now before I call the police.'

'That will be your decision but it won't stop me sharing your family secrets with the press. In fact having me arrested will only add legitimacy to my claims,' Kreon pointed out calmly. 'Your father hates me. I will tell you that for free. But why do you think he leaves me alone? He is afraid of what I might know.'

'You're talking a lot of nonsense and I don't intend to listen to it,' Jax told him, crossing the room to open the door and hasten the older man's departure.

'Your brother, Argo, wasn't your brother because he wasn't your father's child,' Kreon delivered very softly. 'I think Heracles only found that out *after* your brother died and, believe me, he does not want that humiliating truth spread across the newspapers.'

Jax froze, shock washing over him in an almost physical attack that pulled his every muscle taut to breaking point. In a driven movement he thrust the door shut again and swung violently round.

'What do you want?' he demanded of the smaller man, refusing to think of what he had just been told, refusing to join the dots and acknowledge how well that revelation would dovetail with his own quite recent miraculous change of status within the Antonakos family.

'In return for my continuing silence, I want you to marry Lucy.'

Jax stared back at him in savage disbelief. '*Marry*... her?'

'She was a teenager when you wrecked her life. You owe her the security of a wedding ring. It doesn't have to be a life sentence for either of you. But it would give her and Bella the safe harbour and the recognition they need to have a better life—'

'She *wasn't* a teenager!' Jax raked back at him in furious rebuttal.

'Lucy was twenty-one last month. We celebrated with dinner at that hotel where she works.' Kreon shot him a sourly amused appraisal. 'My wife tells me that teenaged girls do lie about their age occasionally.'

'Twenty-one,' Jax repeated thickly, fighting to master the violent anger lashing through him and a powerful urge to strangle Lucy for having dared to lie to him. 'I would require proof of those allegations about my brother, Argo.'

And from an inside pocket Kreon produced a handwritten letter which he handed to Jax. It had been written and sent to Kreon when his father's first wife, Sofia, was terminally ill. Unable to face death with such a weight on her conscience, Sofia had admitted the affair that had led to Argo's conception, although she had not named her lover.

'Why didn't you come forward with this at the time of her death?' Jax demanded harshly a few minutes later. 'With this letter, you were in possession of facts that were unknown to everyone else involved.'

'Sofia couldn't have thought through what she was doing. Your father had just lost his wife and Argo had lost his mother and her letter would have destroyed them both. Back then Heracles had no idea that Argo wasn't his son. What do you think he would have done?' Kreon grimaced. 'He would've disinherited the boy and cast him off.'

Jax stared at the wall, knowing that there was a fair chance his father would have reacted like that in the first heat of his fury. Once Sofia had let that genie out of the bottle there would have been no putting it back.

'I didn't want that responsibility. I'm not a cruel man. It was a secret that shouldn't have been told. I never liked your father and he was a lousy absentee husband but, fond as I was of Sofia, once she was gone I preferred to mind my own business...that is, until an Antonakos threatened the security of my own flesh and blood.'

Long after Kreon had gone, Jax studied the copy of the letter the older man had allowed him to keep. He was still shaken even though the woman had died long before he was born. The contents of that letter would distress his father, although, like Kreon, Jax was inclined to believe that somewhere around the time of Argo's death his father had found out that his eldest son was not actually his son. That would better explain why Heracles had found it possible to move on so fast from that loss and adjust his attitude to Jax almost overnight.

That new knowledge and understanding just about ripped Jax apart, not to mention his view of his family. He had looked up to the big brother he had never really got to know very well and he loved his father. And why *did* he love Heracles, who had proved to be a useless parent when Jax was young and in need of a father? Ultimately, he had recognised that the older man deeply regretted allowing his dented ego and workaholic ways to triumph over the ties of blood. Heracles was hopeless when it came to expressing emotion though and Jax had realised that he suffered from the same flaw. His father had stumbled on blindly after Mariana's infidelity had made him a laughing stock in the media, protecting himself as best he could by avoiding his ex-wife…and unhappily that avoidance had included Jax.

Jax hadn't really thought about how he actually felt about Heracles until that moment, but when he thought of his father being forced to see the tragedy of his first marriage spread across the newspapers he knew he couldn't allow that to happen. Sofia had died after a long drawn-out fight against breast cancer. Heracles was domineering and manipulative and interfering but he had once adored his first wife and the son he had believed to be his.

Jax's first act was to summon Zenas and tell his security chief that he wanted an in-depth private investigation carried out on Kreon Thiarkis and his daughter, Lucy. How the hell had something as basic as Lucy's age been wrong in that file? Her parentage had been incorrectly recorded as well. Lucy *did* have a Greek father. What else could also be wrong? He needed the background and facts he could rely on. He also needed to check out Kreon's ties to his father's first wife, Sofia. And to his father. After all, it was *his* father who had sent that file to him.

Jax began to mull over the other things he had learned. Lucy was still only twenty-one years old? And had been only nineteen when they had first met? Memories swirled in a colourful haze in Jax's head and he marvelled that he had not recognised Lucy's immaturity for what it was. She had been impulsive, outspoken, naïve and unnervingly ignorant about facts he took for granted and a sneaky little unrepentant liar...*obviously*.

And no way was he prepared to marry her! Kreon could not blackmail him into doing what he had never wanted to do, he assured himself stubbornly. On the other hand, Jax also knew he could not stand back and watch his father endure the scandal that would blow up if Kreon went to the press to sell his story. People would enjoy reading about the skeletons hidden in the Antonakos cupboard and his father would lose his dignity. At the age of seventy, Heracles deserved to keep his dignity, Jax decided heavily. He might have been a lousy husband in Kreon's eyes but he had surely not deserved the tragic conclusion to his first marriage. Knowing how badly Heracles had reacted to his own mother's infidelity, Jax could hardly begin to imagine what his father must have felt once he realised that Argo was not his child. Surely Heracles had suffered enough for being a less than stellar husband? How dared Kreon Thiarkis threaten him?

Yet even in the grip of that seething Antonakos rage, Jax could still not stop planning. He knew that it was up to him to control the situation. He reached the stage of listing pros and cons. Were he to marry Lucy, he would get her back into his bed. A sliver of raw anticipation raked through Jax's tense, angry body and he recognised that that was a fringe benefit that he would very much enjoy. At the same time he would also gain a stronger legal right to his daughter and he would not have to fight to gain access to her.

Nevertheless, Jax hated being told what to do and Kreon Thiarkis had just thrown a double whammy at him that came attached to a very high price tag. Primarily he was in a rage because he knew that Kreon had given him a choice but it was the hateful choice of picking between the lesser of two evils: marriage or his aging father's public humiliation. He could tell Kreon to do his worst and then stand by and watch his father get hurt. Unfortunately, family loyalty and a very real affection for his inadequate father warred against that option. But the alternative was to surrender his freedom.

No more hot and cold running women, no more

sexually self-indulgent variety in the bedroom. But then that wasn't quite true, Jax allowed with a sudden strong sense of relief. Even Kreon didn't expect him to stay married to Lucy for ever. Kreon was expecting an eventual divorce, which would still leave Lucy and Bella respectfully acknowledged as members of the Antonakos family and financially secure. *Thee mou*...he could do marriage on a short-term, strictly temporary basis, particularly with Lucy playing the starring role in his bed every night. Furthermore, Bella would have his name and the safeguard of his presence in her daily life. But just how was he expected to cope with a father-in-law he wanted to strike down and kill in cold blood?

As an Antonakos, Jax had little experience of being threatened. He was too rich, too powerful to cross and his father had long enjoyed the same protection. But Kreon was in legal possession of very private and personal information that went right to the heart of Jax's family, the kind of secret nobody wanted exposed and picked over in public. Even worse, one revelation would almost inevitably lead to others. What might be dug up about his own mother? Jax shuddered at the prospect of Mariana's drug-addicted frailties and Tina's death being dragged out into the punishing light of day. At that point it struck him that a wedding ring was a worthwhile sacrifice if it bought peace and left the family's dirty laundry untouched.

Lucy studied the text from Jax with wide incredulous eyes. He had asked her when she finished work.

I'll pick you up when you finish and we'll talk.

Jax? *Talk?* Jax had been known to leave the room or remember a pressing engagement when any form of serious discussion was threatened. Jax didn't believe in talking about stuff. He thought in private and then he acted to fix a problem. He didn't share the reasoning that led to the decision. He believed that talking only heightened the wrong emotions, encouraged divisive stances and made issues seem worse than they were. When she had once tried to talk to him about where their affair was heading he had become angry and he had walked away. Naturally he had, she conceded, because he had known their affair was going nowhere.

But obviously he had to talk to her about Bella, she reasoned ruefully. Even he couldn't make unilateral decisions about the daughter they now had to share. He would want to make arrangements to see Bella again, he would want to ask questions about what the little girl liked and didn't like. That he was prepared to talk was a healthy sign, Lucy told herself heavily, striving to muster some enthusiasm about the idea of sharing her daughter with her father.

Before she even went into work, her own father had lectured her, urging her not to do to Bella what had been done to her. She had grown up without a father because her mother had selfishly chosen not to tell Kreon he had a daughter. Now, quite unnecessarily, Kreon was advising Lucy to take a long-term view and keep her anger and resentment out of the situation.

'I know it's a big ask,' Kreon had conceded, 'but you have to deal with what's happening now and handle it sensibly. Try to concentrate on what's best for Bella.'

Her father's outlook had surprised Lucy because he

seemed to have come to terms with what she had told him about Jax very quickly and had now taken a more detached view of events. Unfortunately everything still felt painfully personal to Lucy. Jax had rejected her but he had *not* rejected their daughter. She knew she shouldn't be thinking that way but she couldn't help it because she was only human.

A car picked her up from the hotel. It wasn't a limo and Jax wasn't in it but she recognised Jax's security guards. She climbed in, smoothed down her denim skirt and worried at her lower lip with the edge of her teeth. She was wondering what Jax wanted while telling herself to keep her temper and her daughter's emotional and physical well-being at the forefront of her mind regardless of what he might say.

Jax had plans as well. He would not confront Lucy about anything until they were safely married. Hopefully by then he would also know how accurate that file he had actually was. But he was also well aware of how deceptive Lucy could be, he reminded himself grimly, thinking of the familiar flash of that red dress below the street lights as she'd walked down that alleyway to have sex with another man. Lucy wasn't the faithful type. Two of his father's three wives had betrayed him with other men and Jax's own mother had never been faithful to anyone. Surrounded from childhood by broken, dishonest relationships, Jax had always tried to avoid emotional involvement and commitment. But when his daughter came into the equation he discovered that he badly wanted to give Bella the storybook family he had never had. Something better, something happier, something lasting…

Lucy walked dry-mouthed and nervous into the

house with the confusing mirrored hall. The elegant drawing room looked more welcoming than it had on her last visit with only a couple of lamps lit to leave the rest of the very large room shrouded in shadow. When Jax stepped out of the shadows, she flinched and stilled on the threshold.

'I ordered supper for you.' Jax indicated the table spread with a selection of snacks.

Jax wore jeans and an open-necked shirt. He shouldn't have taken her breath away in such ordinary garments but he did. The jeans clung to his narrow hips and outlined his long, powerful thighs. The pale shirt accentuated his bronzed skin tone and the blue black of his hair. She sucked in a breath in the tense silence and clashed with shimmering green eyes fringed by black and her heart hammered out a drumbeat inside her.

'Supper,' she repeated, that being the last thing she had expected from him, but she stepped fully into the room to head for the table, grateful to have something other than Jax to focus on.

'Help yourself,' he advised.

Settling down on a sofa, Lucy needed no further encouragement because she was always hungry after work and she was involuntarily impressed that he had remembered that little fact. She filled a plate and poured a cup of tea. 'This is what I call civilised,' she admitted with a wry smile.

'I thought it would be,' Jax said. 'Were you working in that outfit?'

Lucy smoothed a self-conscious hand over her comfy skirt with which she had teamed a black tee shirt. 'Yes…'

Jax gritted his teeth. A tripwire stood in front of

him but he neatly avoided it by refusing to give way to his inner caveman. The short skirt showed off her surprisingly long and very shapely legs and the tee shirt shaped her pert breasts to perfection. Once upon a time he had objected to her wearing the sort of clothing that revealed her body and that had set off heated arguments. Now he was respecting boundaries to preserve the peace. He sank down onto the sofa opposite her while mentally trying to come up with garments that would still be fashionable but which would miraculously shield that glorious body from the visual attention of other men. And he finally registered that there were no such garments on the market. Lucy had always outshone her clothing. From her bright tumbling hair to her luminous skin and radiant blue eyes, Lucy glowed with sheer energy, attracting attention even in a crowded room.

'It's not a short skirt,' Lucy remarked, knowing his flaws.

'No, it's not,' Jax agreed, wishing she hadn't directed his attention to her pale slender thighs and knees because it only made him think about the sheer glory of parting them. Furiously conscious of his growing desire, Jax rocked forward, his lean, strong face taut, green eyes semi screened by his lashes.

'You said you wanted to talk.' Lucy widened her eyes suspiciously. 'Was that a joke?'

'No…' Silence fell while Lucy munched through her third sandwich. 'We have a dilemma and I have come up with a solution,' he spelled out in a roughened undertone as the tip of her tongue chased a crumb from the corner of her mouth.

'Bella isn't a dilemma. She isn't and never will be a

problem,' Lucy assured him quietly. 'I'm not going to be difficult about you seeing her or anything like that.'

Jax breathed in deep, striving to make himself get to the point and bite the bullet. 'If we married, we would be in a position to give Bella far more.'

Lucy put down her sandwich unfinished. *'Married?'* she repeated in consternation. 'But you don't ever want to get married.'

'I didn't plan to have a child either,' Jax reminded her. 'But Bella is here now and that changes the whole picture. I want to give her what I didn't have. A mother, a father and a settled home, all the security that only a traditional family structure can give her.'

Lucy was stunned because she had never dreamt that she would live to hear Jax admit a desire to embrace such conventional ideas. 'Neither of us had that,' she conceded unevenly. 'But life isn't perfect and that's the way it is—'

'But we *can* change that,' Jax sliced in forcefully. 'We don't have to live apart when we could raise Bella together, as a married couple.'

Lucy blinked rapidly, her heart in her mouth, her feet flexing because nervous tension made her want to get up and walk round the room. 'Together?' she repeated in bewilderment.

'We can get married and make a home for our daughter, the kind of home neither of us had the advantage of growing up in,' Jax extended with unearthly calm.

'I don't know much about your background. Well, I know your parents divorced when you were young but—'

Jax stiffened. 'You already know that my mother

was unstable and not a reliable parent. Men came and went in her life. None of them ever stayed. She was too high maintenance. I don't want our daughter to have to adapt to that kind of lifestyle.'

'With respect,' Lucy said uncomfortably, 'I'm not a world-famous, gorgeous actress and I don't think my lifestyle and your mother's would have anything in common.'

Jax released his breath in a small hiss of frustration. 'Do you really believe that your life is going to stay the same now that I know you are raising my daughter?' he pressed in disbelief. 'Do you honestly believe that you can go on working as a waitress and living with your father? Obviously I will take care of all your expenses now—'

'No,' Lucy broke in with a frown. 'I don't want that.'

'But that's what will happen whether you like it or not. Naturally I want my daughter to enjoy the same lifestyle that I enjoy myself and I can't believe that you would deny her what she is entitled to receive. Bella is an Antonakos,' Jax reminded her with pride.

'Yes but...' Lucy's voice ran out of steam as she began to think about everything he had said.

He was asking her to marry him. Jax Antonakos was asking *her* to marry him, offering her the dream conclusion she had once secretly cherished and then buried deep two years earlier. For the space of several frantic minutes Lucy could only stare down into her tea and struggle to come to terms with a proposal she had never expected to receive. A home, two parents and a real family for Bella. That truly was the ultimate ideal for Lucy when it came to her daughter. Her mother had ended up alone raising Lucy and Lucy had ended up alone in the care system because the authorities had failed to trace Kreon. Sometimes she hated herself for making the same mistake with Bella and having to bring her up without a father.

'Are you serious about this?' Lucy asked breathlessly.

'Of course,' Jax asserted levelly.

'But you *never* wanted to get married,' Lucy reminded him helplessly.

'And then Bella came along and turned everything upside down,' Jax confessed with complete honesty. 'This is no longer only about you and me. We have to think about our daughter and about what would make *her* happy.'

'Unhappily married parents wouldn't help,' Lucy pointed out apologetically.

'I see no reason why we shouldn't make a go of it. Even sitting here having a serious conversation I can barely keep my hands off you,' Jax admitted bluntly, his stunning green gaze glittering across her heart-shaped face and watching the flush of awareness slowly build there. 'And if you're honest, it's the same for you.'

Lucy dragged her attention from his sleek, darkly beautiful features with the greatest difficulty. But trying to blank her mind, trying not to look at him was no use when the hunger inside her felt like an insidious virus that refused to die. And she knew what the cure was and that unnerved her. The only cure she knew was the wild, pounding plunge of his body into hers and the explosive release he would give her. And even that wasn't a permanent fix, she thought shamefacedly. She had once craved him as she craved air to breathe. She set her tea down with a jarring crack on the coffee table, her hand trembling.

'Look at me,' Jax urged, breaking the smouldering silence.

And Lucy looked even though she knew she shouldn't, desire clawing at her insides, awakening the yearning buried deep within her body. A ragged breath escaped her, her pulses racing. Her breasts ached but the biggest ache of all was between her legs, at the very heart of her where she was burning with need. That voracious need that hungered for his touch terrified her because it was so ready to rage out of control and sweep all restraint and all common sense before it.

'We're getting married as soon as it can be arranged,' Jax decreed.

Her head flew up. 'You can't just—'

'One of us needs to be decisive. You want to bury your head in the sand and run away from the responsibility.'

'No, I don't.'

'We do it for Bella. Together we make a family,' Jax intoned.

'It's not that simple.'

'Nothing worth having is ever easily acquired,' Jax said drily. 'Everything worthwhile I have ever achieved has come at a cost and there have always been sacrifices involved. Are you willing to make sacrifices for Bella's benefit?'

Lucy leapt upright in frustration. 'Jax! Stop trying to railroad me!'

'In a couple of days the paparazzi will be on to us. I want to pre-empt them with a wedding, a big splashy wedding, which they won't be expecting,' he told her grimly. 'They'll be happy enough to settle for wedding photos.'

'Do you really *want* to do this?' Lucy whispered shakily.

'I want you. I want my daughter. To give her what we both want, to give her what she *deserves*, we have to get married,' Jax countered with measured cool. 'I can handle that. Can you?'

And Lucy thought about that, really seriously thought about that even though her brain did not feel up to that challenge. Even when she had dreamt about marrying Jax two years earlier she had known it was only a dream because Jax had seen too many relationships break down to have any faith in the marriage bond. He had admitted that to her in Spain and afterwards he had seemed unnerved by what he had told her and he had cut their evening short.

'We will fight,' Jax forecast. 'But we're good at making up again.'

Lucy flushed and nodded jerkily and he laughed huskily for they had always ended up in bed after arguments, taking refuge in the sexual unity that bridged their differences.

'And if you don't want to give up work after we're married I'll make a special arrangement for you,' Jax murmured lazily. 'I'll buy a bar and I will be the *only* customer and you can serve me to your heart's content.'

'You say the craziest things,' Lucy muttered, shaking her head while locked to the stunning green eyes gleaming below his black lashes.

'I will say whatever I have to say to get that ring

on your finger,' Jax admitted truthfully. 'The world's your oyster tonight, *koukla mou*.'

But Jax was no perfect pearl for her to acquire, she thought helplessly. Jax was complicated and reserved and unpredictable. Living with Jax would not be easy; it would be a roller coaster of highs and lows. Yet didn't she want to take the chance? It was a chance she had never thought she would have. Yes, Jax had treated her badly in the past but marriage was an equal partnership and this time around she wouldn't have to surrender her independence or her self-respect because money wouldn't be an issue. Giving her daughter the secure and loving childhood she had not had herself would mean so much to her. How could she refuse that offer?

'I'll marry you,' Lucy breathed tautly. 'But you'd better not make me regret it.'

Thinking of the secrets he had withheld and the complete honesty that he would eventually have to practise, Jax breathed in deep. He had given way to blackmail to protect his family but in marrying, he acknowledged grimly, he would be protecting his new family from potential harm as well.

'I should be honest,' Lucy murmured, her blue eyes awash with regret and apology. 'I don't trust you.'

Jax, who had learned never to trust anyone, particularly one's nearest and dearest, almost laughed out loud. Lucy would flourish like a tropical flower in the Antonakos family.

## CHAPTER SIX

EVEN A FEW days before the wedding Lucy still couldn't quite accept that she was getting married. She was very tense and stressed. Jax had insisted on picking up the bill for the hundreds of guests invited and her father had been dismayed to discover that he was only allowed to cover his daughter's more personal expenses. In the same way Jax had organised the church and the venue for the reception.

And he had done all of that from a safe distance, leaving Lucy to handle her father's hurt pride and angry complaints. Jax, after all, was the man who had never planned to marry and since the moment Lucy had agreed to marry him Jax had come no closer to the centre of bridal activity than a phone call because he had hired a wedding planner to take care of everything. Lucy had had the freedom to make her own choices but had relied heavily on the planner's advice because she knew nothing about high-society weddings. Her brain was still stuffed, however, with the turmoil of selecting flowers, colour schemes and table arrangements from frighteningly long lists of options and having to discuss every possibility.

Iola had gone shopping with Lucy for a dress and

Jax had been allowed no input there. Lucy had gone for lace and a fancy pleated train that would be removable if she was dancing and she had picked the sweetest little outfit for Bella.

It was ironic that Jax had pretty much vanished as soon as she'd accepted his proposal and that had really annoyed Lucy. He had said that he had too much work to get through and he had only visited the house once when she had insisted he come and meet her father and her stepmother. That had been a very awkward hour of stilted conversation, she recalled ruefully. Jax had been very cool and polite and her father had been stiff and formal. Iola and Lucy's efforts to lighten the atmosphere had made little difference. It had been painfully obvious to Lucy that her father and her bridegroom didn't much like the look of each other.

And then there was the troubling question of her future father-in-law, Heracles Antonakos.

Lucy had assumed that Jax's father would want to meet her in advance but apparently not, and Jax did not seem to know whether or not his father would attend their wedding, an admission that had made her wince. Obviously, Heracles Antonakos was not impressed by his son's decision to marry a waitress and he wanted nothing to do with the event. But Jax refused to be drawn on the sensitive subject and had urged her to be patient.

'It's a delivery…for you,' Iola called up the stairs to Lucy.

Lucy clattered downstairs and signed for the package she was given, turning it over and back before walking into the kitchen to open it. She extracted a letter and a small jewellery box and frowned.

'Is it a wedding present?' Iola asked.

'No…it's from some woman called Polly, who *says* she's one of my sisters,' Lucy whispered in deep shock, reading the closely typed lines to learn that her mother had only passed away a few years before at a hospice and commenting on the fact to Iola.

'I always assumed that Mum had died when I was a child…possibly during the three years I was adopted because of course I wouldn't have been told about it then,' Lucy confided. 'But according to my sisters they too only found out about her death afterwards because she didn't want to see any of us while she was so ill. But she left us all rings given to her by our fathers…and it was only then that my sisters found out that I existed.'

'Strange,' Iola commented. 'But if she was very ill, possibly she wasn't thinking very clearly. Is there a ring in that box?'

Lucy opened the box and extracted a small ruby ring with a smile. 'It's very pretty. I'll wear it when I get married. It's wonderful to have something that my mother actually wore,' she murmured with a sad look in her eyes.

'Read the rest of the letter,' her stepmother urged. 'Tell me about your sisters.'

Unfortunately Polly didn't offer much information beyond the fact that she was married and had children just like Lucy's other sister, Ellie, who was a doctor. What she did say was that she and Ellie very much wanted to meet Lucy and get to know her.

'She couldn't have chosen a worse time to contact me,' Lucy mumbled, settling down to read the letter again. 'She hasn't given me an address or anything but she has given me a phone number, which I could use to talk to her.'

'You could invite your sisters to your wedding,' Iola suggested.

Lucy grimaced. 'No. I don't know them and I don't think Polly knows I'm a mother as well either. It would all be too awkward for a first meeting and in any case they would need more warning than a few days to attend. I'll call her as soon as we get back from our honeymoon. But my goodness, this is exciting,' she muttered abstractedly. 'I wonder what Polly and Ellie are like. Do I look like them? Do you think they have the same father?'

Kreon walked in and Lucy handed him the letter straight away to read. He stared down at the ring on the table and then he lifted it. 'I gave this to Annabel as an engagement ring. It's not a real ruby, you know, but it looks well. It was all I could afford at the time—'

Lucy laughed and removed it from his hand. 'I will still wear it with pride, Dad.'

'You have your mother's bright and beautiful smile,' Kreon told her fondly. 'But you have a kindness as well, which she never had.'

'Maybe I inherited that from you,' Lucy replied, watching her daughter hug her grandfather's knees and raise her arms to be lifted with all the confidence of a child who knew she could always expect a welcome.

Lucy couldn't sleep that night. Jax phoned and she told him about Polly's letter. It shook her that her most driving instinct was to share that very private news with Jax even when he wasn't around. But then Jax knew better than most about complex family divisions, she reasoned, shying away from the inner awareness that she trusted Jax more and wanted to share everything with him more than she was willing to admit.

Jax urged her to do nothing until he had checked out her sisters and she got cross with him then and told him to mind his own business. Not that he could do anything else, she conceded, when there wasn't enough personal information in that letter to allow Lucy or indeed Jax to identify either of her sisters or even work out where they lived. Polly had kept the letter short and sweet as a first approach and Lucy's mind buzzed with conjecture about the siblings she had never met.

Some of her excitement gradually subsided, however, when she thought about Ellie being an actual *doctor.* Ellie was obviously very well-educated and clever and possibly Polly was as well. Lucy could well be the odd one out, the lesser sister, the oddball who didn't fit in. That idea troubled Lucy because it seemed to her that that was the story of her entire life: never quite fitting in anywhere. Not with her mother, not in the foster homes, not even in the short-lived adoption she had enjoyed until her adoptive parents died in a car crash and she was sent back into care. And she hadn't fitted in with Jax either, had she? He had dumped her and walked away without a backward glance. Yet now, he was marrying her. How did that make sense?

He was only marrying her for Bella's benefit, she reminded herself, feeling her pride sting and her heart sink at that awareness. Could their desire to do well by their daughter be enough to sustain a marriage? Lucy didn't want make-believe and she didn't believe in perfect. She believed that she had realistic expectations. But she did desperately *want* to have a real marriage and be part of a proper family. It was what she had dreamt of all her life and never managed to achieve. Now that Jax was offering her that opportunity she planned to make the most of it.

The morning of the wedding dawned bright and sunny and, having done her hair and her make-up for herself, Lucy donned her gown. It was a perfect fit, swirling round her in delicate shimmering white lace. As a mother she had felt self-conscious about wearing white but she hadn't felt the need to make a statement either by choosing another colour. In any case she was marrying the man who had become her first lover and the father of her daughter and she wasn't ashamed of either fact.

A heaving bunch of paparazzi waited behind crash barriers outside the vast Metropolitan Cathedral in the city where the Greek Orthodox ceremony was being held. Lucy was unnerved by the questions shouted and the flash of cameras and she gripped her father's arm tightly as they negotiated the shallow steps and moved below the arches into the church.

'Royalty once got married here,' Kreon murmured with satisfaction. 'I never dreamt that one day I would see my own child taking her vows below this roof.'

The comment lightened Lucy's tension as nothing else could have done. 'Glad I've finally done something to make you proud but why are the paparazzi so interested?'

'You are about to become a member of one of the foremost families in Greece. Naturally, the public want to know who has captured the notorious playboy, Jax Antonakos—'

'I wouldn't say captured is the right word,' Lucy muttered uncomfortably as they paused at the end of the aisle and her father shook out her small train for her and offered his arm to her again with a proud smile.

'He's a very fortunate man. I hope he appreciates that. You look really beautiful,' the older man declared with satisfaction.

Tears stung the backs of Lucy's eyes because she was touched by her father's faith in her. She watched Jax turn his handsome dark head and look at her and the ability to breathe died in her throat. The closer she drew to him on their slow walk down the aisle, the more gorgeous he appeared, his dramatic green eyes welded to her approach. Colour warmed her cheeks and tingling heat surged low in her pelvis. She felt as if all her dreams were coming true in that moment and she scolded herself for being too emotional and sentimental. Jax was neither sentimental nor romantic. He didn't love her and she didn't love him, she reminded herself firmly, but they had Bella to bind them and, in time, maybe they would find that more than their daughter kept them together.

Jax studied Lucy with heavily lidded eyes, his attention roaming over every exquisite shapely inch of her petite body. The gown was a triumph, a delicate lace affair of simple design that enhanced her slight stature and gave her elegance. He didn't look to see how his father was reacting. Only minutes earlier he had noticed his father's absorption in Bella where she sat on Iola's knee across the aisle. Heracles longed for grandchildren, and the knowledge that he had a little granddaughter he had yet to meet had at the very last minute made him decide to attend the wedding. True, Jax wasn't expecting his father to be in a party mood because Heracles hated Kreon Thiarkis and hated that his son was marrying Kreon's daughter, but Jax was relieved that Heracles had put family first and shelved his reservations to share their day.

Some of the ceremony went over Lucy's head, for which she blamed Jax, who had said he was too busy to attend a rehearsal at the cathedral when the services of an interpreter had been available. She concentrated on the simple Greek words that she knew and smiled nervously up at Jax when he slid the ring onto her finger. Their eyes met and the burn inside her spread like wild fire. It was utterly inappropriate but she had never wanted so badly to be kissed. Jax angled his arrogant dark head back and gave her a teasing smile of naked challenge and she went for it as she had always gone for it when he egged her on. She stretched up awkwardly in her very high heels, her hands clutching at his arms to steady herself, and *still* she wasn't tall enough.

With a husky sound of sensual amusement, Jax gathered her up and raised her to his level to taste her lush parted lips for himself. And for a split second, Lucy forgot everything. She forgot that she was in public, she forgot the guests shifting in their seats and the imposing robed Archbishop who had conducted the service. The taste of Jax's mouth was like a shaft of sunlight bursting inside her after a long winter. It charged her up, rendered her helpless with longing, and the plunge of his tongue into the moist interior of her mouth only multiplied the explosive effect of that kiss on her body. Her heart hammered, her pulses raced as

Jax slowly slid her down his lean, powerful frame to stand on her own feet again.

She caught a glimpse of Iola's grin and just as suddenly appreciated that she was still in public view. A swoosh of mortified pink lit up her heart-shaped face as Jax closed his hand over hers and walked her back down the aisle.

Jax was amazed that he felt so relaxed. He had expected to loathe every minute of the wedding. Knowing he was protecting his father was one thing, doing what had to be done when it went against his own instincts was another. But that hot little taste of Lucy's passion assuaged those feelings. She wanted him, she wanted him just as much as he wanted her, and for the moment that was as much consolation for his sacrifice of freedom as he needed.

He had struggled against anger, resentment and bitterness throughout the two weeks it had taken to set up the wedding. He had kept his distance from Lucy because he was afraid that she would guess that he was not the enthusiastic bridegroom he was purporting to be. Deception of any kind had always been a challenge for Jax. He was very talented at keeping his feelings to himself but he was very bad at *faking* anything. He had found the drinks engagement with Kreon and Iola extremely uncomfortable and Lucy's demands for his opinion on the colour of the bridal flowers and such nonsense had simply exasperated him. For two solid weeks, Jax had rigorously reminded himself that he was acquiring Lucy and his daughter and protecting his father by getting married. But even that couldn't disperse the sour flavour of having to do what he had always sworn he would not do and take a wife.

Outside the cathedral the paparazzi went into a frenzy of excitement when the bride and groom appeared. Jax's father stalked silently from cathedral to limousine without pause. It was ironic that Heracles was furious with his son for marrying Lucy. Only after Jax had pointed out that he had had a daughter with Lucy had Heracles gone from raging to dark muttering, finally accepting that a waitress, who was also the daughter of an obnoxious criminal, was entering the Antonakos family. And having learned about that criminal record, Jax had not argued in his father-in-law's favour. Agreeing that Kreon was obnoxious had somewhat soothed his father's ire.

Jax had been tempted to bring up the file he had been given on Lucy two years earlier but he had decided to take a rain check on that line of enquiry until after the wedding. Getting information about Kreon Thiarkis had been surprisingly easy but getting information on Lucy was proving deeply problematic. She had lived in so many different places and had even been adopted at one stage when her name had been changed. Indeed the discovery of just how grim Lucy's growing years had been had saddened Jax. Some years after the adoption she had gone back to using the name she had been given at birth. But Lucy's frequent childhood moves read like a depressing indictment of social services care and the investigator striving to trace her movements during her adolescence was currently at an admitted standstill.

Of course, you could simply ask her for the details, Jax reminded himself wryly. Could he trust her answers? Or would she lie to mislead him, hoping to cover up conduct she might now be ashamed of? Jax needed the confidence of knowing that he had the *whole* truth. Naturally he expected her to deny the drugs offences but, so far, no official record of any such offences had been found. Was it possible that the detective agency his father had used had confused Lucy's identity with someone else's? Was it even remotely possible that she was innocent of the charges in that file? But then hadn't he been equally shocked when he'd seen her with that man in the alleyway? Lucy didn't wear her sins or her flaws on her lovely face.

With the ease of long practice Jax buried the memory of Lucy's betrayal deep where he didn't have to think about it. If he thought about it, he mused grimly, it would drive him off the edge, the way it had two years ago when he had tried to find solace in the bottom of a bottle: the aftershocks of giving up Lucy had been little short of terrifying for a male who needed to stay in emotional control. For a short while he had been overpowered by his conflicting feelings, not something he was willing to recall or relive. In fact even remembering that made him flinch.

They arrived at the hotel and settled down with Bella in a private room set aside for their use to drink champagne and await the arrival of their guests. Poised by the window, Jax tensed. 'That's my father's car arriving. Come on. I want to introduce you and Bella.'

By the time Jax and Lucy reached the grand foyer, however, Iola and Kreon were already greeting Heracles. And then there was one of those strange little moments of absolute stillness as Kreon said something and Heracles backed up and then suddenly lurched forward and punched the younger man with angry ferocity. Lucy was aghast when the fight broke out. Her father responded, lurching clumsily after Heracles to return that punch and then receiving yet another for his pains, for Heracles was very fit and fast on his feet for his age. Further violence was only forestalled by the Antonakos bodyguards who stood between the two men to keep them apart. Heracles let out an angry roar of frustration.

'Stay back,' Jax warned Lucy, striding in to intervene and grip his father by both his arms to restrain him, since it was obvious that none of their staff had the nerve to lay actual hands on their irate employer.

All red in the face and still patently desperate for a fight, Heracles roared something angry in Greek. Jax stole a glimpse at the guests piling through the entrance doors and then stopping dead to stare at the spectacle and he suppressed a groan. He said something to his father and shepherded him over to a door of the private room. Pushing open the door, he gestured to Lucy's father to follow him. Looking reluctant but red-faced and more than a little embarrassed, Kreon finally did so. Jax was trying to sort the argument out, Lucy recognised ruefully while wondering what Heracles Antonakos had against her father that had so overpowered his manners.

*'Men!'* Iola proclaimed dramatically at her elbow, making Lucy emit a startled laugh. 'Thank heaven, Jax got them out of sight.'

'What sparked off that punch?' Lucy demanded in bewilderment.

'Apparently Kreon and Jax's father have some past history. Kreon didn't go into detail but it's obvious that Jax's father hates him and almost didn't come to his son's wedding because he knew Kreon would be here.' Iola rolled her eyes. 'Don't let it spoil your day.'

'I shan't,' Lucy responded, stroking Bella's curls distractedly while thinking that family relations promised to be taxing with their fathers at odds.

With Iola by her side, Lucy welcomed guests and chatted until she saw Heracles and Kreon emerge again together with drinks in their hands and actually speaking to each other. But when Jax strode back to join her, raw tension was still stamped on his lean, darkly handsome features.

'Evidently you're quite successful in the peacemaker stakes,' Lucy remarked as he steered her into the function room to take their seats, mercifully moving her right before she had to greet Kat Valtinos, who looked ravishing in a cutaway emerald dress teamed with feathers in her hair.

'No, they achieved that without any help from me. I only stayed to ensure that hostilities didn't break out again,' Jax admitted. 'You still haven't met my father and I need to explain what happened out there.'

'Don't break the habit of a lifetime and tell me something,' Lucy urged with helpless sarcasm.

'It's not something I want to talk about but I must,' Jax breathed stiffly. 'However, it's old history and nothing to do with us. No doubt you're wondering why my father went for yours…'

'Kreon does seem to be an acquired taste with some people.'

'This is not a teasing matter,' Jax censured.

As she settled down beside him at the top table Lucy was watching Heracles Antonakos make their daughter's acquaintance. Bella was fearless and she stared up at the older man and handed him her stuffed rabbit. Heracles's craggy face broke into a sudden unexpected smile and he sat down with Iola by his side and accepted the rabbit to make it walk across the seat beside him. Bella started to giggle and clutched at the leg of his trousers to stay upright.

'He likes Bella,' Lucy noted with satisfaction, willing to overlook and forgive a great deal if her daughter was accepted and appreciated.

'He loves children.' Jax fell broodingly silent and she glanced curiously at his lean, taut profile, helplessly admiring the classic perfection of it. 'My father discovered after my brother, Argo, died that he could not have been his child. Argo needed a transfusion after the attack and I suspect it was discovered in the minutes before he died that he did not share my father's or my rare blood group.'

Lucy's eyes widened because she was completely disconcerted by that bombshell. 'My goodness, Heracles must have been devastated to find that out—'

'Particularly as he idolised his first wife and despised my mother...and me...for my mother's infidelity. When he found out that he hadn't fathered Argo he immediately suspected your father because of the close friendship Kreon had had with Sofia.'

Lucy winced. 'I honestly don't think it was that sort of friendship.'

'It wasn't. Kreon saw Sofia as a little sister. His mother, your grandmother on Kreon's side, was Sofia's nanny and as children Kreon and Sofia spent a lot of time together,' Jax told her. 'Unfortunately having married Sofia my father distrusted their friendship and became jealous.'

'In other words, your father is an old dinosaur who can't credit that a man and a woman can have a platonic friendship,' Lucy commented, still watching Heracles as he lifted Bella onto his knee with careful hands.

'I wouldn't appreciate my wife being that friendly with another man either,' Jax admitted.

'Sadly I don't currently have any close male friends to torment you with.' Lucy sighed with unhidden regret on that score.

'You're a little witch,' Jax growled, running his forefinger along the lush line of her full lower lip. 'Why does that make me want to kiss you again?'

'You love a challenge?' Lucy whispered unevenly, meeting those stunning green eyes in a head-on clash and feeling more than a little dizzy with excitement, her lips parting.

'But I don't enjoy an audience,' Jax countered, running a finger back and forth across the delicate bones of her wrist below the level of the table.

Lucy was breathing in rapid shallow little gusts, insanely conscious of her body responding to him on every level. She could feel her breasts full and constricted within the bodice of her dress, her distended nipples pushing hard against the scratchy lace of her bra and then there was the tight locked-down tension and heat between her thighs, not to mention the dulled little throb there that made her ache and stiffen her posture.

'It's showtime—but not for what we want,' Jax murmured drily as Iola took a seat beside him and Heracles settled down beside Lucy with Bella still on his knee.

'She's very cute,' Heracles said of her daughter. 'She knows what she wants.'

'Mum… Mum,' Bella framed, lurching straight off Jax's father into her mother's arms and flopping down sleepily.

'She needs a nap,' Lucy sighed.

'Where's the nanny I hired for the day?' Jax asked.

The older woman was already approaching Lucy, ready to take the tired toddler off her hands, but Lucy stood up. 'I'll come upstairs with you and get her settled.'

'Your bride doesn't take hints, does she?' Heracles remarked with some amusement to his son. 'You'll have your hands full with the two of them.'

Jax, who very much wanted to follow his bride upstairs and have her settle *him* down, grimaced. 'I know it.'

'Well, you can't make worse choices than I did. I won't say anything more,' his father declared piously. 'With my track record, I can't afford to preach, can I?'

'No, you can't.'

'Three marriages ending in one death and two divorces and your mother was almost as bad. We didn't set you much of an example, did we?' Heracles sighed heavily. 'By the way, I've set up the island for your honeymoon—'

Thoroughly taken aback, Jax frowned. 'But you live on Tifnos,' Jax objected, because he had been planning to take Lucy cruising round the Mediterranean on the yacht.

'Tifnos is yours now that you're a father. It was built to be a family home and I'm tired of living there alone in that great barn of a house. I've signed it over to you and I'm in the process of buying an estate outside Athens,' the older man told him in a tone of finality. 'It's time for me to step back and make room for the next generation.'

## CHAPTER SEVEN

LUCY CAME OUT of the room where she had left the nanny watching over Bella and smiled at the sight of Kreon waiting for her. 'Dad? What are you doing up here?' she asked with a grin. 'Are you trying to escape all the polite chit-chat? Or have you heard a rumour that the food's going to be bad?'

Kreon shifted uneasily on his feet, his face grave and troubled. 'I have done something wrong and it concerns you.'

'What on earth are you talking about?' Lucy laughed as he urged her into an alcove with seats.

'Talking to Heracles made me see stuff...differently.' Her father selected his words with an air of discomfiture as he sat down. 'It made me appreciate that we've all had our tragedies and our triumphs but it's how we deal with them that makes us who we are. I'd like to be proud of who I am but right now I'm *not*.'

Lucy narrowed her eyes in confusion. 'You don't sound like yourself.'

'Jax's father neglected Jax because he despised Jax's mother, whom he divorced. He knows he can never make it up to Jax and he has to live with it every day, knowing that all those years he left his boy to deal alone with a very difficult woman,' Kreon told her.

'But you and I have a different history,' Lucy reasoned, tucking that fresh information about Jax into her memory to take out and ponder at a more suitable time. 'You didn't even know that my mother was pregnant when you left London and she didn't tell you later when she could have done—'

'That's not what I'm talking about,' Kreon told her heavily. 'For many years I hated Heracles Antonakos because he put me down over my friendship with his wife. I'm ashamed to admit that I took my resentment out on his son.'

Lucy's smooth brow had furrowed. 'In what way?'

'When Sofia was dying, she had a letter sent to me in which she confessed her darkest secret. She didn't have the nerve to tell her husband so she told me instead.' Kreon drew a crumpled envelope from his pocket and passed it to her. 'Give it to Jax, let him decide what to do with it now. In it Sofia confesses to having an affair and she admits that Jax's brother wasn't fathered by Heracles. I went to see Jax a couple of weeks ago and I threatened to take that letter to the newspapers.'

'Good grief…why would you threaten to do something so horrible?' Lucy demanded in total disbelief.

'I wanted Jax to marry you and take care of you and Bella. I thought he owed you that security and I *still* believe that he does but coercing him into doing it was wrong and unjust. He was protecting his father from more heartache and I shouldn't have put him in that position. He is not responsible for his father's mistakes.'

Lucy had turned very pale and her stomach was

curdling as if she had eaten something that disagreed with her. She studied her father in slowly dawning horror and comprehension. 'Are you telling me that you blackmailed Jax into proposing to me?'

As Kreon gave a guilty nod of silent confirmation, Lucy felt as though the bottom had just dropped out of her world. She stared at the brand-new wedding ring on her finger and felt sick. Jax hadn't wanted to marry her. No, he had been *forced* to marry her. It was ghastly. She looked at her father in stricken condemnation. 'Were you insane? I mean, what on earth could persuade you that *that* was an acceptable way to behave towards Bella's father?'

'I was angry with him. I wanted to punish Jax for seducing and abandoning you. It's not an excuse but at the time I honestly believed I was doing what was best for you and my granddaughter.'

'Because Jax is rich and powerful,' Lucy slotted in sickly. 'And now you feel bad about it because you've realised that rich and powerful people like Heracles Antonakos make mistakes and suffer just like everyone else.'

Kreon sighed. 'That's probably it in a nutshell. When I listened to Heracles talking I felt my anger draining away. He was a workaholic who neglected all his wives. But he came to the wedding today even though he didn't approve of you because he was making an effort to be supportive of Jax as a father should. That was the *right* kind of effort to make for a child, mine was wrong. What did I do today? I made a sarcastic comment and provoked that punch.'

'I'm really upset,' Lucy admitted, breathing in deep and slow to calm herself down. 'You'd better go back down and join the guests before Iola starts wondering where you are.'

'I'm sorry, Lucy. I've just felt so powerless since you came into my life. You had had such a rough time and I genuinely *did* want to make your life better,' Kreon confessed before he walked away.

And she understood exactly where her father was coming from *but* he had blackmailed Jax. Nausea stirred in Lucy's tummy. Jax, who would hold a grudge beyond the grave. Jax, who idolised the father who had ignored him for so many years, had been vulnerable. A deep sense of anguish flooded Lucy and an even deeper sense of shame. The father she had so easily come to love had let her down badly and shown her his feet of clay. That hurt as well. Was she always going to be a rotten judge of character?

But what did she do now? Well, the middle of a wedding didn't seem the ideal venue in which to open a very difficult conversation with Jax. Oh, by the way, my father mentioned that he blackmailed you… Lucy cringed and winced and hurt all over again. She hurt for her father and for Jax and for Bella, for surely the chances of such a marriage working out looked very poor. But most of all, she was discovering that she hurt for herself. Jax's apparent desire to marry her had filled her with hope and even unleashed a few dreams.

Only now it was obvious that Jax hadn't actually experienced *any* desire to put a ring on her finger. Her father had used the nastiest form of persuasion available to get that wedding ring on her hand. Hadn't it ever occurred to Kreon that it would be his daughter who had to deal with the aftermath of what he had done? Hadn't he appreciated how angry and aggrieved

Jax would feel? Lucy shivered, suddenly feeling very alone and without support. She couldn't depend on her father and now it was equally obvious that she could not depend on her new husband either.

For the first time she badly wanted to speak to the sisters she had never met. It was crazy but she wanted to reach out and see if she could connect with a sister as she so obviously had failed to connect with Jax or her father. Kreon had lied when he said that she could trust him. And Jax hadn't meant all those fine things he had said about how they could be a couple creating a secure family in which to raise a child. He had been forced to talk like that to convince Lucy to agree to marry him and she groaned out loud, remembering how unusually understated Jax had been that evening. She had already put her sister's phone number into her mobile for fear that she might mislay Polly's letter and she dug her phone out of her small ornamental bag.

She got a bad case of cold feet while the phone was ringing and almost stopped the call before it connected. And then it was answered by this sunny, confidence-inducing female voice and Lucy froze.

'It's Lucy…er…your sister…if that's you, Polly,' she gabbled in an uneasy rush.

'Lucy!' Polly proclaimed warmly. 'I'm so very happy to hear from you. Do you have any idea how long Ellie and I have been trying to trace you?'

'Why were you trying?' Lucy asked in genuine puzzlement.

'Because you're our sister and part of our family. Ellie and I always had each other but until recently I know you had no one. Of course, I appreciate that you have your father now—'

'That hasn't worked out so well,' Lucy mumbled in some embarrassment.

'I'm really sorry to hear that. Are you all right, Lucy?' Polly prompted anxiously.

Lucy stared stonily at the wall, hot prickly tears stinging the backs of her aching eyes. 'Well, not so great today…to be brutally honest,' she framed chokily.

'You sound upset,' Polly remarked with care. 'Naturally I don't want to pry but—'

'I'm not upset,' Lucy insisted chokingly. 'It's my wedding day—'

'My wedding day wasn't great either,' Polly told her ruefully. 'I assume the ceremony has already taken place? Do you love the man you married?'

It was a simple question but it froze Lucy from head to toe. She started to shiver, feeling cold and clammy. 'No, we're not in love. We got married because we have a daughter…at least I *thought* that's why we got married but seems I was wrong about that too,' she mumbled shakily.

'I can't believe you're already a mother at only twenty-one,' Polly exclaimed. 'Somehow our detective didn't pick up on that. You sound so unhappy though. Please tell me what's wrong…'

And Lucy compressed her lips, fighting the tears positively attracted by that soft, understanding sibling voice. 'I *can't* tell you—'

'You can tell me anything,' Polly assured her. 'Ellie and I are here and ready and willing to help you if you need us.'

'That's good to know but I still can't tell you,' Lucy repeated doggedly.

'Is your child's father abusive?' Polly demanded worriedly. 'Are you at risk in any way?'

'No...*no*!' Lucy insisted, hastening to shut down that suspicion. 'Look, I've just found out that my father blackmailed my bridegroom into marrying me! That's why I'm upset.'

'Right...' Polly's momentary hesitation spoke volumes and Lucy winced. 'But you're not responsible for what your father does. Lucy, you only have to say the word and, wherever you are and no matter what time of day it is, we'll have you picked up.'

'That's a very generous offer,' Lucy framed, deeply touched.

'Please think about coming to stay with us for a while...you'd be very welcome and it would give you a breathing space in which to decide what you want to do next,' her sister pointed out.

'I'll certainly think about it but I have to go now. I'm sorry. I'll phone you again when I have more time to talk.'

Lucy thrust her phone guiltily back into her bag, wondering what had possessed her to say so much to a woman she had never met. Now Polly probably thought she was more than a little weird. She headed down to the powder room on the ground floor to repair her make-up. Her mascara had run and she asked herself why she had been reduced to tears. The shock of Kreon's confession? The knowledge that Jax had only proposed to protect his cantankerous old father from the humiliation of having it known that his elder son had not been his? Whatever, it was her wedding day and she was on show and she had to get over her emotional reactions and behave normally.

'Where the hell have you been?' Jax demanded as he strode out of the function room to intercept her and closed his hands round her arms to hold her still. 'Is Bella OK?'

'She's fine. I was talking to someone,' Lucy told him, colliding with his stunning black-fringed green eyes and experiencing a jolt not unlike an electric shock.

Jax stared down at her. 'Have you been crying?' he asked, noticing the very faint hint of pink round her eyelids, which he was certain hadn't been visible earlier.

'No, for goodness' sake,' Lucy parried with an uneasy laugh. 'Why would I have been crying?'

Jax had no idea but he could see that Lucy's naturally sunny aura had dimmed. Perhaps Bella was playing up, he reasoned. Weddings were stressful and a strange place and a strange nanny could well have upset his daughter. He dropped a hand to Lucy's spine and guided her back into the function room and towards the top table.

The meal was served. It melted in Lucy's mouth but she might as well have been eating sawdust for all the pleasure it gave her. Her father-in-law asked her some very awkward questions about her past life and she answered as best she could, struggling to breeze lightly past her years in care and becoming much more animated when he asked about Bella.

A professional singer entertained them and then the dancing began. Jax had to almost drag Lucy onto the floor because she couldn't dance very well and was covered in blushes at the thought of having to perform in front of people.

'I just wish this day was over,' she confided, pushing her face against his chest, realising that he was so tall that, from one angle at least, she could literally hide herself.

'You and me both,' Jax admitted, wondering if his father had said something cutting to make her appear so subdued and feeling surprisingly angry at that suspicion.

Of course, the wedding he had been blackmailed into agreeing to could hardly be a source of pleasure for him, Lucy reckoned wretchedly. And what must he think of her father now? He probably knew Kreon had already spent a couple of years of his youth in a cell and now he would believe that Kreon belonged in prison and would think less of her because of it. People did judge you on your background and relatives. Not that he had ever thought that much of her to begin with, Lucy reminded herself unhappily, recalling how she had been cast off like an old shoe in Spain.

'In another few hours we'll be on our way,' Jax remarked, long brown fingers sliding down her back to gather her closer.

Heat curled between her thighs as she felt the evidence of his arousal. Her mouth ran dry. Evidently blackmail didn't douse Jax's libido. He still wanted her. Was that something to celebrate? Or something more to beat herself up about? Was she supposed to settle gratefully for being his sexual outlet? Was that all she was worth? All she deserved? She didn't know any longer. Her brain in turmoil, she forced herself to relax into the hard, muscular warmth of his hold and allowed him to slow-dance her round the floor. Other people were dancing now as well and she no longer felt like the centre of attention.

'Where will we be on our way to?' she asked belatedly.

'That's a surprise,' Jax admitted, still taken aback by what his father had done.

The little island of Tifnos was the Antonakos home but Jax had yet to even spend a night there. As a boy he had been ferried out there but only on day trips to attend several big family social occasions and as an adult he had flown to the island regularly to consult with Heracles about business. But it had never been *his* home because when he had been young he had been lucky if his father even acknowledged his presence among so many other guests. In truth he had always felt like an intruder and an outsider in his father's house and the startling concept of making Tifnos his base raised all sorts of conflicting feelings.

'Oh...' Lucy framed, drinking in the scent of him with flared nostrils. There was definitely something scientific in the effect of pheromones on attraction, she conceded ruefully. She loved Jax's smell; that indefinable combination of designer cologne and husky male had called to her from his first kiss.

Her eyes prickled again and she wrinkled her nose to hold the stupid tears back. Her husband, *blackmailed* into marrying her. Knowing that, she found it a challenge to believe that she could be a true bride and wife. In fact, Kreon's intervention and use of pressure made a nonsense of the entire day. She felt utterly humiliated. She wondered when she would work up the nerve to discuss what Kreon had done with Jax and how he would react when she did. He could well be furious that she had found out. His ferocious pride would rebel against her knowing that he could be forced into doing anything.

She was heading for the bridal suite to get changed for their departure when she saw Kat Valtinos walking towards her and suppressed a sigh because she wasn't in the mood to be patronised or bitched at over the head of Jax.

'Lucy…' Kat murmured with a bright artificial smile. 'Your big day's almost over.'

'Yes. We're leaving soon.' Lucy busied herself fishing out the card to open the door. Kreon and Iola had already taken Bella home for the night and her daughter would be staying with them for the first week Jax and Lucy were away.

'Well, enjoy it while you can,' Kat advised with saccharine sweetness. 'It's not as if your marriage will last long.'

As Lucy thrust the door open she simply ignored the brunette, refusing to be drawn into an exchange with her. Kat had hated her two years ago in Spain for attracting Jax and, from what she had seen of Jax and Kat in the newspapers, Kat must still have cherished hopes of something more coming from their long friendship.

'Jax will take the kid and dump you again,' Kat murmured lethally. 'Don't say you weren't warned.'

Lucy closed the door firmly behind her. Pale and shaky after that nasty little threat of what could be, she concentrated on removing her gown and freshening up. She pulled on a light dress and thrust her sore feet into sandals, touching up her make-up with a light hand. Kat was such a shrew, she reflected ruefully. Jax would *never* try to take Bella from her. Why would he do such a cruel thing? Or even think about separating a mother from her child? It wasn't as though she was an unfit mother. All right, she wasn't perfect. She had been known to snarl a little when Bella tried to get her out of bed at dawn but she *loved* her daughter. Nothing pleased Lucy more than the ability to give Bella all the little things she had never had herself, the small stuff like bedtime stories, favourite foods and lots of hugs.

Her luggage packed and then collected, Lucy went to meet Jax. A limo ferried them to the airport, where they boarded a helicopter.

'Are we going on the yacht?' she asked before the noise of the engine made any conversation impossible.

'No. Tifnos,' Jax told her simply.

And Lucy nodded, secretly intimidated by the prospect. She had read about the fabled private island Heracles had bought as a base in the eighties. Her father-in-law was reputed to live in feudal splendour there in a house that had never been photographed or shown in any publication. But it was supposed to have gardens that could rival the Garden of Eden, a private zoo and literally hundreds of staff.

Lucy felt inadequate. She was far too ordinary for such a backdrop. She had always been ordinary and had once thought that that was what attracted Jax to her. She didn't put on airs, she didn't say things she didn't believe to impress and when she didn't know something she admitted it. Unexpectedly, Jax closed a large hand over hers and then slowly laced his fingers with her own. His thumb massaged her inner wrist soothingly. It was as if she had hoisted a flag telegraphing panic and he had picked up on it. Or as if he was a little apprehensive too…

An idea she swiftly dismissed, for Tifnos was the Antonakos home and he had to be well accustomed to it.

It was fully dark by the time helicopter landed and Jax scooped her out onto the helipad. Momentarily she was thrilled by the dark heavens filled with thousands of the stars that were never visible in the city. Their luggage was piled into a beach buggy and Zenas took the wheel to drive them up a steep hill road hedged in by a forest of pine trees.

And then at the top the Antonakos house stretched like a giant illuminated cruise ship.

'It's big,' she said abruptly.

'Yep, for a man who doesn't like to entertain, Heracles built a very large house,' Jax conceded wryly.

They stepped into a foyer glossy and glittering with pristine marble and chandeliers. It looked exactly like a plush hotel reception without the desk. A double staircase swanned up to the next floor, each tread wide enough to march an army.

'Think movie set,' Jax urged. 'My mother redesigned the entrance, so there are some very theatrical touches.'

A small middle-aged Greek man approached them with a tray of welcoming drinks. Jax passed her a champagne flute but demurred on his account. 'I don't like champagne,' he admitted.

Lucy drank down hers to be polite while she peered into rooms furnished with the kind of opulence that just screamed old money to her. There were statues and collections and cabinets and elaborate artwork everywhere she looked. Suddenly she understood why there were supposedly hundreds of staff. It would take a fair number to look after so many possessions.

Jax set down her glass for her and closed his hand over hers and told the hovering manservant whom he addressed as Theo that they were going to bed.

'Wasn't that a little…offhand?' she pressed self-consciously as they climbed the stairs.

'It's one in the morning and it's our wedding night,' Jax intoned, his hand tightening on hers. 'We can get chatty tomorrow.'

She thought about what she had been avoiding thinking about and colour mantled her cheeks as Jax walked her into a vast room overflowing with urns of white roses and lilies, ornamented with trailing ivy. It was magnificent but not as magnificent as the vast divan bed on the dais scattered with rose petals.

'Heracles wasn't joking when he said he'd set the house up for the bridal couple,' Jax conceded with forbidding cool.

'It's beautiful,' Lucy muttered, because it was and she was grateful that her father-in-law had been prepared to make the effort on their behalf. 'But maybe a little too grand for the likes of me.'

'The "likes of me" now happens to be my wife,' Jax reminded her in reproof. 'And nothing is *too* grand or *too* good for my wife.'

'I'll get used to it…it's just a little overwhelming coming to a house like this,' Lucy confided.

'It's ours now,' Jax revealed, sharing his father's plans with her. 'I think he's hoping we'll go forth and multiply now for him.'

Lucy shrugged a slim shoulder, making no comment on that possibility.

'I think Bella's enough for us at present. I still have to learn how to be a father,' Jax completed, making his opinion clear. 'Do you want a drink or anything to eat? There're snacks waiting on the trolley.'

'No. I only want to get my shoes off,' Lucy admitted, dropping down into a luxurious armchair with a sigh. 'My feet are hurting.'

'Let me...' In the most disconcerting way, Jax crouched down lithely at her feet and unfastened her shoes to slip them off. 'You have such tiny feet. They used to fascinate me.'

Long brown fingers gently stroked the back of a delicate ankle and Lucy snatched in a sudden startled breath because her skin felt super sensitive, as though he had touched her somewhere much more intimate.

'All that got me through the day was the glorious thought of sating myself inside you again, *koukla mou*,' Jax said huskily, rising to lift her bodily out of the chair and settle her down on the huge bed.

Eyes flying wide, cheeks flushing, Lucy stared up at him with bright blue eyes.

'So, why do you look like a cornered rabbit?' Jax asked pleasantly. 'You've been acting strangely all day.'

## CHAPTER EIGHT

'I...I FELT OVERWHELMED,' Lucy told him and it was true.

The cathedral wedding, the sleek bejewelled Antonakos relatives and guests and the absence of any actual friends aside of her father's had weighed her down. The constant stares and the low buzz of conjecture hadn't helped either but when someone as rich as Jax married a waitress, who was the mother of his child, people stared and speculated. The wedding had been a strain and her father's confession of wrongdoing had crushed her. It had been the ultimate humiliation to learn that only Kreon's criminal act had made it possible for her to marry Jax.

And yet what could they possibly *do* about it now? Kreon had confessed too late to change anything. If she and Jax were to part this very night, it would cause a major scandal and she knew Jax wouldn't want to invite that media attention, which meant that at the very least they would have to stay married for a few months to make any breakup appear less worthy of comment.

'I can understand that,' Jax conceded, removing his jacket in a lazy fluid movement.

And Lucy watched him with a fast-beating heart,

still wondering what she should do and how she should be behaving. Yet with a good ninety per cent of her being she craved the intimacy that being with Jax would give her. She wanted forgetfulness. She wanted to sink into the comfortable depths of the massive bed and shut the rest of the world out to take refuge in Jax. Even if he wasn't really hers and possibly wouldn't be hers for very long. His dazzling green eyes gleamed in the low-lit room, so bright against his dark bronzed skin, and her mouth ran dry.

Tugging his shirt from his waistband, he came back to the bed and sank down behind her to unzip her dress. She sat there like a little statue, her heart thudding like crazy in her chest as he lifted the garment up over her head, leaving her clad only in the white lace lingerie she had worn with her wedding gown. Sliding upright again, he unbuttoned his shirt, displaying a wide slice of his torso, well-defined muscles coming into view as he shed the shirt.

And she was as entranced by his sheer male beauty as she had once been in Spain, feasting her eyes on him with feminine appreciation. Jax worked out and it showed. He was all lean muscle and controlled power.

'Take the rest off,' he urged. 'I want to look at you.'

Her face burned as she reached behind her back to unclasp her bra. She had never done that before in front of him. Her clothes had once vanished beneath his skilled hands and she hadn't had to think about it or ever feel particularly naked. But there in that silent bedroom she was insanely aware of her body and its deficiencies as she let the bra fall. Most of the pregnancy weight had fallen away but there was no denying that she was curvier at bust and hip and there was an obvious scar low on her belly from the Caesarean she had had to have. Her waist was bigger too, she thought nervously, anxiously cataloguing every flaw. And this was a guy accustomed to the flawless female bodies of underwear models.

Jax studied the pouting swell of her pink-tipped breasts with intense pleasure, arousal flashing through him with storm-force potency. Everything about her daintiness appealed to him because her slender lines became lush in all the right highly feminine places. And he knew exactly what would happen when he touched her. He knew she would respond to him in a way no other woman ever had and that there would be nothing fake or exaggerated about it. Anticipation gave him the ultimate high.

'I'm not perfect,' she warned him tightly as her fingers flirted with the band of her knickers. 'Well, I never was, but—'

A flashing grin flared across Jax's lean, darkly handsome features as he came down on one knee on the bed and yanked her playfully to him by her ankles. 'You're perfect for me…I only want to see you.'

Sharply disconcerted by that teasing assault, Lucy looked up at him with apprehensive eyes of blue. He hooked his hands into her knickers and dragged them off, lowering her back gently against the pillows and then rearranging her to his own satisfaction, her legs parted and her hands by her side.

'I'd love a painting of you looking like this, all spread out and waiting for me, but I couldn't stand the artist seeing you naked,' he admitted thickly, peeling off his trousers and his boxers in an impatient movement.

Lucy lay there feeling like a sacrifice and yet she was quite ridiculously excited by his scrutiny and the thrusting fullness of his arousal. He was so ready for her, was always ready. He made her feel as though her body were flawless and the desire he made no attempt to hide warmed the sore place inside her where her father's betrayal had contrived to undermine her self-esteem.

Jax joined her on the bed and went straight for her mouth with hungry, driving kisses that parted her lips and sent a current of high-voltage expectation flying through her trembling length. Her fingers clutched into his spiky, messy black hair and tears burned behind her lowered eyelids because she wanted him so much that she hurt with the wanting. It felt too intense, too desperate and that wasn't what she wanted to feel. She needed to stay in control, she told herself, remember what was real and what wasn't real. And what they had now *wasn't* real. Why did thinking that drive a knife through her when it was only the truth?

'I can't get enough of you,' Jax growled between the urgent biting kisses that bruised her lips and the devastating plunge of his tongue that made her slight body jackknife in reaction beneath his.

'We've got all night,' she whispered through rosy swollen lips, eyes glazed with passion.

'I've got a hunger that one night won't come anywhere near satisfying,' Jax told her rawly, fisting a hand in her tumbling curls as he snaked a string of kisses down over her collarbone and found a plump, pointed nipple to torment with attention.

'Oh… Jax,' she gasped, a fire trail of tingles lighting up from her breast to her pelvis where a warm damp sensation pulsed.

With difficulty Jax dragged his lips from her writhing body and stared down at her. She was his wife now. Signed, sealed and delivered. In the strangest way, he registered, he *liked* that, liked that ring on her finger that marked her as his and loved the way she was looking up at him as though he had hung the moon.

'You will be very tired tomorrow,' Jax forecast without hesitation. 'I'm planning to take everything you can offer and then some more.'

Without hesitation, Lucy leant up and claimed his sensual, taunting mouth for herself, revelling in the instant rush of hungry need he betrayed. He scored the edge of his teeth across her full lower lip, dallied over the sensitive skin below her ear and then returned to his self-imposed worship of her full breasts. He lashed the hard little tips into swollen, throbbing sensitivity and her hips rose beneath his long, lean physique until he settled a leg between hers, giving her the pressure she craved at the crux of her body.

The demanding ache at the heart of her spread, sending little tingles through every skin cell, building and building her tension. He teased her nipples with his teeth and the heat of a climax simply exploded through Lucy in a glorious rush that made her cry out and jerk under him.

'That's one…' Jax husked with satisfaction.

'You're counting now?' Lucy mumbled distractedly, dragged into brain-dead lethargy by the shimmering backwash of sheer pleasure.

'I always was goal-orientated,' Jax reminded her, working his passage slowly down her quivering length.

Tell him you know about the blackmail, a guilty little inner voice urged her. But that would unleash a very difficult conversation after an extremely long and trying day. In any case Jax was reasonably happy at this precise moment, she decided, and she didn't want to spoil things. Later they would both be more relaxed and less tense. He tugged her thighs apart and buried his mouth there and suddenly her brain didn't have any space left in which to be rational. Suddenly she became a twisting, gasping creature at the mercy of her own sensual responses.

Jax slid a finger through her silky folds. He stroked her, smiling as she moaned and shifted, striving to urge him on, but in bed Jax was always in control, most particularly because Lucy had no control.

'Torture!' she muttered between gritted teeth, a rosy flush and perspiration slicking her skin as she thrashed under his ministrations, gasping as he hit the exact spot where she was most sensitive.

'I love the taste of you,' Jax growled, the vibrations of his dark deep drawl pulsing through her tender flesh.

Involuntarily, her body erupted again, driven to the point of explosive climax by the intensity of her excitement. She screamed his name and jerked and then fell still, wonder creeping over her that anyone could possibly wreak such havoc with her system and give her that much pleasure.

'*Thee mou*, I want you so much,' Jax ground out as he slid over her, his hands strong on her hips to angle her back.

He entered her slowly, urging her tender flesh to open for him and stretch, and the sensation made her dizzy with yearning and wildly impatient for more. He eased back and then pushed in hard and deep and her body convulsed and tightened round him, intense sensation ravishing her. A string of tiny sounds was wrenched from her parted lips as he ground into her and picked up the pace, raw excitement flooding her as she tilted up to meet him, hot, damp and abandoned as the wild roller coaster of sensation raged on and on. He slammed into her with primal force and her body just splintered from the inside out, taking her apart in pieces so that she slumped back on the bed, barely aware of his muffled groan of completion but welcoming the warm, heavy weight of him.

Empty of all conscious thought, Lucy skated her hands over Jax's smooth damp back and then wrapped her arms round him tightly. He was struggling to catch his breath close to her ear and she smiled and twisted her head to kiss him on the cheek.

Jax froze as though she had crossed some invisible boundary line. He refused to do that stuff with her again. Bone and sinew he rejected any show of affection that came from her and he yanked back from her and rolled away. He wasn't buying into that again with her, no way! She had given him that same hugging and petting and apparent warmth in Spain and he knew it was meaningless. He had known that when he saw her in that alleyway having sex with another man. As that cringe-making memory returned, Jax wanted to smash a fist into the wall.

That was better left buried and he knew it, particularly now that they were married. When he thought about it, he felt seething anger and violent. Forgiveness wasn't in his vocabulary and forgetting wasn't in his nature. There wasn't any reason for him to think about that sordid episode, he told himself grimly. All he had to do for his own protection was remember that she was treacherous and watch out when she was around other men.

When Jax jerked away from her and headed for what she assumed was the bathroom, Lucy felt as if he had slapped her in the face. He had recoiled from her as if she were contagious, as if he couldn't *bear* her touch. After such intimacy, that hit hard and hurt, spelling out the message that once he had had sex, he was up and away, any pretence of courtesy or caring set aside and rejected.

She felt hollow and very, very foolish. This was the aggressive male her father had blackmailed into marrying her and this was the payoff, she assumed sickly. Evidently he had taken the only thing he actually wanted from her and now she was like an abandoned toy, a distraction good enough only to be tossed back in the cupboard until the next time he wanted to take her out and play with her.

'You don't like it when I touch you after sex,' she accused baldly.

Jax shot her a winging glance from narrowed green eyes that glittered. 'Because it's fake.'

Lucy sat up. 'It wasn't fake,' she told him but he had already vanished into the bathroom and within seconds she heard the sound of a shower running.

Well, Jax needn't think that was the end of the conversation just because he wanted it that way, Lucy thought angrily. She scrambled out of bed and grabbed up her handbag to extract the letter that Kreon had given her. Whether she liked it or not, it was time to be open and honest. She opened the bedroom door and found their luggage piled outside. She lifted a case and dragged it in, opening it up to remove a light cotton robe. Nothing slinky about her nightwear, she reflected ruefully. Iola had insisted on buying her some stuff and the prospect of Jax gazing in disbelief at her chain-store PJ's had persuaded her. She wrapped herself in the robe, watching out of the corner of her eye as Jax strode naked into what sounded like an en-suite dressing room because she could hear drawers being rammed open and shut and cupboard doors being slammed. My goodness, he was in a bad mood… so much for her assumption that intimacy would bring relaxation and a release of tension!

Jax reappeared, clad in a pair of faded jeans and a black tee shirt that clung to his muscular torso. He headed straight for the trolley and opened it before lifting a plate and piling food on it. 'Would you like anything?' he asked with studious politeness and she wanted to slap him for his tone.

'Not right now, thanks,' she murmured tightly. 'I have something for you… Kreon gave it to me today.'

Jax swung round, fully acknowledging her for the first time, his lean, darkly handsome face guarded until he saw and immediately recognised what was in her hand and he stalked forward to snatch it from her with a profound look of revulsion.

'Were you in it *with* him?' Jax shot at her accusingly, for most ironically that possibility hadn't occurred to him and right there and then he called himself an idiot for not having suspected her active involvement in Kreon's blackmail threat.

Lucy's chest swelled on a stark indrawn breath of shock as she drew herself up to her full unimpressive height. 'Are you certifiably insane?' she demanded in fiery rebuttal of that suspicion. 'Yesterday, *after* the wedding, Kreon told me what he had done to you because he felt guilty. He knew he'd done wrong—'

*'Diavolos...'* Jax derided. 'Kreon felt guilty? You will never know what a comfort that is to me!'

'He did wrong but he's not a bad man and the mistake you made was in not immediately coming to me about my father's threat and the existence of that letter,' Lucy condemned with conviction. 'I believe I could've stopped it because he would have been too ashamed to continue with it once I knew about what he was doing.'

'And pigs fly and there's two blue moons in the sky,' Jax scorned, shaking his tousled dark head in wonderment, green eyes as cutting as sword blades. 'I'll ask you one more time…were you aware of his intentions?'

'No, I blasted well wasn't!' Lucy shouted back at him, her blue eyes flooded with angry, defensive discomfiture. 'How can you even ask me that? I wasn't expecting you to ask me to marry you, wasn't even thinking along those lines!'

Jax cocked his proud dark head back, black curling lashes semi-screening his stunning eyes. 'It's done now.'

'Yes,' she acknowledged uncomfortably. 'But I had nothing to do with the blackmail or any idea of what was going on behind the scenes—'

'But it all worked in your favour, all the same,' Jax spelt out with contempt. 'You got to marry into the Antonakos family.'

'Well, from where I'm standing now, on my wedding night, marrying into the Antonakos family is not the triumph it's purported to be!' Lucy shot back at him furiously, an angry flush mantling her cheeks. 'In fact it feels like hell, most particularly when I seem to have a husband who can happily have sex with me and then virtually push me away afterwards!'

'I don't cuddle...*ever*,' Jax stressed.

'Bella needs cuddles so you'll have to revise your rule and I need them too,' Lucy flung back at him rawly. 'So, if you want sex, you'll do it.'

An unholy flare of rage lit up Jax's eyes, lightening them to the brilliance of sea glass gleaming in sunshine. 'I've put up with a hell of a lot but I won't stand for *that*!' he raked back at her, every word slicing through the air like a knife. 'I married you. Be grateful for it because you're getting nothing else from me but the name and the money and a father for your child!'

And as Lucy stood there staring at him, involuntarily unnerved by the sheer force of his rage, she stilled a shiver, appalled by that assurance. 'That's not enough for me,' she muttered shakily.

'Tough,' Jax enunciated with clarity. 'That's all you'll be getting now and in the future.'

With that final statement of punitive intent, Jax strode out of the room and just left her there. Lucy ate through a whole plate of profiteroles and drank coffee and then felt sick. Her whole world had fallen into pieces round her feet and, with it, any sense of security. She lurched into the bathroom where she was sick and when she felt strong enough to stand up again she went for a shower. She knew she would never look at a profiterole again. She would never look at Jax the same way again either for she had just seen a side of him that he had never shown her before.

Now she knew what she really *hadn't* wanted to

know. He hadn't wanted to marry her. In fact he had absolutely hated and thoroughly resented having to marry her. He had suppressed that fury successfully throughout the day and she had provoked him into expressing it by asking for something more: a stupid cuddle, of all things. Her eyes stung and she looked heavenwards as she struggled to control her wildly see-sawing emotions. As far as Jax was concerned he had already given her more than enough: his famous name, his great wealth, his readiness to be a father. *Your* child, he had called Bella, not *our* child.

Why would he care that none of that would be sufficient to make her happy? Why would he care that she was hurting so bad that she wanted to scream with the pain of it? He hadn't asked her to care about him and she didn't know when or how she had started caring again. In Spain it had begun with a smile, a shared look of understanding and discussion, a touch of his hand, six weeks of breathless excitement and more happiness than she had ever experienced before she lost it all again.

But, Jax had reappeared in her life and somehow shreds of those old feelings had taken root again deep down inside her where she didn't explore very often. *She* cared. Much more than he deserved. But was that a true or fair view? Kreon had been vicious and Jax had been strong-armed by family affection into making a sacrifice he didn't want to make. Sadly, Jax wasn't any keener on the concept of marriage than he had ever been.

So, what did that leave her to work with? Lucy blinked back tears and went to clean up her face again, dashing on a little make-up in a desperate hope of relocating a hint of a lingering bridal glow. Unhappily she looked tired and heavy-eyed and pale and even bronzer didn't help. In the end she washed it all off again before she went to look for Jax.

It was the early hours of the morning but everywhere was lit up. She didn't even know what she was going to say to him but she knew that she had to deal with the situation and make something out of the mess Kreon had created. After all, they had Bella to consider and while Lucy was prepared to let go of her own dreams she wasn't prepared to give up on her dream of giving her daughter a normal family life.

She peered into empty room after empty room on the ground floor and then she found him, sprawled with a glass in his hand on a huge fancy padded lounger sited on a wide terrace from which he was watching the sun come up in a glorious multicoloured reflective rainbow over the dark sea far below the house. She hesitated beside the patio doors and then noticed that the phone he was studying was displaying a wedding photo of their daughter. And that discovery softened her and empowered her in a way nothing else could have done into moving forward.

'Jax?' she murmured uncertainly.

'We have to make a go of it…or at least *try*…for her,' Jax breathed in a raw undertone without turning his head.

'Yes…' It was exactly what Lucy wanted to hear and yet she still felt as though her heart were breaking inside her because she knew that she wanted so much more from him.

'I'm drunk,' Jax confided gruffly, wishing he weren't, wishing he were better at handling his own emotional turmoil. 'But drowning your sorrows doesn't help. It only darkens everything more.'

In the tense silence, Lucy dropped down onto the smaller lounger beside his. She didn't recline, she sat on the side of it, rigid-backed and still. A photo lay on the table between them and she lifted it. It was a picture of another little girl, a little girl who looked similar enough to Bella to be her sister.

'Who's this?' she asked worriedly, immediately wondering if Jax had another child.

'My little sister, Tina. The reason why I didn't need to wait on DNA test results to know that Bella was mine,' Jax explained reluctantly.

'I didn't know you had a sister.'

'Hardly anyone knows. When she died it was hushed up,' he muttered.

Lucy frowned. 'Your father's child?'

'No. From my mother's second marriage to an actor. He was half her age. It fell apart quickly. By then Mariana was accidentally pregnant and as a devout Catholic there was no question of her not giving birth. Valentina was born the summer I was twelve. Mariana was determined to keep her a secret because she couldn't bear the idea that her adoring fans would pity her for being abandoned a second time with a child. Unfortunately, she could never keep household staff for long. I looked after the baby that summer—'

'At twelve years old?' Lucy gasped although she was trying hard not to react to what he was telling her. 'Where was your mother?'

'Zonked out of her skull on prescription drugs…the way she always was,' Jax confided grudgingly. 'I got attached to Tina. She was a sweet kid. Mariana got another nanny before I went back to boarding school and for a couple of years everything was fine. I saw Tina in the holidays. And then Mariana had a fight with the nanny the day before she held a pool party…and Tina drowned because nobody was looking after her. My mother was a legendary star and the studio ensured that the death and the burial were dealt with very discreetly.'

'I'm so sorry, Jax,' Lucy whispered shakily.

'The worst part of it was that nobody ever mentioned Tina again. It was like she'd *never* existed.'

Lucy slid to her feet and settled on the big lounger by his side, one arm draping over him protectively.

'I don't cuddle,' he told her argumentatively.

'You're not cuddling,' Lucy assured him. 'I'm cuddling you.'

'I really don't need *or* like that sort of stuff,' he growled.

'Of course you don't. You're just tolerating me to be polite.' Lucy sighed, feeling the rigid tension in his muscles ease and snuggling into the powerful heat of his long, lean frame. 'You have such good manners, Jax.'

'I *do*?' Jax said in surprise, flipping over to face her, green eyes clear as emeralds in the dawn light.

'Most of the time,' Lucy murmured with amusement, colliding with those gorgeous eyes of his, eyes full of so much hunger and uncharacteristic uncertainty. 'I *wasn't* part of the blackmail plan.'

'I know…' Jax rubbed his dark stubbled jaw against her shoulder as if in apology. 'But I think I preferred you not knowing about what your father did.'

'I would've preferred that too,' Lucy admitted. 'But it happened and we have to deal with it.'

Assertive hands tugged at the edges of her robe and the sash before sliding beneath the crisp fabric. 'Naked,' Jax savoured. 'I like, *glyka mou*.'

Lucy bridled. 'I wasn't thinking about that when I came looking for you. I couldn't be bothered poking through another case to find clothes…'

'Shush…' Jax murmured, long brown fingers rubbing with devastating expertise over the most sensitive spot on her entire body to set off a devastating tingling awareness before sliding down below. 'I want you.'

*'Here?'* she gasped in consternation even as her slender thighs parted and her hips shifted in a rhythm as old as time.

'I sent the staff to bed when we arrived. Poor Theo had kept them all up,' Jax told her. 'I don't need attention twenty-four-seven…except from you.'

Lucy's rosy lips parted on a helpless gasp. 'Twenty-four-seven?' she framed with difficulty.

'I'll make it well worth your while,' Jax promised, crushing her ripe mouth urgently under his as he unzipped his jeans and shifted over her with urgent intent. 'Let's take this back into honeymoon territory…'

And Lucy, at that moment malleable as clay in his expert hands with her body rising and burning and already defencelessly eager, had no objection to that plan. They had weathered the first storm, learned that for both of them Bella was their main focus. That had to be enough, she told herself urgently, a strangled sound escaping her convulsing throat as he pinned her under him and plunged into her with raw, hungry energy.

Pushing for more would only strain their relationship, which meant that *she* had to learn to settle for what she could get. And if that meant forgiving his suspicion that she could have been involved in her father's blackmail, she had to do it. It was early days, she reminded herself.

Yet how could he suspect her of such dishonest behaviour? And why did he assume that her affection was faked? Was his past so littered with unscrupulous lovers that trust was impossible for him?

# CHAPTER NINE

'YOU WERE TELLING me about your adoptive parents,' Jax reminded her as they walked along the deserted beach three weeks later, walking Bella between them to keep the little girl steady.

'Was I? They were good people. I was nine years old and very fortunate to get a home at that age,' Lucy declared wryly.

'I imagine you were a very pretty little girl. I'm sure that helped.'

Lucy shrugged, thinking back to that brief three-year period when she had been part of a family. 'They were very academic. When they took me on they were warned that I'd fallen behind at school and straight off they decided to hire tutors for me in every subject.'

Jax frowned. 'Impatient, were they?'

'No, they were trying to help but it put me under a lot of pressure. I was trying very hard to be everything they wanted and then I failed an important exam, which meant I couldn't get into the school they had set their hearts on and they were really disappointed. I don't think I was the right child for them,' she admitted ruefully. 'But when they died in the car crash, all that ended and I went back into care because none of their relatives saw me as being part of the family. At the end of the day and whether you agree with it or not, blood counts.'

'Yes, doesn't it?' Jax agreed, thinking of his late brother, Argo, a good-natured, indolent young man, who with hindsight had been remarkably dissimilar to Heracles and Jax in nature.

Bella tugged her hand free of her mother's and pulled at Jax's jeans to be lifted. He hoisted her high and she giggled and rested her curly head down sleepily on his bare shoulder. Their interaction was so relaxed and natural now, Lucy thought with satisfaction, that it was hard to believe they had only met a month ago.

She and Jax hadn't lasted a whole week on the island without Bella. Lucy had never been separated from her daughter before and had decided a week was unnecessarily long when there was a nanny on the household staff, willing and able to give the honeymooners a break from childcare: Heracles had prepared for every eventuality when he entertained. But the rumour of a private zoo had proved to be just that—a rumour.

The gardens, however, were spectacular although Jax and Lucy had spent more time on the beach, crunching through the pale sand to the water's edge where Lucy, who could not swim, liked to paddle. Never having enjoyed many such opportunities, she was not keen on trusting her body to either a swimming pool or the sea, but Jax had insisted that her learning to swim was a safety issue more than anything else. So, Lucy had braved swimming lessons with Jax, which they had both found equally trying,

Jax because he was naturally impatient and Lucy because she was nervous.

Over the past three weeks they had learned so much about each other, she acknowledged cheerfully. Jax was a morning person, Lucy was a night person. They had spent a wonderful ten days cruising round the Mediterranean on his father's yacht, *Sea Queen*, docking at different islands to see the sights, dine out and shop. She loved to dance and they had enjoyed several really late nights out at clubs. He had bought her loads of clothes in hip boutiques on Crete and Mykonos and he had had a jeweller flown out to Tifnos for her to choose what he deemed to be the basics. A gold watch now encircled a wrist and gold hoops ornamented her ears. She had a diamond pendant, bracelet and earrings as well, which he had referred to as a 'belated' wedding gift. And Bella had a nursery overflowing with toys and clothing and picture books to go with the designer furnishings.

In fact, Lucy believed she already had almost everything she had ever wanted or ever dreamt of having. Jax had spoiled them both. He was marvellous with Bella, far more patient with her than he was with anyone else. He was making a huge effort to be a dad and she appreciated that when so many of his friends, smooth sophisticates whom they had met in the clubs where he was well known, had yet to even settle down. For a man who had never wanted to marry, Jax was settling down into family life remarkably well, she reflected gratefully.

Yet she couldn't forget that Jax was the same guy who had dumped her for 'boring' him two years earlier, the same guy who had seemed perfectly content with her one day and who had then cut her out of his life only days later. That past still made her insecure because she had no faith that she could accurately read Jax and estimate his state of mind with regard to her and their marriage. Of course, he seemed to do and say all the right things, but then he had done that before in Spain and look how that had ended!

'I'm hungry...' Jax curved a hand to Lucy's shoulder and steered her up the beach towards the buggy that would waft them up the steep hill. 'And I think our daughter needs a nap...and maybe I need one too, *glyka mou*.'

Lucy coloured. Heat licked at her feminine core as Jax sent her a glittering green glance of sensual enquiry. Dampness gathered between her legs, anticipation rising because that side of their relationship was outrageously healthy. He still wasn't doing the cuddling thing the way she wanted. No, with Jax what might start out as a cuddle invariably turned into sex. He said he couldn't be that close to her and touch her without wanting to get naked and energetic. There was nowhere they hadn't made love. They had indulged on the beach, in the pool, in the pine forest, in the labyrinthine privacy of the lush gardens, but most often in the delicious comfort of their own bed. The simmering flare-ups of passion that wound through their days felt so natural to her. It was as if Jax couldn't get enough of her, a thought she kept tactfully to herself, and that made her feel safer. She couldn't help viewing sex as a barometer to gauge the health of their marriage because Jax certainly wasn't any keener to discuss such things than he had ever been.

'It's those freckles. I can't resist them,' Jax said huskily, skimming the bridge of her nose with a teasing finger.

Lucy laughed because she hated her freckles, seeing them as imperfections, but Jax thought they looked delightfully natural, which of course they were. Did anyone draw in freckles? She thought not and smiled as they piled into the buggy. A pang of sadness infiltrated her mood because the honeymoon as such was almost over. Jax was meeting with Heracles about some big project in Athens the following morning and she was accompanying him because she planned to take Bella to visit her father and Iola. She was hoping that the passage of time since her wedding day and Bella's noisy presence would make the occasion less tense and awkward.

In actuality, Jax wasn't looking forward to the next day either. He intended to confront his father with the file Heracles had had sent to him on Lucy two years before. From what he had so far managed to establish the file was full of inaccuracies and outright lies and he needed to know if those lies had been a deliberate attempt to break up their relationship or the simple product of a lazy investigator and a case of mistaken identity. He could scarcely censure Kreon's ethics if his own father was guilty of the same lack of moral scruple when it came to getting the result he wanted most.

Even so, he still could not have said which answer he wanted to hear from Heracles because if the older man actually *believed* the contents of that file, it outraged Jax in a way he could not rationally explain. Yet he, more than anyone, knew Lucy was far from perfect. His mind skipped superfast over that acknowledgement and tucked the memory of that alleyway encounter back into the box where he kept it locked away. She had made an unforgivable mistake and he *had* to live with that...for Bella's sake, he told himself urgently, *only* for Bella's sake.

Bella's nanny took the little girl off to bed. Lucy went for a shower because she was hot and sandy and she wasn't at all surprised when Jax stepped into the shower with her, all lithe, wet bronzed skin and rippling muscles. She ran her hands up appreciatively over his torso and as the water jets shot at them, sprinkling even their faces with droplets, his mouth came crashing passionately down on hers. He tasted her with raw driving need and as always the strength of his hunger for her disconcerted her. He gathered her slippery body up and pinned her against the cold tiles, lifting her thighs round his waist while rocking and grinding against the tender triangle of flesh at the heart of her.

That fast she wanted him intolerably and with every probing plunge of his tongue she wanted him more. Evocative little noises were wrenched from low in her throat as skilled fingers teased and played to prepare her for his entrance. And then he tilted her back and thrust into her with vigour while she clung to his shoulders, her ankles wrapped round him. He grunted with raw male satisfaction, his hand supporting her hips as he pounded her yielding body with delicious force. Excitement writhed through Lucy in an unstoppable surge and she reached her peak with an involuntary cry, convulsive waves of exquisite pleasure rippling through her lower body as an orgasmic flush spread over her sun-dappled skin.

'I didn't use a condom,' Jax groaned in her ear as

he slowly lowered her back to her own feet. 'Is that likely to be a problem?'

'Hopefully not,' Lucy muttered after doing some quick calculations and without looking directly at him as she stepped out of the shower and grabbed a towel. 'It's the wrong time of the month.'

What had he meant by that question? Was he asking her if she was willing to get pregnant again? Or was he worrying that she *would* conceive? And for that matter, was she willing to take that risk? Lucy thought not. She had not had an easy pregnancy the first time around and was not in a hurry to do it again, particularly when she did not yet feel secure with Jax. Even so, if she did conceive she would still welcome and love her baby.

But then what would it take for her to feel truly secure with Jax? she asked herself. Perhaps she was her own worst enemy and had quite unrealistic expectations of a marriage in which only one of them loved. She might not like the reality but their relationship was bound to be unbalanced with one of them wanting and hoping for more than the other.

'Did you know that the contents of that file were a complete fiction?'

'What do you want me to tell you?' Heracles slapped the file on Lucy back onto his desk and sighed heavily. 'I will not lie. I did what I felt I *had* to do.'

Sharply disconcerted, Jax tensed even more, anger roaring through his tall, powerful frame because he had somehow expected the older man to try and evade his very direct question. 'Why did you think you *had* to do anything? Why did you even think that it was your place to interfere? It wasn't as though I was talking about marrying her—'

'Jax…in the space of two weeks, you flew back to Spain *five* times to see her,' Heracles traded defiantly. 'That was enough for me to view her as a serious contender for something and when I discovered that she was the daughter of Kreon Thiarkis, well, to be really blunt…that was that. Thiarkis is a slippery customer, always has been, always will be and I will not apologise for not wanting a criminal's daughter involved with my family.'

'I know Kreon's history,' Jax interposed harshly. 'I know what he is and I can understand your concern but I was twenty-six years old, *not* a teenager, and you had no right to interfere.'

The older man stood his ground. 'I know I had no right but I didn't care. Years ago I watched Thiarkis charm my deluded first wife into paying for his legal representation in court when he was charged with fraud—'

'Two years ago, Lucy hadn't even *met* her father,' Jax pointed out rawly. 'What I had with her was our business alone, nothing to do with your ongoing distaste for Thiarkis. And far be it from me to say a word in Kreon's defence but for over thirty years he held onto a letter that would have made his fortune had he sold it to the press…'

Jax settled the letter Lucy had given him down on the desk. 'Your first wife confessed her sins on paper during her last days.'

His father turned grey before his eyes and dropped down suddenly into his office chair, studying the letter as if it were a cobra likely to strike out at him. 'Sofia was never discreet,' he muttered heavily. 'Are you telling me I have to thank Thiarkis for his restraint?'

'No,' Jax breathed in a driven undertone, having decided not to reveal the secret of Kreon's blackmail. 'But it's time you came to terms with the fact that he is Lucy's father and stopped visiting your experiences and your resentments on *my* life. I'm not Argo—'

'I know you're not,' Heracles acknowledged grimly. 'Argo always did as he was told and you *won't*, which is why I went behind your back in the first place. I assumed she would be wrong for you.'

'She's not,' Jax bit out curtly. 'But because of that file I treated her badly and now I have to tell her why.'

Heracles compressed his lips in disapproval. '*Do* you? I don't think that's a good idea. A wise man shares nothing with his wife but a bed.'

'Three wives and you *still* don't know better?' Jax derided with seething bite. 'Well, I do know better and I will not tolerate your meddling in my life. If you ever do anything like this again, I'm *out*.'

'You can't mean that,' Heracles breathed in consternation.

'I do. Blood counts but family counts more and you were out of my life for too many years to be considered family in the same way that I consider my wife and my daughter. They come first…*always*.'

Simmering with angry frustration, Jax sat in his limo in the heavy Athens traffic mulling over that confrontation. Heracles had finally apologised and at least his father had at last told him the truth. Jax hated secrets. He had grown up in an atmosphere of secrecy, continually urged never to tell anyone that his mother was 'ill', pregnant or involved with a man. As a boy, he had reacted to those warnings by deciding to never tell anyone at school that the famous Spanish movie star was his mother. It had been a rather pathetic ploy considering that the name Antonakos was too well known and just about everyone who was anyone knew his father had divorced Mariana for having an affair with one of her co-stars. But the practice of keeping his thoughts and feelings and personal details strictly private had been taught to him when he was very young and had become a habit he couldn't shake…until he'd met Lucy and told her things he had never told anyone before.

And if he was honest that experience had totally unnerved him two years earlier. He had seen that he was veering into dangerous territory and had feared getting too involved with a woman again. *Feared?* No, obviously he had been in no hurry to admit that to himself. His mother had been frighteningly volatile, constantly ranging between high and low moods while using drugs as a crutch to get her through the day. Freed by Mariana's death from the powerful conviction that it was *his* responsibility to look after her, Jax had decided that emotion was a weakness and that a sensible man steered clear of it. Most of the time that had worked very well for him.

*Until* he'd met Lucy…

*Until* he'd met Bella…

Jax poured himself a stiff drink and drank it down. He *had* to tell Lucy. How could he *not* tell her? He reminded himself that she had married him even after what he had done in Spain. He reminded himself that she seemed happy. He didn't have to love her to make her happy. Hadn't he already proved that? Together they had the fathers from hell. Not her fault, not his fault either. He would give her the facts. She would be angry and hurt but she would forgive him. Jax knew he wasn't the forgiving type but he was convinced from recent experience that Lucy *was*. They had signed up to be a family for Bella's benefit. And that would be Lucy's bottom line because more than anything else, Jax reminded himself doggedly, after a life of turmoil Lucy craved security.

And he offered security, he offered a *lot* of security, he reflected with growing assurance. But it still really bothered him that she wasn't clingier and more open with him. The Lucy he remembered in Spain had been distinctly needy and clingy and, although he ran a mile from that trait in other women, for some reason he had liked that attribute in Lucy as much as he had liked her once flaky tell-all chatter. He had liked it when he was the first person she looked for in a room, when he was the only one she really smiled at or noticed, when she wrapped herself round him all night as though she was afraid he might attempt an escape. He had liked being told that he was loved even if in the end it had all turned out to be a lie.

But she didn't do those things any more even though he wanted her to. She was wary. Of course she was, he conceded, struggling to be fair, so, putting the truth out there was a sensible move, he told himself squarely. He would tell her what had really happened and she would forgive him because that was what Lucy did. And what choice would she have? a more cynical voice enquired. After all, she had betrayed his trust too…

* * *

'He's treating you well?' Kreon prompted while Iola was playing in the garden with Bella.

'Yes,' Lucy told her father flatly. 'But I won't discuss Jax with you.'

'A wife should be loyal to her husband,' Kreon remarked equably. 'I simply wanted you to be happy—'

'I can only be happy with a man who is happy to *be* with me,' Lucy countered drily, resisting the urge to remind him that he hadn't thought of that angle.

But with Jax being the very practical but reserved male that he was, he was more likely to make the best of a bad job than try to wriggle out of the commitment, particularly when his daughter was involved. Lucy showered and changed while telling herself that she had absolutely nothing to complain about. Whatever else, she was married to the love of her life. There was nothing she could do about the fact that she had only gained a wedding ring through her father's dirty tricks. But she knew that somewhere in the back of Jax's astute brain he would probably *always* associate her with her father's treachery and would never quite forgive her for his lack of choice and loss of freedom.

'He gave in to me very easily. That is *not* an Antonakos trait,' Kreon argued.

'Obviously he cares about his father.'

'I believe he cares more about you.'

Unconvinced by that startling claim, Lucy returned to the city villa with nerves run ragged by the strain of pretending for Iola's benefit that everything was fine between her father and her. She had been surprised that Jax hadn't objected to her visiting Kreon and Iola and then relieved because her father was still her father even though he was imperfect. *Imperfect?* Manipulative, sneaky, quick to jump on a golden opportunity even if it entailed blackmail, Lucy's brain added unhappily. But until she had met her father and learned about the existence of her sisters, she had believed that her father was her only living relative and his support and acceptance had meant a great deal to her. That he was capable of going to such lengths to secure a very rich husband for her still devastated her because of course it had to make a difference to her marriage and the light in which Jax saw her.

If Kreon hadn't interfered, who knew what might have happened? All right, they would clearly not have got married, she allowed ruefully, but at least Jax wouldn't have felt forced into doing something he didn't want to do.

Lucy had only just finished drying her hair when Jax strode into the bedroom. He paused for a second, appreciating the sight of her small slender figure in a summery blue dress, tumbling ringlets framing her piquant face. 'You look ridiculously pretty,' he heard himself say stiltedly, and he almost winced at that ill-timed opener because he had come upstairs to give her the investigation file.

Lucy angled her head to one side and gave him a questioning look. 'You never pay me compliments. What's wrong?'

He had called her pretty, not beautiful, and she was more than happy with that, well aware that her looks weren't on the beauty level. In marrying Jax, she had boxed above her weight because *he* was the beautiful one in their relationship, standing there in his exquisitely tailored silver-grey suit, his stunning bone structure accentuated by a shadow of black stubble, gorgeous green eyes glittering like stars in his lean bronzed face.

*'Never?'* Jax was taken aback by her claim, only belatedly recognising that she was right. He thought such things but he very rarely voiced them out loud. 'I have something for you to read.'

He looked so very serious that Lucy's heart gave a sudden lurch inside her chest. 'OK,' she said apprehensively.

He extended the file. 'My father sent this to me two years ago in Spain. It's why I didn't turn up that last night.'

Lucy grasped the slim file and sank down heavily on the foot of the bed. 'Your father?' she queried with a bemused frown.

'He had discovered who your father was and apparently he was determined to break us up,' Jax explained flatly. 'The file is filled with what I now know to be lies about you.'

Lucy lowered her shaken gaze to the file, thoroughly off balanced by what he was revealing because it was coming at her out of nowhere. Suddenly he was talking about what had happened in Spain and admitting that he hadn't ditched her simply because he had got bored. 'You *now* know…?' she questioned with an uncertain questioning glance.

'I had my own investigation carried out,' he admitted smoothly.

And Lucy was even more shaken at the enormous amount of stuff that Jax had been hiding from her, not to mention the lowering reality of just how much his father had not wanted her in his family. She swallowed hard and, breathing in bracingly, she opened the file and straight away she could not credit what she was reading. It was a seriously exaggerated character assassination in print, from the outrageous allegation that she had convictions for drug dealing and soliciting sex to the fact that her age was quoted as being twenty-five.

'But how could you possibly have believed *any* of this?' she heard herself whisper with incredulous emphasis.

'It was in the early stages of my new relationship with my father and I trusted him. I had no reason to be suspicious of his motives because I had no knowledge of his acquaintance with your father or his dislike of him,' he pointed out flatly.

Lucy shook her head very slowly, an almost dazed light in her luminous blue eyes as she focussed on him. 'You misunderstood my question. I'm not asking why you believed your father but how on earth you could believe that kind of nonsense about *me*? Soliciting *sex*? I was a virgin when we met!' she reminded him with sudden resentful heat. 'And you knew that!'

Jax compressed his lips, wearing the aspect of a male who would have liked to be anywhere but where he was at that moment. He shifted his feet uneasily. 'A woman can fool a man over stuff like that. She can pretend,' he began uncomfortably.

'Then you must have assumed my acting ability rivalled your mother's!' Lucy slotted in a little shakily because anger was rising now to cut through the shock of what she was learning. 'I just don't know what to say about all this…*stuff*!' she selected jaggedly, tossing the file down on the floor in disgust. 'I thought you *knew* me—'

'I thought I knew you too until I read that file,' Jax admitted curtly. 'But I had no good reason then to suspect my father of setting me up.'

'So, you're telling me then that he was responsible for me losing my job?'

'I didn't go into that with him… I was far too angry,' Jax confessed. 'But it's probable that he *was* responsible for that and for the manner in which you were treated as you were put off the yacht. If I had stayed long enough to get into that kind of detail I probably would have *hit* him…'

'Oh…' Lucy was a long way from forgiving him for having had so little faith in her but she was certainly mollified by that little speech.

'You were pregnant,' Jax pointed out, still stuck on that offence with an anger she could see making his lean, darkly handsome features rigid. 'You could have been seriously hurt. He could have killed his own grandchild…we could have lost Bella!'

Lucy warmed up to him a little more in response to that additional really quite emotional exclamation. Jax had only known her for six weeks in Spain. Six weeks and a handful of dates. They had finally become intimate during the final two weeks of that time frame. Why would he have distrusted his father? The father then riding high on the wave of finally deciding to accept and welcome the younger son he had once ignored?

Lucy felt that she had to be fair to Jax. After all, she had not distrusted Kreon when she first came to Greece, had she? It occurred to her that Jax was probably feeling much as she had felt on their wedding day, angry and hurt and defensive while wondering how someone he cared about and respected could have done such a thing to him.

'I think the very least you could have done was speak to me about the file and give me the chance to answer those allegations,' Lucy told him firmly. 'There is no excuse whatsoever for you failing to tell me about that file two years ago.'

And Jax's long, lean, powerful physique went rigid, shoulders squaring, legs straightening. 'Actually there is…'

'No, there's not.' Lucy could understand and forgive a great deal but he could not justify his complete failure to tell her what was going on either in the past or the present. 'You didn't even send me a text in Spain to tell me we were finished, for goodness' sake!' she exclaimed.

'I had my reasons,' Jax breathed in a raw undertone, his eyes gleaming like polished gems.

'Unacceptable reasons.' Lucy refused to give way. She often gave in to Jax because he had a very forceful personality but she knew she couldn't go through life without disagreeing with him occasionally. 'You owed me an explanation of some kind—'

'I owed you *nothing*!' Jax shot at her with sudden derision. 'I did come to see you the night after I received that file.'

Her brow had furrowed because she was beginning to feel a little lost in the dialogue, as though she had misinterpreted some crucial sentence. 'You *didn't* come to see me—'

'And do you know why?' Jax's hands knotted into

fists because he felt like a volcano about to spew lava and somewhere in the back of his mind lurked a tiny voice asking him if he *really* wanted to say what he was about to say. But Jax didn't back down, had never learned *how* to back down. He only knew how to come out of a corner fighting and how to win. He had had a hell of a day and it wasn't getting better the way it was supposed to, it was only getting *worse* and that thought did nothing to cool his temper. He had done nothing wrong with Lucy, he was, in his own opinion, the injured party. He was not a vengeful man but he would not be accused of something he wasn't responsible for.

'If I did, I wouldn't be arguing with you or trying to get you to see my point of view,' Lucy parried.

'I bet you don't even remember that night…'

'I remember it very well,' Lucy admitted, lifting her chin. 'What's this all about, Jax? I'm getting confused—'

His eyes narrowed, his mouth flattening. 'I drove over to the bar and before I could get out of my car, I saw you walking down the alleyway in your red dress—'

'It wasn't me you saw,' Lucy sliced in thinly. When Jax had failed to turn up to see her the night before Lucy had stayed in her attic room after doing her shift, frantically hoping that Jax would magically appear with an explanation. Like a child waiting for Santa Claus she had refused to believe he wouldn't show up eventually and she had been terrified of somehow missing him. She had had that much faith in him, that much *trust*…

'It was you. You were with a man—'

'You're mistaken,' Lucy told him confidently.

'I followed you because I assumed you were heading for the entrance that led up to your room but you weren't,' Jax informed her stonily. 'You stayed outside to have sex with the man you were with against the wall.'

Her lashes fluttered up on disbelieving bright blue eyes and she stared back at him. 'You think that I had sex with some guy in the alley?' she demanded with a revulsion she couldn't hide. 'Are you kidding me?'

Lean, strong face shuttered and forbidding, Jax stood his ground because naturally he hadn't expected her to own up to her behaviour. 'You know I'm not kidding and what I saw that night is why you never heard from me again. There was no point in showing you that file when you were already with another man,' he proclaimed harshly. 'I don't need to apologise or make excuses for not approaching you again.'

'I agree,' Lucy said with wooden diction, shattered inside herself but holding it all together out of pride. 'If I had been with another man that soon, you owed me nothing. Clearly, it suited you very well to assume that night that the girl in the alley was me—'

'And what's that supposed to mean?' Jax shot at her suspiciously.

'Well, you'd seen that file and learned that your precious father did not approve of me. It was really incredibly convenient for you that in spite of everything you knew about me you decided to accept that file and *assume* that I was the sort of young woman who would have sex in an alley.'

Lucy could feel her cheekbones ache with the strain of keeping her face composed but there was a much deeper ache of pain inside her chest. She knew he didn't love her. She knew he had never loved her. That wounding knowledge had chipped away at her upbeat outlook on their marriage and she had fought it off, telling herself to settle sensibly for what she could get. But for the first time ever, Lucy decided that Jax was *bad* for her.

Never mind the Antonakos fame, the money and the gorgeous looks. Two years back, she had told Jax that she loved him and she *had*, but he had given nothing back, not the words nor any other form of commitment. He had held back from her, he had always held back from her and now she finally knew why. But she deserved better. She deserved a man who would, at the very least, refuse to *believe* that she would have sex in public with some chance-met stranger. And Jax hadn't had that faith in her and probably never would have. A horrible sense of emptiness spread inside her. *Her* loving him wasn't enough.

'It *was* you. I recognised the dress,' Jax bit out, exasperated by the stretching silence and the strange way she was staring at him.

'Yes…you may have done but it wasn't me *wearing* the dress,' Lucy countered tightly. 'I loaned it to Tara that night because she had a hot date and I imagine she was fooling around in the alley because she could hardly bring a man back to the room we shared when I was there. Not everyone has a private room or a yacht available for these things…'

Jax froze. 'It *couldn't* have been her! Why would she have been wearing the dress I bought you?'

Lucy sent him a weary glance of exasperation. 'Because we shared our clothes. We didn't have much but what we had, we *shared*. Half the clothes you saw me wear that summer belonged to Tara.'

'It couldn't have been her,' Jax repeated again doggedly, struggling to remember her friend before dimly recalling the much more worldly blonde whom Lucy had worked and lived with.

Lucy shrugged a shoulder in a jerky movement. 'Well, it doesn't much matter after this length of time, does it?' she traded.

'It matters to me. And it *must* matter to you,' Jax told her with assurance.

'No, it doesn't,' Lucy responded heavily.

Jax hovered and clenched his teeth hard. He wanted it dealt with and then never mentioned again. But could it have been Tara in that stupid dress? It had been dark and Tara had had long blonde hair too. Between the street lights and the shadows, it was possible that he had been mistaken. And if he had been mistaken, it would be the very first time in Jax's life that he would ever be *grateful* to have made a mistake. Didn't she appreciate that? Didn't she understand what believing she would behave that way had done to *him*? Refusing to look at him, Lucy was staring at the tiled floor instead as if she were expecting it to start showing a movie and frustration racked Jax's tall powerful frame. *Women!* She had gone into a weird mood now and he would probably get nothing more out of her.

'I have a meeting. I was planning to reschedule it and take us back to Tifnos—'

'No, go to your meeting,' Lucy urged, her throat convulsing, and she still wouldn't let herself look at him because she didn't want what she felt in her heart to show.

'We can fly back in the morning,' Jax commented. 'The timing would probably suit Bella better than a late flight.'

Lucy listened to the door close on his exit and continued to sit there with tears rolling silently down her cheeks. Jax had just shown her how he really thought of her and how he saw her and it was…it *was* ugly, uglier than she could bear or forgive or comprehend. To think that all those weeks on the island he had believed that she had been unfaithful to him and yet he hadn't said a word, hadn't even given her the chance to explain or defend herself. It was so cruel, so unfair but you couldn't change a man, couldn't alter what went on inside his head.

Jax didn't trust her, had never trusted even a word she'd said. He had been her one and only lover and he couldn't even believe that. She had been too young and immature at nineteen to recognise how cynical and distrustful Jax was. She had realised that he was pretty jealous and possessive but her awareness had gone no deeper than that. She thought of him seeing Tara in that grubby alley and believing it was her and a stifled sob of pain and regret and humiliation was wrenched from her. That hurt so much and it seemed with Jax at that moment that he did nothing but hurt and disillusion her. She didn't want to stay married to a man like that, she *couldn't* stay married to a man who thought so little of her…

And when the wave of conflicting emotions began to tear at Lucy more than she could stand she dug out her phone and rang her sister, Polly, desperately needing a shoulder to cry on.

Polly was a terrific listener. Lucy let the whole

sorry story of her relationship with Jax and Kreon spill out and, very satisfyingly, Polly was even more appalled by the alleyway accusation than Lucy had been.

'Come and stay with us, Lucy,' Polly suggested warmly. 'You need a holiday. I know you felt that you were happy with him at first but Jax doesn't seem to appreciate you the way a husband should. It's possible that he resents you for what your father did.'

To Lucy in that instant the prospect of walking away into a different environment shone like a bright welcoming light. 'I don't even know where you live, Polly,' she pointed out unevenly.

'In a country called Dharia. It's one of the Gulf States,' Polly explained.

Lucy was flummoxed by that news. 'I don't know how I'd get there or even how I'd get away from here.'

'Don't you worry about that,' Polly told her assertively. 'I will arrange everything. If you leave tonight, we'll be having breakfast together in the morning and I can get hold of Ellie and she could be here by this weekend. We really do want to meet you and your daughter, Lucy.'

'Leave...*tonight*?' Lucy gasped in astonishment, wondering if it would be wrong of her to take her daughter with her as well and then deciding that, just at that moment, losing both of them was what Jax deserved for his distrust.

'I don't think you should waste any more time on the Antonakos family. They don't love or value you but we *will*.'

And Polly's enthusiasm was the deciding factor for Lucy, who usually took more time to decide anything of a serious nature. But at least she didn't feel like crying any longer, she registered with relief, because crying after Jax had gone over her like a steam roller with his nasty allegations seemed feeble. Jax didn't want her and his father didn't want her in his precious family and her own father had seriously disappointed her. A fresh start and the friendship of her sisters looked a lot more promising than her current situation.

'Tonight will be fine,' she assured Polly. 'I'll start packing. I suppose it will be very hot?'

'Yes, but the pal—er…my place is air-conditioned,' her sister informed her.

# CHAPTER TEN

JAX WAS STUNNED. He ran through the empty wardrobes again as if he expected to find Lucy curled up below the empty coat hangers in hiding. He wandered back to the empty nursery, stared into the even emptier cot and then hurriedly strode back downstairs again.

'Take me through it again,' he urged Zenas jerkily, struggling to master the kind of emotions he generally never allowed to see the light of day. Emotions like panic, fear and insecurity that could tear a man to pieces as they had once torn apart the boy he had been. Having frequently lived those emotions in childhood and adolescence, he had sworn never to give them space again. But there they were still inside him, he discovered, just waiting their chance to jump on him and either paralyse him or urge him to make fundamentally stupid decisions…

Zenas breathed in deep, a wary eye on Jax, who was visibly pale and stressed. 'A diplomatic limousine with a foreign flag drew up. An Arab man in a suit and a crowd of heavies got out. The man had diplomatic credentials but he spoke neither Greek nor English and was unwilling to engage with my questions. Your wife opened the door with your daughter in her arms. She had a stack of suitcases waiting in the hall—'

'And you just let her *go...?*' Jax repeated incredulously. 'You let a bunch of foreigners *kidnap*—'

'She wasn't kidnapped. She went of her own free will,' Zenas told him apologetically. 'We followed the car to the airport where the whole party proceeded through VIP diplomatic channels to which we were denied access. From what we can establish a private jet flew Mrs Antonakos and the little girl to Dharia.'

The name of that country rang a bell of familiarity with Jax. His brow furrowed. There had been some connection. *Thee mou*, his one-time business partner, Rio Benedetti, was married to the sister of the Queen of Dharia...who was coincidentally called... Polly, just like Lucy's long-lost sister. No, he shook away the suspicion until he thought about that slick diplomatic kidnapping—he refused to accept that Lucy had willingly left him—and then the suspicion lodged deep.

Lucy was making a statement, he told himself grimly. He should do nothing and wait for her to get in touch. Lucy would not walk out on him, he told himself. She was annoyed with him. There was nothing he could do about that. He was merely paying the price for having finally told her the truth and if she didn't like the truth, what was he supposed to do about it? Satisfied that he had reached a mature and measured decision, Jax poured himself a stiff drink.

Within the hour he was back pacing the empty marital bedroom. He should not have been imagining Lucy there because they had never yet spent a night in his Athens villa. Yet inexplicably memories of Lucy were everywhere around him. He pictured her on the bed, the softness of her pouty lips, the delicate paleness of her skin, the silky fall of her hair running between his fingers. He snatched in a stark breath. There was a tiny spiralling blonde hair on the dressing table and the scent of the perfume he had bought her in Mykonos still lingered on the air. The bedding was still creased from where she had sat while they'd talked that very afternoon.

*Talked?* Well, she hadn't really talked, he acknowledged tardily, indeed had been remarkably quiet for a chatterbox. With hindsight it became clear to Jax that she had been upset, *seriously* upset. And he hadn't picked up on that. How could he *not* have picked up on that?

Still locked in the mindset he had had for two long years, Jax had continued to feel like the victim of her treachery. But what if there had been no betrayal in the first place? What if that ridiculous story about sharing clothes was genuine? What if he had abandoned her in Spain two years earlier without any excuse for doing so? And what if he had blown up his marriage over a stupid red dress and a mindless need to finally confront Lucy?

Jax paced, feeling in dire need of another drink but knowing he shouldn't have one when his brain was already leapfrogging all over the place. Lucy and Bella were gone and he could live with that, couldn't he? A divorce, shared custody, parental access…?

Suddenly feeling very short of breath, Jax froze. There was a tightness in his chest and a dryness in his throat and his heart was thundering in his ears. No, he couldn't live with that option, he decided with dizzy abruptness.

And as so often before when life challenged Jax, anger came to his rescue. He wasn't letting the queen of some tinpot country steal his wife and child! Lucy had been lured away from him and misled and he was going to get her back pronto where she belonged, which was in Greece with him.

'By the sound of it, Jax really doesn't know how to deal with the emotional stuff,' Ellie remarked with a wry smile on her lips.

'That's an understatement,' Polly inputted with a sniff. 'That alley business…accusing her of *that*—'

Ellie laughed and Lucy looked at her red-headed sister in surprise. 'But don't you see? It was all still as fresh as yesterday for Jax, which tells you that he never got over it. Two years on he's still agonising over that alley…yet he still decides to *stay* married to you, he takes you on a honeymoon, acts happy, treats you decently in every other way. It took the equivalent of torture to get the story about the alley out of him because he's *ashamed* that he still wants you, regardless of what he supposedly thinks you did. No, really, Lucy…you can learn a lot from reading between the lines.'

Lucy smiled at that more optimistic viewpoint even if she didn't quite believe in it. She coiled back into her comfortable corner of the sofa in the beautiful room with its impossibly high domed ceiling and wished that she could see what Ellie appeared to see in Jax's behaviour. Her two sisters were so different. Polly was warm and caring, almost motherly, while Ellie was very clever and sympathetic and their children, *her* nephews and nieces, she noted with pleasure, were simply gorgeous.

Polly's boys, Karim and Hassan and Ellie's daughter, Teresina were playing out in the shaded courtyard on trikes. Ellie was feeding her baby boy, Olly, with a bottle while Polly was nursing her newborn daughter, Haifa. Bella was watching the older children scoot around on their bikes while chasing a ball. Karim got off his bike simply to move Bella back a little with her toys, looking out for the toddler in the most considerate way for a small boy.

Lucy was shaken to admit that she would have been crazily happy in her sister's gorgeous royal palace were it not for Jax's absence. The discovery that her eldest sister was a ruling queen with her husband, Rashad, and that Ellie was the working wife of a fabulously wealthy Italian had certainly helped to take Lucy's mind off her own problems. The three women had sat up into the early hours the first night they were all together, exchanging histories, talking about the three rings they had inherited and catching up on a lifetime of different experiences.

Talking about Jax had come later and had sent Lucy's mood plummeting again because, even though she still felt that walking out on Jax had been the only thing she could do, there was a hollow place inside her where her heart had been ripped out.

In the back of her mind lurked the conviction that Jax had been hurt so much in life just like herself yet they dealt with emotions in very different ways. Jax buried his, hid troubling issues and lived in virtual denial of his feelings. Lucy wore everything on the surface and picked herself up again emotionally no matter how often she was kicked. But she hadn't reacted that way at her last encounter with Jax, she acknowledged.

He had hurt her too much and for the first time ever with Jax she had hidden her feelings as well.

In a sense that had been cruel of her and hitting him over the head with something large and heavy might have been kinder. Feelings had to be shoved in Jax's face like placards for him to read them. He had probably been very shocked by her departure and he was probably furious that she had taken their daughter with her. But he still wouldn't understand *why* she had left, which bothered her. The truth was all that had mattered to Jax and he had finally told it without grasping the damage he was doing. He had expected her to excuse him for past events soured by their fathers' machinations. He had not been capable of realising that she had been devastated because everything he had said had spelled out the message that he had never loved, respected or even understood her. How could she possibly love someone like that?

'He's a man. He might as well be from another planet,' Ellie mocked quietly. 'Rio was exactly the same, hiding things, holding onto the past—'

'Rashad too,' Polly admitted ruefully. 'So, perhaps Jax *could* be rehabilitated…'

Lucy studied her linked hands, unable to imagine Jax budging a stubborn inch from his own convictions.

The door opened, framing Rashad, the King of Dharia. Tall and very handsome, he flashed a smile at his wife. 'Polly…we have a visitor. He thinks we kidnapped his wife. What would you have to say to that?'

'Lucy's my sister and I didn't kidnap her…I offered her sanctuary,' Polly declared loftily.

*'Sanctuary?'* Rashad echoed, visibly appreciating

that choice of word. 'I don't think I would employ that particular word with Jax, Lucy.'

'Jax is here?' Lucy flew off the sofa as though jet-propelled and then stilled, colour rising in her cheeks below her sisters' interested scrutiny.

'Let the rehabilitation commence,' Ellie remarked softly.

'*Have* I been interfering?' Polly asked worriedly.

'No, I was hugely grateful for the support,' Lucy told her warmly.

Lucy couldn't think straight. It had taken Jax less than forty-eight hours to come out to Dharia and she was sharply disconcerted. In the back of her mind, she had feared that he would let her go and write off their marriage as a mistake. After all, how could he possibly *want* to stay married to a woman whom he had such a low opinion of? But then letting her go could well be what he had arrived to discuss, she reasoned unhappily.

Jax was in no better mood after his long flight to find himself in a room decorated like something out of an Arabian Nights' fantasy, which dovetailed beautifully with the royal palace of Dharia. Rashad, the King, had seemed fairly normal though, acknowledging that he too would have been very 'put out' to find his wife and child had staged a vanishing act.

And then Rashad had murmured, 'But now that you're part of the family I should warn you that when the sisters get together, they plot and plan. You're either with them *or* against them.'

'You're my brother-in-law...well, *half*-brother-in-law,' Jax adjusted, recognising that the three sisters had all had different fathers.

'They don't think of each other as half anything,' Rashad cautioned him.

'Catching up?' another voice interposed, a voice that Jax recognised and he tensed, slowly turning round to arrange his thoughts before meeting the eyes of his former business partner, Rio Benedetti. 'Well, isn't this a small world?' he breathed uncomfortably.

'Relax,' the Italian billionaire urged. 'I ran into Franca last year and she brought me up to speed on past events. No disrespect to Franca intended, but I had the lucky escape and *you* had—?'

Jax winced. 'I owe you a wholehearted apology for what happened but let's not talk about it,' he retorted wryly of that sobering experience.

'Let's not,' Rio agreed, leaning closer. 'A word of advice though,' he added in a rueful undertone. 'The word "alley" will be etched on your gravestone…'

Momentarily, Jax froze as if a gun had been angled at him and faint colour rose over his sculpted cheekbones. 'Is that so?'

'The sisters don't keep secrets,' Rio imparted. 'Nothing is too sacred to be discussed. Cross one and you cross all three and none of them are batting for you.'

That was information that Jax could well have done without. He knew he had messed up but everyone else knowing how badly he had messed up made him feel worse. He had had forty-eight hours in which to think and he had done more thinking within that forty-eight hours than he had done in all his twenty-nine years. And having reached obvious conclusions, had even decided what to say.

But Jax's prepared speech flew right out of his head

when Lucy walked into the suite he was wafted off to. Lucy was wearing a long flowing dress in shades of blue and it fluttered round her as she moved and just seeing her again, just looking at her again, made Jax feel stuff he couldn't suppress any longer.

'I came because…' he began.

Jax looking gorgeous as usual, Lucy was noting, striving to be cool and composed after Ellie had advised her to play hard to get. But she couldn't play hard to get with Jax, which was the crux of her problem where he was concerned: she loved him. She had always loved him and what had been rather insta-love in Spain when she barely knew him had turned into something much deeper and more binding the second time around. Jax might be hopeless at some things, like talking about feelings and paying compliments, but he was very, *very* good at other things.

'Yes…you were saying?' Lucy prompted, striving to take control of their meeting.

Jax raked a deeply frustrated hand through his tousled black hair, green eyes glinting from below black lashes, and her heart jumped. 'I don't know what I was going to say. I had it all planned out but now it's gone. This is all new to me,' he muttered in a sudden surge. 'But the only really important thing I have to say is that I love you and I need you and I want you to come home with me…'

And just like that and with the unexpectedness of an explosion, Jax stole the wind from Lucy's sails. She didn't have time to try and work out how to play hard to get. He took the breath from her lungs and the arguments from her brain because what he had just said was what she felt as if she had been waiting all her life to hear.

'I've never said those words to anyone else,' Jax admitted gruffly as the silence dragged. 'I married you, not because of your father's blackmail, but because somewhere deep down inside me I *wanted* to be married to you. My head was telling me I didn't want to get married but my instincts were pushing me in a very different direction. Is that weird?'

'No…' Lucy almost whispered the word, scared to move, scared to speak lest she interrupt him and stop him speaking.

'My father reminded me that over one two-week period I flew back to Spain five times to see you. My attachment *was* obsessional,' he conceded grudgingly. 'I loved you then but I was afraid to accept that. Possibly when you said it suited me to believe that file and…*the other stuff* there was a shred of truth in that. Love has always been something that hurt and damaged me. I loved my mother, my father, my little sister, my half-brother and years before I met you I fell for a woman, who turned out to be a very troubled alcoholic, whom I had to place in rehab for recovery. I was determined not to get hurt again.'

Lucy nodded like a vigorous little marionette, wanting so badly to reach out to him and hug him and cover him in kisses but knowing it was wiser to let him say what he needed to say to explain the past and the present. 'I can understand that—'

Jax released his breath on a hiss. 'How can you? You keep on caring about people even when they hurt or disappoint you. That's brave—'

'Or plain stupid,' Lucy slotted in wryly. 'That's just

me. I tend to look for saving graces in people and stay optimistic but you're a giant pessimist, who always sees the worst possible conclusions.'

'Pretty much,' Jax conceded.

'And thinks the worst,' Lucy added with spirit, thinking about the alley. 'Even if there's no justification for it.'

Carefully avoiding the word Rio had advised him to avoid, Jax straightened his shoulders. 'The alcoholic that I fell for was repeatedly unfaithful to me. She couldn't help herself—she was a mess until rehab. But like my mother before her she conditioned me to distrust women. I'd seen that file. I saw a woman I thought was you and it seemed to fit, it seemed to be exactly the sort of thing that happened to me—I had got in too deep and you weren't who I thought you were—'

'Like with this alcoholic lady? That would be… er… Franca?' Lucy checked. 'Rio told Ellie about her and Ellie told me.'

Jax took on board the second of Rio's warnings. 'Yes, it was Franca. After her I was very wary and cynical with women. I didn't have faith in my own ability to read a woman, to really *know* her and, life being life,' he groaned, 'that meant I screwed up very badly with you. I ran when I should've stayed. I thought I was protecting myself but you had already burned me.'

'Burned you?'

'I never got over you. I kept on thinking about you at random times and reminding myself how bad you were…you know the—?'

'*Alley* stuff?' Lucy enunciated with precision, bright blue eyes gleaming.

'Yes, that,' Jax muttered, desperately keen to move on. 'Obviously I was wrong and I am very sorry that I believed that was you. I just saw the dress and the blonde hair and—'

Lucy moved closer and closed both arms around him. 'It's all right,' she murmured softly because his voice was ragged and too troubled for her to bear without touching him. 'It's all right. I forgive you. You made a mistake. It's over, done and dusted—'

Jax stared down at her with suspiciously bright green eyes. 'I don't deserve you. You probably don't even believe that I love you and that I loved you right from the start and I don't know how to prove it to you.'

But Lucy didn't need any more proof. Jax had wanted to stay married to her even though he believed she had once been unfaithful to him and that spoke volumes on its own. He had loved her warts and all, carefully schooling himself to overlook what any man would have seen as a monumental flaw and betrayal and predictably keeping his thoughts to himself. And then he had come clean and what he had been keeping secret had shocked and distressed her but at the same time it had set both of them free.

'I love you too,' Lucy whispered, planting a flyaway kiss on his freshly shaven jaw line, which was as high as she could reach even on tiptoes. 'So much that when you're not there it hurts.'

Jax carried her hand to his lips and kissed the back of it in the most un-Jax-like tender manner. 'You didn't even leave me a note. I felt sick. I didn't know what to do. I experienced pure panic—'

'I would've phoned eventually,' she confided. 'I was so upset but you were right to tell me. It all needed to come out for us to deal with it and then put it away again.'

'Your departure in a royal private jet was fairly straightforward when it came to tracking you,' Jax admitted ruefully, and then he gathered her up into his arms with the attitude of a male who couldn't keep his hands off her any longer.

'The bedroom's next door,' Lucy told him helpfully.

'I even told myself I was only marrying you for Bella's benefit,' Jax confessed. 'I lied to myself all the way down the line.'

'I persuaded myself I was only marrying you for our daughter's benefit as well, so you're not the only one.'

'How's Bella reacting to being here?' Jax queried.

'She's got six cousins to watch and loads of toys to steal. She's having a whale of a time.' Lucy laughed, blue eyes sparkling, and Jax looked down at her with his heart in his own eyes and adoration there, a brilliant smile on his lean, darkly handsome features.

'You are a very special woman, Tinker Bell,' Jax declared, settling her down on the bed with that same heartbreaking smile dazzling her. 'And the saddest element of all this is that my father is now going to be battering down our doors for invites.'

Lucy studied him in bewilderment. 'How? *Why?*'

'Heracles is the son of a pig farmer,' Jax told her with a chuckle. 'Yes, he keeps that little fact well under wraps because he is an enormous snob. When he discovers that your sister is a queen, he will be horribly friendly. He's very easily impressed in that line.'

Lucy shifted an unconcerned shoulder. 'I can live with that. It's not as though either of us can change our fathers. They are what they are but neither of them is going to get the chance to spoil our happiness again.'

'*Can* you be happy with me?' Jax pressed with touching anxiety. 'You do know I'll screw up again. I won't mean to but I will because I won't always get it right—'

'Neither will I,' Lucy pointed out equably as she struggled to get him out of his jacket and tie and then, when he got helpful, embarked on his shirt, spreading her fingers lasciviously across his muscular torso. 'Love is all about making allowances and compromises. We'll get there. Nobody has to be perfect.'

'I think you are. You have a heart as big as any country, *khriso mou*,' Jax told her with a blissful sigh as she knelt over him, cheerfully stripping him.

'And so have you,' Lucy countered, much amused. 'The difference between us is that you put your heart in a cage to keep it safe—'

'And you still worked your way through the bars of my cage,' Jax reminded her appreciatively. 'You've got more power than you realise.'

Lucy let a small hand stray and he arched up against her as if she had pressed a switch and she laughed as he sat up, wound both hands punitively into her hair and kissed her into breathless, leaping excitement. There was no more conversation then. They were both much too involved in sharing their bodies as they had shared their love.

'I suppose we should get up for dinner…or whatever they call it here,' Jax mused hours later. 'I'm being a very rude guest.'

'No, I know my sisters and they know me. They'll have tucked Bella into bed and gone on as normal.

There's no pressure, no expectations. Everyone's family here and that's just the way it is. I *love* it, especially because you're here too now,' Lucy confided, tucking a sleepy head into the crux of a strong brown shoulder and dreamily taking in the familiar scent of his skin, soothed by his proximity and the glorious high of knowing herself loved at last.

'I love you,' Jax muttered, easing her closer, marvelling at how easy it had become to say those words that he had refused to think about for so long.

'Love you,' Lucy whispered, dropping off to sleep, because she had lain awake sleepless while they were apart.

And Jax smiled in the darkness, recognising that for the first time in his life he was truly, joyously happy.

'This place looks amazing,' Polly carolled as she stood in the marble hall of the house on Tifnos and admired the fabulous Christmas decorations and the glittering tree. 'It's wonderful that you have a home big enough to take us all too, so we can get together like this to celebrate.'

'You can thank my father-in-law, Heracles, for that. He built *big*.'

'Was that the little man who kept on bowing to me?' Polly whispered uneasily.

'Yes, that was him, very subdued at being in the royal presence,' Lucy remarked, stifling her amusement.

In the three years Lucy had been married to Jax a great deal had changed. Her father-in-law was a frequent visitor, their children providing a major draw. Lucy had warmed up to Heracles considerably once she'd realised that he genuinely adored children and his grandchildren most of all. Yes, she had had another baby, a little boy called Dmitri, who was almost two years old. Their lengthy unplanned holiday in Dharia after their reconciliation had extended the family. She had enjoyed her second pregnancy much more than the first because she had had Jax by her side and Jax had been scientifically fascinated by every change she had gone through on the road to producing his son. He had shared everything with her and supported her right through the nausea in the early stages to every medical appointment and finally the birth.

During those three years only Lucy's son had been born but Polly was expecting again, freely admitting that she wanted a large family. Ellie had declared that two children would do her nicely but one never knew with Ellie, who could be prone to saying one thing and then quietly doing another. As for Lucy and Jax, they were still young and, while being quite happy with the children they had, they thought that some day they might plan a third child. Ellie had already lectured them hilariously about birth control, pointing out that *two* accidental conceptions was inexcusable, and her audience had only laughed.

Kreon and Iola were regular visitors on the island and Kreon and Heracles politely avoided each other at family gatherings. Her father had faced bankruptcy proceedings the year before and Jax had bought a small business for him and placed him in it, pointing out that Kreon needed to be kept occupied and independent. His kindness had almost reduced Lucy to tears and she was relieved that Jax had finally begun to see and understand Kreon's essential good-heartedness.

'He's your father and you love him,' Jax had said to Lucy. 'We have to do our best for him. After all, you put up with my father and forgive his foibles.'

Jax was a wonderful husband in every way, Lucy reflected gratefully, feeling very blessed. After spending so many years of craving the feeling of being special to someone she had finally found a safe harbour.

Leaving Polly to get settled in with her children and explaining that Ellie had gone straight to bed after a hospital late night shift, Lucy went off to put Dmitri down for a nap because he got very cross and whiny when he got too tired and with all the children in the house and the excitement of the Christmas season, he needed more sleep. The little boy snuggled into his cot, clutching his toy elephant. He was as blonde as his mother, which had been a surprise to his parents, but he too had Jax's green eyes and olive complexion.

Lucy looked out of the window and saw the older children down on the beach with Rashad and Rio. She could just make out four-year-old Bella in her yellow dress skipping through the surf with Polly's younger son, Hassan, and Ellie's Teresina. The cousins had all become fast friends and playmates, which made family get-togethers run more smoothly.

Recognising that she finally had the family circle she had dreamt of having all her life, Lucy vented a contented sigh and went to freshen up before dinner. She was in the shower when another body stepped in beside her and she spun round with a delighted smile of welcome.

'Jax…thought you were going to be late tonight!' she gasped.

'No, I looked round my office, thought of you all here enjoying yourselves without me and decided I was needed at home. I saw the children down on the beach as we flew in.'

'Dmitri's having a nap. He was throwing tantrums all over the place,' his mother confided ruefully.

'I swear he's got my mother's temperament,' Jax said worriedly.

'No, don't be silly,' Lucy soothed, aware that he had that little fear that he might somehow pass on some troublesome gene. 'He's a toddler with a short temper and he hasn't learned to control it yet. When he's not tired he's very good-natured. And, hey, did you join me in the shower to talk about the kids or—?'

'Or, *agapi mou*,' Jax chose, plastering her back against the shower wall and tasting her lush mouth with hungry urgency.

Lucy melted every time he called her his love. He was hot and wet and gorgeous and all hers. Excitement rippled through her in seductive sensual waves.

'Birth control,' Jax growled, lifting her out of the shower and throwing a heap of towels down on the tiled floor as he dug into a drawer for the necessary.

Lucy arranged herself on the towels and giggled like a drain. 'Ellie really got to you with that lecture, didn't she?'

'Ellie knows how to make a man feel irresponsible,' Jax responded. 'And I will *never* be irresponsible with you again but don't tell her that.'

'I promise I won't.' Her amusement dying as they joined, Lucy lifted tender fingers to stroke his jaw line. 'I love you, Jax Antonakos...I love you so much.'

He was too otherwise engaged to speak at that moment but his emerald eyes telegraphed love and passion and need and that was more than sufficient for Lucy, who knew a good man when she found one and held fast to him because he gave her so much happiness.

* * * * *